# THE DREAMCATCHER

# THE DREAMCATCHER

## *BARRETT*

SAPPHIRE BOOKS

SALINAS, CALIFORNIA

**The Dreamcatcher**
Copyright © 2017 by Barrett All rights reserved.

ISBN - 978-1-943353-67-5

This is a work of fiction - names, characters, places, and incidents are the product of the author's imagination or are used fictitiously. Any resemblance to actual persons living or dead, business, events or locales is entirely coincidental.

All rights reserved. No part of this publication may be reproduced, distributed, or transmitted in any form or by any means, including photocopying, recording, or other electronic or mechanical methods, without written permission of the publisher.

Editor - Heather Flournoy
Book Design - LJ Reynolds
Cover Design - Treehouse Studio

**Sapphire Books Publishing, LLC**
**P.O. Box 8142**
Salinas, CA 93912
www.sapphirebooks.com

Printed in the United States of America
First Edition – January 2017

This and other Sapphire Books titles can be found at
www.sapphirebooks.com

# *Dedication*

My parents, Peg and Jim Magill: You taught us well in
the short time you had.

# Acknowledgment

My journey as a writer has crossed the paths of so many inspirational and supportive people. With each new story I have new thanks to share.

This project was begun almost five years ago for fun. A dear friend and I shared ideas about some young women with uncommon adventures in a quiet Midwestern town. We wrote and shared excerpts on a regular basis trying to escalate the drama and humor. There was never any talk about publishing, but we did invent some other scenarios. I learned so much from that project.

The intervening years did not diminish my love for these characters. With a generous nod from my talented collaborator, I set about the task of preparing the story for submission. If you are reading this, you'll have already figured out that the astute publisher at Sapphire Books Publishing accepted the story and welcomed me into the talented and skilled family. The admirable story of Sapphire's growing influence in the writing community is one of hard work and determination.

Many thanks to my supportive friends, most especially my trusted Lodge sisters for their unflagging support.

To my editor, Heather: Thanks for the mind-meld and considerable skill to find the weak spots. . It was a pleasure to work with you. Thanks as well to the entire production team for their excellent support: Lori, Shawn Marie, Peggy, Chris (PR/sales), Sallyann, and anyone I may have forgotten.

To Chris: "Thank you" sounds too simple. I'm very grateful.

To Ann McMan and Treehouse Studio: Once again, my friend, you have brilliantly provided exactly what I wanted for my cover.

I want to add a very special thank-you to Susan X. Meagher for not only teaching me about humor, but very graciously allowing me to use excerpts from Awakenings, the first book in her *I Found My Heart in San Francisco* series. You are a generous friend and colleague.

Most of all, to my loyal readers: Through good times and bad, it's always been FOR YOU.

# *Disclaimer*

This novel is a work of fiction. Any resemblance to real people or places is unintended. The legends and Native American references are essentially fiction based on factual details.

The author regards the Lakota Sioux Nation with the utmost respect and admiration. Accordingly, a percent of the sales will be donated to a Standing Rock and Pine Ridge charity for the care of their children.

If fiction could come true, the souls of the warriors would return to help defend the the land for future generations. Absent that, it falls to the neighbors and friends of the indigenous people to help preserve their heritage.

# *In the Beginning...*

Pale morning light slowly crept across the velvet sapphire sky. The White Crow Nation gathered in silence to sing the dawn. A fierce wind exploded from the west blowing dust and cold, and with it came billowing dark clouds that would threaten the breaking dawn.

Distant rumbles of thunder warned of a gathering storm, but this time, it was the Black Crow nation amassing and advancing toward the sacred eastern plains to regain power.

Since the beginning of time, forces representing Dark and Light sides of the Great Sioux nation battled for control. The struggle replayed with every generation, as new leaders came to power. In modern times, the war continued with clever medicine people using every trick to manipulate and gain more power.

The tribal elder sat high above the plain and waited. A young woman approached, leading her pony. "You asked for me, Grandfather?"

"Yes, Wind Horse, it is time," he whispered and extended his hand with a bundle wrapped in deerskin. "You must take this and ride east for seven suns. It will protect you until you can pass it on to a new generation. Our people will need a strong leader to defeat the dark forces of Black Crow. This Black Obsidian amulet must remain hidden from him until then. He cannot hurt anyone without this totem."

Without words, she accepted the bundle, mounted her pony, and turned eastward into the rising sun.

# *Chapter One*

The last bell rang as Kai Tiva opened her locker, stuffed in her math book, and grabbed her peacoat. Ending the day with one of her best subjects was a good thing; she liked math, plus it was on the main floor. The first year at Lindan High couldn't have been better.

A loud noise followed by a yelp caught her attention, and Kai turned in time to catch Zach Coho shoving Johnny Little Elk into the lockers. *Damn it. I told him to leave that kid alone last week. And the week before that.*

She dropped her peacoat and ran toward the group of kids forming a circle. Over the hooting and yelling, she could hear Zach's sarcastic voice.

"Quit whining, you half-breed midget. Nobody gives a crap what you have to say."

"Leave me alone!" Johnny cried as Zach yanked away the backpack.

"Or what, you sniveling little mama's boy? What're you gonna do about it, call squaw momma?"

Zach swung the backpack and hit him just as Kai pushed through the students standing around taunting or watching in horrified silence.

"Let go of him, you feeble little dickweed. Why don't you pick on someone your own size?" She leaned down and pulled Johnny to his feet. "Are you hurt?"

The smaller student cowered by his open locker,

crying. He shook his head and swiped at the tears with his sleeve.

Zach jeered at her. "Why should I listen to you, you big ugly redskin?"

"Because the last time you did this, I told you to stop so I didn't have to hurt you." Kai took a step closer to him.

Zach Coho was easily a foot shorter than she was, and teased her about it constantly.

He laughed. "And what's the gigantor dyke gonna do about it?" He shoved her.

Kai swallowed hard and her pulse pounded in her head. She looked around at the kids watching her. Anger bloomed and her arms tensed. Like a reflex, her right arm shot out and her fist slammed into Zach's face. She felt the snap of a breaking bone. Zach's eyes were wide and bright red blood ran across his lips.

The sudden silence got her attention. Then someone jerked her by the arm down the hall.

Mrs. Klein's bombastic voice shouted orders. "Someone take Zach to the nurse's office. You come with me."

Kai tried to pull her arm free from the vice grip of the school's iron-fisted enforcer and grumbled, "Why am I the one getting in trouble?"

"Because you're the one that hit Zach." Mrs. Klein gripped her arm tighter as she picked up her pace.

"Ouch!" Kai yanked again to no avail. "But he was bullying that kid—again. It wasn't fair and nobody was trying to stop him."

"Enough," Mrs. Klein said, opening the office door and pointing to a line of plastic chairs against the far wall. "You sit there and don't move until you are told to."

"I didn't do anything wrong." Kai groaned, and then huffed once as she slouched into the familiar chair.

Mrs. Klein stood at the counter, tapping her foot as she waited for the secretary to hang up.

The principal's office door swung open and he stuck his head out. "Call the vice principal and tell him I need to talk to him now." He stomped back in his office and Kai could hear him on the phone. "Yes, Miss Pettibone, I'm sure the rat's frightening, but I am sending Mr. Hammer to the cafeteria...No, I don't think rats are that large but you just stay in your office...No, we do not need the police. Please try to stay calm."

"I have Mr. Hammer on line one."

"Jack, you have to get down to the cafeteria right now. Ms. Pettibone swears there is a rat as large as a house cat in the kitchen...Of course I don't, but she's hysterical...Yes, call animal control if necessary."

The school secretary carefully hung up the phone and came over to the counter.

Kai didn't know whether to laugh or be concerned. Rats in the cafeteria? Aunt Tilley would love to hear about that story.

"Adela, Ms. Tiva will need to speak to the principal. Again. She punched Zach Coho and may have broken his nose this time."

Kai watched as Adela lifted a hand to her prim, red-rimmed mouth. "Oh, my. Again? It's a good thing his father is a doctor." She adjusted her glasses and nodded firmly. "I'll make sure she speaks to Mr. Higgenbottom immediately."

"Thank you, Adela. I would hope this is the last time I have to come down here." Turning around, she cast a trouty glare. "Kai, this is your final warning. This kind of behavior will not be tolerated in this school. Next time you feel compelled to act like a vigilante, I will personally see to it that you are expelled. Do I make myself clear?"

Kai met the fishy stare with a dark look of her own as she warred with telling *Der Henker* what was really on her mind. *Right, that would get me expelled for sure.*

This was definitely one of those times where it is best to have half—or more—of the conversation in your head. Why would anyone take her word for it anyway? The Great Zach Coho never did ANYTHING wrong. Stupid waste of skin! Huffing a deep sigh of resignation, she looked down at the floor. "Yes, Mrs. Klein."

Kai heard the door open, and looked up to see Riley James, easily one of the prettiest and most popular girls in her class, breezing in. *Shit. The only things I'm missing are zip-ties and an orange jumpsuit.* Her stomach knotted and her face burned as she tried to will herself invisible.

"Hi, I'm supposed to meet someone from *The Daily Herald Gazette*?"

Adela and Mrs. Klein turned in unison. Kai caught the starstruck look on Mrs. Klein's face before she turned and cast a final withering glare at her.

"Adela, let me know if Mr. Higgenbottom needs to speak to me further about this incident." She turned and marched priggishly to the door. With a supercilious smile she said, "Ms. James, you look lovely today, dear."

"Have a seat, Riley." Adela motioned to the chair next to Kai. "Mr. Higgenbottom is on a conference call, and the reporter from *The Daily Herald Gazette* is running behind.

"Okay, No prob." She turned around and smiled brightly at Kai. "Hey, mind if I sit here?"

Kai looked up. "Um, okay. Yeah. Sure. You can sit here. By me. It's okay. Really." Her face flamed red as she forced herself to stop babbling.

Riley pulled her pink hoodie off, and sat down. She pointed to Kai's right hand, leaned over, and whispered conspiratorially, "You know everyone's talking about the girl that totaled Zach Coho with one swing. I've wanted to do that for such a long time." Glancing at the desk, she whispered, "He's in my homeroom. O. M. G. He is the meanest kid I've ever met. I've complained so many times, but my homeroom teacher never sees it."

"Uh..." Kai rubbed her tender knuckles, and looked up at Riley and the prettiest smile. "Um..." She sighed. "Yeah, I know. He's a total dickweasel and deserved it."

Riley smiled brightly and offered her hand. "I'm Riley. I've seen you around, you're in Mrs. Klein's homeroom, but I don't remember your name."

Kai looked at the offered hand, then into Riley's eyes. They were a soft, mossy green, and had a slight impish gleam to them, "Uh. I'm Kai. Kai Tiva." She tentatively shook, and said a silent prayer that she didn't sound like an idiot.

Riley's smile brightened again. "I'm guessing that punch's the reason you're down here. Bummer. You deserve a medal because that little weasel deserved it. Probably more."

Kai couldn't stop the flash of a smile before a more serious expression pushed it away. "Yeah. Nobody will believe me, though. Zach is a total plank, but he gets away with everything at this school, the same as he did in junior high."

"Don't worry too much. The fact that he got punched out by a girl is making him look pretty lame right now. I think he's a serious tool, so do most of my friends. Is your hand alright?" She took Kai's hand and ran her thumb lightly over the scraped knuckles.

Kai's stomach tightened. She licked her dry lips. "It's, um, it's okay. I'm okay. You know. It's…it's fine."

Kai saw the hallway door open and a tall blond boy walked in and set a stack of papers on the counter. "Mr. Pedersen told me to bring these down to be copied." As he turned to leave, he smiled and nodded. "Hey, Riley. 'Sup?"

Riley released Kai's hand, and looked up briefly. "Oh, hey, Brock. Nothing much." She turned back to Kai, her eyes wide. "Hey, I just remembered where I saw your name. OMG! You're the one with the highest score on the National Science Exam, totally awesome!"

Kai flushed a bright red, and looked down at her raw knuckles, flexing them, then back to Riley. "Yeah. It was luck, mostly."

"Hey, Riley, I'll see you later, okay?"

Riley gave Brock a quick nod, and turned back to face Kai. "Seriously? That test was so hard. I did okay on most of my tests, but I totally hate science and bombed, majorly." She tilted her head, and gave Kai a look. "You must be pretty smart."

Kai swallowed hard, feeling suddenly very exposed, and murmured, "Not really."

The principal's door flew open, "Adela, is that reporter—" He stopped in mid-sentence and looked blankly at Kai, then Riley, then back to Kai. He cleared his throat. "Is that reporter here yet?"

"No, Mr. Higgenbottom, he's running late, and should be here soon."

Mr. Higgenbottom looked at his watch and sighed dramatically as he adjusted his baggy pants. "Well, Ms. Tiva, I don't know exactly why you're here but I'm quite sure it could have been avoided."

Adela puffed up. "Um…Mrs. Klein reported that Ms. Tiva…well, she punched Zach Coho in the nose. May have broken it."

He pinched the bridge of his nose, groaned, and gestured to his office. "Come in so we can get started."

Kai looked forlornly at Riley then back to Mr. Higgenbottom. "Yes, sir." She stood and strode into the office as Mr. Higgenbottom followed and slammed the door solidly.

❧❧❧❧

Riley cringed when the door slammed. Mr. Higgenbottom was always going on and on about his "Creatively Resolving Conflict Program," but she suspected that Kai tattooing Zach with a right jab wasn't what he had in mind. *God, I hope she doesn't get in too much trouble for teaching that punk a lesson.*

She watched the second hand on the Regulation school clock that now read 3:15. Riley wished she hadn't agreed to the stupid interview, but she was determined that her performance in the Winter Fest Concert would be even better than the one her sister— the favored child—had "starred" in last year. And if that meant singing "O Holy Night" and talking to a dumb reporter…then she'd sing "O Holy Night" and talk to the dumb reporter.

She bit her bottom lip and mentally rolled

her eyes. There was never any doubt that her sister, Rebekah, was her parent's favorite. In fact, until she was ten, Riley swore they'd adopted her. Rebekah is the pretty one. Rebekah is the smart one. Rebekah has all the boyfriends. What-EVER.

"Rebekah stuffs her bra," she mocked under her breath.

Mr. Higgenbottom's voice was getting louder. *Bummer.* Riley cringed and looked at the door and thought about the girl she just met. When she watched her walk into the office, Riley was astounded by Kai's height. She was taller than Mr. Higgenbottom. But there was something else about her, something different. She wasn't as scary as everyone made her out to be. In fact, she seemed kinda shy, but in an alternative, cool kinda way.

The volume inside the principal's office increased even more. Riley crossed and uncrossed her legs, then began tapping her fingers on the arm of the chair. It wasn't fair that the only person who stood up to Zach Coho was getting in this much trouble. She glanced at the desk and saw the secretary hang up the phone. Without another thought, she stood up. She started toward Mr. Higgenbottom's door.

"Ms. James! You can't go in there."

"Excuse me, Adela, I don't mean to interrupt, but I just have to say something."

"Ms. James, this does not concern you."

"You know what? It does. It concerns me and every other student at this school who's seen the bullying that goes on, especially by Zach Coho. He taunts every kid that is smaller, handicapped, or different than he is. Today was Johnny Little Elk. Not only is he Native American, he also has trouble hearing.

It's at least the second time I've seen Zach pick on him. Even the upperclassmen have commented on it." Riley knew her voice was loud enough to be heard inside the principal's office by now.

Adela began Xeroxing the papers on the counter. "Ms. James, that's enough. It's not a matter we should be discussing."

Riley crossed the office until she was standing in front of her desk. "It should be the topic everyone is discussing. Why should one of Johnny's classmates have to defend him when the teachers should be doing it?" Riley slapped her hand on the counter. "If it wasn't for Kai—a freshman girl—Johnny would probably be the one at the nurse's office, while Zach was off bragging to his friends."

Adela's face paled in shock, her shoulders sagged. "I appreciate you offering your opinion, and I will make sure the principal is aware of your concerns. I think you should return to your seat now."

Riley could feel her pulse pounding in her neck; she knew she'd said more than enough. "Alright, I'll go, I just wanted you to know what was going on." She returned to her chair. It was embarrassing, but she felt good about speaking her mind.

The hallway door banged open, startling her from her thoughts. A skinny, bald-headed guy dropped a notebook on the floor as he tried to shove a camera back into the case. His nerdy glasses were crooked on a really long nose, and he had an oily, thin little mustache. *Oh God, that has to be Clark Kent.*

He approached Adela's desk. "Um, hello, my name is Tyrrell Burkbinder from *The Daily Herald Gazette.* I'm looking for..." He fumbled with a notebook. "Riley Beth James."

Riley groaned and wanted to slink under the chair.

"Mr. Burkbinder, we're so pleased you could make it," Adela said with great relief as she pointed. "This is Ms. James. Riley, this is Mr. Burkbinder from the newspaper."

Riley stood up, grabbed her jacket, and slung her backpack over one shoulder. "Hey. Nice to meet you."

Adela came out from behind the counter and pointed to a ledger on the counter. "The principal arranged for you to use the conference room across the hall. If you'll just show me photo identification and sign in, I'll get your visitor's badge and escort you. Mr. Higgenbottom will join you both as soon as he's available."

❧❧❧❧

Kai grimaced when Mr. Higgenbottom slammed his fist down on the metal desk. "THIS." Slam. "MUST." Slam. "STOP." Slam. "Do I make myself clear?" His face was purple, and his puffy frogeyes looked like they were about pop out of his head.

Kai nodded.

"No, Ms. Tiva. I want to hear you to say it out loud."

She set her jaw and stared at him. His comb-over was standing up like Snookie's poof, it kind of looked like a hairy door to his brain. *Serves him right.* A big part of her wanted to just get up and walk out, but that would get her expelled for sure. *I don't want to get expelled, Aunt Tilley will totally freak on me.* She sighed.

"I'm waiting, Ms. Tiva." He reached up and

smoothed his comb-over back into place, then steepled his pudgy fingers in front of his nose.

Kai bit her bottom lip and took a deep breath. "Yes, sir."

A dark look crossed his face, but his voice was calm. "Yes, sir, what?"

Kai mentally rolled her eyes. "Yes, sir, I understand that any further violence will not be tolerated…even if I am only standing up for a special needs kid that Zach Coho is emotionally, verbally, and physically bullying." She met his eyes, and returned his dark look.

He took a deep breath and sat back in his chair, watching her carefully. "Kai, what Zach Coho does or does not do is of absolutely no concern to you." Kai started to protest, but he raised a finger to silence her. "In the future, you will take your concerns up with one of the teachers or with me, but you will not take justice into your own hands. If it happens again, you could be expelled, and if that happens, you will not come back for the remainder of the term. That means you fail your classes and you don't play basketball. Do I make myself clear?"

This was her third time in Mr. Higgenbottom's office this semester, and every time it was because of that tumor, Zach Coho. She could tell Higgenbottom was super serious this time, and it kind of scared her. She looked down at her lap and nodded. *Zach wins again. Big surprise.*

"All right then." Mr. Higgenbottom picked up a pen and started scribbling furiously in her student folder. "Let's talk about your punishment. I will talk to the teachers." He sighed heavily. "But you will write an apology for assaulting Zach…before we're all sued."

***

Riley cut the interview short by telling the skeevy reporter she had cramps and had to use the washroom. She didn't, but he didn't have to know that. She waited awhile before scurrying back past the conference room, and let out a sigh of relief that it was empty. As she rounded the corner to the main hallway, she saw her friends Amber and Meghan standing in front of the trophy case.

"Hey, guys."

Amber put a hand on her hip and Meghan mirrored the move. "Riley, where you been, girl? Brock was waiting for you at your locker after last period."

Riley shrugged. "Yeah, I know, but I had to go talk to some guy from the newspaper."

"Too bad." The two girls giggled in unison. "Hey, guess what? We totally got the scoop on Tiffany's breakup with Devon."

Riley mentally gagged. She could care less about why Tiffany broke up with Devon—again. "Cool. Hey, sorry I missed it but I really have to get home. Text me with the four-one-one." She waved over her shoulder, and the two girls immediately started jabbering about cheerleading.

"Later guys," she muttered as she continued down the hall to her locker. Most of the time she liked hanging out with her friends, but lately everything they did just seemed so stupid and juvenile. Tiffany was the worst, but since school started, she and 'Devon The Boyfriend' had been attached at the hip, so that at least made it a little easier. *Please get back together, if not for each other, for me.*

As she pulled her coat out of her locker, she noticed someone down at the end of the hall. There was no doubt who it was by the dark shaggy hair just visible above the top of the locker door. Riley snapped shut the combination lock and shrugged into her Mr. Rat backpack. As she got closer, she could hear Kai muttering to herself.

"Hey, you okay?"

Kai stuck her head around the locker door looking startled. Her dark brown eyes narrowed, then softened. "Oh...uh...hey."

Riley leaned against one of the lockers. "Didn't mean to freak you. Have you been in the principal's office all this time?"

Kai looked down at her shoes as a shock of hair fell across her forehead. She brushed it back behind her ear. "Yeah, he made me write an apology to the dick Chiclet."

"Wow. That royally sucks!" Riley said.

Kai closed her locker and buttoned her peacoat. She reached down and picked up her backpack. "Yup. Nothing I can do about it though."

Riley laughed. "It won't help, but I sure piled it on the poor receptionist. I'm sure there won't be a smiling reception next time I go down there."

Kai looked up. "That was you? I heard yelling and thought it was another potential kid ready to be expelled, or the skeevy rat they were all jacked about."

"Is he expelling you?"

"No, but I really have to watch it."

They started down the hall to the entrance. "Is someone picking you up? What rat?"

Kai shook her head. "Supposedly there was one in the cafeteria. And no, I usually walk home."

"Me, too. My mom doesn't get home till after four thirty." Riley looked up at the tall girl striding next to her. *Man, she's a giant.* "Can I ask you something?"

"Sure," Kai said with a shrug.

"How tall are you, Stretch?"

Kai grinned. "Five feet, fourteen inches."

Riley groaned. "God! She makes me do math."

Kai laughed and pushed open the door, then followed Riley through. "Which way do you go?"

Riley pulled out her mittens and pointed down the street. "That way. I live right off Tremont."

"Really? Cool, me too." Kai shoved her hands in her pockets. "I'm on Raand, by the park."

Riley looked and grinned, realizing the Kai was matching her much longer strides to her shorter ones. "I'm on Bellegrade. That's so wild. We only live like two blocks apart!"

Kai grinned back. "Yeah, I've seen you walking home before."

Riley threw her shoulder into Kai. "Really, you goof? How come you never walked with me before?"

Kai shrugged and stopped. "I dunno, I guess because you always have a bunch of friends with you."

Riley stopped and looked up into Kai's dark eyes. "Well, if it means anything, I kinda like talking with you a whole lot more than them."

Kai grinned from ear to ear.

A laugh bubbled out of Riley. "Dude, you really need to smile more, you know that, Stretch?"

A blush rose up Kai's neck.

Riley grabbed Kai's arm and pulled her down the street. "Do you walk to school in the morning?"

"Yeah." Kai nodded.

"Wanna walk with me tomorrow?"

"For realz?"

Riley pointed down the street. "I have to turn here. Seven ten?"

Kai nodded. "Yeah, sure. Okay. Seven ten."

Riley smiled and started walking. "I'll see you tomorrow at seven ten. Oh, friend me on Facebook, okay?"

Kai nodded and give a quick wave. "Okay, sure. See ya."

# *Chapter Two*

"All right, what gives?" Riley's mom slathered peanut butter on the newly popped toast. "This makes two weeks in a row that I haven't had to nag you to get ready for school." She narrowed her eyes and crooked an eyebrow. "You are going to school, aren't you?"

Riley gulped the orange juice, zipped up her jacket, folded the toast in half, and grabbed her backpack. "Yes, Mom, I'm going to school. Sheesh. Why is it you always think I'm doing something wrong? Rebekah never got grilled like this."

"You, young lady, are not Rebekah. Your older sister was very serious about school, and never gave me a reason to worry. Recently, you've done a complete one-eighty, and I'd like to know why." Her mother stood with her arms folded across to her chest and glowered.

Riley hated that look. She shrugged. "It's no big deal. I just found out that one of my friends from school lives over on Raand so we walk to school together. Is that a major crime?"

"Of course not," her mother tutted. "It's just curious how responsible you've suddenly become without threats or bribes." She picked up her coffee cup. "What's your friend's name?"

"Kai Tiva. She's in the same grade as me, but a different homeroom. I gotta go."

Her mother's brow furrowed. "Why does that name sound so familiar?"

Riley turned. "I don't know, but I've gotta go. Bye, Mom."

Riley didn't expect the wind gust and the snow flurries that buffeted her, but she didn't care as she jogged to make sure she wouldn't be late. She liked having someone to walk to school with, especially Kai. The night before, they had IM'd till after ten. Kai was funny once you got to know her, but she was also really super smart. Well, smart and way shy. But that was cool too, because Riley didn't have to pretend she cared about stupid stuff when they hung out. When Kai said something, it was usually for a reason. She smiled to herself. Kai also got nervous sometimes and babbled. That was kinda cool too, but she wasn't sure why. Maybe it was her voice. It had a sing-songy sound and was kinda low pitched.

A smile bloomed on her face as she remembered the funny story Kai told her about showing up at basketball practice with her shorts turned inside out, and the epic ribbing she took from everyone. She giggled as she turned the corner and saw her gigantor friend waiting for her. She broke into a jog.

"Hey, Stretch. G'morning," Riley said as she deliberately bumped into her.

"Watch it, Shorty. Do you want to knock me over?" Kai grabbed her arm to keep them from veering into the bushes.

"Sorry if I'm late. My mom went all five-oh on me this morning. Apparently, getting up on time is a big deal. Give me a break."

"Tell me about it. My aunt thinks I'm going in early because I'm in trouble again."

Riley laughed. "Don't tell her you're with me, she'll know you're in trouble."

Kai snorted. "Yeah, hanging around with you is totally wrecking my rep."

As they approached the school, Riley saw Kai stiffen. Lately they'd both been getting teased by some of the kids. Their height difference was always good for a few lame jokes, but some of the cracks were starting to get mean, especially the ones making fun of the fact that Kai was a tomboy, was Native American, dressed weird, and played on the basketball team.

"Hey, Riley, that your new boyfriend?" The group of boys obstructing the hall burst into hysterics as Brock looked on and said nothing. "Do you call her Tonto or Toto?" A chorus of hoots followed.

She saw Kai's fist clench. "Just ignore these dickheads," Riley whispered hotly as she shot them the bird, then elbowed through the group.

When they got to Riley's locker, she said, "Hey, I've got choral practice this afternoon, so I'm gonna be here late."

A nod. "That's okay. I have b-ball practice, and if I finish up early, I'll just go to the library for a while and study. I don't want you to have to walk home in the dark by yourself."

Riley cocked her head as she grabbed her algebra book and shut her locker door. She looked up into Kai's sincere brown eyes. "That's really nice of you. Nobody's ever cared if I walked home alone before." She tugged the end of Kai's multicolored scarf. "Then I guess I'll see you later, Stretch."

A blush appeared on Kai's strong face, replacing the fierce look that had lingered.

"Yeah, I guess you will, Shorty. See ya."

Riley started to track down the hall and turned. "By the way, I didn't forget that you play Dalton Prep tomorrow. I'll be there."

Kai stood at the free-throw line and tried to focus on the two upcoming shots. They were up by three with forty-two seconds to go. A five-point lead was two possessions and a lot safer than a one-possession game, especially since their starting point guard was out of the game on fouls.

"We're shooting two," the official said as he handed her the ball.

She dribbled once. Twice. A third time, then twirled the ball once. She lifted the ball over her head and launched a soft rainbow that bounced off the rim onto the backboard, then in.

A roar went up from the crowd, and her teammates all stepped in and slapped her hand, then returned to their positions along the lane and at the half-court line. The official approached her again with the ball. "This one's in play."

She dribbled once. Twice. A third time, then twirled the ball once. She lifted the ball over her head, and heard a familiar voice. "YOU CAN DO IT, KAI!" She grinned to herself, and brought the ball back down into her dribble routine, then lofted a perfect swish.

As she ran to the baseline to get into position for the press, she glanced up in the stands and saw Riley jumping up and down furiously as she let loose with a piercing two-fingered whistle. Kai couldn't keep the wide grin off her face as she waved her hands in front of the player trying to inbound the ball over her. The much shorter girl tried a football throw over her head, but she jumped up and batted the ball to herself. As she wrapped it up and waited for the sure foul, she made eye contact with her new best friend in the stands and nodded.

❧❧❧❧

The gymnasium exploded with cheers as the home team claimed the Lindan Holiday Tourney crown for the first time in more than a decade. Fans from the opposing team began to trail out as the Lindan High band stumbled through the school song in various stages of pep. The four cheerleaders did their best to encourage the students and parents to sing along, but the majority of the crowd was more concerned with scrambling down the old wooden bleachers to help their team celebrate the unexpected win.

Riley beamed with pride as she watched her classmates surround the suddenly popular Kai. She shook her head at how changeable everybody acted. Yesterday at lunch, a bunch of her friends were dishing about how Kai's dad was a lame-o magician and one of his stupid tricks backfired and blew him up. They laughed, and joked that she should keep her distance just in case one of Kai's science labs went nuclear. Well, they could laugh all they want, because if Kai weren't such a good player, then they wouldn't have won the Lindan Holiday Tourney.

Riley made her way down the bleachers as the janitor and several teachers helped erect a small platform at the north end of the gym. Feedback from the microphone squealed through the large space, and Riley slowly pushed her way to the front of the crowd.

She had gotten used to Kai's lanky form in her standard uniform of jeans and T-shirts, but she was surprised at how much different she looked in the gold and blue basketball uniform. She felt an unfamiliar swirl low in her belly as she took in the long, toned arms and legs of her friend. *Duh. Of course, she has arms and legs. She just looks so…well, geez, so not like anybody else.*

Kai raised a hand and waved, and a warm glow rippled through Riley. A giggle bubbled out as she waved back. It made her feel special that of all the people in the gym right now, Kai singled her out. Kai gave her the thumbs-up, and then lowered her head to say something to one of her teammates.

The microphone squealed again. "Ladies and gentlemen, I'm David Graham, superintendent of the Lindan City School System. Thank you for supporting the Lindan City School System and all of our fine student-athletes and coaches. As many of you know, I've been affiliated with this school district for more than ten years, and I will tell you, it is my honor to present, for the first time, the Trophy for the Annual Lindan Holiday Tournament to Coach Logan and the Fighting Polecats of Lindan High." The superintendent hefted a large, gaudy trophy and handed it to Coach Logan, who was wearing her bright gold blazer.

Riley zoned out briefly as the coach rambled on about school spirit, the importance of teamwork, and blah blah. But her ears perked up when the superintendent picked up a smaller trophy, and said, "And I'm equally proud to award the Tournament MVP trophy to Kai Tiva of LHS." Without thinking, Riley let loose another loud whistle, and screamed, "Way to go, Tiva!"

The gym erupted again in applause as the tall,

exotic-looking girl made her way to the stage. She shook hands with Superintendent Graham and accepted the trophy as he pushed the microphone into her face.

"Thank you, Mr. Graham. This should really be a team award. Thanks, Coach, for letting me play on your team." With that, she stepped back with her teammates.

༄ ༄ ༄ ༄

Riley waited for Kai to change clothes and meet up with her in front of the gym by the weird blue polecat statue. As Kai jogged down the front steps, she brushed wet hair off her forehead and flipped her scarf around her neck.

"Way to go Stretch! I'm really proud of you," Riley said as she grabbed a friend's arm with both hands. "Wanna go celebrate? Pizza at Carmine's?"

"Cool. I'm starving. You sure your mom won't mind?"

"Nah, she has her DAR meeting on Saturday afternoons, and won't be home till dinner time. What about your Aunt Tilley?"

Kai beamed at Riley, "She's working, so I'm on my own. I just have to be home before dark."

As they sat in a booth near the back of the restaurant, Kai bubbled over with details about the game, and Riley listened with rapt attention because she'd never heard her friend so stoked. It was so cool to see Kai so unguarded and playful.

Riley took a sip of her soda as Kai plopped the last pizza bone down on the empty tray. "I can't believe how good you are," Riley said. She leaned forward and began folding and unfolding her paper napkin. "I've never really been into sports, but you know, it's kinda different when you know somebody on the team." She laughed and felt herself blushing. "Especially the most excellent player on the team."

Kai had pushed her plate away, and was leaning on crossed arms. She swallowed hard, and slowly moved her hand until one finger touched the back of Riley's hand. "I've played on a bunch of teams since I was a little kid. Anyway, I'm pretty sure this is the first time anyone has been there to watch me. I'm really glad we're friends."

Riley felt something funny in her belly when she saw the way Kai was looking at her. She turned her palm up, and Kai didn't pull away. "I know. Me, too." The fluttering was stronger, and it felt like her heart was going to beat out of her chest. She looked up to see Kai's dark brown eyes staring at her, and laughed lightly. "I really like you a lot."

Kai gulped so loudly Riley could hear it. Her fingers stopped moving and then she squeezed Riley's index finger. "Ri, I really like you a lot. Like, more than I've ever liked anybody." She pulled her hand away and grabbed her soda cup in a death grip.

Riley sighed with relief as a huge smile spread across her face. *That wasn't so hard. It was scary, but Kai feels the same way, so that's good. Right?* She curled her fingers into a fist to preserve the warmth of Kai's touch.

Kai slowly looked up and their eyes met. They didn't speak, but Riley knew they were still somehow connected. It felt cool but it kinda weird at the same time.

She had all kinds of friends, but she'd never told anyone she liked them. Ever. The truth was, she really did feel closer to Kai than anybody, even more than her sister. And when Kai had touched her hand, it made her stomach get all tight and tingly inside. It was a feeling she really liked.

Kai walked her all the way home, the long way. While neither one said anything more about their conversation, they playfully bumped shoulders and agreed to IM after dinner.

# *Chapter Three*

Sunday felt like the frickin' longest day in the world. Kai slept in until almost eleven, and then tried to focus on doing homework but she couldn't. Then she tried getting into a good game of *Portal 2*, and then *Deus Ex*, but they both seemed just as pointless. She even thought about doing some laundry. It felt like she was coming out of her skin. She'd probably checked her phone and Facebook page every ten minutes since noon, hoping for another message from Riley.

She picked up her phone and let out a deep sigh. Nothing since

Riley: TTYL. Mom on rampage.

The longer she waited, the more she paced. *I bet Amber and Meghan came over to listen to music.* She threw a dart at a picture of Mrs. Klein on the back of her bedroom door. No, Tiffany probably invited her out to a movie. *Stupid Tiffany, with her stupid whiney voice and her stupid Nicole Scherzinger boob job!* She threw another dart that missed far left and bounced onto her bed. "Dammit!" She sighed again and threw her head back.

She picked up her iPod, slipped the ear buds in, and selected MCR's "The Black Parade." A couple of days ago, Kelly, the point guard, asked her if she knew if Riley and Brock Jones were hooking up. Kai let her know Riley wasn't really into anybody.

Still, Kelly swore that Riley and Brock were making out at Amber's birthday party right before Thanksgiving.

A sick feeling swamped her stomach.

Sometimes Riley took hours to IM back. She always said it was because her mom was on a bitch-bender about something. She yanked the ear buds out and tossed the iPod on her desk. MCR was just depressing her more, and she sighed heavily. *No wonder Brock is always staring at her with that stupid look on his face.*

She picked up her dad's old goat head drum and drumstick, and started a soft, familiar rhythmic beat. It was a simple, redundant harmonic that instantly starting soothing her jagged emotions.

What did Riley really mean yesterday when she said she "liked" her? Did she mean she "liked" her liked her, or did she mean she simply liked her? The drumming took on a slightly different timbre as she closed her eyes and focused inward.

*I don't want Brock looking at her like that. It's creepy, and I want to punch him out.* The timbre changed again. *Riley deserves more than a spoiled rich kid with Bieber swag who smells like a goat.* Her breathing slowed but the drumbeat remained steady. *The truth is, I really like her. More than a friend. I think about her all time. Everything is tied to her. When I'm with her, I want to touch her. No, more than touch her. I want to kiss her.*

The drumming stopped.

Kai opened her eyes, swallowed hard, and then took a deep breath. Lately she'd had to admit that she'd been having a bunch of girl crushes, but this thing with Riley was way beyond that. Way, way beyond that. She wanted to be with her all the time, and kiss her, and hold her, and she wanted Riley to want that with her. She looked down at the drum and set it back on her desk. Unexpected tears spilled down her face, and she angrily swiped at them with the palm of her hand. If she wanted to keep Riley as her friend, then there was no way Riley could ever know how she really felt. Ever. A sob bubbled up from her chest, and she hurled herself onto her bed as harder sobs racked her body.

❧❧❧❧

"I already cleaned up my room!" Riley screamed as she ran up the stairs. "Why don't you just leave me alone?" She slammed the door, and then for good measure opened it and slammed it again, jarring three stuffed animals off her bookshelf.

Her mother's voice echoed. "If you want to be in the Holiday show, young lady, you will get that room clean."

Once the hot tears dried, she sat up and looked around. It didn't look that bad. Sure, there were a few clothes on the floor and a pile of schoolbooks. The Holiday show was the biggest production her school did every year, and she really wanted to be in it. She sighed dramatically, then halfheartedly picked up two sweaters, folded them, and stuffed them into a drawer.

Her older sister, Rebekah, starred in the production her junior year. Of course, Mom and Dad still bragged about her amazing voice. "She sings like an angel," she mocked. "Like Rebekah was better than Beyoncé or something. I sing better than she ever could, but does anyone ever notice? Nooo."

She'd show them that she could do more than draw pictures and get passing grades.

Riley sighed and looked at the other twin bed, the one Rebekah slept in until three months ago when she went off to college. As much as Rebekah annoyed her and as much as she loved having her own room, it was pretty lonely. It had been really cool for the first week or so, but now she began to notice how much she missed her. Rebekah wasn't all bad; she really was a pretty cool big sister. It wasn't really her fault that Mom and Dad worshiped her. She picked up her stuffed Mr. Rat and squeezed him to her chest. *God! If it wasn't for Kai, this would be the worst year ever.*

On impulse, she peeked out her bedroom door to make sure she could hear the TV set the living room, then grabbed her cell phone and closed herself in the closet as she dialed Kai's phone number.

"Hey," Kai said. Her voice sounded a little funny.

"Hey. It's me, what're you doing?" Riley whispered.

"Playing a game. Why're you whispering?"

"I'm not allowed to talk to you until I get my room cleaned up. Stop laughing. It's not funny."

"Ri, it's not that big a deal, why don't you just do it?"

"Easy for you to say, Ms. I-Alphabetize-My-Locker," she teased as she sat down on the laundry basket in the closet. "I wish I was a superhero and I could do this in three seconds."

"Yeah. I'd help you if your mom would let me."

Riley sat up as a grin blossomed across her face. "That's a great idea, why don't you just come over?" Riley chuckled.

"Because last time I did that she told me you were too busy and couldn't have guests." Her voice trailed off, and she said softly, "I don't think she likes me."

"Don't be a goof. She's stoked that my grades have been going up since we met." Riley giggled. "She thinks you have some sort of magical powers. Hey! I've got an idea, bring your Earth Science book, and we'll say we need to study for the quiz tomorrow."

"We already did that Friday in study hall." Kai's voice trailed off again.

"I know, Kai, but Mom doesn't. It's perfect. You can help me clean my room, and if she comes up, we can be studying. Come on...it'll be fun." She waited a beat, but Kai didn't respond. "Seriously, Kai, I really have to get this done or she won't let me be in the Holiday production." Another silent beat. "And...I really want to see you today. Please?"

"Okay, Ri. Let me call my aunt and tell her where I'll be, then I'll head on over."

As soon as she had Kai's agreement to come over and hang out, Riley grinned widely and headed downstairs to find her dad. She could usually get his approval on things if she gave him a rational explanation.

"Hi Daddy," she called as she walked into the living room.

"Hi pumpkin, how's it going?" He muted the football game

She sat down on the arm of his chair. "I know Mom's upset about my room being a disaster area and everything and I'm almost done, but I also have to study for a science test. Can I have my friend Kai come over and help me? You know how smart she is."

He took off his glasses and pinched the bridge

of his nose then sighed. "Honey, you know how your mom feels about having your friends over when you have things to do."

She grabbed his hand and squeezed. "Please, Daddy. You know how hard I'm trying to get better grades. I promise I'll get my room cleaned up, and we'll be really quiet. Please?"

Her dad chuckled then winked. "All right, all right, but you better not be getting me in trouble with your mother or I will disavow all knowledge of this conversation."

Riley threw her arms around her dad's neck. "I love you, Daddy, you're the best."

"Don't forget to clean the room!" he shouted as she sprinted upstairs laughing.

# *Chapter Four*

Kai shook her head and smiled. Resistance to anything Riley wanted was futile, and she knew it the minute she heard the question. Picking up the stuff in her bedroom wasn't the problem. Trying not to act on these weird feelings? Well, that was getting to be the problem.

Kai took a deep breath as she raised her hand to ring the doorbell. She was so nervous she felt like she was going to throw up. *That'll impress her, for sure.* She put her finger on the button, but hesitated. She hoped she looked okay. She pulled her hand back and looked at her reflection in the storm door, then reached up to brush the hair off her forehead. She'd changed shirts three times before she settled on the long-sleeved tee that said: "The only thing we have to fear is fear itself …and rats." Riley thought it was hysterical. Riley also thought rats were cool. Kai shivered. If Riley had one flaw that was it. Rats. Why did she have to like rats? Kai grimaced. *The one thing that truly skeeves me out.* Oh well, Riley with rats was still a heck of a lot better than no Riley at all.

She reached out and pushed the button.

"Hi, Mr. James," Kai said as the door opened.

"Come on in, Kai. Riley's up in her room and her mother is at the store. I would suggest you two get that room squared away quickly so we can avoid upsetting the boss," he said and winked.

She grinned at him, realizing that he was only a little taller than she was. "Okay, we will." Kai took the stairs two at a time, and found Riley sitting in the middle of her room sorting CDs. "Hey, Shorty. Probably not the most productive use of your time..."

Riley's face lit up. "Kai! You made it."

Kai laughed as she hung her jacket on the doorknob and surveyed the disaster. "Your dad suggested we get moving before your mom gets back. Let's start with the clothes on the floor then move up. You decide where they go and I'll put away." She walked over to the closet, knelt down, and picked up a rumpled pair of jeans. "Laundry or hanger?"

They worked quickly as a steady stream of music blasted from her computer. Kai was into The Airborne Toxic Event, so they were listening a CD she'd ripped for Riley. When the floor became visible, Riley ran downstairs for the vacuum and some rags. Riley's second trip down produced two cans of soda.

"Thanks." Kai popped the tab and sat on Riley's bed. When she looked up at Riley, she saw her friend grinning from ear to ear.

"You are a total genius, Stretch. I never would've thought of cleaning up this way." Riley lifted her can in a toast.

Kai felt warmth spread across her chest and down into her belly, and took a deep breath. "Organization. That's the key. Besides, it's kinda fun when it's somebody else's stuff." Kai offered one of her rare smiles.

Riley smiled back. She sat on her sister's bed and crossed her legs. Kai watched her, but didn't say anything. Riley took a sip of her soda. "Can I ask you something kinda personal? It kinda feels important."

Kai quirked an eyebrow. "How personal?" Her face was steady, but her heart thudded painfully against her chest. *She's going to ask me if I like girls, I just know it.*

Riley watched her. "I don't know. I guess it's pretty personal."

Kai studied Riley. She looked a little nervous, but not upset or anything. The truth was, she didn't want to lie to Riley. *And, if Riley is really a friend, she'll find a way to accept me. Right?*

Riley bit her lip. "It's okay, don't worry. Forget I said anything."

The sound in her voice made Kai's stomach twist painfully. "No. Really. You're my best friend, Ri. You can ask me anything." *I hope.*

Riley studied her friend's eyes, seeming to seek out sincerity. She nodded her head. "Okay, but if you don't want to answer, that's okay. All right?"

Kai nodded. *Does she have any idea how pretty she is when she gets that serious look on her face?*

"Okay, here goes." Riley took a quick sip of her soda. "How come you never talk about your parents?"

Kai choked on the mouthful of soda she was sipping.

As she started coughing, Riley jumped up and ran over to pat her back. After a few hard pats, Riley asked, "Are you okay? You don't have to tell me anything, it's okay. But I wondered why you never mention them."

Kai swiped her sleeve across her mouth and considered Riley's serious expression. She started to take another sip of Sierra Mist, and then paused just to make sure Riley wasn't going to lob another surprise at her. Convinced she was only waiting for her answer, Kai took a small drink and set the can on the desk. She turned back to look at Riley.

"Um, well…I…I don't know. I mean, it was a time ago, you know, and I don't remember a lot."

Riley nodded solemnly and placed a hand on Kai's knee. "Hey, I really don't wanna make you uncomfortable and stuff. Okay?"

Kai nodded a silent offering of thanks.

Riley squeezed her knee gently. "The only reason I'm asking is because I want to know more about you."

Kai looked at Riley's hand on her knee. She wasn't really sure she wanted this conversation to go on, but she'd do just about anything to keep Riley's hand there. She looked back up to her green eyes. "It's okay. I really don't remember much, but I'll try to answer your questions." She lifted her hand and gently put in on top of Riley's. "Seriously, Ri, what do you want to know?"

Riley bit her bottom lip. "Well, I was at lunch last week. A couple of the kids were giving me a hard time about us being friends…"

Kai's eyes shifted into a serious stare.

Riley caught it and spoke quickly. "Really, it was just stupid stuff. You know?"

Kai's didn't know how to react.

Riley turned her hand over to take Kai's. She laced their fingers together. "Hey. It was stupid, and so are they. Okay?" She held Kai's dark look.

"Look Kai, they said your dad was a magician, and that he was trying to do some escape trick that didn't work."  She looked down at her lap and Kai waited. "They said he got killed, and that you didn't have a mom because she left him because she didn't want to be married to a guy that pulled rabbits out of his hat for a living."

The swell of emotion rolled up and across Kai's face faster than she could process. Her vision darkened and faded.

Kai felt herself imploding.

Jumbled memories—hard to sort, faded, but very dark.

She didn't remember her mom at all, but she remembered her dad. He was a big man, but gentle. He used to put his thumb and index finger together and chase her around the apartment saying the "pinchey bug" was going to get her. That always made her giggle. But there was more.

She flashed to him drumming and chanting, sweat rolling down his face. Another of him in a trance, ignoring her as she played with his necklace.

Another to a dark, thrumming dream of rats and snakes and spiders, everywhere. She could hear his voice: "I love you, little one." "You are the power of the sun." "This is who you always have been, who you always will be."

She remembered him putting her to bed with the broken rattle, the face of a laughing raven. Then, nothing.

Riley wiped Kai's cheeks. "Kai, what's happening? Are you okay?"

The voice seemed distant. Kai looked into her friend's eyes and saw only genuine concern. She'd never talked to anyone about her dad or her memories or her visions. Not even Aunt Tilley. She'd tried once when she was younger, and Tilley told her to let it go, to move on, to live in the here and now.

She took Riley's hand, and moved it back to her leg. "My mom left after I was born, so I don't really know anything about her. I was still pretty young when my dad died. It's like he was there, and then he wasn't. I went to stay with Tilley, and never left." She looked directly Riley. "Ri, my dad wasn't a magician. I mean, yeah, he did stupid birthday parties and stuff, but that was just to pay for things. I remember him taking me to an old shop that sold magical stuff. I don't remember what was in there, but it smelled old. When I was older I rode my bike by there, but was too scared to get close."

Riley held her eyes, and nodded.

"Dad was a shaman, Ri. He had powerful medicine, like my grandma. He would tell me stories, and it feels like I should remember them, but I don't. Something very bad happened to him that day, and no one, not even Tilley, will tell me what or why."

Riley shivered, and held Kai's hand tighter. "Wow, Kai. I'm sorry, I didn't realize what I was, you know, asking."

Kai took a deep breath, and forced a light smile. "It's just that I've never talked to anybody about it. No one ever asked. But, well, I thought I could tell you."

Riley smiled. "That means a lot. Thanks for trusting me."

Riley continued to ask questions while they finished cleaning, and Kai continued to answer as best she could until they both grew silent.

"It looks good, Stretch. I hope it's good enough for the warden."

Kai laughed out loud.

Riley beamed. "You are totally awesome, the room has never looked this good, and I like the new arrangement. I never would've thought of moving things around, but I like the desk by the window."

Kai stretched her arms over her head. "Yeah, it

gives you a little more space to store your clothes and CDs on the floor."

Riley picked up her stuffed Mr. Rat and threw it at Kai.

Kai caught it in one hand, grabbed the tail by her thumb and index finger, and tossed it quickly on the bed. "Gross."

Riley giggled, and she collapsed on the bed. "So tell me more about that weird magic store your dad used to take you to. I've lived in Lindan my whole life, and I never even knew a place like that existed."

Kai flopped on Rebekah's bed and crossed her long legs. "It's really close to school. We can head over there sometime, if you want."

Riley kicked off her shoes and stretched out on her bed. "Suddenly I'm tanked. That was so hard."

Kai banked her empty soda can off the door and into the wastebasket. "Come on, Riley, it only took us like an hour."

The bedroom door opened suddenly and Mrs. James popped her head in. It took a second to register, but the look in her face was priceless.

Riley sat up. "Hi, Mom."

Kai jumped to her feet.

"Oh. My. God! Riley Beth James, I never would've thought you could pull this off, especially when your dad told me you had company. It looks wonderful," she proclaimed dramatically as she walked around, nodding and wiping her finger across different surfaces. She turned to look at Kai.

"Kai, I guess I have you to thank for this. I just hope Riley didn't strong-arm you into doing it for her."

"No ma'am, I just made a few suggestions and pushed furniture around. Riley mostly did everything else." Kai blushed.

Riley bumped her. "Come on, Kai is being modest. I mean she has been a totally good influence on me, don't you think, Mom?"

Her mom looked from Riley to Kai, and smiled brightly. "Well it is true that Riley's grades have improved." She winked at Kai. "And I don't have to spend nearly as much time nagging her." She patted Kai on the shoulder. "Thank you, Kai. Oh, maybe you'd like to join us for dinner?"

Riley jumped up. "That's a great idea, Mom. Can you stay? I mean you said your aunt was working. Come on. Please!"

Kai felt a twinge of anxiety growing deep inside. She'd never been invited to a friend's house for dinner. *Oh, God, what if I say something stupid?* She wasn't sure how to act around someone else's parents—especially Riley's. One glace at Riley was all it took to make the decision. How could she say no to that smile? "Um, that's really nice of you Mrs. James. I don't want to intrude...I mean—"

"It's no trouble, honestly. I invited a coworker to stop by, the more the merrier."

"Then I should probably call my Aunt Tilley first to make sure it's okay."

"You're certainly welcome. Dinner will be in about thirty minutes. I'm proud of you, honey." She leaned over and kissed Riley on the top of the head, then turned and moved briskly out the door.

Kai looked back to Riley, and noticed she was smiling but had tears in her eyes. "Ri, what's wrong? Don't you want me to stay?"

Riley sniffed and gave her an exasperated look. "Of course, you goof!" She smiled. "I just don't think she's ever said that to me before."

Kai nodded and slipped her hand into her pocket for her phone. She dialed quickly and waited for someone to pick up. "Hi, Ms. Majors, it's Kai. Is my aunt available? I have a quick question for her." She nodded. "Uh, huh." She slid her right hand into her pocket. "Okay, thanks, I'll make it quick." She looked at Riley. "Even though I'm nervous about having dinner with your parents, I'm kinda excited, too.

"Aunt Tilley, hi, it's me, sorry to bother you again. I'm still over at Riley's, and her mom just asked if I could stay for dinner." Kai nodded. "Thanks, Tilley. Uh huh, promise. See you later. Okay. Bye." She ended the call and grinned. "She said it's okay as long as I'm home by nine."

※ ※ ※ ※

The dining room table was set for five, and Riley pulled Kai into the kitchen.

"You can help me with the silverware. We usually have spaghetti on Sunday night. Hope you like that."

Kai looked around the large kitchen. It was homey and it smelled wonderful. Mr. James was fiddling with the wine bottle and Mrs. James was dumping a big pan of spaghetti into a colander.

"Uh...I really like spaghetti, it's one of my favorites."

Riley handed her a stack of napkins and pulled silverware from the drawer just as the back door opened.

"Anybody home? Homeless detective looking for a hot meal." A tall and very attractive dark-haired woman stood stamping her feet by the back door.

"Hi, Sela, come on in. We're just about to eat."

"Hi, Aunt Sela," Riley said and gave her a big hug. "What a neat surprise. Mom didn't mention that you were gonna be here. I'm stoked."

The woman hugged Riley tightly.

"It's great to see you too, little one. Boy, have you filled out. What happened to that skinny little kid I used to carry around?"

Riley laughed and hung onto her arm. "Oh c'mon, I was never that skinny. But I did like being carried around. How come we don't see you very much?"

Mr. James gave Sela a one-armed hug. "Good question. We sure haven't seen much of you since you got the promotion."

The woman slipped off her leather jacket and Riley took it to hang up while Kai continued folding the napkins.

"Thanks, honey. I'll tell you, Richard, I thought the hard work would be studying for the detective exam. Turns out the job is just as hard."

"Come on Sela, this is Lindan, Minnesota. How much detective work could there possibly be?" He laughed.

"Let's move it inside everybody," said Mrs. James, carrying a large serving dish filled was steaming hot pasta and sauce. "Girls, would you grab the salad and the bread?"

Once they were seated, dishes were passed around and everyone helped themselves.

Kai watched carefully to see just what the protocol was for family dinners. She was on one side of the table with Riley, and across from them sat Mrs. James and Sela. Mr. James was at the head of the table and put his hands out, taking Riley and her mother's hands. Riley took Kai's hand and Sela reached across the table for the other one. It felt kind of weird to be holding hands of the perfect stranger, but she liked holding Riley's hand. A lot.

He mumbled a really fast prayer and suddenly everyone stopped holding hands and started eating. *Well, that was interesting.* She looked over Riley, who just smiled.

"Riley, I don't think you introduced your friend to Sela," Mrs. James said with a nod of her head.

Riley took a quick drink of water and swallowed. "Oh my gosh, that was so rude. I'm sorry. Aunt Sela, this is my friend Kai Tiva from school. We just met recently but she lives like two blocks from here and helps me some with my homework and stuff." Riley turned to face Kai. "Aunt Sela isn't really my aunt, but she's known me since I was like little. And she's mom's best friend from work. She used to take me camping for my birthday every year and it was so much fun. Why don't we do that anymore?"

"I'm not sure, do teenagers like camping? It's nice to meet you, Kai," Sela said. "Lizzie has told me a lot of nice things about you."

Kai could feel the heat rising up her chest to her neck and knew everyone was staring at her. "Thank you. It's nice to meet you, too."

Sela cocked her head to one side. "I hope you don't mind my asking, are you Lakota?"

Kai choked on a piece of garlic bread. No one had ever asked her. In fact, she wasn't sure anyone in Lindan would have a clue about the different tribes. "Yes. But I've been living here since I was two years old, so I don't remember too much. How did you know?"

"My mother was Lakota; my father is German."

"Well that's an interesting coincidence don't you think?" Mrs. James reached for the salad bowl. After serving herself, she said, "Kai, it looks like you're ready for a little more," and passed her the bowl.

"More wine, Sela?" Mr. James asked, handing her the bottle. "Lizzie tells me you were voted MVP of the Lindan PD softball league. Congratulations."

"Thanks, Richard. I think it was because I was the only woman on the team and they took pity on me."

Mrs. James leaned over and put her arm around her friend. "That's not true. You're the best pitcher that team has ever had, and a better athlete than most of the guys."

"That is so cool, Aunt Sela. Why didn't you ever tell us about your games? I would love to come and cheer you on. Kai isn't that cool? Kai plays basketball, like she's almost the star—"

"Riley!" Kai said as every muscle seized.

"I had no idea." Mr. James leaned back in his chair and gave her a big smile. "I hope we can catch a game sometime."

❧ ❧ ❧ ❧

Dinner was over by eight thirty and Riley walked Kai to the front door. "I'm really glad you could stay. That was fun. My parents aren't too bad once you get to know them."

Kai bumped her shoulder. "I had a really good time. Your dad's pretty cool and your mom is an awesome cook. I'm stuffed," she said, zipping up her jacket. "And your Aunt Sela is pretty neat, too."

"Thanks, I just love her. She so much fun it's like having an older sister that's cool." Riley handed Kai her gloves. "I wish you didn't have to leave already,"

"I know, me too." Kai nodded. "I've got a lot to do to get ready for school and I…well, I think I just better go." She took the gloves, touching Riley's hand as she did.

Riley started to say something, but clearly changed her mind, "Okay. Bye, Stretch. Look both ways before you cross the street."

"Will do. See ya, Shorty." Kai gave a quick finger wave.

Kai looked back at the house when she crossed the street. She guessed that the fancy pickup truck belonged to Sela. She was really kind of interesting and kinda familiar. *I wonder what that's all about.* She continued to move through the park as the conversations from dinner played over and over. Sela never mentioned a husband or roommate or anyone really.

Kai liked the way she dressed in jeans, turtleneck, and a really nice wool shirt.

She stuck her key in the front door lock and stopped. "Shit, I think Sela's gay. Wow."

꘎꘎꘎꘎

Riley watched as Kai trotted down the steps and across the front lawn, leaving footsteps in the fresh snow. The warm spot in Riley's chest began to ache, but it wasn't a bad ache, just a lonely ache. *I wish you could have stayed longer.*

As a special treat for doing such a good job on her room, Riley didn't have to clean up the kitchen. She kissed her mom and Aunt Sela on the cheek, then ran up to her room and closed the door. She grabbed her phone and sat down on her bed, and lay back against her pillow. She sent Kai a quick text, then grabbed Mr. Rat to her chest as a slow smile spread across her face.

The streetlight lit up the front yard, and it occurred to her there was something magical about the glittering snow that still fell lightly. Riley thought back to the afternoon she spent with Kai—her best friend.

They had so much fun, but it was more than that. She had fun with her friends, but it felt different with Kai. She smiled to herself. Everything reminded her of Kai, and her other friends were always teasing her that everything she talked about had something to do with her new "sidekick."

"What do you think, Mr. Rat?" she asked her fuzzy friend.

He looked at her with his beady little black crystal eyes, but said nothing, which was okay since he was a stuffed rat.

"She's just so cool, you know?" The rat continued to stare at her. "I mean she's really smart, and super nice, and when you get to know her, she can be pretty silly and make me laugh like crazy. You know?"

Mr. Rat continued to answer her by not saying a word.

"I can really be myself around her, and when we hang out together, it makes me feel really good inside."

She scratched Mr. Rat's belly. "You don't say much, do you?" She grinned. "How come I've never felt funny inside when I hang out with Amber and Meghan and Tiffany?"

On impulse, she got up and sat Mr. Rat on her desk, and opened the iPhoto app on her Mac. After they'd finished with the room, they had taken turns posing and making goofy faces. She scrolled through each one until she came to the one they took by accident. She looked carefully at the photo and the expression on Kai's face. They were sitting facing one another, less than a foot apart, and the look in Kai's deep brown eyes was…really sweet.

Riley felt her pulse quicken as a flush rode up her neck. She cropped the photo until it was just Kai's face. "What is she looking at, Mr. Rat?"

His expression remained steady, serious, knowing. "Is it me?"

Riley picked up Mr. Rat, pushed away from the computer, and plopped down on her bed. "It is, isn't it?" She held Mr. Rat up. "I like it when she does that. It makes me feel…" She rubbed a thumb between his eyes.

A slow, building wave of strange sensations began rippling inside of her, tingling and warm, then sharp and unexpected. She released a soft gasp. It was the touch. *When Kai left, the way she touched my hand… it felt the same way as it did at the pizza place.* Riley straightened, and looked at her fuzzy little confident. "Am I crushing on her?"

Mr. Rat's knowing stare said it all.

Riley took a deep breath and then released it slowly. "I am."

"And it's not like I just think she's cool and want to be like her, it's like I want her to touch me, and be here all the time, and…geez, everything."

She glanced over at the image the computer, then back to Mr. Rat. "What if I'm wrong?"

"Why earth would she like me? Gaak! She's tall. Completely good looking. God. When she smiles I want to wrap myself around every part of her!"

"Ugh! What am I? Well, for starters, you're short, dumb as a post, and a lame freak that people only like because you're Rebekah's sister! Face it, she's only hanging around with you because she knows you're lonely."

As she said those words, she felt a sharp pain in her chest. *What's so wrong with me?*

She hugged Mr. Rat to her, and knew that he somehow understood everything had just changed for her. *Please just make her like me!*

# *Chapter Five*

By twelve thirty on early dismissal days, the school cleared out quickly, but Kai and Riley were still sitting in the library finishing homework. On their walk to school that morning, Riley had seemed kind of down, so Kai had asked her if she was interested in learning a little more about her Native American heritage. That had really seemed to perk her up, because she'd been asking Kai nonstop questions all morning. It made Kai feel good knowing that Riley was interested in knowing more about her.

"Girls, it's after twelve thirty now. You need to finish up and be out of here by one, okay?"

"Yes, ma'am." Kai started stuffing books and pens into her backpack. She hesitated for a second, then unzipped the front pocket of the pack and pulled out a small object wrapped in newspaper. She held it out to Riley. "Here, I made this for you."

Riley smiled. "What is it?"

Kai shrugged as she handed it to Riley. "I just wanted to give you something that has a very powerful meaning to me."

Riley touched her hand as she took the small package. "That really means a lot to me, you know?"

Kai smiled solemnly and nodded as Riley pulled the tape off one end, and pulled out a small leather pouch with a long leather string. She turned it over in her hand and inspected it. The pouch was small, maybe only one inch by two, and made of soft, buttery leather. There was an image of a paw print on the small flap, and the pouch was cinched by a leather string.

Riley released a soft gasp as she inspected it closely. She whispered, "It's so cool." She looked up at Kai. "What it is?"

Kai grinned. "It's called a medicine bag. It's pretty much for talismans. You know, stuff like stones, herbs, things that have some sort of special meaning."

"Is it a necklace?"

Kai nodded. "Traditionally, they are used to bring protection, good luck, and healing. Stuff like that."

Riley nodded as she looked down at it again. She continued to finger the soft leather.

"I put a few things in there for you, but you can add or take out anything you don't want."

"Can I open it?" Riley's eyes met Kai's.

Kai nodded. "You can show people what's inside, and tell them about the things in it, but you can't let anyone else open it."

"Why?" Riley's forehead furrowed.

"Everything in there is a talisman."

Riley nodded yes, then shook her head no.

Kai smiled. "And talismans have sacred power. If someone else removes them from your medicine bag, they steal that power from you."

"Wow, that's intense."

Kai laughed lightly. "Yeah, it is." She pointed to the bag. "Go ahead and open it up."

Riley loosened the leather cord and opened the flap. She looked in, and then gently shook the contents into her left hand. "What is all this stuff?"

Kai reached a finger out and gently separated the items in Riley's palm. She pointed to each item.

"This is corn, it's the symbol of life. This little thing is a smudge stick; it's made of tobacco, sage, cedar, and sweet grass, the four sacred herbs. This one is crystal, and it gives energy and protection." She touched a small black stone. "This one is jet, which protects you against injury and illness, and this one is turquoise. It brings clarity."

She picked up a small fetish. "And this little guy is a bear, and he's made of malachite, which represents prosperity and creativity." She pointed to a small square. "And this little silver token has a raven's foot." She graced Riley with a serious look. "The raven means a lot of things to us. They bring light, help us see the truth, they represent change, and they are the bearers of magic. They're probably our most sacred animal spirit."

Riley seemed mesmerized by the small items in her hand, and by the soft tone of Kai's voice. She pointed to a small bright blue stone streaked with lines of white and gold. "What's this one?"

Kai's face warmed as a light blush rose up her neck. "Um, yeah. That's a little piece of lapis lazuli."

"It's really pretty." Riley picked it up and looked at it closely. "What does it do?"

Kai felt a little off-center. "Um, lots of thing, I guess."

Riley eyed her suspiciously. "Like what?"

Kai shrugged and looked down at the leg of her jeans, and started playing with a frayed piece of fabric above her knee. "Well, some people think it can bring inspiration, prosperity, healing, and other stuff."

Riley cocked her head. "Like what other stuff?"

Kai swallowed audibly. "I don't know. Stuff, you know, like love, I guess."

A warm glow bloomed on Riley's cheeks, and she reached over and hugged Kai. "You are the coolest friend ever."

Kai leaned into the quick hug and soaked it up. *You might not think so if you knew why I put that stone in there.*

As she sat back, Riley started carefully putting each of the small items back in the bag. "Do you have one?"

Still reeling from the quick hug, Kai simply nodded an affirmative, and tugged on the leather string around her neck. She held the small pouch out. "It used to belong to my dad, but Tilley gave it to me a few years ago."

Riley reached out and touched it. "It has a paw print on it, like mine does."

Kai smiled. "Yeah, it's a badger paw." She pointed at the print. "See the long claws?"

Riley nodded. "Does it have a meaning, too?"

"Yeah." Kai slipped the necklace back over her head and then under her shirt. "Badgers are really tough and aggressive, and seeing their print is a sign that you can do anything you put your mind to. It's kinda like knowing their animal spirit has your back."

Riley laughed and slipped her medicine bag around her neck. "I like that. If only it could help me with science."

Kai laughed with her. "I think it would probably work better for you if I was the one that helped."

Riley laughed while she gazed at the details of the small pouch. "I thought you told me your Aunt Tilley didn't believe in Native American stuff."

Kai shrugged. "She wanted me to have something to remind me of my dad."

"How come you know so much?" Riley picked up her backpack and zipped it.

Another shrug. "Even though she doesn't much believe in it, she thinks it's important for me to understand my heritage, and be prepared for how it affects me."

Riley's brow furrowed. "What do you mean?"

"Face it, Ri." She looked her in the eyes and spoke softly. "I'm not really like anybody else around here."

"Hey." Riley bumped her with her knee. "That's not a big deal."

"That's the thing, Riley, it is a big deal. Around here"—she gestured in a wide arc—"I don't look like anyone else, I don't talk like everyone else, and I sure as heck don't act like everyone else." Kai's voice trailed off. "You've heard them, half the kids in this school think my name is Tonto, Sacagawea, or Pocahontas."

A hurt look crossed Riley's face. "That's not true." She placed her hand on Kai's forearm. "The kids that say that are just stupid jerks. They think it makes them cool and—"

"No, Ri. They do it to remind me I don't belong here." Kai's voice was firm.

Riley shook her head. "But you do, Kai." She squeezed her friend's arm again. "You do belong here. Do you have any idea how lonely I'd be if you hadn't punched Zach?" A tentative smile creased her face.

Kai felt her heart thud hard against her chest. *God, Ri, do you have any idea how lonely I'd be if I hadn't punched Zach?*

"Look." Riley leaned forward and held eye contact. "I know I probably don't get it, but I want to because I really care about you." She moved her hand down Kai's arm and took her hand. "Please know I'm on your side, okay?"

Kai felt the air leave her chest, and struggled to center herself. A few deep breaths. Two more. She nodded, then words failed her.

Riley sat back. "Hey, I think it's really cool that you have your dad's medicine bag."

Kai sat up a little straighter, and took the opportunity to pull in a few more cleansing breaths. She appreciated how Riley backed off the subject. "Yeah."

She smiled lightly, almost sadly. "I don't really remember much about him, but I've always had these, I don't know, dreams or whatever where it seems like I see parts of his life. I guess…" She shrugged. "I guess it makes me feel closer to him." She sighed as she started picking at the threads of her jeans again. "Sometimes I just wish…I don't know…that maybe my dreams were happier." She felt a hot stab deep inside her chest.

Riley took Kai's hand. "What do you mean?"

Kai gave her a light squeeze, more for herself than for Riley. "No one's really ever told me how he died, you know? Just that he had an accident doing some new trick for his show."

She looked into Riley's warm eyes and felt a surprising flood of comfort. "But, in my dreams, I see him running. Scared. Begging for his life. Then…"

Riley waited, watching.

Kai's expression tightened, and her voice softened to a whisper. "Then nothing."

Riley leaned in and gave her friend another quick hug. "I want to say something, but this is one of those times where words just aren't there."

Kai responded to the hug, then took a breath and leaned back. She felt the hole in her chest closing again, and smiled. It was the first time she'd ever trusted anyone enough to try to explain was going on inside of her. *Please don't run away.*

"Hey." Riley brightened. "Why don't we get out of here and go check out the freaky magic store you were telling me about?"

Kai suddenly felt much lighter and gave Riley a bright smile. "Yeah, come on, before we get detention for spending too much time in the library."

A bubble of laughter escaped from Riley as she grabbed her Mr. Rat backpack and pulled Kai up by the hand.

# *Chapter Six*

T ake a left here." Kai gently placed a hand on Riley's lower back and gestured down a short street.

"Mystic Lane?" Riley looked tentatively down the street, then back up at Kai. "Seriously?"

Kai shrugged. "Corny. I know. Come on." She nudged Riley down the dark, narrow street. On one side loomed the brick back wall of a large mercantile exchange, and on the other several smaller, mostly boarded up specialty shops. It ended in a "T" intersection with even darker alleyways.

"Dang, this neighborhood must've seen its day in the sixties or seventies. Look at the shops with faded, cracked psychedelic paint jobs." Riley pointed. "Must've been a rockin' place back then, but it now just looks kind of worn out and discarded."

Kai pointed to a wood sign. "Agrippa's Natural Magic — Unique Items Both Mystic and Occult." It was barely legible because of the old-fashioned printing, and it had suffered enough weather damage over time to make it look at least a hundred years old.

A tilting weather vane atop one of the buildings moved, catching Kai's eye. A large black bird flapped its wings and cocked its head. She was certain he was watching them, and she shivered.

Riley paused as they neared the door and shivered as well. "Have you been here since you were a kid?"

Kai scuffed her heel against a bank of snow. "Sorta."

Riley looked up and tugged Kai's multicolored scarf. "Sorta yes, or sorta no?"

Kai shrugged. "Both, I guess."

"You're killing me, Stretch." Riley gave the scarf another firm tug.

"I've come down here a couple of times." Kai looked to the door, and then back to Riley. "But I never went in."

Riley halted the tugging, but held onto the scarf. "How come?"

Another shrug. "Dunno, I guess I just didn't know what I was looking for."

Riley bit her bottom lip and looked up at her. "Tell you what. Let's take a quick look around, and if you want to leave, we can. Okay?"

Kai smiled. "Okay." When she reached for the door and pushed, a small bell jingled and the hinges creaked loudly. Kai stepped in and Riley followed. She closed the door, and both waited for their eyes to adjust to the dark.

Riley sneezed, and started waving at the dust motes floating through the air on the watery sunbeams from the front window. "Do you think they forgot the pay the electric bill?" she whispered. "I mean, I get the mysterious vibe and all, but how can anybody find anything in here?"

There was a large counter running across the wall on the right, which featured bins full of gaudy, eye-catching magic paraphernalia. There were colored scarves, balls, plastic and metal wands, packages of cards, fake coins, linked metal rings, flash powder, and shelves of books and DVDs.

Riley wandered down the counter in sheer amazement. "Ouch," she said as Kai poked her in the ribs. "What was that for?"

Kai simply tipped her chin and looked to the back of the shop where a man stood backlit between two parted velvet curtains. He looked totally creepy and more than a little menacing.

He started toward them. "There something you kids want?" His accented voice was oily and so low it seemed to vibrate.

Kai stepped between Riley and the approaching man. "Uh, yeah, do you have any drums?"

"What kinda drums?" He stood almost as tall as Kai, with greasy coal-black hair and watery eyes. His skin was very pale and he had long, yellowed nails.

"Plains Indian."

He looked at her warily and answered tersely. "No. Don't carry that stuff here."

The bell on the door jingled, and a man backed in pulling a hand truck with half a dozen large boxes. He bumped into case of swords, daggers, and knives, and cursed under his breath.

The shop owner gave the girls another nettled look, then walked over to the deliveryman and ushered him behind the long counter and into what was surely a storeroom.

Kai grabbed Riley's elbow. "Shh! Follow me." She pointed to the old wood spiral staircase on the far side of the shop that led a balcony. Riley hurried up the steps behind Kai. The small, dusty, dimly lit area contained several glass cases with an odd assortment of artifacts and objects. The far wall showcased books floor to ceiling, and an old desk.

"Dude, this is a so cool!" Riley began to tiptoe

past each case slowly. "But majorly creepy." She bent down to examine a pile of bones and feathers in one of the display cases. "Gross. It looks like something died in here." She looked back over her shoulder at Kai. "What're you doing?"

"I wanna make sure he doesn't catch us up here," Kai whispered, glancing over her shoulder.

"Eww, he's even got shrunken heads," Riley whispered loudly. "And that one looks like a fetus."

Kai tiptoed across the room and looked over Riley's shoulder into the case. She felt her stomach drop, and whispered quietly, "This isn't the kind of magic I was expecting, Ri."

"Why, what's wrong?" Riley said as the front doorbell jingled again.

"Thanks, I'll see you next week."

Kai turned quickly and crept back to the balcony in time to see the very angry owner glance up and meet her eyes with a cold, dark stare. A flush rose up his pasty face, and Kai felt waves of angry energy hit her.

She turned. "We've got to get out of here!" Kai grabbed Riley's elbow and pushed her toward the rear wall of the store where a burned-out exit sign dangled.

"You're not supposed to be up there!" the owner screamed as he started up the staircase.

The door was padlocked on the inside. "Shit!" Kai looked around frantically until she spotted an old-fashioned fire axe leaning against one of the display cases. "Get back." She raised the axe over her head and powered it into the hasp holding the lock. The rusty lock shattered, and Kai kicked the door open.

She grabbed Riley's hand and pulled her out onto the fire escape. "We gotta hurry, Ri."

The ladder hit the ground at the same time the

owner stepped out on the fire escape, and the girls took off running down the alley. Kai pulled them behind a pile of empty produce crates and cautiously peered around the edge as she tried to slow her breathing. "I don't think he followed us." She turned to check Riley out. "You okay?"

Riley giggled. "You sure know how to show a girl a good time."

Kai wheeled around. "God, Ri, I didn't know the dude was bat-shit crazy!"

Riley put her hand on Kai's shoulder. "Hey, I'm just kidding." She locked eyes with Kai and smiled gently. "Crazy Creepy Guy aside, that was kinda fun. He's got some wicked cool stuff."

Kai took another quick look around the edge of the crates, then back.

Riley stood up, and reached a hand out to Kai. "Wouldn't it be wild to take my dad in there sometime? I bet Crazy Creepy Guy'd tinkle into his cheap tassel loafers."

A slow smile spread across Kai's face as she let her friend haul her into standing position. "Tinkle?" She started to laugh. "Trust me, Ri, guys like that don't tinkle."

Riley put her hands on her hips and gave her friend an incredulous look. "They do so."

Kai shook her head. "No, they don't."

"Yes, they do!" Riley huffed.

Kai mimicked Riley's position. "No, they don't"

"Yes, Kai. They do."

"No, Ri, they don't."

Riley folded her arms across her chest and glared up into Kai's amused brown eyes. She fought a smile. "Well, if they don't tinkle into their cheap tassel loafers, what do they do, Ms. I-Hang-Around-In-Skanky-Alleys-Holding-Axes?"

Kai looked down at the axe she still held a death grip on, and started laughing. She leaned the axe against the brick wall and brushed her hands off on her jeans. "Well, Ms. Look-At-The-Cool-Shrunken-Heads-Ooh-Is-That-A-Fetus?" She dodged a playful slap from Riley. "Crazy, creepy, bat-shit guys like that are a lot more likely to piss, poop, crap, dump, whiz, or even drop a pile. They don't, in my humble opinion, tinkle."

Riley howled as she swiped at the tears rolling down her face, "God! You are such a—"

A blood-curdling scream pierced the air.

Kai took off running in the direction of the sound. "Call for help," she yelled as she sprinted down the dark alley.

⚜ ⚜ ⚜ ⚜

Riley took off after her friend, trying to get the phone out of her backpack.

As she skidded around a rusted Dumpster, she saw a burly figure in black wrestling with an older woman in bright yellow, with Kai barreling toward them at full speed. Kai hit the man in black with a flying tackle, and the little old lady in yellow slumped to the ground.

The momentum drove the man into the brick wall, and he released a loud grunt. Kai tried to force him to the ground, but he elbowed her once hard in the face. Kai's head snapped back, but she held her grip.

The man pivoted and pushed Kai hard into the wall. Her head hit the bricks with a thud and the air gushed out of her lungs as she slid to the ground. The man in black kicked out and connected hard with her thigh. A second kick landed on her shoulder.

"NOOOOOOO!" Riley screamed as she sprinted past the little old lady, smacked the man across the shoulders with her backpack, and then tried to push him away from Kai. He pushed at her, but stumbled over Kai's feet.

Riley swung the backpack again, and he fell to one knee. She swung a third time, but he grabbed at one of the straps and tried to pull it out of her hands. Riley kicked at him as she yanked back on her backpack. He pulled hard again, and Riley flew into him. As he stood up, he shrugged out of her grasp, and took off down the alley and around the corner onto Mystic Lane.

As the echo of the man's footsteps faded, Riley fell to the ground beside Kai. "Oh, God!" She touched her shoulder and shook her lightly. "Hey, are you okay?"

Kai didn't respond.

A frightened sob bubbled up from Riley's chest. "Kai?" She brushed a lock of dark hair off Kai's forehead. "Please be okay, please."

When Kai didn't move, Riley scrambled over to her phone. "Damn it!" she muttered when she saw she didn't have any bars.

"Hey." A soft voice came from behind her.

Riley looked back at Kai and saw dark eyes staring at her.

Kai sat up a little straighter. "Where'd you learn to talk like that?" She reached up and rubbed the back of her head, then looked at her palm.

Riley scrambled back to Kai's side and engulfed her in a huge hug. "Are you alright? Are you hurt? Are you bleeding? Can you move? Should I—"

"I'm okay, Ri." Kai cut her off as she returned the hug.

"You are?" Riley pulled back and fixed a questioning gaze at Kai.

Kai nodded.

"Really?"

Kai nodded again.

Riley punched Kai hard in the shoulder.

"Ouch!" Kai rubbed her arm where the fist made contact. "Why'd you do that?"

"You idiot! What did you think you were doing?"

Kai blinked as she continued to rub her arm.

"That guy was huge, he could have really hurt you." Riley pointed at her for emphasis. "He could have had a gun, or a knife, or a TASER, or God knows what else." She took a deep breath. "He could have."

Riley saw Kai's eyes grow wide and slowly move up to a place several feet above her shoulder. She turned, dreading the return of the man in black just in time to see a huge one-eyed rat fly off the edge of the Dumpster and onto Kai.

Kai screamed as the rat landed on her chest. She started clawing at it, but the rat eluded her swatting hands. She rolled onto her knees and tried to stand up, but slipped and went down hard on her shoulder. The rat clambered onto her shoulders as her screaming and swatting continued.

Riley ran over, grabbed the squirming rat by its long thin tail, and yanked. Its nails dug into Kai's jacket as Kai let out another howl. Riley grabbed the rat with both hands and yanked again, harder. It lost its tiny-fingered grip on Kai's wool coat, and Riley held it out as she ran over and chucked it up and over the edge of the trash bin.

Kai continued to scream, covering her head with flaying arms. "Get him off me! Get him off of me!"

Riley ran back and knelt down beside her. "He's gone, Kai. He's gone, you're okay." Kai tried to scramble past Riley, who reached out and grabbed her shoulders. Kai tried to pull away, shaking and sobbing.

"Shh, it's okay. It's gone." Riley wrapped her into a hug and held on. Kai tried halfheartedly to pull away, but Riley held on for dear life. She continued to whisper reassuringly into her ear, "It's okay. Relax. It's gone now. I've got you."

After a minute, Kai's shaking began to lessen, but she still sobbed quietly.

"I've got you, Kai," Riley whispered into her ear soothingly as she shifted to get a better hold and hugged tighter. "I promise I'll never let anyone or anything hurt you. Ever." She softly kissed the top of Kai's head.

Kai tentatively reached out and put her arms around Riley's waist, and tucked her head beneath Riley's chin.

Riley continued to rock her until Kai finally took a deep breath and leaned back. "Are you okay now?"

Kai looked at her with red eyes, and batted long wet lashes at her several times. She sniffed and wiped her face with her sleeve, then looked into Riley's eyes and smiled unconvincingly. "I feel like a total idiot."

Riley raised a hand to Kai's face and gently wiped at a stray tear that was about to roll down her cheek. "No. You're not. That was…"

Suddenly, they heard scuffling and a frustrated moan a few feet away. A bright yellow coat and hat rose from a pile of discarded boxes on the far side of the Dumpster. The little old lady, much less than five feet tall, even in her sensible yellow pumps, stood unsteadily, her hat tipped jauntily to one side.

Riley turned quickly to Kai. "Are you okay, can you get up?"

"Yeah, I'm fine," Kai said, using the side of the Dumpster to steady her.

Riley made sure Kai was steady, then turned to look at the little old lady in yellow. "Where'd she go?" Riley turned back to Kai, her eyes wide.

Kai looked to where the little old lady in yellow had been, rubbed her eyes, then back to Riley. "I think I hit my head harder than I thought I did. Wasn't there a little old lady in sunshine yellow that looked like the queen over there in those boxes?"

Riley looked back over at the pile of discarded boxes. "Maybe she fell down again?"

"Right," Kai said as she limped over to the pile of crumpled cardboard. She kicked a few of boxes around, and then looked back at Riley. "Nada."

"Really?" Riley cocked her head and walked over to where Kai stood.

Kai rubbed her shoulder as she looked around the alley. "This has been the weirdest damn afternoon ever!"

Riley picked up a big "Processed Meat Product" box, and tossed it aside. Wiping her hand across her jeans leg, she knelt down. "Hey! Take a look at this." Riley held up a slim twelve-inch wand covered with sparkly glitter and tiny jewels of all colors.

Kai looked at the wand, then at Riley, then back to the wand, and back to Riley. She scratched her jaw, and surveyed the alley. "I'm not being Punk'd am I?"

Riley turned in a slow circle, and then looked up

at Kai. "No...am I?"

Kai shook her head slowly.

"What are we going to do with this?" Riley said.

Kai shrugged. "It's gotta be part of the little old lady's costume or something."

Riley turned it over in her hands a few times. "It's heavier than you'd think, pretty fancy for a prop. Here, take it," she said, handing Kai the wand.

"What am I gonna do with it?" Kai recoiled and handed it back.

"Well, we have to find the lady and give it back to her," Riley said, reaching down to brush some melting snow off her jeans. "Did you see which way she went?"

Kai walked to the corner and looked around. "You wouldn't think a little old lady like that could move so fast." She turned to look back at Riley. "She should be easy to find though, especially in that bright yellow coat and hat."

A dark cloud passed over the sun as a gust of wind swirled bits of paper and leaves through the alley, causing them both to shiver. Riley moved a little closer to her tall friend.

"I'd feel better if you held onto this," she said, pushing the wand toward Kai again. "Do you think we should go back and ask Crazy Creepy Guy in the magic shop?"

Kai stopped, took the wand, gave it a quick once-over, and then shoved it in her back pocket. "I don't think so, Ri. He might know where it came from, but I don't want to go anywhere near him again. I got a real weird vibe off him." She pulled her collar up against the wind. "Maybe we should put a note up on the street sign saying we found something at the end of Mystic Lane and tell the owner to contact us. I don't think we should say what it is."

Riley watched carefully as her friend's face settled into dark mask of apprehension. She didn't recognize the expression, and it made her a little uneasy inside.

"We better head for home. This place is creeping me out a little," Riley said as she tugged on Kai's arm.

# *Chapter Seven*

Kai nodded and pointed the opposite direction. "Let's go this way so we don't have to walk by the magic store."

As the girls began to put some distance between them and the alley, the wind began to let up, and the sun started to poke through dissipating clouds.

Kai pulled the wand out of her pocket, and began studying it as they walked. "You're right, this thing weighs a ton." She pointed it at a bush and flicked her wrist. "Abracadabra!"

Nothing happened.

"What were you trying to turn it into?" Riley asked.

"Anything but a rat," Kai said dryly.

"Hey, you're one for one!" Riley smiled.

Kai ran her thumb across several of the shiny jewels. "Man, this thing is totally blinged out."

Riley nudged Kai with her shoulder. "I think it's cool. And it totally completes your urban grunge look."

Kai stopped and stared at Riley, a hurt look spreading across her face.

Riley turned back to look at Kai, and stepped forward. "Hey, I was just joking." She grabbed Kai's forearm and squeezed lightly.

"Yeah, sure." Kai nodded, her smile not quite reaching her eyes. "Come on, let's go." She started walking again. "You said you had to be home by four thirty."

Riley jogged a few steps to catch up. "Come on, Kai. Slow down."

Kai released a deep sigh and turned around as large shadow from the west eclipsed the sun. Kai glanced up at the rapidly approaching object and shouted, "Run!"

Riley saw an ominous black bird swooping toward them, screeching an unearthly warning. She started to run, but was already ten feet behind Kai's long loping gait. She heard the whoosh of flapping wings, and could feel the bird getting closer with each step.

"KAI!" Her scream was lost in another chilling screech. She turned to see how close the big bird was, and threw her hands over her head as it swooped down, talons extended.

"Hit the ground!" Kai whirled around at Riley's second scream. The black bird banked hard, and moved into position for another strike.

Riley clambered to a sitting position, and glanced from the approaching bird to Kai, a look of stark fear fracturing her features.

Kai started running back to Riley, but realized she wasn't going to make it in time. She stopped and threw the heavy, stone-studded wand at the lunging bird. The wand stuck its intended target with a thud. A glowing yellow orb swallowed the squawking creature, and just as suddenly, collapsed in on it. With a loud crack of electricity, a bright yellow finch emerged and darted away, and the wand clattered to the pavement.

Kai dropped her backpack, ran over to Riley, and knelt down next to her. "Ri, you okay?'

Riley was breathing hard, and trembling. She looked at Kai and nodded, then laid her head on her shoulder.

Kai put her arms around Riley and gave her a protective hug, rubbing her back gently. She looked up and down the street, but saw nothing out of place. "It's gone now, okay?"

Riley nodded into Kai's shoulder, and then pulled back to look at her. She started to speak, but stopped short. She started again, with the same result. She released a pained sigh and nodded.

"Are you okay? You fell pretty hard." Kai started looking her friend over for obvious injury.

Riley ran a hand across her face, then looked at her palm. It was bruised and raw, but not bleeding. She noticed the tear in the knee of her jeans, and poked at the hole. "A little bruised, but nothing broken."

Kai smiled lightly, and rested her hand on Riley's thigh. "I was pretty scared when you fell, Ri."

Riley crooked her head, and gave Kai a smile. "Me, too." She laughed lightly.

"Can you stand up?"

"Yeah." Riley offered a hand. "Help me."

Kai stood, and took hold of Riley's hand. She tugged as Riley stood, then started brushing the snow and slush off her coat.

Riley tucked her hair behind an ear and looked around, then up at her friend. "Kai? What the heck just happened?"

Kai blinked hard several times, then shrugged. "No clue."

Riley felt a bubble of exasperation rise in her stomach. "Where did that vulture thing come from? Where did it go? What did you do to it?"

"I don't really know."

"Well, you've got to know something, Kai." Riley's voice was getting louder.

"I told you, I don't know any more than you do." Kai's voice stayed soft. "I just looked up and saw that thing when you screamed. We ran. When I turned around you were on the ground. It was going to attack you, so I threw the wand at it."

Riley's fierce look told Kai to explain the rest of it.

Kai let out a deep sigh. "Well, you saw it! The wand hit the bird, and there was a crack, like lightening, and a burst of something yellow."

"When I looked again, the bird was gone," Riley added.

"It flew that way." Kai pointed in the direction they had come from. "At least that's what I think happened."

Riley licked her lips and started to say something, then stopped. She looked down at the wand lying on the ground, then back to Kai. "What is that thing?"

"I have no idea," Kai said, bending over to pick up the wand. "I don't think it's a prop though."

Riley nodded. "I think we better get going." She just wanted to get home, crawl under the covers, and think about everything that had just happened. Medicine bags, creepy guys, muggers, rats, disappearing little old ladies, angry black birds, and the stupid wand thing. *Geez.*

Kai nodded her head in agreement, and picked up their backpacks. "Yeah, let's get going."

Riley started walking, and noticed Kai quietly fell into step with her. She had a really bad feeling, sort of like when you know you flunked a test by one question before you found out your grade.

As she unzipped her coat to cool off a little, Riley glanced over at Kai. Looking at Kai always made her feel good, even with all this weird stuff going on. Still, she noticed that her head was starting to hurt, and she was starting to feel like she'd walked a hundred miles.

When Kai stopped, Riley noticed they were already at the park, and reached for the backpack that Kai was still carrying for her. "I'll see you tomorrow, okay?"

Kai let her tug on the backpack, but she didn't un-shoulder it. "You know, Ri, I think I'm gonna walk all the way home with you. If that's okay, I mean?"

Riley looked up into the brown eyes, and tugged again. "That's okay. I can make it from here."

"No," Kai said a little more firmly. "It's starting to get dark, and I'd feel a lot better if I knew you got home okay."

A soft smile crossed Riley's face. "Then who's gonna make sure you get home okay?"

Kai shrugged. "I'll just run, it's only a couple of blocks. No one will bother me."

"Okay." Riley started walking again.

When they finally got to her house, Riley climbed the first step, turned, and took hold of Kai's jacket collar. "Where did that vulture thing come from, Kai?" she asked again. She stared into her eyes, hoping for an answer that made sense and fearing one that didn't.

Kai shook her head slowly, and looked down at her shoes. "I really don't know. Maybe it was just a scavenger that got turned around because of the sudden wind change…"

"I better go in. Maybe we can talk later, okay?" Riley said, suddenly letting go of Kai's collar and turning to climb the rest of the steps. The feeling in her stomach made her want to cry, and she just wanted to lie down for a while. Everything about today would make more sense when she felt a little clearer.

She hurried up the steps without looking back.

# *Chapter Eight*

Riley closed the front door and leaned her forehead against the jamb as she closed her eyes. The vibration started in her legs and soon it felt like the whole house lurched. *Oh, God, what's happening to me?* She jogged up the stairs to her room, hoping to avoid any questions from her mom. As she hit the top step, she shouted, "I'll be back down in a little bit to help you with dinner. Okay? I've just got to lie down for a while."

It was getting dark, but she left the light off as she tossed her coat on Bekah's bed. Riley kicked off her shoes, flopped onto her bed, and curled into a ball. So much had happened since they left the library, and none of it made any sense. Tears welled up in her eyes, and she grabbed Mr. Rat and pulled him close.

For some reason, the things Kai said about her dad and her heritage intrigued her, but left her feeling a little edgy. She reached for the medicine bag hanging beneath her shirt, and clutched it tightly. It was obviously something that meant a lot to Kai, because she'd put a lot of thought into the things she put in it.

Riley sniffed as she swiped at a tear.

Getting Kai to talk about herself wasn't easy. So the fact that she trusted Riley with such personal stuff must be pretty huge. She nuzzled Mr. Rat. No one had ever trusted her like that before, and it made her feel really special. "So why do I feel all jitsey like I'm waiting for the gross one-eyed rat-man to jump out of the closet any second now?"

She rolled onto her back and stroked the soft fur of her stuffed confidant. "Mr. Rat, I gotta tell you, we had a pretty freaky afternoon. Kai took me to a really wicked cool magic store, but the guy who ran it was a major creepy dude. And he chased us like he was ready kill us or something." She cringed as she remembered Kai grabbing the axe to break the door lock.

"Then...there was a little old lady getting beat up in the alley by some huge, ugly guy, and Kai went all ballistic on him without even thinking. What a dork! Then he knocked her down and started wailing on her until I smacked him with my backpack. I think he kinda got spooked or something 'cause he just ran away."

Mr. Rat looked at her with serious, beady little eyes.

"Oh, God, like that's not enough drama...this humongous one-eyed rat totally hurled himself off the Dumpster right onto Kai and she totally freaked out."

Mr. Rat looked at her skeptically.

"I mean, seriously freaked out." She kissed him on the forehead. "He was totally not cool like you."

The sight of her best friend screaming and cowering next to the trash container squeezed her heart. Kai always seemed so brave and in control. "I tried to hold her and stop her from being scared, Mr. Rat."

Riley felt an unexpected tingle low in her belly as she remembered was how good it felt to hold Kai. She stroked Mr. Rat's ears as he patiently waited for her to continue.

Even in her winter coat, Kai's muscles were strong, and as Riley held her, she caught just the faintest hint of her shampoo. Something clean and fresh, something that just fit her. She remembered noticing how Kai's black hair had almost royal blue streaks in the alley lighting, and smiled lightly as she remembered how good it felt when she stroked her fingers through the silky strands.

Riley blushed lightly at the memory of kissing Kai on the head. She hadn't really thought about it, but it made her feel like she was somehow really capable of protecting her friend. "Mr. Rat, can I tell you a secret?"

She had his full attention.

As she started to speak, a fluttering started in her chest and she felt an unfamiliar quiver low in her belly. It felt really good, but confusing at the same time. "I know you know I think about her all the time, right?"

Mr. Rat's silence was his acknowledgement, so she scratched his fuzzy chest. "Sometimes I think about kissing her. Not like I did in the alley, but really kissing her. Like on the lips and stuff."

She took his tail and tickled his nose with it, a familiar thank-you for not judging her.

"Anyway, we took the long way around the block, so we didn't have to walk past the magic store and run into that skeevy guy who chased us." She shuddered and rolled over onto her side, clutching Mr. Rat protectively to her chest.

"And then, as we were walking down Western Avenue, this huge, ugly, stinky vulture thing came out of nowhere and started chasing us." She swiped at a tear that was ready to spill down her cheek. "Kai took off, and I tried to keep up, but she can really move when she wants to. I guess I tripped or something and went down."

Mr. Rat settled into her arms, engrossed by his

person's horror story.

A cold wave passed over Riley as she remembered the large black bird with blood-red eyes swooping down toward her, sounding like it was shrieking, "*Raghallaigh.*"

She and Mr. Rat bolted upright. *My name.* She forgot the bird called her by name. *Did Kai hear that? Why didn't she say anything when I asked about what happened?*

Riley laid Mr. Rat against the pillow and grabbed her backpack. She rummaged around until she found her cell phone, and then stopped. She turned to Mr. Rat, her voice becoming hoarse. "If Kai knew what was going on, why didn't she say anything to me?"

Mr. Rat couldn't answer that question.

Riley released a frustrated breath. Lately, whenever anything came up—at all—she immediately grabbed her phone to text Kai. It was a no-brainer.

This time something stopped her.

*Why do I have a bad feeling about all of this?*

As she stared down at the phone, she tried to make sense of the weird events of the day. It wasn't all bad, really. Up until the guy in the magic store freaked out, she and Kai were having a lot of fun.

A sudden wave of nausea made her reach out for her desk for support. The low-grade headache she'd had for a while began to intensify, and she turned and wrenched open the bedroom door and lurched for the bathroom across the hall. She didn't have time to lift the seat before she fell to her knees and her turkey tacos from lunch were violently deposited into the bowl.

When she stopped retching, she leaned her forehead across her arms, fighting the feeling that her stomach was turning inside out. Another wave of nausea bubbled up, and she began dry heaving. As she sat up a second time, she felt the cramps in her belly beginning to ease a bit.

"Honey, what's wrong?"

Riley turned and looked into the concerned eyes of her mother kneeling next to her.

She leaned into her mother's arms and began to cry. "I don't know, Mom."

Her mother rubbed her back, then reached up and placed a cool hand on her forehead. "You feel a little feverish." She kissed Riley's sweat-soaked hair. "Why don't you get into your PJs and climb into bed, and I'll get the thermometer. Okay?"

Riley nodded and gingerly stood up. She brushed her teeth quickly, and then went back to her room. She grabbed her favorite jamblies, changed, grabbed Mr. Rat, and pulled the covers back. She snuggled down, clutching her fuzzy friend beneath her chin. The flannel sheets and thick comforter felt good, and she felt a little better knowing her mom would take care of her.

Within a few minutes, her mom returned with a tall glass of icy 7-Up and the temporal thermometer. She placed it softly against Riley's forehead. "One hundred point four. You better take some Tylenol and stay in bed for a little while, honey."

Her mom went into the bathroom and called over her shoulder, "That was Ruth Thorsen on the phone earlier. She's letting everyone know that Mr. Winkler was called out of town for a family emergency."

Riley sat up. "What? He can't leave now, what about the concert?"

Her mom returned with two tablets. "Swallow these," she said and handed her the soda. "Family emergencies happen, Riley. It's no one's fault and I can assure you he didn't do it on purpose. There's no need to worry about it tonight, I'm sure they'll figure something out."

"But Mom, I've been practicing really hard. We have to do this, it's really important to me." She put the tablets in her mouth and washed them down with the cold soda.

Her mom leaned down and kissed her forehead, then took the glass. "Honey, this isn't about you, it's about Mr. Winkler, and I'm sure they'll do everything they can to avoid disappointing the students." She smoothed her daughter's hair off her face. "Now, lie down and get some rest. If you still have a fever tomorrow, I don't want you going to school."

As the bedroom door closed, hot tears began to slide down Riley's cheeks. What else could possibly go wrong? Kai was acting all weird and lying to her, stupid birds were swooping out of nowhere after her, and now her solo was being flushed down the toilet with her stupid turkey tacos.

Mr. Rat let her hold him tightly against her chest. The one stupid chance in her whole stupid life to prove that she could be as good as her stupid sister, and it was all over because of some stupid "family emergency." And on top of that, her stupid best friend probably didn't even care that she barfed up a stupid lung.

Riley reached under her pajama top, pulled out the medicine bag, and clutched it in her fist as the toll of the day's emotion and excitement came out in tortured sobs.

Kai punched her pillow hard a few times until she could lay her head on it without wincing. The knot on the back of her head from where she'd hit the brick wall was throbbing. At least the headache wasn't as bad as it had been.

She closed her eyes and tried to figure out why she felt so out of balance. It could have been any of a number of things that had gone down during the day.

*Let's see, for starters I had to give her the medicine bag with the stupid lapis lazuli in it. She probably thinks I'm a deranged, lovestruck, gigantor, idiot geek.*

Kai released a heavy sigh.

"Then I just had to go all Native American on her, and skeeve her out with the stuff about my dad. That was pretty freakin' brilliant of me."

"I have dreams. I see him running. Blah, blah, blah. Welcome to my freak show," she mocked herself and then scowled at the dark ceiling.

And what was up with that creepy dude at the magic store? He was throwing off some seriously damaged vibes.

She cringed as she thought about his oily hair and watery eyes. *Damn, that look in his eyes when he realized we were upstairs was demented. I totally thought I was going to pee myself when he started screaming at us.*

Kai bit her bottom lip. And what was he doing with all those old books? *Geez, there must have been a hundred of them on those bookshelves.*

A light smile crossed her face. *And, God, Ri is so funny sometimes. She's the only person I know that can be totally grossed out and fascinated at the same time. She's such a dork.*

A sudden tightening swept through her belly as she remembered the look on Riley's face as she tugged on Kai's scarf in the alley. *She's so amazingly hot, but when she gets that mischievous look those green eyes... Man, oh man, I'm totally worthless after that.*

Kai yawned and rolled over onto her side with a grimace. *But damn, did she have to hit me after I jumped that guy mugging the little old lady? Sheesh, what was I supposed to do, tap him on the shoulder and gently remind him that wasn't polite behavior?*

She groaned. *And, God! I still don't know whether Aunt Tilley wanted to ground me or chew someone's butt off when I told her I lost my phone and got the crap beat out of me when I was trying to help out.*

Kai pulled the blanket up under her chin and tucked a shock of hair behind her ear. *I guess I actually got off easy since all she did was ban me from ever going to that creepy magic store again. Well, that and making me wait until Monday for a new phone, since that huge rat is probably hocking my old one on Rat-Bay right about now.*

A swift wave of fear bubbled up inside of her. *I swear he was looking at me like he knew me and wanted to kill me.* She took a few deep breaths to try to push down the unsteady feeling. *But that's ridiculous. Other than that dime store punk, Zach Coho, I'm not on a first name basis with any rats.*

The humor wasn't making her feel any less shaky. The truth was she didn't remember much after the rat hurled himself at her. It was sort of like she was suddenly watching the scene in the alley from above, and the rat was relentless as he bit and scratched at her face and her eyes and her mouth. He just kept attacking, and nothing she did could get him to stop.

Kai felt a cold chill cross over her face. Her heart was beating, and she began to breathe harder. *The rat wasn't just biting at me. It was really and truly trying to eat me alive. And then Riley just walked up and pulled him off me. Like she had some weird power over him. He didn't try to bite her or anything, he just let her chuck him back into the Dumpster.*

Kai rolled onto her back again, careful not to put too much weight on the lump. As she thought about it, she could remember seeing Riley putting her arms around her and whispering to her. Then she was back in her own body, and she felt Riley give her a soft kiss on top of the head. God, that rat was pure evil, but it was worth it just to feel that kiss.

The twitter in her belly returned. *She said something about not letting anything hurt me, but she couldn't really mean it—she's like half as big as I am. I'm the one who should be protecting her.*

Kai thought about the blinged-out wand thing hidden in her sock drawer. *So what happened with that lady in the alley? Riley said she saw her, but I think she was just saying that if to make me feel better because I hit my head. But, if I didn't see the lady, then where did the wand come from?*

Part of her wanted to get up and go check to make sure the wand was real, but she knew it was. She'd stared at it for half an hour before turning in for the night.

*So, if we suspend the laws of physics and energy and say the wand is real, what does it do?*

She thought about the big black bird that came out of nowhere. It had kind of looked like a black vulture on steroids, but the black vulture habitat doesn't extend into Minnesota. *Geek much, Tiva?*

She rolled her eyes. *It could have been someone's pet that got loose, and had some sort of weird visual recognition on either Ri or me.* She bit her lip and shook her head, not really believing that idea. *Or maybe "Urban Grunge" is another term for "looks like carrion."*

Every time she remembered Riley's comment, it felt like another gut punch. *I'm so freakin' pathetic. She tells me I dress like a street person, and I offer to carry her books home. "Thank you very much, Miss. May I have another?"*

She felt like she wanted to throw up, but knew she wasn't going to get that lucky.

"Okay, but to the bird. What I don't get is what happened to it. I swear it was dive-bombing Riley, and then I threw the wand. That much I know for sure. But when it hit the stupid thing, there was some sort of ectoplasmic burst, and presto change-o, big, ugly, stinky bird vanishes and little yellow finches tweets its feathery ass up the street."

She shook her head slowly and thought drily, *Well at least it didn't turn into a one-eyed rat.*

And that walk home…AWK-ward. Riley didn't say ten words the whole way. Usually it took her ten words just to say hi. Riley's silence—that's really what was eating at her.

*If she really cared anything about me, she would have checked in to make sure I made it home okay.* Kai had checked Facebook and email several times throughout the evening, but nothing from Riley. She'd thought about sending her a message, but the way Riley ran into the house made it clear that she didn't want to have anything more to do with her.

Kai rolled carefully onto her belly, and made a silent invocation for sleep. Anything was better than lying there thinking about what she would do if Riley were really done with her.

❧ ❧ ❧ ❧

"Hmm, your temperature is still one hundred," Riley's mom said, sitting on the side of her bed. She stroked the auburn hair off Riley's forehead. "That's still a little high. How do feel?"

Riley pulled the comforter up around her neck. "I kind of feel cold, and I'm hungry but every time I think about food I wanna throw up."

Her mom leaned down and kissed her forehead. "You still look a little pale." She stood up. "I'm going to call the school and let them know. I'll stay home this morning, and if you're not better by noon I'll take you to the doctor."

"Mom, I really don't think it's a big deal. I'll probably be okay in a little while."

Her mother stopped at the door and turned around. "Sweetheart, do you even remember the last time you were sick? It was over a year ago. You don't get sick that easily. Besides, there's a nasty flu going around and you may have picked it up."

Riley rolled over on her side, triggering a wave of nausea. She groaned. "Mr. Rat, I feel awful. I hope you don't catch it." Her eyes flew open and she thought about Kai—maybe she was sick too. She pushed off the comforter and tried to stand. Big mistake. Her knees buckled and she landed back on the bed.

Her mother returned with some ginger ale and Tylenol in time to see Riley fall ungracefully onto the bed.

"What happened?" she said, helping Riley into the bed and pulling up the covers.

"I need to call Kai. She could be sick, too."

"I'm sure her aunt will take care of her. You two don't have to talk a dozen times a day." She sat down on the bed. "Did you eat anything unusual yesterday?"

Riley groaned. "Nooo, just the turkey taco you put in my lunch." She settled Mr. Rat under the cover. "Please Mom, I need to call her."

Her mom adjusted the covers. "Riley, I want you to tell me where you went yesterday afternoon after school."

"We just walked downtown." She looked up into her mom's eyes. "We went to an old magic shop in the warehouse district."

"Why on earth would you go there?"

Riley suddenly felt that she'd said too much. "No reason. It sounded kinda fun."

Her mom started to speak, and then stopped. She stroked Riley's flushed face. "Has Kai mentioned anything to you about her father, you know, about his accident? Is that why you two went down there?"

"I don't feel so good. Would you help me to the bathroom?" Riley felt the nausea along with some stomach pains. She was pretty sure this was not the flu.

The leather string on the medicine bag was tight around her throat. She gasped and pulled it free as the shadow of a big black bird blocked the sun. It was moving fast toward her, its eyes focused solely on its target. But as it started its high-speed descent toward her, Kai lifted Riley around the waist and they flew away. They were faster than the ugly black bird and easily escaped, skimming above the treetops.

She looked at Kai, but it wasn't Kai. She had transformed into something else, something huge, white, and birdlike. It occurred to Riley that she should be scared, but she wasn't. Something about this Kai thing made her feel safe.

She started to ask Kai what was going on, but stopped short. It was her voice asking the question, but Riley didn't recognize the words coming out of her mouth. It was like she suddenly knew some new language.

Kai began to take them higher, and banked hard to the right. Riley looked down at the rapidly retreating ground. She expected to see Lindan, but instead saw nothing but trees, rivers, lakes, and dark mountains on the horizon.

Riley awoke with a start. The sheets and her pajamas were damp; so was her hair. At least she didn't feel that icy chill inside. She sat up carefully, and was surprised to realize she no longer felt like she was going to barf. "Mr. Rat, I think I'm going to live." It was almost four o'clock according to the clock on her desk. "Wow, I can't believe I slept all day." Riley picked up her little stuffed rat buddy. "Why didn't you wake me up?"

# *Chapter Nine*

More snow had fallen overnight, and the bright morning sun made the white fluffy flakes glisten like billions of sequins. Most of the leaves had fallen except for the stubborn oak leaves; they flittered on the breeze but refused to fall.

With Mr. Rat and her yellow fleece bathrobe, Riley sat snugly on the heated window seat in her room. She loved Saturday mornings because it meant two whole days without school. It also meant she'd normally have rehearsal for the holiday concert, but not today. Her mom told her that the school had hired a replacement music director, but they wouldn't start practicing again until next week.

The school choir director had been really cool and helped Riley polish her solo. The last-minute change to "O Holy Night" turned out to be a good thing. She liked it a lot better than "Ave Maria," and knew that it showcased her voice better.

But now she was sick. Damn it all, why now? Rebekah would never let her forget it if she blew this performance. Rebekah. Riley looked around her bedroom and sighed. Those three months sure went by awfully fast. In a few hours, she'd be sharing her room again.

"Kai, where are you? I need to talk to you."

Riley hit speed dial for what it must've been the millionth time. "The mailbox of the cell phone customer you are calling is full. Please try again later."

"Crap," she said, tossing the phone on her desk. After booting up her laptop, Riley started typing. "Why aren't you picking up your cell messages?"

"Riley, are you sure you don't want go with your dad to pick up Rebekah?" her mother called from the foot of the stairs.

*No, I don't want to. I want to talk to Kai. Where is she?* She stood up and walked out in the hall and over to the banister. "I don't think I should, Mom. I still feel kinda yucky and I have a bunch of reading to do for school Monday."

"Okay, honey. Get back in bed and I'll bring you up some tea. Remember we have a nice dinner planned tonight to welcome Rebekah home."

"I remember." Riley headed back to her room. "A nice dinner to welcome Rebekah home. Great. That's just what I need. Rebekah, everybody's favorite," Riley muttered.

She pulled the covers up and tucked Mr. Rat next to her. Riley reached for her social studies book. After she opened it, she looked down at the deerskin medicine bag hanging from her neck. She closed her eyes and thought about the conversation at the library. It was sad thinking that Kai was pretty much alone. She always acted like nothing bothered her, like it didn't matter. It wasn't true.

Riley's life had been so different from Kai's. Even though Rebekah annoyed her most of the time, at least she was someone to talk to about stuff. Kai never had anybody other than her aunt. Her throat felt tight thinking about the stupid comment she'd made about Kai's clothes. *I wonder if that's why she won't call me back. God, what if I really hurt her feelings? What if she never wants to talk to me again? She's my best friend. What would I do?*

She began to cry.

❦ ❦ ❦ ❦

"Hey pest, is that any way to greet your loving sister? Wake up," Rebekah said.

Riley jumped at the sound of a suitcase hitting the floor, and rolled over. She propped herself up on one elbow. "Leave me alone, can't you see I'm sick?"

Her sister jumped on the bed and began to tickle her. "You're not that sick, runt. Come on, get up. I have tons of stuff to tell you. I met the most amazing guy. Omigod, he's awesome. Just wait till you see his picture." She jumped up and began pulling things out of her backpack and tossing them onto her bed. "His grandparents live in Lindan, and he'll be here most of break, staying with them. I can't wait for you to meet him."

Riley pushed a lock of hair off her forehead and behind her ear as she watched Hurricane Bekah storm around the room making a huge mess—and knowing her mother wouldn't say a word. The Amazing Bekah could do no wrong. Before the thought was completely out of her mind, a lump formed in her throat as she remembered how much fun it was when she and Kai had completely rearranged the room. *Guess Bekah doesn't notice.*

"Knock, knock," her mother said, standing at the door with a bright smile on her face. "Are you getting settled in?"

"Yeah," Bekah greeted her mom with a blazing smile. "I just hope the runt hasn't turned my room into a petri dish."

Mom rolled her eyes as she waived Bekah off. "I'm sure the worst of it is over." She turned to her younger daughter. "Riley, did you tell your sister how much you missed her?"

Riley groaned. "Yeah, like a throbbing toothache."

Rebekah tossed a pair of dirty socks at her. "Brat."

Her mother shook her head and laughed. "Oh, how I've missed that." She turned and started for the stairs, calling over her shoulder, "Dinner will be ready in half an hour, and I want you both downstairs setting the table and getting the drinks ready."

꧁ ꧂

Kai held the kitchen door open with her elbow as the diminutive caterer hobbled through on his crutches. Eleven, no thirteen, trips to his van, and she'd had to carry everything as well as opening and closing all the doors for him.

*If he wasn't an old friend of Tilley's from college, I'd seriously consider "accidently" knocking out a crutch from beneath him.*

"All right, you long, tall, studly drink of water, set that pallet of glassware on the island by the sink." He pointed dramatically with his fuzzy soul patch.

She set the plastic pallet down, being careful not send the basket of fresh produce hurling across the kitchen floor like she did half an hour ago. *Sheesh, you would've thought I mixed stripes with plaid.*

She rolled her eyes, and glanced at the phone on the wall. *Eventually he's got to start working, and then I can slip off and call Ri. Why wasn't she at school yesterday? I mean, I know she was freaked out and everything, but she'd still talk to me, right?*

A wave of queasiness rolled through her belly.

Tilley pushed through the swinging door into the kitchen. "Do you have everything you need, Brad?"

"Oh, just about." Brad sighed heavily and he struggled to the center island on his crutches. "My delightful little helper only has another half dozen or so trips to the van for the shrimp, mascarpone, tuna, and the duck for the ravioli, and then we can start cooking and preparing the serving stations."

"How is your leg holding up?" Tilley asked as she walked over to join the two at the island.

He threw his head back and laughed jauntily. "Only I would dare trip over Mr. Poopy-pants and break my leg during the absolute height of my busiest season!"

Tilley threw her head back and laughed with him.

*Mr. Poopy-pants?* Kai made a face.

Taking pity on her poor niece, Tilley put her hand on her shoulder. "Mr. Poopy-pants is a teacup Chihuahua with socialization issues."

"Pshaw! He's just misunderstood." Brad waved a hand in dismissal.

Kai nodded. "I should probably go out and get the rest of the stuff out of the van." *So I can finally get a chance to talk to Riley.*

"Okay, sweetie," Tilley said as went up on her tiptoes to kiss her on the cheek. "When Brad's done with you, could you make sure all the twinkle lights in the living and dining rooms are twinkling?"

Kai nodded. "Sure."

"Oh, and when the bartender gets here, could you show her where to set up and make sure she has everything she needs?" Tilley squeezed her forearm.

"Yeah, no problem." Kai smiled. She could tell that Tilley was pretty nervous. This was the first open house she'd had since she made partner, and she wanted it to be perfect. Kai wanted it to be perfect, too. Tilley had worked really hard to get where she was, and she still found a way to make sure Kai had everything she needed. Wanted for, even. She sighed inwardly. That pretty much settled it for her. As much as she wanted to talk to Ri, it would have to wait until they had everything taken care of for the party.

Kai leaned over and gave her aunt a hug. "Anything else you need me to do?"

Tilley returned the hug vigorously and then leaned back to look up at Kai. "We'll see what's left after I finish vacuuming and cleaning the bathrooms. Okay?"

"Okay." Kai nodded, and started for the kitchen door and yet another trip to the catering van from Hell.

"Oh, Kai?" Tilley called out.

Kai stopped and turned. "Hm?"

Tilley wiggled her finger at her niece. "What were you going to wear tonight?"

"Um," Kai looked down at her ripped and faded Levi's, Doc Martens, and "Got Pi?" hoodie. "I don't know." She shrugged. "Maybe my black jeans and a button-up shirt."

"Oh, honey, do I need to step in here with some fashion advice for the lost among us?" Brad trilled at Tilley.

Kai gave him a long-suffering look, and Tilley ignored him. "That's fine, just no rips in your jeans. Okay?"

Kai nodded her consent. "Sure. My black jeans are in good shape."

Tilley smirked. "And maybe your new black loafers?"

"You're pushing it, lady." Kai grinned at her aunt.

"So makeup and nail polish are out of the question?" Tilley laughed as Brad sighed painfully at the thought.

Kai pushed open the door and started out to the van. "If you know what's good for you!" she yelled over her shoulder.

# *Chapter Ten*

Rebekah spent most of the morning texting, talking on the phone, and IMing her friends from school. Riley tried to study, but even with her iPod turned up, she could still hear her sister laughing and talking. She tried downstairs, but her mother was working on her laptop in the dining room and her dad was watching football while he untangled Christmas lights.

The refrigerator offered nothing interesting, so she poured some orange juice and sat at the kitchen counter. With a burst of inspiration, Riley reached for the phone book. Kai hadn't answered her cell phone and hadn't been online all weekend. *They have to have a landline. Everyone does.* She thumbed through the book until she got to the Ts, "Tiva, Tiva, there must be something…" Finding nothing, she picked up the phone and tried directory assistance. "Unlisted, crap."

Riley walked over to the patio door leading to the backyard. Another eight inches of snow had fallen overnight and the lawn looked like a winter wonderland. It was cold enough that the fluffy snow covered every branch and leaf. Her dad had mentioned earlier that he had cleared the driveway and that the city snowplow had gone through.

Riley walked over the sink and rinsed her glass. In just that instant, she knew what she had to do. Walking into the dining room she said, "Mom, is it okay if I go for a walk? It's so pretty outside."

Her mom took off her cheaters and looked up. "Are you sure you feel up to it, honey?"

"Yeah, I feel pretty much normal, and I'm tired of sitting around."

"Did you finish your homework?"

"Yes. What're you working on?"

Her mom put the glasses back on and returned to the computer. "A new software program the comptroller ordered. I'll be darned if I can figure out how to launch it, I've reinstalled it twice, and your father refuses to mess with it."

"Sorry I can't help. Kai probably could."

Her mom pushed back from the table and threw her hands in the air.

"Okay, go ahead, but be sure to bundle up. You can't afford to get sick again and you have rehearsals this week."

Riley ran up the stairs. Ignoring her sister, she rummaged through the clothes on the floor and grabbed her jeans. Another idea. She tossed the jeans on her bed and rummaged through her bottom drawer for the long underwear from last Christmas. She had never actually been to Kai's house but knew where it was, and with the snow the walk would take longer.

By the time she left the house, it was almost nine thirty. The streets were pretty deserted, even for a Sunday morning. Riley figured most folks must have put their cars away because of the snow. By the time she got to the park her feet were chilled, but the rest of her was still pretty toasty.

The walk was only a couple of blocks, but Riley went over what she was going to say several times, changing it every few steps. Everything inside of her felt confused, jumbled. Something had gone way wrong, and she couldn't figure it out why Kai was avoiding her.

She stopped on the corner of Kai's block, and looked up as the shadow of a large bird disappeared into the shade of large spruce tree. A cold breeze whipped her auburn hair around her face and made her eyes water. *What if she really doesn't wanna see me anymore? That's like the worst thing in the world. Besides, I just know she's my friend…but what if she's really mad about me for insulting her? She has to know I didn't mean it the way it came out. Everything about her is totally cool. I've told her that like a thousand times!*

She stamped her feet and started walking again. This was just crazy, and Kai was just going to have to put on her big girl panties and talk to her!

Halfway down the block she spotted it: a brown stucco Craftsman with white trim. It wasn't huge, but you could tell it had been renovated fairly recently. The double doors on the small porch had green wreaths with red bows, and a pine garland went up the side of one door, over the half-moon transom, and down the other side. Riley took a deep breath and started up the walk that looked like it had been shoveled last night but not yet this morning. She reached into her coat pocket with a mittened hand to check the time on her cell phone. *I wonder if they're awake. Or maybe they're not home.*

She took a deep breath, determined to find out what was wrong with Kai, and headed up the steps.

A beautiful dark-haired woman in slacks and a cashmere sweater answered the door. The resemblance was amazing, and Riley knew instantly that it was Aunt Tilley. The woman smiled brightly. "Can I help you?"

"Uh, hi. I'm Riley James. I'm a friend of Kai's… from school. Is she at home?"

"Riley. Of course, come in. I'll call her for you. Maybe having company will get her out of bed." The woman smiled warmly and pointed to the living room. "Make yourself comfortable," she said and disappeared up the stairs.

Riley looked around the small but comfortable living room. The furniture was modern and pretty stylish, but really different from her house. As she looked around, she noticed there were some pretty cool pictures and the built-in book shelves were full, but there weren't any family photos or anything like that.

She spotted Kai's science book on the coffee table and went over to sit on the couch. She unzipped her jacket and picked up the book. *Of course. I'm barfing up a lung and she's studying chemistry.*

Tilley walked back into the living room carrying her coat. "Kai will be right down. I'm running out to pick up a *New York Times*, but I'll make you girls something to eat when I get back."

Her stomach lurched. "Oh, okay," said Riley, unsure of how long she'd actually be talking to Kai.

"Take your jacket off and get comfortable," Tilley said as she opened the front door and walked out.

Riley shuffled out of her coat and laid it across the arm of the sofa. *Okay, just keep to the facts. Give her a chance to explain. And, whatever you do, don't cry.*

A minute or two later Kai ambled down the stairs. Riley's heart began to beat faster and she crossed her arms to keep her hands from shaking.

Kai's long black hair hung loose around her face,

framing her high cheekbones and deep brown eyes. A black hoodie hung below her narrow hips and topped a faded pair of jeans.

"Hi," Riley said in a bizarre scratchy voice. She immediately flushed, feeling stupid.

"Hey," Kai murmured.

It seemed like an eternity as they stared at each other. The silence was horribly uncomfortable.

"I…" they both sat at the same time, then laughed.

"You go ahead," Kai said, gesturing to Riley as she walked farther into the room.

"Okay." Riley didn't really feel okay, but she came here for a reason and she was determined to sort this mess out. She took a deep breath. "I just want to know why you've been avoiding me. You're supposed to be my best friend, but you sure don't act like it." Her face flushed, and quickly she was almost yelling. "Why haven't you returned my calls? I seriously called you like a hundred times. I left so many messages your mailbox is full and it keeps hanging up on me. I sent you text messages. I wrote you a bunch of emails. I IM'd you. I've even been freaking stalking you on Facebook!"

A half-sob slipped out, but she pressed on, determined to get it all out. "Is it that easy for you? Just flip a switch and walk away? Did I embarrass you or something? Is it because I'm not as smart as you? Because I'm not as cool as you want me to be? Was I some stupid pity project?" Hot tears threatened to spill down her cheeks.

Kai's mouth hung open. Dumbfounded, she shook her head as she plopped down in the closest chair. "No, Ri… I didn't think—"

"Of course you didn't think!" Riley's voice

became even louder and she swiped angrily as a tear rolled down her cheek. "That's the problem, Kai. You didn't think! Didn't it ever occur to you that I'd be worried?"

Kai's mouth moved, but nothing came out.

Riley pressed on, the momentum too much to stop. "With all the weird shit that happened on Thursday, I was really freaked out. And you? You just disappeared. I didn't know where you'd gone and why you suddenly hated me. Is it because I made a stupid crack about your clothes? I said I was sorry! And, God! I was really sick and you never called! Didn't you even notice I wasn't at school?"

She wiped the tears with her sleeve. "Why? Don't you ever want to see me again?" Her final entreaty was almost a whisper.

The final question roused Kai. She stood and quickly moved over to the couch and sat next to Riley. She tentatively put a hand on her friend's forearm. "You've got it all wrong, Ri. You didn't want me to walk you home. I thought you blamed me—"

Riley's eyes got huge and she pulled her arm away. "I've got it wrong! How can you say that? You never tried to call or—"

"I couldn't—"

"Couldn't or wouldn't?" Riley growled. "The last time we talked was Thursday afternoon. Are you trying to tell me your aunt had you locked in your room with no phone and no computer for three days?" She was practically shouting and she knew it. Her throat was tight and her body shook with anger.

Kai turned and grabbed Riley shoulders. "Listen to me, Ri! I said I couldn't—"

"But I—"

"Riley, I lost my phone Thursday!"

Riley stopped struggling. "You could have sent me an email or something," she said petulantly.

Kai gently laid a hand on Riley's thigh, but stayed focused on her green eyes. "A water pipe at the end of the block burst Thursday morning, and they cut through the cable when they were fixing it."

Riley looked at her warily.

Kai pressed on. "And then right after school on Friday, we had a game at Otter Tail. I swear, by the time we got back and I walked home it was almost midnight."

Riley sniffled. "Yeah, but what about—"

Kai brushed some loose hair behind Riley's ear. "Tilley made partner at the firm a few months ago, and she had this huge holiday party here last night. It was the first thing she's hosted since she made partner, and it was a really big deal. I promise, I was up before seven and we didn't finish cleaning up until after midnight."

Kai wiped a stray tear away with her thumb. "Honest to God, I've been thinking about you nonstop, I just didn't have time."

Riley turned to face Kai and tucked under one leg so they were even closer. All she could see was sadness in Kai's eyes. "I don't understand. Why did run away from me?"

Kai bit her bottom lip and shrugged. "It sorta felt like you were brushing me off, and I guess I kinda thought you hated me. All the weird stuff that happened at the magic shop and in the alley, I thought you blamed me, like somehow I caused it." She looked down at her lap.

It was Riley's turn to reach out and touch Kai's arm. "Why on earth would you think that?"

Dark hair masked Kai's face. "It's…well…after I gave you the medicine bag and explained it to you, it just seemed like everything spazzed out. I mean, the crazy creepy guy chasing us and the fight with that dude." She grabbed her head with both hands. "That one-eyed rat…geez." She shivered.

"And the wand and that freaky vulture thing." Riley squeezed her arm reassuringly.

Kai pivoted to face Riley and continued. "Yeah, and you just kept asking me over and over what was going on, like you thought I should know. I don't know, maybe I should. But honest, something truly weird is going on and I don't get it. Sometimes I get this…I don't know, feeling or something that I *should* know. Ri, you have to believe me, I don't know, but it just feels like I should."

Riley's heart clenched; she hated the pain she saw in her friend's face. The thing was, just looking at Kai she knew she believed her. "Can I ask you something?"

Kai took a deep breath and nodded.

"Do you think that bird was going after me, or you?"

Kai looked directly into Riley's eyes and shrugged. "I don't know. I've gone over it a bunch of times, and I still don't get it." She bit her bottom lip again. "I really want to tell Aunt Tilley, but I'm kinda freaked out that she'd call someone and I'm not crazy, and neither are you."

Riley felt a chill run down her spine as she thought about everything. "This is really some intense stuff, but I think I'll be okay as long as we face it together and be honest about with each other."

Kai nodded.

"And, maybe," Riley said as she graced Kai with a

soft smile. "Trust each other a little more?"

Kai sat up straighter, her expression serious and her voice reverent. "I promise you, Ri, you can have absolute faith in me to be there for you, no matter what."

Riley could barely contain the thudding in her chest. She looked into Kai's eyes and saw the truth of her words. In slow motion, she raised both hands and placed them on either side of Kai's face. Their faces were only inches apart and Riley could feel warm breath on her face. She couldn't look away but leaned closer. Kai never blinked.

Riley's breathing became rapid and shallow and she licked her lips. *Now.* She closed her eyes and softly kissed Kai. Her hands trembled as she tightened her touch and felt Kai's soft lips surrender.

Everything stopped—her breath, her heart.

Everything.

⁂

Kai felt lightheaded as she melted into the sweet lips that pressed against hers. The room spun and everything inside of her was trembling. She whispered a silent prayer to the Great Spirit that this moment might never stop as the exquisite velvety touch sent hot currents through her body.

Kai felt the rush of a shared eternity in a moment.

Then it was over.

Riley pulled back slightly and the sweet connection was broken. Kai opened her eyes and looked at the greenest eyes she'd ever seen. She heard rather than felt the groan as the breath she had been holding escaped. She had never begun to imagine the harmony she felt at that moment, but she couldn't speak. She raised her hand and placed it softly on the side of Riley's face. Soft auburn curls filled her fingers.

Neither spoke.

Riley's eyes expressed emotions that words could not convey. Kai knew that they somehow understood an unexplainable connection between them that was profoundly deep and inherently destined.

And then it was over. They both slowly leaned back and dropped their hands as their breathing returned to something more normal.

The flushed red face of her best friend fascinated Kai, and it occurred to her that she wanted to jump up and do a supremely goofy happy dance. Someday, later, she would tell Riley about all the nights she'd dreamt of this very moment, and how it somehow erased all the pain and humiliation caused by the people who ridiculed and taunted her for as long as she could remember.

It no longer bothered her.

Riley James had kissed her, and nothing in the world could change that. The smile started deep inside her soul, and she felt it surround her heart and stretch across her face.

Then, it was there—a twinkle in Riley's eyes, and she knew from that moment, everything would be all right.

Riley grinned brightly at Kai, and reached out for her hand. "Your aunt said she was going to fix something for us to eat when she got back, but I think I better go."

Kai felt a sudden loss at the thought of Riley leaving, but couldn't resist her amazing smile. "Oh, okay. I... I'll tell her. Look, Ri, I'm sorry..."

Riley stood up and Kai handed her the winter jacket. Riley slipped it on and zipped it up. "No, I am."

Kai stood up and Riley reached out to squeeze her arm. "I shouldn't have gotten all crazy and assumed the worst, you know? We'll figure this out."

Kai nodded and gave her a warm smile. "Wait a minute! I just thought of something."

Kai turned and sprinted up the stairs, taking two at a time. *Might not help, but it sure as heck won't hurt.* She rummaged through her top drawer and unwrapped the wand they had found.

She bounded back down the stairs, returning to the living room and skidding to a stop in front of an adorably bundled Riley. "I think it would be a good idea for you to keep this," she said, handing the blinged-out wand to Riley. "I'm really not sure how to use it or if it's even real, but I want you to hold onto it and case you need it."

Riley looked at her skeptically.

Kai's eyebrows twitched comically. "If nothing else, just throw it."

Riley burst out into a loveable giggle.

"Thanks, Stretch." At the front door, Riley turned suddenly and threw her arms around Kai's neck and pecked her quickly on the lips. Just as quickly, she released her hold and ran out the door.

Kai stood motionless as her best friend jogged down the sidewalk to the end of the block. She watched her stop, turn, and wave. Kai's heart thumped happily. After a slow wave and watching Riley disappear down the sidewalk, she gently closed the door, slid to the floor, and hugged her knees close. It was impossible to remove the goofy grin covering her face.

❧❧❧❧

Riley kept running until she reached the park. Once she crossed the street she flopped back on a huge snowdrift and began to laugh. She had been grinning since she ran out the front door and could no longer contain it.

How awesome was that! *I kissed a girl. And I really liked it.* She giggled wildly.

She kicked her feet in the snow and tossed handfuls in the air. She stared up at the clear blue sky as the fluttering in her stomach both tickled and warmed her. *It was just a stupid misunderstanding. She was totally thinking about me the whole time.*

She cackled like a chimpanzee, then sat up and looked around quickly, realizing that if anyone saw her they'd probably think she was a total dork. *Who freakin' cares? I feel different inside. Good different. Really and truly good different.*

The thought that Kai dumped her and didn't care had been making her sick. Not the barfing kind—that had been something else—the kind of sick that made her feel like her chest might cave. *But she likes me, and she totally kissed me back!*

Riley lay back down and made a snow angel, then rolled over and scrawled "RJ + KT" in the snow next to it. She got up, made a note to drag Kai past here tomorrow morning, and then skipped the rest of the way home singing, "I Kissed a Girl."

❧❧❧❧

*Holy shit! Riley James kissed me. The single most awesome, beautiful girl in the whole freakin' world kissed me. Oh my God, it really happened, I can't believe it.* She touched her lips with her fingers and closed her eyes.

Laughter bubbled up from deep inside and she hugged her knees closer, reliving that amazing moment when their lips met and jolts of electricity shot through her body lighting her up like a Christmas tree. There was no feeling like it in the world. It occurred to Kai, at that moment, that she could fly—actually fly. Her body tingled and the blood in her veins seemed hotter. Everything looked different, the colors were brighter, the wood floor was shinier, the sun beaming through the front window made everything glow, and Kai had never felt more alive in her whole life.

She heard a soft swoosh as the door from the kitchen opened, and looked up to see her aunt standing in the doorway with her head cocked to one side. She had a newspaper in one hand and a cup of coffee in the other. "Are you okay, sweetie?"

Kai knew she was grinning like a fool but couldn't seem to do anything about it. "Yeah, I'm fine. Most excellent."

Her aunt shook her head as a knowing smile traced her lips. "Alrighty then." She motioned toward the kitchen with her coffee. "Come on in and we'll scare up some leftovers for brunch."

Twenty minutes later, they sat at the kitchen table enjoying the shrimp, vegetables, sesame tuna skewers, and duck ravioli left over from the party. Aunt Tilley wiped her mouth with a paper napkin and took a slow drink of her coffee. She cleared her throat. "Your friend Riley seems very nice."

Kai looked up at her aunt, eyes wide. She felt herself starting to blush, and nodded quickly before stabbing a tiny ravioli and plopping it in her mouth.

Tilley put her coffee down. "She's the girl you've been studying with a lot lately, right?"

"Uh-huh," Kai murmured as she speared a grape tomato.

"She's also really cute," she said, raising one eyebrow.

Kai took a huge swig of milk and swallowed. "Yeah. She's really pretty cool and everything." She went back to stabbing at her raviolis.

"You know," Tilley said, "I know how tough it's been for you to fit in here in Lindan. I went through a lot of the same stuff when your grandparents sent me away to high school."

"Why'd they send you away from Pine Ridge?" Kai asked, studying her aunt's face.

Tilley shrugged. "Oh…a lot of reasons I suppose. Mostly, I think they wanted me to get a better education so I'd have more of a chance." She picked up her coffee and took a long swallow. "I'm glad they did, but it wasn't always easy being different from everybody else."

Kai nodded.

Tilley went on. "You are an amazing young woman in so many ways, and I'm so proud of who you've become. I just want you to be happy."

"I'm doing good." Kai smiled as she looked into the eyes of the one person who had had always been there for her.

Aunt Tilley smiled back. "I know you are. Your grades are great, and your coach told me you've really won over your teammates. I just want you to know that I'm proud of you, and I'm happy you have a friend like Riley in your corner."

"Riley's cool, you know? She really gets me and doesn't care that I'm different." Kai shrugged as she put her fork down.

Tilley folded her napkin and placed it on her plate. "I just like how you light up when you talk about her." She grinned evilly. "Just like you're doing now."

Kai felt heat rising up her neck and face. *If you only knew why I'm lit up.*

Suddenly feeling like the duck ravioli was going to make an unexpected reappearance, Kai jumped up and began to clear the table. "It's just that Ri's a really good person, you know? She does what she thinks is right, and doesn't care what other people think." *Oh, God! Babble much?*

"I know, sweetie. Sit down for a minute and just talk to me."

Kai sat down next to her. *Oh, crap. Puhleez don't say anything that includes the words penis or vagina!*

"You're not a little girl anymore." Tilley laughed and rolled her eyes. "Well, you haven't been little for a long time."

*Here it comes. Oh, God! Bad choice of words!* Kai suspected her face was turning an unattractive shade of puce, but she smiled at her aunt's tease. Tilley just had that way about her.

"Every day I see you maturing into a really amazing woman."

Kai knew she was still blushing, but had a surprisingly hard time pulling her eyes away from her aunt.

Tilley stroked Kai's long black hair behind her ear. "You're smart, you're beautiful."

Kai looked down at her lap.

"And you have a strong and gentle spirit."

"I —" Kai started.

Tilley rubbed her shoulder. "God, every day I wish your dad were here to see you grow up."

Kai looked up at her aunt, unexpected tears threatening.

"He would be so proud." Tilley swiped at her own tears.

Kai leaned in and wrapped her aunt in the strongest hug she could. "It's okay, Tilley," she whispered.

Tilley kissed Kai's cheek and leaned back. "Kai, I just want you to know that I love you and…" She took in a few breaths as Kai reached for her hands. "I love you just as you are, okay?"

Kai gulped and nodded. "I love you, too, Til."

The two women sat back and gauged each other. The both sniffed, and released a soft laugh at the unintended mimic.

Kai smiled at her aunt. *I really do love you. You're like the best thing that ever happened to me… Well, you and Ri.*

Tilley nodded at the unspoken words and let out a deep breath. With a brighter voice, she said, "Oh, hey! I nearly forgot, I ordered another phone for you and cancelled the service for the one you lost. It should show up tomorrow afternoon, okay?"

Standing up, Kai smiled and grabbed the remaining dishes. She turned toward the sink. "I really appreciate that, and I'm sorry for being so careless. I'll be more careful with this one, okay?"

Tilley smiled. "Yeah."

After finishing the dishes and putting the remaining leftovers away, Kai trotted up to her room and closed the door. She felt like she was a little fish in the middle of a twenty-foot wave. One second she was thinking about Ri and the kiss. *Man, I have never felt that kind of schwing, ever.*

And the next she was thinking about Aunt Tilley and what she said. *Sometimes I really miss my dad, but I totally lucked out with someone as great as Til for a mom.*

*I really need to read before my English final.* She released an inward groan, and a grin warmed her face. She reached out and booted up her Mac. *How do I tell Ri that I'm totally in love with her?*

*Hey Shorty,*
*I'm really glad you came over to kick my butt. I know I was total jerk but only a friend like you would totally forgive me. And, well, I really liked it.*
*Stretch*

Then she hit Send.

# *Chapter Eleven*

**B**ekah was talking with Wesley when Riley came in, which meant no privacy for either of them. Riley started fumbling through her schoolbooks, shuffling papers, and trying not to listen. *Oh, Wesley! You're so strong and handsome! Barf.*

"Bye, Wesley. I'll call you after lunch." Rebekah snapped her phone shut and rolled over. "Hey brat, how come the back of your jeans are wet? I thought you were too old for accidents."

Riley looked down at her jeans. They were pretty soggy. She shrugged. "It's kind icy out there and I fell in the snow on the way back."

"Way back from where?" Bekah cocked her head.

"I went over to see Kai, as if that was any of your business."

Rebekah sat up and crossed her legs Indian style. She leaned her chin on her fist and teased. "When do I get to meet this mysterious Kyle of yours? Mom says you guys are together all the time. Is he cute?"

"It's Kai, she's my best friend, and not a boy." Riley felt her face flush with a wave of anger and pride.

Rebekah yawned, barely paying attention. "So, do you wanna hear about Wesley?"

Riley rolled her eyes as she struggled out of her wet jeans and grabbed a pair of sweats from her dresser. *No, I really want to lie here by myself and think about the awesome kiss.* Instead, she grabbed Mr. Rat and flopped onto her bed. Feigning interest, she said, "Sure, sounds like you guys are pretty serious."

A dreamy look came over Bekah's face. "God, Ri, he is totally awesome. He's a little taller than I am, and has long blond hair and gorgeous blue eyes." She sighed audibly. "We met in an art history class. And then ran into each other about a million times before midterms. I thought I was going to die when he finally asked me to the Sigma Chi Halloween mixer." She giggled. "It was so cool, because we dressed up as Thor and Sif, and we had so much fun because we were totally comfortable."

Bekah looked at Riley, her cheeks pink and eyes wild with excitement. *Is it just me or does Bekah look a little crazy?*

"When he took me back to my dorm, he actually asked me if he could kiss me good night." She rolled her eyes dramatically. "Some of the girls on my floor warned me that he was a real player, so I was a little nervous. But, my God, can he kiss." She fanned herself. "Within ten seconds my knees went all rubbery. He held me and we just kept kissing for ages."

Bekah looked at Riley. "When we finally had to stop, he asked if he could call me when he got back to his dorm. No games or anything, he was just really sweet and super nice." She laughed and put both hands on her cheeks. "I don't even remember how I got upstairs to my room. But he called like five minutes later and we spent half the night talking. He said he didn't want to just hook up, he wanted to be like totally exclusive with me, and everything."

Riley watched in wonder. Brock Jones had been after her since school started, and she'd made out with him at Tiffany's Halloween party when they played

Truth or Dare. *Ugh! That was so gross, it was all wet and sloppy, and he kept trying to shove his stupid tongue down my throat.* She shuddered as she remembered him pressing her against the wall and grinding his crotch into her. All the kids at the party had been egging them on, and Brock really wanted her to go to Tiffany's parents' bedroom with him. *Thank God I told him my uterus was probably sloughing off or something.* She smiled inwardly at the slightly green look he got on his face. *I wonder if he even noticed I never came back after I offered to go get him something to drink.*

Bekah had continued droning on about Wesley this and Wesley that.

Riley looked down at Mr. Rat and stroked his ears. The kiss with Kai was totally different. *I didn't even know I was going to do that, but I don't think I could have stopped if I tried.* Kai's lips were so soft and the kiss was warm and gentle. She felt a soft surge in her belly as she remembered the lingering touch of Kai's lips. It was kind of like they were both taking time to memorize the feeling before they parted. *Why did I leave so soon? I could have kissed her like that forever.*

"And then he told me that he talked his dad into letting him spend Christmas break here in Lindan with his grandparents so we could be together. Isn't that the most romantic thing ever?"

Riley looked up at her sister, and realized she missed most of what she'd said about the Great and Powerful Wesley. "Are you in love with him?"

Bekah swooned and lay back across the bed. "God, Ri, I never thought I could feel this good. I totally think I am."

Riley nodded. "That's really cool, Bekah." She hugged Mr. Rat. *That's kinda how I feel when I'm with*

*Kai. I wonder—*

"Dinner's ready, girls." Riley's dad stuck his head in the door and smiled brightly. "Mom's made a homecoming feast, and I'm about to chew a hole through the wainscoting, so come on!" Both girls hopped up and trotted after him.

❧❧❧❧

They hadn't actually discussed it yesterday, so Riley assumed business as usual and that she would walk to school with Kai. She listened distractedly as her mother and sister negotiated Christmas shopping. Bekah wanted to spend more time with Wesley, but Mom had other ideas.

Riley slowly chewed a bite of waffle, and thought about The Kiss. At first, she was really pretty jazzed about it, and then Kai had sent the email. But Kai's email was kinda weird, and now Riley was starting to think about the different responses she might have if Kai didn't show up, or did show up but pretended like nothing happened. *I'm totally into her, and she's probably scared to be within fifty feet of a spastic little freak like me.*

"Don't forget you have rehearsals this afternoon and your new director is going to be there." Her mom handed her fifteen dollars for her weekly allowance. "Try to be on your best behavior, and remember that she might want to do things a little differently, so give her a chance." She winked at Riley. "Okay?"

"Hey, squirt! If I can escape from the mall, I'll try to swing by your rehearsal," Rebekah said around a mouthful of waffle.

"That's cool, Bekah," Riley said, slipping into her

coat and grabbing her backpack. "But no big deal if you can't. We're probably just going to be doing a lot of standing around today, you know."

Bekah shrugged and speared another chunk of waffle. "Sure, whatever."

Riley kissed her mom on the cheek. "Gotta go, bye."

She found herself walking a little slower than normal to meet Kai. *Crap. She's got to think I'm the biggest tool ever! I stomp over there, yell at her for being an unfeeling creep, and then totally jump her. Freak show much?*

There was a tiny part of her that hoped Kai had already gone on without her so they wouldn't have to talk about "it." Riley stopped on the corner and looked both ways before crossing the street, and then noticed that Kai wasn't waiting on the bench as usual. She let out a sigh as she first felt a sense of relief, then felt her stomach clench as the sense of sadness. She was scared to death to see Kai, but not seeing her felt ten times worse.

Just as Riley felt a huge bitter lump of anxiety rise into her throat, she caught a glimpse of someone skidding around the corner. She turned and saw Kai leap over a pile of snow, a huge grin plastered on her face. The lump in Riley's throat melted into warm, sweet goo at the sight of Kai loping gracefully down the sidewalk toward her. She slowed and walked the last four feet.

"Hi, Shorty," Kai said with a huge, goofy grin on her face.

"Hey, Stretch. Glad you decided to make it," Riley teased as she started to reach out to grab Kai's arm, and then pulled her hand back.

The grin on Kai's face melted, and she looked down and started scraping chunks of snow into a pile with her foot. She shrugged. "I had to shovel the driveway for Aunt Tilley, so I got a late start. You know."

Riley saw Kai's smile fade. She took a deep breath and touched Kai's arm. "Hey, I got your email yesterday afternoon."

Kai looked up, seemingly somewhere between hope and humiliation. "I guess I feel a little embarrassed, you know, like I don't know what say and stuff."

Riley looked around and slid her hand down to grab Kai's gloved fingers.

Kai's look softened a bit and she nodded. "I know, lame, but it's all I could think about yesterday. Well, last night, too. And this morning." She moved them off the sidewalk toward the bushes.

"Really?" Riley's voice brightened a bit.

"Well, yeah." Kai squeezed Riley's mittened fingers. "It's just, well, that, uh…" She stopped and looked away, and then slowly back into Riley's eyes. "It's just that I really, you know, totally like you. A lot. Probably more than I should, you know?"

Riley bit her bottom lip and nodded softly.

Kai took a deep breath and released it with a whoosh. "I've never kissed anybody before, and it was like completely amazing and it's…really all I can think about."

"Really?" Riley cocked her head in amazement. "No way you've never kissed anybody!"

Kai's eyes narrowed at the strange look on Riley's face, and she pulled her arm away. "Look, let's just forget it ever happened and that I said anything." She turned and started in the direction of school.

Riley grabbed the sleeve of Kai's coat and yanked her back, almost slipping in the process. "Wait a minute!" She moved directly in front of Kai and grabbed her other arm. Her voice was agitated. "Oh, no, you didn't just blow me off like that!"

She poked a mitten into Kai's chest. "I don't care if you've never kissed anybody before." Another poke. "This isn't just about you, so you can get over yourself." A third poke. "I didn't even think I would kiss you until I did." A fourth poke. "And you know what Stretch?" A fifth poke. "I thought it was the most amazing thing I've ever..." Poke. "Felt." Poke. "In." Poke. "My." Poke. "Life."

Kai grabbed the poking mitten. "Are you done poking me?"

Riley looked at her mittened hand, then up into Kai's dark brown eyes. She nodded a bit sheepishly.

"Look." Kai sighed. "I'm not popular like you, and I don't have any experience when it comes to making out and stuff."

Riley cocked her head, not quite sure where Kai was going with this.

"I'm just a stupid, freakishly tall science nerd that can dribble a basketball. I haven't done all the stuff with people like you have."

Riley tried to poke Kai again, but was thwarted by a firm grip. "Where did you come up with that completely insane, wing-nut idea?"

Kai shrugged. "Well, Keisha Taylor said that you and Brock were really hot and heavy at Tiffany's Halloween party, and that you were doing like all kinds of stuff."

"And what else did Keisha Taylor say about my

love life?"

"Nothing much." Kai released Riley's mittened poking hand, defeated.

Riley knew there was more and waited. She sighed audibly. "And?"

Kai shrugged and looked down at her feet. Her voice became almost a whisper. "Well, just that you were kissing him, and that he was telling everyone that you gave him a BJ."

"That little bitch!" Riley stepped so close to Kai their chests were almost touching. "You wanna know what?" She poked Kai again, hard. "We were playing a stupid game, and I had to kiss him." She tried to make a finger through her mitten, and pointed it up near Kai's chin. "It was gross." Point. "It was sloppy and slimy." Point. "He kept trying to shove his tongue down my throat." Point. "He smelled like a goat." Point. "And I left the party!" Point. "Also. No. Blow. Job." Point, point, point. "And." Point. "No penises! That's just disgusting!"

Kai's eyes widened with each emphatic point, and she nodded silently as puffs of steam rose from Riley's flared nostrils. Finally, when she clearly thought no more pokes or points were coming here way, she bit her bottom lip. "Do I smell like a goat?"

Riley glared up into Kai's eyes, steam continuing to puff from her nostrils like an enraged bull.

"No, Kai." The first traces of a smiled played on Riley's lips. "You totally don't smell like a goat."

She slowly took hold of the lapels of Kai's peacoat and looked up at her. "Yesterday, I found out what it was like to really kiss somebody." She licked her lips. "And it was amazing."

Kai's brown eyes softened, and she nodded as she

put her hands on Riley's hips. "I thought so, too, and it's all I've been thinking about." She grinned. "You are all I've been thinking about."

Riley blushed bright crimson, and then pulled down on Kai's lapels. She softly pecked Kai on the lips. "Good. Me, too." She released the lapels and stepped back. "I think we better get to school right now, or we'll be late for homeroom."

Kai nodded, still grinning.

Laughing out loud, Riley looped her mittened hand around Kai's arm and pulled her down the sidewalk.

# Chapter Twelve

As the girls turned the corner on Madison, the mood had lightened significantly and Riley was on a mission to convince Kai about the superiority of Aquafresh toothpaste.

Kai held firm to her scientific argument. "Colgate has a higher concentration of fluoride and a much better whitening ingredient."

"Well, Aquafresh has the whitening ingredient and mouthwash." Riley poked her tongue out.

Kai stopped in her tracks and looked down at Riley with a goofy grin. "Yeah, I noticed. You taste pretty good."

Riley snorted as she punched Kai in the shoulder, which sent her loping away down the sidewalk howling in pain. Riley shook her head and adjusted her backpack. As she did, she noticed an unusual shadow across the sidewalk. She followed the shadow up the trunk of the tree on her left and spotted a large black vulture with its enormous wings spread in the morning sun. It emitted a low growl, which sent a cold shiver down Riley's spine.

She carefully moved past the tree and began to run. Her heart hammered in her chest as she looked over her shoulder to see the giant bird bobbing its head up and down. "Kai!"

Kai wheeled around with an alarmed look on her face. "What is it?"

Nearly breathless, Riley said, "That bird!" She turned around and pointed back to the tree. But it was gone. "Kai, it was here again. I swear to God, that creepy bird was sitting up there waiting for me!"

Kai jogged back toward Riley and put her hand on her shoulder. She gave a reassuring squeeze as she squinted up in the direction of the tree. "I believe you." Kai's voice took on a low ominous sound. "Come on, Ri. I think we better get to school. It'll be okay."

Riley looked up into Kai's dark eyes and felt a little less freaked out. Then she grabbed her friend's arm tightly and tugged her on toward the school.

☙ ☙ ❧ ❧

The school day passed quickly without further smelly bird incidents, but Kai couldn't quite shake the creepy feeling she had. There was no doubt that Ri was telling the truth because the look of abject terror in those green eyes made her stomach feel sour. Or, it could have been the Fiesta Chicken at lunch that made her stomach sour, but she was pretty sure it had been heading that direction way before fourth period.

Kai slammed her locker shut and glanced up at the big clock in the main hallway. She didn't have basketball practice today because Coach was having her wisdom teeth taken out and Assistant Coach Tyree threw his back out shoveling snow over the weekend. *Oops, better get a move on. Promised Shorty I'd meet her in the auditorium in three minutes.* She shoved her chemistry book and a copy of *To Kill a Mockingbird* into her backpack and zipped up.

The halls were crowded after the last bell and she had to wind her way through throngs and waves of kids jamming the hallways. More than once, she picked up bits and pieces of snide comments that were slung her way, but she clenched her jaw and kept moving. *Tilley is right; I can't beat the snot out of all of them…at once.* Their stupid comments still hurt, but it occurred to her that she was spending a lot less time caring about it than before she met Riley.

That revelation brought a smile to her face.

As she rounded the corner, Kai glanced up toward the top of the stairs and saw Riley standing there with a ginormous smile and twinkling green eyes. Kai's heart thumped like a Triumph in overdrive, and she grinned back as she took the steps two at a time.

"Hey, sorry I'm late." She tossed her head toward the lower hallway. "Heavy traffic you know."

"I had faith in you, Stretch," Riley said as Kai pulled open the back door to the auditorium. They stepped inside the dark cavernous space and waited for their eyes to adjust. A large group of kids were mingling around on the stage, talking and goofing off.

"It sure his dark back here," Riley whispered, putting her arms around Kai's middle.

"What are you doing? Do you want to get us kicked out of here?"

Riley giggled. "Maybe. I was just thinking about kissing you again."

"Riley!" Kai hissed, but a smile spread across her face.

From the apron of the stage Mr. Higgenbottom said, "Ms. James, would you care to join us?"

Riley slipped off her backpack and handed it to Kai. "Wish me luck," she said, and hustled down the aisle to the stairs at the side of the stage.

Kai slid into a seat in the back row and draped

her long legs over the seat in front of her. She openly grinned as she watched Riley move into a group of girls on one side of the chorus. Everyone smiled and greeted her, and several hugged her.

Kai reached up at felt her face, and realized the soreness was because she'd been smiling like a deranged goober for the last twenty-four hours. A giggle bubbled up and out. *Yep, that totally hot girl down there kissed me. Smack. On. The. Lips. She said it was amazing, too!*

"People, can I have your attention. Take a seat, it doesn't matter where." Mr. Higgenbottom waited as thirty-five students agonized over the life and death decision of which chair to sit in.

"Please sit down and stop talking," he said in a much louder voice. "I know you are all aware that Mr. Winkler was called out of town and we missed a lot of practice last week. We have only one more week before the performance. Mr. Jackson, put your phone away. Do I need to remind you that all cell phones need to be turned off?"

There was a flurry of activity as a dozen students quickly complied.

He continued pacing in front of the chorus. "We have been very fortunate to secure the services of a well respected musical director. Ms. Byrd has directed performances at the university as well as choruses in several cities. I would like you to give her the respect she deserves. Students, may I present Ms. Loliy Byrd." He turned and gestured to someone in the front row.

Kai could barely see as a little woman stood up, but even from that distance, she recognized the sunshine yellow coat and hat. Kai untangled her feet and legs from the chair in front of her and stood up so she could see the tiny figure march primly up the steps and across the stage to the podium. *Holy shit. That's the little old lady in yellow from the alley!* She immediately looked at Riley and saw the same wide-eyed expression on her face.

Riley snapped her head toward the back of the auditorium and mouthed at Kai, "Little Old Lady in Yellow!"

Kai nodded and gave Riley a "what now" shrug. *This is seriously too weird!*

Ms. Byrd shook hands with Mr. Higgenbottom and he turned to go. "That was a lovely introduction, Mr. Higgenbottom." Kai was immediately intrigued by her accent, but couldn't quite place it exactly. English? Irish? Somewhere in the British Isles. "I am so very pleased to be here. Thank you." She turned to the students. "Good afternoon boys and girls. Let's get started." She unfolded a piece of paper from her pocket. "I'd like to start with the opening number and then go right into the finale. After that, I want to go through each solo starting with Ms. James and her rendition of 'O Holy Night.'"

She removed her yellow coat and carefully draped it across the rail on the back of the podium. She picked up a small, nubby baton, tapped it briskly on the music stand, and nodded to the accompanist.

Kai settled back into our seat. *What the heck is going on?* The music began and Kai's attention focused on Riley, who stood up straight and sang her heart out. Kai tried to multitask and think about where this Mrs. Byrd lady came from, but all she could do was stare at Riley and grin like trained harbor seal waiting for someone to launch a mackerel her way.

Mrs. Byrd stopped the choir several times and made them redo various parts of the songs with different inflections and different combinations of sopranos, altos, and tenors. Kai sighed painfully when they launched into the chorus of "Winter Wonderland" for the sixth time. Finally, Mrs. Byrd thanked the students for their patience, and then called Riley to her mark on the stage for her solo. Kai sat up straight and brushed an unruly strand of hair behind her ear. The fluttering in her chest began as Riley made her way to the front of the stage.

Kai couldn't hear what Mrs. Byrd said to her, but saw Riley bob her head in agreement several times. Even from the back of the auditorium Kai could see the pink flush on Riley's cheeks contrasting with her green eyes and wavy auburn hair. *She looks beautiful.*

Riley's voice began softly and expanded as the music did until she filled the auditorium. Kai's mouth hung open in wonder. All the time they spent talking and she never really thought about what Ri's singing voice might sound like. It was angelic and amazing. *So that's what a mezzo-soprano sounds like.* Tears welled up in Kai's eyes. She swiped furtively at them with her sleeve and looked around, hoping nobody was watching her. She couldn't remember the last time she had felt this gooey and happy.

Mrs. Byrd had Riley repeat one last part and then excused her. Instead of going to her seat, Riley stealthily angled off stage.

Kai continued to watch as one student after another ran through their solos. She felt something and turned to see Riley slip into the seat next to her. "What are you doing out here?" Kai asked quietly.

"She said I could go." Riley pointed at the stage. "Do you know who that lady is?"

"Of course I do. What the hell is she doing here?"

Kai's voice came out almost harshly.

"Damned if I know. I thought maybe we should wait around and ask her."

Kai slumped down in her chair and leaned closer to Riley. "Just what exactly do you think you're going to ask her? Excuse me lady, how do you go poof in alleys, or why are you stalking two teenagers who are royally freaked out?"

"I don't know." Riley's impatience wasn't masked, but she quickly noticed the hurt look on Kai's face. She took a deep breath and exhaled slowly. "I just thought we could ask about the, you know, wand and stuff."

"Did you bring it?" Kai asked.

Riley scrunched down and leaned her head on Kai's shoulder. "Well, no."

Kai's belly felt warm as the scent of Riley's shampoo drifted over. She really wanted to put her arm around the soft body leaning into her. *That is so not a good idea right now, cowgirl.*

Instead, Kai rested her chin on top of Riley's head. "I really liked your solo, Ri. I knew you'd be good, but you could be on *American Idol* and stuff."

Riley tipped her head up and smiled. "Was it really okay? Do you think I'm good enough for the show?"

"Are you kidding? My God, your voice is awesome! You should be recording that stuff." Overcome with the moment, Kai reached over and took Riley's hand very tenderly.

Neither spoke for a moment, but the reflection of the stage lights in Riley's eyes told Kai what she wanted. It was all she could do to keep from touching her face. She pulled back slightly and lowered her eyes.

"Man, I'm in so much trouble."

"Why, what's wrong?" Riley said.

"Geez, I just really wanna kiss you," Kai said quickly before she could change her mind.

Riley squeezed her hand and giggled. "I know. I really wanna do that, too." She looked around. "But I don't really think this the right place. Know any place we could we sneak off to?"

Kai's eyes lit up like a Christmas tree. "Can you leave?" she asked hopefully.

"Well, not yet. What are you thinking?"

Kai closed her eyes and tried to think of any place in the school that would be private, where they would not be caught. A slow smile crossed her face. "What about that bathroom on the third floor outside the yearbook office? It has a lock and no one ever goes up there."

Riley's face lit up and she giggled. "That's perfect, no one should be up there now." She looked up at the stage and saw kids starting to wander around. "Looks like we should be done pretty soon. Can you wait?"

"Geez, yes. Of course I can…if I have to."

They both laughed and then Riley said, "Hold that thought. I better get back up there."

Kai grabbed her arm. "Wait. What about talking to the little old lady?"

"Crap, I forgot about that. Hang around and I'll try to talk to her." And she was gone.

Kai slumped back in her seat. It was probably a good thing that Riley left. The heat in her belly spread through her chest to her arms and legs. She'd felt it before and it was uncomfortable. Kai knew that when she told Riley she wanted to kiss her, she wanted to kiss her hard. She wanted to kiss her gently, too, like their first kiss, but the feeling in her belly told her she wanted more…passion. *Is that the right word?*

She was confused and felt uncomfortable sitting there. The ache got stronger and she was afraid it might be cramps. *Shit, not now.*

She opened her eyes when clapping, hooting, and scraping chairs got her attention. Kids were filing out the doors, but she couldn't spot Riley or the little old lady. She stood up and looked carefully. Soon the stage cleared completely, and she saw Riley hustling up the aisle toward her.

"Did you get to talk to her?" Kai asked.

"No, she disappeared again. She went over to talk to the accompanist, and when I got there she was gone."

Kai just shook her head and rolled her eyes. "That is just too weird."

Riley just sat looking at Kai with her head cocked. "Still up for a trip to the third floor?"

The butterflies started before the sentence was through. "Well…yeah. Are you?"

"Of course, goof." Riley looked around the auditorium one more time. "First let's check downstairs and see if Mrs. Byrd is anywhere around. I'm totally dying to find out who she is."

Kai gave her a dubious look.

Riley nudged her friend with an elbow. "Aren't you the least bit curious?"

Kai's stomach lurched and sunk like an iron anchor. "Yeah, but I was kinda hoping she was gone…"

"Come on." Riley pulled Kai's sleeve as she trotted toward the exit.

They rounded the last landing and saw a flash of yellow in the main hallway.

"I see her," Kai said, taking the last three steps in a leap.

They caught up at the front doors.

"Mrs. Byrd," Riley called out. The woman in the doorway turned, and quickly looked around.

"Can we talk to you a minute?"

"Oh, my, I do need to hurry..." She looked over her shoulder to a cab idling at the curb.

"Please, it will just take a minute," Riley said.

Mrs. Byrd closed the door and moved to the side near a large statue of a huge grinning polecat. The hall was empty except for two custodians pulling out their carts and the floor buffer.

Riley moved closer. "Do you remember seeing us? We were in the alley behind the magic shop the other day."

The petite little woman inched closer to Riley and adjusted the thick black frame of her glasses. "Why yes, I think I do remember you." She turned around and looked straight up at Kai, towering above her. "I'm not so sure about you..." Her eyes tracked from the top of Kai's head to the Doc Martens on her feet. And she smiled. "I do remember those large feet. You must've been who tussled with that ruffian."

Kai smiled. "You can say that again. Unfortunately, I was the one on the losing end."

"Oh dear, I'm sorry. Were you hurt badly?"

"Nah, not bad," Kai said, reaching for the tender knot on the back of her head. "Just some bumps and bruises."

"We just wondered if...maybe you had lost something that day?" Riley said.

Ms. Byrd looked around. "Oh, well now, I'm not sure. Did you find something, perhaps?"

Riley looked up at Kai with a you-tell-her expression on her face.

Kai just shrugged and shook her head.

Leaning a little closer, Riley whispered, "We found something, you know, shiny on the ground… And, we thought you might have dropped it."

"Perhaps. Could you describe it?" The tiny woman cocked her head to one side, pursing her lips together. The awkward motion caused her yellow narrow-brimmed hat to shift into a jaunty position She shifted the lemon-yellow pocketbook to her other arm, and Riley noticed the handle had the same kind of jewels as were on the wand.

Kai thought Riley was reluctant to describe the object as a magic wand because that sounded pretty weird. Of course, there was no other way to describe it, she clearly just didn't want to give away too much.

"Well I guess it was kind of an ornamental thingy about this long." She held her hands about a foot apart. "And it was very brightly decorated."

Loliy Byrd cocked her head the other way and a tiny twinkle appeared in her warm grey eyes. Her small mouth with the pursed red lips spread into a tiny smile. "I believe that might be my…" She paused. "Let's just call it my baton." She looked from Riley to Kai. "Do you have it with you, dear?"

Kai shrugged. "No, I mean we wanted to find you, but you disappeared. It was a total surprise when you popped up at the rehearsal."

Mrs. Byrd actually giggled. "Yes that was quite unexpected, but isn't this a nice coincidence? You know I would love to talk to you more." She looked out at the cab. "I really am in quite a rush. Perhaps we could get together some other time. Do you know that little tearoom on the corner of Cedar and First?"

Riley nodded and grinned. "My sister and I went there last year when my grandmother was in town." She glanced up at Kai, who was looking at her with a bemused expression. "Don't laugh, Stretch. It was really cool."

Mrs. Byrd patted both girls on the arms. "Why don't you meet me there Wednesday afternoon after school? And I think it would be wise not to mention this to anyone." With that, she pressed through the doors and flew down the sidewalk and into the waiting cab.

Kai and Riley looked at each other and shrugged.

"Man, for a little old lady she moves faster than anyone I've ever met!" Kai said.

Riley looked around. The halls were deserted and the streetlights were starting to pop on outside. "You know, Stretch, I think we ought to get out of here. I'm kinda creeped out."

Kai buttoned up her peacoat and tied the scarf around her neck. "Yeah, it's getting late. We'd better get home." She glanced at the stairway in the hall and sighed heavily. Her heart tugged a little with the memory of their first kiss almost thirty hours earlier.

Riley followed her gaze. "I know, I wanted to go up there, too."

Kai opened the door and held it as Riley passed through. Their eyes met and Riley took Kai's hand as they trotted down the front steps of the school.

# *Chapter Thirteen*

After dinner, Riley and Bekah cleaned up the kitchen while their parents got dressed for a concert.

"We'll be home by eleven. Riley, get your homework finished and be in bed by then. We have our cell phones," her mother said.

"I'll pull the car around, Lizzie."

"Be there in a minute," Elizabeth chimed as she sprinted upstairs.

Riley followed her up and leaned on the doorjamb to her parents' room. "I'm almost done with my reading. You guys have a good time."

Her mother stopped on the landing and turned around. She brushed a lock of hair off Riley's forehead and kissed her. "Then you might want to go to bed a little early. I don't want you to get sick again. I love you, sweetie."

Riley was searching her dresser drawers for the second time when her sister sashayed into the room.

"Suddenly decide to sort your socks by color and fabric?" Bekah said, flopping onto her bed.

"I'm looking for something." Riley slammed the bottom drawer.

She started for the closet and began going through the dirty clothes in the laundry basket. She slumped down in the doorway. *I can't believe I lost that thing. I know I stuck it in my sock drawer. Crap, what am I going to do? Kai's going to kill me for losing it.*

"Maybe mom washed it," Bekah said, grinning at her sister.

"Mom wouldn't wash it," Riley called over her shoulder. She reached into her pocket for her cell phone. She tapped in Kai's name and started poking the keys.

Riley: Hey, did I give the wand back to you?

A moment later the reply came.

Kai: No. I gave it to you for protection. Remember?

*Crap.*

❧❧❧❧

"I don't know! I looked everywhere. I was sure it was in my drawer." Riley grabbed Kai's arm and pulled herself up over the snowdrift.

Kai shrugged. "Don't worry about it now, we're gonna be late. I'll come over after school and we'll find it." The first bell rang and they broke into a run.

Riley waved and then threw her jacket into her locker. The hallway was slippery from all of the wet boots and she struggled to keep from falling. She caught a glimpse of the hall clock as she swung around the doorframe into her algebra class. The clock buzzed loudly just as the bell rang.

Mr. Flegal glowered at her as she slid into a chair.

"Pass your homework to the front of the room. Today we will be discussing…"

Her shoulders slumped and she sighed loudly as

the teacher droned on about graphing linear equations and slope-intercept forms. *Where the heck did I put that freaking thing?*

They were meeting Mrs. Byrd tomorrow, so she had to find it tonight. *Sorry ma'am, I lost your priceless doohickey, would you like another spot of tea?* She groaned inwardly. *Kai will help me find it. She's a total genius and will probably just walk into my room and point at it. Sheesh, I really need to get my act together and keep my room clean like she does hers.*

Riley grinned as a warm spot blossomed across her chest and belly. Whenever she thought about Kai it happened, and it had been happening a lot lately. She glanced at the clock on the wall. *Twenty-six minutes and forty-two seconds until the bell, and then I get to eat lunch with Kai. I bet she offers me her carrot sticks again, and then I can give her my Oreos.* Riley bit her bottom lip and grinned. *Ms. My-Body-Is-A-Temple can't resist my Double Stuff, can she?*

⁂

Kai was sitting at the back table in the library when Riley arrived. She was bent over a huge book, and her thick black hair that was so neatly pulled back in the morning was now loose and hid her face. Riley smiled at how serious she looked. But then Kai always looked serious when she was studying.

"Hey, Stretch," Riley said, poking her in the shoulder.

"Ouch." Kai rubbed her shoulder. "How is it you keep forgetting that the Alley Dude kicked me there?"

Riley sat her books down and pulled the chair out. "Sor-ry. Geez, I didn't mean to cause you undue pain and suffering, stud."

Kai's eyes grew large and a blush rose up her neck.

Riley winked at her, and plopped down in her chair. With a giggle, she reached out and tried to tug Kai's book to her side of the table.

Kai playfully slapped at her hands, and then smiled. "Hey, Shorty."

"What are you so busy studying? You look super serious."

"It's for English." Kai sighed heavily. "I have to write a two-pager about Romeo and Juliet, you know, what it was like for them"—she made quotation marks with her fingers—"as teenagers in love." She shrugged. "Anyway, I'm trying to find something about that time period. It's hard, it's like ancient history!"

"Want me to help you?" Riley said grinning.

Kai raised an eyebrow. "Don't you have homework?"

"I did it in study hall." Riley stuck out her tongue.

Kai grinned as she shuffled a pile of paper. "Okay then, since you're a free agent, think you could find some details about coming of age in fifteenth-century England?"

"I'm on it, cowgirl." Riley jumped up and started toward the librarian's desk but stopped. She stood there for a second, then turned around and walked back to Kai's table.

"Stretch?"

Kai looked up at her. "Yeah."

Riley folded her arms across her chest, and then unfolded them. She looked into Kai's eyes quickly before looking at a point somewhere on the table in front of Kai. "Does it bother you when I call you 'cowgirl'?"

"Look at me, Ri."

Riley glanced up at Kai, feeling contrite.

Kai gave her a soft smile. "It's okay. Really."

Riley gave her a skeptical look.

Kai's grin grew a little wider. "Really. Just because I'm Lakota, it doesn't mean I'm offended by being called a cowgirl." She waved playfully waved at Riley. "Really. I kinda like it."

"Really and truly?" Riley asked, then bit her lower lip.

"Really and truly, Little Bit." Kai winked at Riley.

"I could call you Buckaroo." Riley's grin widened.

"No." Kai shook her head and tried unsuccessfully to hide a wide smile. "No. Seriously, 'cowgirl' is better. Buckaroo makes me sound like a six-year-old with poopy pants."

Riley released a bark of laughter as she wheeled around and trotted off the librarian's desk.

❧ ❧ ❧ ❧

Kai closed the book and rubbed her eyes. When she looked at the clock, she realized Riley had been gone for almost half an hour. She was nowhere in sight. *Where is that little imp?*

She stood up, stretched, and then took off on her search. She swung past the reference desk to find out where she could find the History section. *Of course, 900s are on the balcony level. Riley is probably curled up on a shelf napping between the British Isles and England and Wales.*

As Kai poked her head around the stacks, she spied Riley sitting on the floor near a window, totally engrossed in a book.

"I can't believe English history is that fascinating. Where've you been?" Kai whispered as she walked up.

Riley looked up. Her face was all red and her eyes were huge.

"Check this out, you totally won't believe what I found!" Riley said in a loud whisper.

Kai laughed and slid down until she was sitting next to her. "Must be something good, 'cause you look like you just found the cheat sheet for your algebra test."

Riley shoved the paperback into Kai's hands. "Read this!"

Kai laughed and took the book. As she scanned the page, she could feel her own heart pounding in her chest. She turned the page, and then flipped back and started again.

"Well?" Riley said impatiently, poking at Kai's arm.

"Sssh, let me finish." Kai couldn't believe what she was reading. Her pulse raced as she flipped page after page. When she got to the end of the chapter, she swallowed hard and closed the book.

Riley's eyes were still huge as Kai turned and looked at her. "Where did you get this?" She waved the paperback at Riley.

Riley pointed to one of the upper shelves. "I was trying to get that big blue book down, and it fell on my head."

For a long moment they sat and stared at each other, breathing heavily.

Kai broke the silence. "Your face is all red."

"I know, so is yours," Riley said as she continued to stare at Kai.

They were so close together; Riley's face was less than a foot away from Kai's. Her green eyes looked dreamy and her lips looked so soft. Kai could feel the fluttering in her chest and then felt an ache in her gut. "I know. I feel really hot and kind of uncomfortable. Maybe we should get out of here."

"Kai, I feel kind of weird too…"

They started to get up at the same time and banged heads.

"I'm sorry." "Damn."

Kai began to pack up her books. Her hands were shaking and all she knew was that she wanted to get out of the library. She looked over and saw a Riley standing on the other side of the table staring at her with a funny look in her eye.

"Are you okay?"

Riley just nodded.

Kai returned the reference book and they quickly headed out to the hallway. Without discussion, Kai grabbed Riley's arm and pulled her to the staircase. They ran up two flights of stairs to the third floor. When they reached the landing they were both out of breath.

The third floor mostly contained offices and storage. The only kids that ever went there were the kids working on the yearbook. Kai peeked around the door and the office was empty. They walked a little farther, listening for voices.

"Are you sure you wanna do this?" Kai said.

"Yes. Are you?"

Kai nodded and tapped on the bathroom door.

"C'mon."

The room was small with one tall window with an industrial frosted glass window. Below it was a bench covering the radiator. The rest of the room contained one stall, a pedestal sink, and what looked like some kind of vanity with a mirror.

"Kai, the book...I couldn't believe, well it sounded like those girls really liked each other a lot. I mean, oh, I don't know what I mean. It's just when I read it, all I could think about was how it would feel, you know, if we were those girls."

"I thought the same thing. When I was reading it all I wanted to do was kiss you." Kai felt her face burn and her hands were shaking.

Riley shrugged off her backpack and dropped it on the floor. "I think I better sit down."

Kai sat her backpack on the floor and sat down next to Riley on the bench. "You look so pretty right now." She took Riley's hand and slowly brought it to her lips. She kissed it gently and heard Riley's breath catch.

"I'm nervous and excited all at the same time. You know I think about you all the time, and mostly I just want to be alone with you," Riley said as she stroked Kai's cheek with her other hand.

Kai was afraid her heart would pound out of her chest. It was hard to breathe, and there were spots before her eyes. She put her arm around Riley's shoulders and pulled her closer. The bench was warm, Riley's breath smelled like spearmint, the soft fabric under her fingers was smooth, and Riley's green eyes flashed as she begged. "I want to kiss you so badly..."

Riley slipped both arms around Kai and tipped her head. "Oh, do it."

The first touch was soft and wet. Kai inhaled deeply and pressed her lips tighter as Riley seemed to melt against her and she felt soft breasts against her chest. With her other hand, she cupped the back of Riley's head to pull her closer.

Riley moaned from deep in her chest.

They stopped, an inch apart. Both breathless. Eyes open. Kai tightened her grip and pulled Riley's swollen lips closer. Riley responded by opening her mouth just enough. Kai turned her head and carefully touched Riley's upper lip with her tongue. Riley's response was immediate, and their kisses deepened as they each took a turn exploring.

Kai's entire body was vibrating. All she wanted was to have Riley's body nearer to her. She moved her arm down to Riley's waist in an effort to pull her closer. Riley groaned, and Kai felt a wave of dizziness wash over her.

A door slammed in the hallway and they both froze.

"What was—"

"Sssh."

They were both panting. Kai was on alert as she felt a drop of sweat roll down her chest. She whispered, "I think they're gone, but let's wait a minute."

Riley leaned her head on Kai's shoulder. "I feel so dizzy…and so good."

Kai smiled. "Me, too. You're amazing." She leaned over and pressed her lips to Riley's forehead. Hugging her tightly, she took a deep breath and let it out. "Wow."

Riley sat up and traced her fingers across Kai's forehead. "You're pretty amazing yourself. But I guess we better go."

Kai smiled. "One more?"

Riley laughed. "Yeah, but a quick one." She pulled Kai's face closer and pressed her lips tightly against

Kai's.

By the time they had gathered coats, scarves, and gloves, fresh snow had started falling.

"Sure is pretty, looks like a white Christmas." Kai tightened her scarf.

"I almost forgot," Riley said, and handed Kai an envelope. "My mom wanted me to give you this. It's an invitation for our Christmas open house on Saturday."

Kai took it. "Really?"

"Of course really, goofball. My mom really likes you and since we hang out together, she thought it would be nice to meet your aunt. Do you think she'll wanna come?"

"I think so. I mean, she really likes you and she's really glad that I made a friend." Kai giggled. "Especially if she knew what those friends were doing fifteen minutes ago."

Kai watched Riley start to zip her bag. "Wait a second, isn't that the library book?"

"Actually, no. It's a book from the library, but it's not actually a library book. See? No barcode." Riley held up the book.

"Ri, you can't take books from the library without checking them out!"

"It's not a big deal. I'll take it back, but I really wanna read the story. Don't you?" Riley was grinning impishly.

Kai sighed. "You are a bad influence on me, you little imp."

Riley looked up at her hopefully.

Kai rolled her eyes. "But, yeah. I kinda want to read it too."

⚜⚜⚜⚜⚜

They walked for two blocks in silence as light winds carried a few snowflakes with them in the late afternoon twilight. When they neared the park, Riley slowed down and reached for Kai's hand.

"Kai? The girls in the book, the one from the library…they're gay aren't they?"

They stopped walking and Kai turned to her. "Well, yeah, I guess so."

The question on Riley's mind was slow to formulate. She knew what she wanted to ask, she just didn't know how to ask it. There was a knot forming in her stomach. "I just wondered if, you know, since we kissed and stuff, does that mean we're gay?"

Kai leaned against the mailbox and squeezed Riley's gloved hand. She looked around to see if anyone was watching them, and bit down on her bottom lip for a second. "Here's the thing, Ri. I'm pretty sure I am."

Riley looked up at her and nodded.

"But I'm not really sure about you."

Riley shrugged, but squeezed Kai's hand a little tighter. "Do you think I am?"

Kai smiled and shook her head. "I kinda think you're the only one that can figure that out."

"Why do you think you are?" Riley cocked her head to the side and scrunched her eyebrows.

"Well…" Kai looked up at the sky and contemplated for a minute. She looked down toward Riley and fought back a grin. "Well, I guess mostly it's because I think a lot about kissing girls, and I kind of have these, I don't know, fantasies about touching them and stuff."

Riley looked up at her, and blinked rapidly.

Kai's smile widened. "And when I think about

boys, I mostly think about practicing my cross-over dribble."

"Wow." Riley released a deep breath and nodded her head.

"Are you okay with that?" Kai brushed a strand of Riley's hair behind her ear. "About me being gay?"

"Of course." Riley matched Kai's smile. "Yeah. I mean, Aunt Sela is a lesbian, and she's one of the coolest people I know."

Kai bit her bottom lip. "Yeah, but you're not kissing your Aunt Sela, are you?"

Riley blushed and let out a nervous laugh. "No, but I thought about it a few times."

"Really?" Kai quirked an eyebrow.

"Well..." Riley buried her head against Kai's chest. "Yes." She leaned back, and looked up into Kai's eyes again. "Does that make me a lesbian?"

Kai tried unsuccessfully to suppress another grin. "Not necessarily, but..."

"What?" Riley reached up to brush away a strand of hair that had blown into Kai's mouth.

"It makes me kind of jealous." Kai stood a little straighter.

A bright smile spread across Riley's face. "I think I've always kinda had a crush on Aunt Sela, but you're the only one I really want to kiss and stuff."

"What kind of stuff?"

Riley motioned for Kai to lean down closer, pulling her scarf until she was close enough to whisper into her ear. "The kind of stuff you don't want to do with boys."

Kai swallowed hard. "Oh, man."

"So." Riley leaned back a bit, but yanked on Kai's scarf again for emphasis. "I kinda think that means I'm gay too."

"Uhhh." Kai continued leaning in, blinking rapidly.

"Are you okay, hot stuff?"

"Uhhh, yeah. No! I mean, I'm okay. I'm fine."

Riley pecked Kai quickly on the lips, and gave her a top-to-bottom once-over. "Yes, you are."

A blush crept up Kai's face, and she backed away a few inches.

"Does it bother you?" Riley cocked her head.

Kai shrugged. "Not really. I mean everybody at school already thinks we're together all the time anyway. But if it's a problem…"

Riley shrugged and took Kai's hands. "Look, Stretch, I know it sounds really lame, but I never thought of myself as gay, you know?"

A nod.

"I mean, I've always had friends that were boys and friends that were girls."

Kai nodded again.

"And I never really thought that much about kissing and stuff until we got to high school."

Another nod.

"Once the school year started, Brock and a bunch of the other guys started asking me to football games and dances and stuff."

"Hey, I get it, you know, it's no—"

Riley put a finger to Kai's lips. "Let me finish, okay?"

Kai nodded, and Riley removed her finger. "It was just kinda what I thought I was supposed to do. You know?"

"That's just it, Ri, I don't know." Kai's eyes looked almost angry. "I've never wanted to do stuff with boys.

Ever!"

Riley placed her hand in the middle of Kai's chest and looked directly into her eyes. "Look, it's not like my mom gave me a manual called *How I Stopped Worrying and Learned to Love Being Lesbian!*"

Kai's nostrils flared, and she pointed a finger at Riley. "Well, maybe she should ha—" Kai stopped midsentence when she registered the playful smile in front of her. A slow grin spread across her face. "Did you just make a joke about being a lesbian?"

Clearing her throat, Riley dramatically flipped her hair over her shoulder. "Yes. Do you have a problem with that?"

A soft chuckle erupted from deep inside Kai's chest. "Where the hell did you come up with that one?"

"Bekah and I were watching this super old movie the other night, and my dad kept saying all the lines with the characters." Riley rolled her eyes. "He's so wacked out sometimes. He kept muttering that it was 'culturally significant' and we needed to pay attention."

Kai shook her head. "Tilley watched that movie with me last year when I had the flu. It was pretty cool."

Riley nodded and rubbed her mittened hands together. "Yeah, it was." She looked up into Kai's eyes. "Are we okay?"

"Yeah," Kai reached out and wrapped her in a hug. "We're always good."

Riley wrapped her arms around Kai's waist and hugged her as tightly as she could. "You're my best friend, and the only person I feel this way about."

Kai kissed her softly on top of the head, and stepped back. "Me, too. Really and truly."

Riley nodded. "Really and truly."

"Come on, Shorty. We'll figure this out." She

grabbed Riley's hand and pulled her down the street. "It's getting dark, so we should get going. I think we better find that wand and then I have to study for my science final."

Riley stopped abruptly. "I'm okay. You go ahead and get your studying done. I'll ask Bekah to help me find it." She smiled. "Thanks for the talk. I think I really needed it."

Kai shrugged. "Me, too. I guess I kind of needed to hear you say some of that stuff."

As they approached the park, Kai stopped and looked around. "This is where I get off. You sure you don't want me to walk you home?"

"Yeah, I know you're totally stressing about your AP finals."

"Okay." Kai nodded and gave Riley a quick hug. "Text me later, especially if you find the missing item of amazing mystery and wonder."

"Huh?" Riley looked up.

Kai rolled her eyes. "The wand, Shortstop."

"Duh!" Riley laughed and waved as she turned toward home. "I'm on it. Study hard, Einstein. Catch you in the a.m."

❧ ❧❧ ❧

A car turned a corner and the headlights caught Riley's retreating figure as Kai stood and watched her disappear into the swirling snow. "Later, peanut."

A not-so-little voice inside her head strongly suggested she follow Riley home and maybe just stand outside her window for a while. That was the thing about Riley: she didn't have to be touching or talking to her all the time, but just being close made her feel like all the pieces were suddenly sliding into place. She smiled to herself. Of course kissing her and touching her wasn't too bad either.

*Damn, if I knew how great that felt, I would've busted Zach's face back in September!*

Kai stepped off the curb and began to jog down the plowed street toward home. Since the summer, she'd been having a lot of dreams about flying, and the feeling she got when she thought about Riley was a lot like the feeling she had in those dreams: soaring with arms stretched wide, chasing the wind, the sanctity of space, and the delirium of blueness stretching as far as the eye can see.

She began humming "How it Feels to Fly," the old Alicia Keys song that Ri gifted her on iTunes last week, then jiggled the key in the front door lock, flipped on the light in the foyer, and tossed the mail she'd retrieved onto the hall table. A white envelope with dark blocky printing caught her eye. Remembering the invitation, she pulled Riley's envelope out of her pocket and put it on the table.

After unbuttoning her peacoat and putting it in the hall closet, Kai returned to the small table and picked up the mysterious envelope. The only name on the envelope was Tiva. It was the correct address but no return address. The hair on the back of her neck stood up and she felt an unsettling feeling rise inside of her. She tossed the envelope on the table and went out to the kitchen.

Aunt Tilley had left a note on the refrigerator:

*Kai, should be home by 7, don't wait to eat dinner. There's a casserole in the refrigerator. Love, T*

Kai didn't hesitate—she was starving. She dished up a large serving of the casserole, covered it with a paper towel, and stuck it in the microwave.

While it heated, Kai went back to the hallway to get her science book. She glanced at the hall table and after picking up her book, grabbed the envelope and took it back to the kitchen.

Her fingers tingled as she held the envelope. It didn't have her name, but she was a Tiva. Her instinct told her to open it but to be careful.

Running her finger under the edge, she slowly pulled back the flap, and removed a four-by-six-inch card. It contained only one sentence.

*As night follows day, darkness follows light.*

Kai felt a sudden burning sensation in her fingertips and dropped the card. Looking down at her fingers, everything looked fine. *What the hell?* She had no clue what the message meant or what it was even referring to, but a feeling of dread settled deep inside. She started to reach again for the card. The timer on the microwave sounded and she jumped.

# *Chapter Fourteen*

R iley slipped her phone out of her pocket and
started to text Kai.

Riley: You will not believe it. Mom dragged me to
the European market to shop for her party. Gag. Guess
we can talk in the morning. Thinking about you. :(

"Go and get three bags of those small dinner
rolls—not the big ones. Make sure they're no larger
than this." Elizabeth James held both hands out
making a small circle with her fingers. "And get an
extra package of butter."

"Whatever…" Riley mumbled as she headed off
to the bakery section. She watched the display on her
phone, hoping for response from Kai. It finally came
when her arms were full of dinner rolls and butter.

She juggled the groceries until she could see the
screen.

Kai: Bummer. Waiting for Tilley. Got a mondo
weird card in the mail. Tell you about it tomorrow.
Can't study, thinking about your lips.

Riley felt the blush in her cheeks, and snickered
to herself as she shoved the phone in her pocket. All
she wanted to do was get home to replay their third-
floor adventure as well as read more of the book they

found.

Her mom was having an intense discussion with a butcher as Riley dumped her contribution into the grocery cart. She wandered over to the book carousel near the checkout counter. Scanning the titles, even a fourteen-year-old could guess that romance sells. As she continued looking at the book covers with naked guys' chests, she shivered.

Her mind flashed back to the basketball game and Kai's body dressed in shorts and a tank top. She'd never thought about it before, but suddenly the lean muscular body held a lot more interest. Riley imagined what it might feel like to touch those muscled shoulders and narrow hips. Warm sensations flowing through her body replaced the fluttering feeling in her chest. She crossed her legs as she felt an ache between them. It felt a little uncomfortable and embarrassing. She looked around to see if anybody noticed. The physical sensations were new to her, but not that unpleasant. She wished she knew how to make them go away. Sort of.

Her mother came up behind her. "I think that's everything. We need to get you home because it is a school night. Did you get your homework finished?" she said as she started tossing items on the conveyor belt.

"Um, yeah."

"Riley, do you feel all right? You face is a little flushed. You're not getting sick again are you?" She reached over and pressed the back of her fingers on Riley's cheek.

"I'm okay. It's just warm in here with my coat on."

꙰ ꙰ ꙰ ꙰

Kai was waiting at her locker when Riley came running up from PE.

"Sorry I'm late. Ms. MacAvoy made us swim extra laps while she waited for Penny to dive off the low board. Geez, what a wimp. You know, just do it, why make everybody late?"

"I guess that explains why your hair is still wet." Kai smiled. Riley looked beautiful with her wavy chestnut hair pulled back, leaving a couple of waves to curl across her forehead. Flushed cheeks made her eyes look dazzling. It was all she could do to keep from grabbing her.

"Well, duh, I didn't wanna be any later." Riley was struggling with the strap of her backpack and Kai reached over to hold it. "How long will it take us to get to that tea shop?"

"It's only about three blocks, it shouldn't take long," Kai said as her hand lingered on the strap over Riley shoulder. *All I need to do is pull and she'd be in my arms.*

"Let's get going, Stretch." Riley had pulled out of her grasp, and was making her way down the hall.

"You didn't tell me. Did you find the wand?" Kai asked.

Riley slowed her pace. "No. I looked again and couldn't find it. I didn't have a lot of time and Bekah didn't get home until midnight. Her boyfriend is in town. She's being insufferable. All she can talk about is Mr. Wonderful. Do you think Mrs. Byrd will be pissed? I really tried."

"I don't know. I mean, we'll find it. It's got to be somewhere. Anyway, she wasn't worried enough to go back and look for it, I don't think."

"Wait, is that the tearoom? The little house with a pink sign?" Riley said, pointing to a small two-story building that looked like a gingerbread house with all the traditional decoration. Ornately carved trim surrounded each window and the eaves on the front of the roof. A dark magenta paint contrasted with the pale pink of the wood exterior. Four steps led to the front porch where a stained glass door welcomed them.

A small chime announced their arrival as Kai and Riley stepped through the doorway. A dark-haired young woman came out to meet them. Kai thought she might be Middle Eastern.

"Do you have a reservation?" Her accent was unfamiliar. Kai watched as her long dress shimmered in the dim light.

Riley step forward. "We're meeting someone… Mrs. Byrd?"

"Ah, yes. She's expecting you. Please, come this way." She led them down a dark hallway to a staircase that curved up to a second floor. Another hallway took them to the back of the house.

Kai leaned over and whispered, "This place sure is bigger than it looks."

"I know. I hope we don't have to get out of here in a hurry."

They passed through one room decorated in old Victorian style with a fainting couch and two chairs beside a round coffee table, then entered a similar size room.

"Mrs. Byrd, your guests have arrived."

"Thank you, Hettie. Whenever you're ready, we will have the standard tea. Please come in girls, and have a seat."

The only remaining seat was a small sofa. Mrs. Byrd was perched in an elegant armchair with a small footstool. She looked even smaller in the large chair. Her white hair was coifed neatly on top of her head, with small rimless glasses perched on her nose that magnified her soft grey eyes. Neither girl was surprised that she was wearing an expensive-looking wool skirt and silk blouse of matching sunshine yellow. Her patent leather pumps and earrings also matched.

Riley took off her parka and hung it on the coat tree by the door, placing her book bag on the floor. Kai followed her example, and they sat down side by side.

The room felt like a movie set with antiques on the bookshelves and an odd-shaped mirror hanging over a tiny fireplace that was burning coal with a soft crackling noise. A small crystal chandelier with very low watt light bulbs was suspended above the table.

Heavy dark fuchsia velvet drapes hung beside the window, partially hidden by an intricate lace curtain. Kai took a deep breath, recognizing cinnamon and cloves scenting the air.

Mrs. Byrd just smiled. "Ms. Tiva, it would appear you've never been here before. Do you like it?"

"It's beautiful. Kind of old fashioned, huh?"

"I believe that's the look they wanted. I hope you girls are hungry. The food is scrumptious."

Hettie returned carrying a three-tiered server. Each shelf held a different assortment of sandwiches, breads, and desserts. A younger woman followed her with a large teapot covered with a hand knit tea cozy.

As she poured, Hettie described the unique Earl Grey lavender tea they were drinking, along with a little history. Satisfied that her guests were comfortable, she vanished.

"I generally start with the little sandwiches on top—I love the cucumber ones. Then I work my way down through the breads to the desserts. You may do whatever you wish."

Kai just looked at Riley and nodded, hoping she'd go first. Riley followed Mrs. Byrd's example, and Kai followed Riley's.

After one bite, Kai smiled. "These are really good."

Mrs. Byrd chuckled and dabbed at the corner of her mouth with a starched white napkin. "I thought you might like it."

There wasn't much conversation as they ate, but when Mrs. Byrd poured the last cup of tea, she folded her napkin, sat back in her chair, and crossed her legs. "I know we don't have very much time so I'd like to get to the point of this get-together. I chose this place because we would have some privacy. In the future, we may need to meet elsewhere.

"Right now, I'd like to ask you girls to keep this conversation secret. It is important that no one else know that I'm talking with you, at least for now."

Riley nodded, so Kai did too, but she also felt a prickly kind of warning. This odd lady was going to tell them something important.

Looking straight at Kai, Mrs. Byrd said, "The scuffle in the alley was not an accident, and it was not a coincidence that you girls showed up. It is also not a coincidence that you two have become friends." She smiled at both of them. "I will explain everything in much more detail. For right now, you need to know that you both have shared many lifetimes together. The reason that you are together now is to help Kai."

When Kai heard Riley gasp, she moved closer,

and without thinking put her arm around her.

Mrs. Byrd lowered her voice and spoke more softly. "Riley, some of the things I'm going to tell you may be somewhat surprising and I don't want you to be frightened." She turned and looked at Kai. "I'm not sure how much your family has told you, but you will soon be playing a very important role in their future."

Kai sat up straight, bristling. "What do you know about my family? Do you know what happened to my father?"

Holding up her hand, Mrs. Byrd said, "In time I will tell you everything. Please be patient. Right now, you need to know that dark sources are watching you. There are enemies who do not want you to succeed. I am here to teach you."

Kai suddenly felt faint. "The card…where did the card come from?"

"What card is that, dear?"

"Yesterday, in the mail, it just was addressed to 'Tiva.' Remember, Riley, the one I told you about?"

Mrs. Byrd leaned forward. "What did the card say?"

Kai closed her eyes. "As night follows day, darkness follows light."

"I see." Mrs. Byrd bit her lower lip and shook her head. She stood up abruptly and moved to the coat tree where she grabbed her matching yellow coat. "I can see there are a number of things we need to discuss. I'm afraid I must dash off now. We'll have another opportunity to talk soon. Don't forget our rehearsal tomorrow, Ms. James." She buttoned her coat, straightened her hat, and said, "Remember, not a word of this to anyone right now."

Kai looked over Riley and they both shrugged.

When she looked back, the little old lady was gone.

"Well, this has been about the strangest afternoon," Riley said, reaching for another cookie. "I thought she was much older. When you see her up close though…she seems younger. Don't you think?"

Kai was still looking at the door. The conversation was evidently more unsettling to her than it was to Riley.

"Kai? Are you okay?"

"I'm not really sure." Kai shook her head. She felt dizzy, almost as though she was floating. The room looked normal, but when she looked at Riley she felt as though she was far away. She reached her hand out and Riley took it, bringing her back to reality.

"Hey, Stretch, you look like you've seen a ghost or something. Can you talk?"

She shook her head again and took a deep breath. "Yeah, I'm okay. Dude, that was weird. It was kinda like I was in a dream or something. You looked so far away but I could hear you. I think we better get out here."

When they reached the front door, the dark-haired lady was waiting. "I hope you enjoyed your tea."

"It was wonderful. What do we owe you?" Riley asked.

"It's all taken care of. You girls have a nice afternoon."

As they walked through town, Riley pointed out various Christmas decorations that she liked. Kai just listened with one ear as her brain replayed the conversation at the tearoom. Her head felt tilted or unattached, and it made her kind of dizzy.

There were two voices in her head. Arguing. What possible use could she be to her tribe? *The old lady must be mistaken, and what's the crap about past lives? Who believes that kind of stuff?* She glanced at Riley who was being uncharacteristically quiet. She was probably scared, and it was all Kai's fault.

Kai ducked when she heard the flapping sound at the same time a shadow passed over them. "Wow, that was close. What was that?" She quickly looked up and Riley was standing motionless with a blank expression. "Are you okay? Riley, answer me."

"Huh, where are we?" Riley mumbled.

Kai looked around. Everything looked the same. Shoppers were moving along the sidewalk with them, cars were moving through the intersection in front of them, and the late afternoon sun dipped behind the trees along the river. "We're still in town, two blocks from the tearoom. Do you feel okay?"

When she looked up, Kai noticed Riley's eyes looked funny—her pupils were dilated. "Damn. I wonder if there was something in that tea 'cause I think we're hallucinating. Let's hurry up." She grabbed Riley's arm and pulled her across the street.

When they got to the playground, Riley stopped and turned to Kai. "My folks are taking Bekah and her boyfriend out for dinner. Do you wanna come over for a while?"

Kai nodded. "That's a good idea, I don't think we should be alone right now."

"Good," Riley said, taking Kai by the hand. They walked in silence the rest of the way to Riley's house. "I almost forgot, do you have a game Friday afternoon?"

Kai stopped. "I'm glad you reminded me. I almost forgot, too, and we have practice after school tomorrow."

Riley unlocked the front door and took off her

jacket. "You can just toss your stuff on the chair." She hung her coat on the banister. "Do you feel as cold as I do?" She continued toward the gas fireplace.

They both curled up on the couch and Riley pulled the afghan from the back of the couch to cover them. "Do you think you could put your arm around me again?"

Until she heard those words, Kai had only been half-listening and half-aware of Riley's presence. She reached out and pulled her closer. The warmth of her body connected them and Kai began to relax. She hadn't realized how tense her body was until that moment. With her other hand she reached for Riley's and leaned her cheek against Riley's head. "I'm glad you suggested this 'cause I was feeling really weird."

Riley snuggled closer. "I know what you mean. Can I tell you something?"

"Sure."

She looked up at Kai. "That stuff about past lives… Do you think we've been together before? I don't really understand."

It was a strange concept to most people, but Kai had heard about it when she was younger. She wasn't sure how to explain it. *Is this the right time to talk about my vision quest?*

Kai stroked Riley's hair and gazed at the flames in the fireplace—they reminded her of the nights she spent on the plateau in the desert. "I think I understand, a little. When she said that, I knew it must be true that I knew you before now. You know it's not like you looked familiar or anything, it's just…I don't know… you *felt* familiar, like we'd known each other for a long time. You know what I mean?"

"I think so. Because it was much easier to get to

know you, and sometimes when you say something, I feel like I already knew you were gonna say that. Y'know?" Riley moved closer and put her arm around Kai's waist.

The words gradually began to form in Kai's brain. She spoke slowly and softly. "Last summer I had the opportunity to go to the Minnesota Lynx basketball camp. A week after I got home, we had a visitor from my tribe in South Dakota. I didn't know the lady, but Tilley did. She was one of the Elders, Wakanda. It was her job to initiate the girls when they turned fifteen. She and Tilley talked for a long time. I was upstairs but I could hear some of the words. Tilley didn't want me to go but I guess there was no choice." Kai pulled her legs up and crossed them under the blanket. She pulled the blanket higher and Riley closer.

"Gosh, I never knew you were from South Dakota. And you lived on a reservation?"

Kai nodded. "We left shortly after I was born— my dad took me to live with his sister, Aunt Tilley. I never knew why. When I was older I'd find out, that's what I was told.

"Anyway, we took a really long train trip to Rapid City, where her grandson met us and drove us through the Badlands to Pine Ridge. Nothing was familiar to me. We spent the night at someone's house and in the morning, Wakanda drove me out to Slim Butte. It took forever."

Kai closed her eyes and drifted. Soon she heard the sound of the flute.

The cold night sky was as black as anything she'd ever seen. Pinpricks of light filled the canopy. They sat on the ground on heavy blankets.

Wakanda played the flute while Kai poked at the

small fire. They hardly spoke. The pungent smoke was the rich smell of sage and sweet grass.

The visions frightened her at first.

A large black bird circled overhead. Closer and closer. The whooshing beat of its wings distorted the column of smoke rising from the fire.

She was alone except for the drumming. One drum. Horses, many of them, racing across the prairie. In her hand a spear, in the other her fist gripped the horse's mane. Her bare legs pounded against the sides of the animal beneath her.

Battle cries and screaming as the horses pounded across the dry earth. Her lungs burned from the smoke. From the yelling. As the smoke cleared, she could see the outline of a large white crow glowing against the night sky.

She gasped as her head fell forward.

"Kai, breathe! Can you hear me? Please answer me." The familiar voice was very far away.

Her eyes fluttered open to see Riley's frightened expression. Riley was holding her face between her hands. Kai gasped, then took a deep breath.

"I was so scared, what happened to you? Oh my God, Kai, do you want me to get you some water or something?"

Her throat was still dry and sore. "I don't know what happened, did I faint?"

"No, you were just staring at the fire, but you wouldn't answer me. It was like you were in a trance or something. Kai, you really scared me."

The blanket suddenly seemed too warm, and Kai pulled it off.

Riley ran out to the kitchen and returned with a glass of water. "Here, you better drink this."

The water was cool and felt good on her raw throat. "Thanks. Come here," she said, reaching for Riley. "I know it looked weird; it was kind of like a dream or a nightmare, but I'm okay. I can't remember everything, but there was a large white bird."

Riley moved close and wrapped Kai in her arms and kissed the side of her head. "You were telling me the story about the lady who came to get you last summer, and you only got as far as saying that you went out to some place called Slim Butte, and then your eyes glazed over. Do you think something bad happened to you?"

"No, it's a tradition for girls coming of age to have a vision quest and then have those dreams interpreted by one of the elders." Kai paused, thinking that was more than enough information for the time being; Riley was already confused. "I'm okay." She pulled the blanket back over both of them and kissed Riley's forehead. "Let's not think about that for now and just watch the fire."

⚜ ⚜ ⚜ ⚜

"Kai," a voice whispered.

"What?" She dragged herself up from sleep to see Mr. James kneeling in front of her.

"It's almost ten o'clock. Why don't you let me drive you home? I don't want your aunt to worry."

She looked down and saw Riley sound asleep on her lap. She gently lifted her head, and slipped out from underneath. She tiptoed into the hallway and grabbed her coat. Mrs. James handed her the backpack.

"You girls must've had a busy day."

"Yes ma'am, we were both exhausted. Tell Riley bye."

After being snuggled under a warm blanket, the cold night air shocked her awake. Fortunately, the car was still warm. "I really appreciate the ride. It's gotten pretty cold, huh?"

"Yup, there are freeze warnings tonight. Your street is the one after the park?" he said as he steered around the corner.

"It's the brown house halfway down the block on the right."

Tilley's car was parked in the driveway and Kai was glad she'd left a message.

"You know Kai, Elizabeth and I are delighted with how well Riley is doing in school this semester. You've been a good influence on her, and we both like you very much."

"Thank you, sir." Kai could feel herself blushing.

"It's obvious that you girls are very fond of one another and...well, I'm glad you're such good friends. We're looking forward to meeting your aunt on Saturday."

Kai unbuckled the seat belt and ducked out of the car. "She is, too. Thank you for the ride Mr. James. Good night."

"Good night, Kai."

❧❧❧❧

Riley yawned and stretched then looked around. "Where's Kai?"

"Your dad took her home. Come on, you need to get to bed. It's late and you have rehearsal tomorrow. The kitchen looks clean; did you have anything to eat?"

*Cucumber sandwiches and tea cake, not exactly a balanced meal.* "We grabbed something on the way home." Riley started up to her room as her mom followed.

"I was rather surprised to find you both asleep so early. Usually I have to hound you to get to sleep," her mom said as she began hanging up the clothes that were strewn about the room.

"We were both exhausted, but Kai was telling me about growing up on a reservation. Did you know that she was born in South Dakota?"

"Really? I didn't know that. What reservation was it?"

Riley pulled on her Joe Boxers and a Vikings T-shirt. "Oglala Sioux, I think. It's somewhere south of Rapid City."

Her mom sat on the foot of the bed. "You seem very fond of Kai. I don't remember you ever spending so much time with any of your other friends."

Riley tossed her clothes into the hamper. "I suppose. I hadn't really thought about it. It's just that, well, Kai is so different than the other girls. She's really smart and we just always have something to talk about. Most of the other kids just want to gossip and it gets so boring." Riley smiled. "And she's a terrific basketball player."

"Okay, honey, don't forget to brush your teeth, and get to sleep. I love you," her mom said and kissed her forehead as she walked out.

"I will, Mom. Good night," Riley said, and trotted off to the bathroom. When she returned to her bedroom, the light was on in her parents' bedroom and her dad was talking. She couldn't hear what he was saying and moved closer to their door.

"…Yes, she lives just on the other side of the park so it didn't take long. Roads are getting slippery, though."

Her mother's voice sounded fainter. Riley figured she must've been in the bathroom talking because she could only hear her father.

"...I'm not concerned. She seems like an awfully nice young lady, a bit shy, but very polite."

Riley heard the back door close and hurried back into her room, knowing Bekah was on her way up. She shut off the light and grabbed Mr. Rat. She curled up and began to replay the afternoon and the conversation they had.

Her new best friend was more mysterious than anyone she'd ever met. But honestly, she couldn't remember ever liking anyone this much. Anyone.

# *Chapter Fifteen*

Kai, hurry, you don't want to be late," Tilley said, wrapping a sandwich and putting it into an insulated bag. "Do you have a game tomorrow afternoon?"

"Yeah, with Saint Luke's, should be an easy win," Kai said, tucking in her shirt. She picked up the toast and peanut butter, and stuffed half in her mouth.

Tilley leaned against the sink and smiled. "You'd think I never fed you. Would you like two sandwiches for lunch?"

Kai shook her head and picked up the glass of orange juice.

"You look nice in that new shirt. I like purple on you, makes you look a regal. Listen, I have an appointment tomorrow afternoon here in Lindan with the bank. If I finish early, I'll try to get to your game."

Kai remembered Riley's invitation. She swallowed what was in her mouth. "Did you see the invitation we got from Mr. and Mrs. James?"

"No I didn't," Tilley said, rinsing her coffee cup.

"They're having a holiday open house on Saturday and wanted us to come, because they wanna meet you. Can we go?"

"You really want to, don't you? Of course, we can. I'd like to meet Riley's parents since you two spend so much time together."

"Okay, I'll tell Riley to let them know." Kai

paused. "What do you suppose people wear to parties like this?"

Tilley laughed. "Oh dear, you really are growing up. Do you realize this is the first time you have ever asked me what you thought you were supposed to wear?" She put her arm around Kai's shoulders and hugged her. "Is there hope that my little tomboy will develop a sense of style?"

Kai pulled away. "Oh come on, I don't dress that bad! It's just…I don't wanna embarrass Riley. I don't even know if there'll be any other kids there."

"Don't worry honey, we'll find you something to wear. We can stop at the mall after your game. Now, you better hurry."

"I'm fine," Kai said, sticking her foot on the kitchen chair in order to tie her boot, then repeated it with the other foot. She hated talking about clothes; first it was Riley teasing her, now it was her aunt. Kai just liked comfortable clothes. *I don't know what the big deal is, who cares anyway?* she thought as she pulled the leg of her jeans down over the top of the boot.

Kai pulled her peacoat out of the hall closet and looked in the mirror. After buttoning up, she pulled her hair out of the back of the collar and tilted her head to one side. *I don't think I look so bad, Riley likes the way I look. And I like the way she looks.*

"Bye," she said to Tilley.

"Have a nice day, honey."

The sun was out and the temperatures were in the mid-thirties as she turned onto the main sidewalk, which was clear so it took less time for her to get to the park. The center of the park had been leveled by some of the dads with garden variety snowplows and shovels. They created an odd-shaped circle surrounded by snow banks, then the village president asked the fire department to flood the area, making a small ice rink. It was a perfect size for the little kids, but too small for hockey or anything interesting to older kids.

The shiny surface reflected the blue sky and fluffy white clouds. Kai looked up to watch as the clouds sailed overhead and she drifted into remembering.

Last summer. She was lying on top of the butte, watching cloud formations. She had studied the shapes and tried to identify them as different animals or birds.

Some of those summer memories were pleasant. Wakanda had showed her how to cook simple food on a small fire.

They had taken very little in the way of supplies, but after four days, she was no longer hungry—the sweat lodge ceremony they performed purified her. So by the time Wakanda had taken her out to the plateau and left her alone on the butte, Kai thought she would be ready for the vision quest.

It was harder than she thought. The first night was the worst because of the noises. She didn't sleep. By the second night, the boredom had exhausted her.

When Wakanda finally returned, Kai had been hallucinating and shaking with cold. Even in the middle of summer, weather extremes in the Badlands can be brutal. Kai shivered at the memory of the harsh experience.

Wakanda made Kai recite every vision, hallucination, and dream to find the symbolism. It seemed like an endless ordeal, then one day it was over and Wakanda brought her home.

The cold fresh morning air jarred Kai into the present. Her torturous dreams from the night before were less threatening. Still, she desperately wanted to tell Tilley about the hallucination she had with Riley, just to share it was someone. She didn't know what it meant and it scared her. *Past lives with Riley—how can that possibly be?*

"Hey, Stretch. Sorry I'm late," Riley shouted from the sidewalk.

Kai turned around and waved, then jogged over to her. "I thought maybe you were sleeping in."

"Yeah, fat chance of that. Was your aunt upset that you came home so late?"

"Naw. I left her text message. She was already in bed. How about your folks?"

Riley stopped walking and looked at Kai with a puzzled expression. "I think they're okay. My mom followed me upstairs and made a couple weird comments about us being good friends but she seems to like you pretty well. When my dad got home I heard them talking, but all I heard was my dad saying he thought you were really polite."

Kai laughed. "I guess that's a good thing. I think your folks are kinda cool and I can't wait for my aunt to meet them."

Riley took Kai's arm. "Stretch...are you okay today?"

Kai looked down at her. "Sure. Why wouldn't I be?" She knew why Riley was asking her didn't want to talk about it. Maybe later.

Riley just grinned. "Good. I'm glad." Then she squeezed Kai's arm and bumped her with her shoulder.

❧❧❧❧

They passed Zach Coho with his friends giggling at the flagpole, and were starting up the front steps of the high school when Kai was hit by a snowball in the back of her head. She stumbled on the top step and fell forward.

"Shit!" She wheeled around as she shrugged off her backpack. "Asshole, I'm gonna—"

Riley grabbed her arm. "Don't! Kai, remember what the principal said. You can't afford to get in trouble again."

Her arms were shaking with rage, and she glared at the little weasel doubled over with laughter. "I'm gonna kill him," she muttered under her breath.

Riley moved in front of her and said with a very low voice, "Pick up your backpack and go inside."

That got Kai's attention. "What?"

"Please, just go inside."

Kai picked up her backpack and watched as Riley marched down the steps and straight up to Zach Coho.

"Listen, you dickless wonder, you're just lucky that you got an early Christmas present," Riley said loudly enough to get everyone's attention. "You think you're such hot shit because you bully little kids and girls, and you're just pathetic. No wonder nobody'll go out with you." She wheeled around and started back up the stairs.

"What's the matter, Tiva, you need your little girlfriend to defend you now?" Zach taunted.

Before anyone knew what happened, Riley lurched at him and dropped him to his knees with a punch in the gut, causing the circle of students to break into cheers just as the bell rang.

Kai just puffed up and grinned. *Way to go Ri!*

Riley grabbed her arm. "Let's go."

"Okay. I'll see you later, tiger. You totally rock!"

After the three-thirty bell, Riley opened her locker and a note fell out on the floor. *I had practice. I'll meet you at rehearsal. K.*

She folded the note, smiled, put it in her pocket, then ran up the stairs to the auditorium. All day she'd waited for a "summons" from the principal that fortunately never happened.

It was a crazy thing for her to do, but Zach deserved it. Creep. She'd surprised herself with her own anger. *I didn't know I had it in me. Cool.*

When he had shouted the taunt at Kai, Riley had experienced an almost primal sense of protectiveness. At that moment, she believed she could've torn him apart.

She rubbed her right hand, which was tender, and wondered where this new fury had come from. In the past she'd had huge fights with her sister and her mother, but she'd never felt like this. It was a little frightening.

As she walked down to the stage area, she looked over her shoulder, hoping Kai would appear soon. She really wanted to talk to her.

"Let's get started," Mrs. Byrd said as she appeared from offstage. "Please find your seats. Mrs. Schumacher, let's start with 'Sleigh Ride.'"

The rehearsal went quickly now that the students were used to their new direcctor. Riley was surprised that Mrs. Byrd completely ignored her until it was time for her solo.

"Ms. James, I've decided to move your solo to just before the finale. Everyone please pay attention. Mrs. Schumacher and I have changed the arrangement so that as soon as Riley finishes her solo we will move right into the finale of 'Silent Night.'"

They went through it twice with a few stops for corrections. Riley had to admit the new arrangement sounded good and it made her solo a little more dramatic. Secretly she was excited about the prospect of her parents hearing her sing.

"All right, people. Remember that the performance is next Thursday afternoon at four o'clock. School will adjourn at one and you will have just enough time to get home and change your clothes. Remember, you will need to wear a white shirt with a collar, and Mrs. Schumacher will provide everyone with red ties. Boys, black trousers, and skirts for the girls. There will be a full rehearsal Monday and a short one on Wednesday afternoon."

Tiffany was waving her hand. "Mrs. Byrd, my mom wants to know if she can get extra tickets."

"Have her call the main office. They can let her know what's available."

Mrs. Byrd stepped down from the podium carrying her baton and her yellow coat. Riley watched but said nothing as a wave of guilt washed over her. *Where in the hell is that damn wand?*

She wandered back to the rear of the auditorium and found Kai slumped in a middle seat of the back row. That tall body scrunched in the seat made her laugh. "Why are you hiding back here?" she asked, slipping into the seat next to her.

Kai whispered, "I just saw two guys super gluing Zach's locker. I don't wanna be anywhere around there when he finds out."

Riley laughed, thinking about how pissed he'd be. "Serves the little shit right."

"Ri, I was so proud of you this morning. You were awesome."

"You know what's weird?" Riley said, tucking her knees under her and facing Kai. "At the time, I was so furious I really think I could've killed him, you know what I mean? I've never been that mad in my life. It scared me a little."

"I think I understand. It's kinda the way I feel when he picks on little kids. It's just so wrong."

"I wonder if our past lives included being soldiers or warriors or something."

Kai looked around the empty auditorium and took Riley's hand. "I think there's a lot of stuff we don't understand and I'm hoping Mrs. Byrd will tell us. Did she say anything to you today?"

"No, it was kinda weird. She pretty much ignored me. Oh, she did move my solo to the end and I think it sounds kind of cool." She looked at Kai's strong profile and the way her dark hair hung across the front of her purple shirt. She reached over and stroked the sleeve. "Is this new? It's really pretty."

Kai looked down. "Not really, I guess I haven't worn it this year. Do you really like it? I thought it looked sort of…foofy."

Riley had the fluttery feeling and smiled. "I really like you, Tiva," she said and leaned close enough to kiss Kai's cheek.

"What are you doing?" Kai whispered loudly.

Riley leaned closer. "It's your turn."

Kai looked around nervously, then moved closer and pressed her lips to Riley's.

A rush of warmth spread through her as she welcomed Kai's mouth.

After one more look around, Kai cupped the

back of Riley's head and pressed her lips firmly over Riley's as she moaned softly.

Riley followed her lead as she caressed the side of Kai's soft face and she became aware of an aching sensation as their passion grew. She couldn't breathe, felt dizzy, and never wanted it to end.

Kai took her face in both hands and pulled back, panting. "We can't do this." She sat back then reached for her coat. "Ri, we have to go now."

Riley grabbed her arm. "Why? Did I do something wrong?" The aching was bad.

"No, nothing is wrong. I just, I can't…when I kiss you, I get really turned on. Geez, Ri, we're in the auditorium."

Riley's heart was pounding and she wanted to be lost in Kai's arms. She sat back and folded her arms over her head. "I know. You're right, but sometimes—"

Kai took her hand. "I know, Ri, believe me I know. But please, come on, we have to go."

As they turned the corner toward the park, Kai said, "Did you ever find the wand?"

Riley kicked a chunk of snow. "No, damn it. I tore my room apart and now it's a total mess. I know I wrapped it up and hid it because I didn't want to explain it to Mom."

Kai shrugged. "I don't know what to tell ya, but sooner or later she's gonna ask us for it. Do you want me help you?"

"Nooo, I'll ask Bekah. Kai are you mad?"

"Nuh-uh, I just can't imagine where it could've gone. Maybe it is magic, and maybe she got it back already. Do you want me to walk you all the way?"

"No. I'm fine. We'll talk later, 'kay?"

"Fershure, Shorty," Kai said and started down

her street. And turned back. "Thanks for…you know." Then she started to run.

❧ ❧ ❧ ❧

Riley waved and felt a twinge of the ache. Wouldn't it be cool if Kai lived closer? She decided to read more of the scene from that library book, hoping to find out more about these strange feelings. She picked it up, tracing the letters of the title with her fingertips: *Awakenings: I Found My Heart in San Francisco Book One* by Susan X. Meagher. She began to read:

"I went to an all-girls Catholic high school. I knew that I was different from my friends but it didn't bother me. I thought I was just unique," she said as she gave Jamie a crooked little grin. "I didn't ever have a crush on a guy or have any desire to go out with one. Luckily we didn't have the pressure of having guys around all the time, so the issue was never forced. I honestly never considered that I might be gay, though. I just thought I was… me. I thought everyone had crushes on their girlfriends and teachers. I honestly thought everyone scheduled their week around *Cagney and Lacey*," Ryan said with a small laugh.

Jamie didn't understand the reference, but she nodded to encourage Ryan to continue.

"Anyway, as the years passed I began to feel more than close to Sara. I wanted to be 'with her,' even though I didn't really know what that meant or how to go about it. I was really naïve when it came to sex. That was one area that Da did a crummy job with. And the boys were certainly no help. It might have been different if I was a little worldlier, but my whole universe was sports and Sara. I didn't watch TV very often or go to many movies or participate much in community events, so I was just not clued into lesbianism."

"You must have been so confused," Jamie empathized.

"In a way I was, but in another way I assumed Sara felt just like I did. We were so close it was like we shared a soul." Ryan dropped her head a little, but continued. "I was finding the temptation overwhelming just to touch or kiss Sara. She was all that I thought about. I wanted to let her know how I felt, but I was so confused about what this thing was, that I didn't feel able to."

Riley folded the book on her chest and pulled Mr. Rat closer. "One soul. That's how I feel sometimes, like Kai and I are sharing some kind of special…I don't know, maybe it is a soul. Because she is what I think about all the time." She pulled him up to face her. "Do you think I'm a lesbian?"

His silence spoke volumes.

She rolled onto her side and hugged him closely. "I knew you'd understand. I don't think that would be so bad, I mean after all there's nobody I'd rather spend my time with than Kai. Certainly wouldn't be Brock the Goat Boy." A laugh bubbled up with that thought.

Riley sat up and looked at the clock on her desk. It was a little after eight, Kai was most likely studying, but what the heck? She reached for her cell phone and hit speed dial.

"Hey, Riley. What's up?"

"Are you busy? 'Cause I just wanted to talk to you."

Papers shuffled. "I always have time for you. Are you okay?"

"Uh huh. I was just reading—you know, the book from the library—and wanted to talk to you. I was reading some more and I think we might be lesbians. Because the girl in the story is talking about how she feels about her friend and…well it sounds like the way I feel and I think the way you feel and how we always wanna be together and are best friends and stuff…but we also like to kiss."

Kai cleared her throat. "That is the way I feel. I wasn't sure that you did."

The fluttering began in Riley's chest. "I do, that's what so weird. Can I read you something?"

"Sure, go ahead."

Riley sat up, holding Mr. Rat in her lap. She opened the book to the page she was reading and began.

"After a minute I reached for her and I kissed her. I had never kissed another person in my life and it was kind of overwhelming." She shook her head and stared at the floor.

"I was shaking so hard she must have heard my teeth chattering, but I could tell she was nervous, too. But God, Jamie." She took a deep breath and let her head drop back against her shoulders. "Nothing since has ever felt that good to me."

"I thought she was enjoying it as much as I was," she said with a rasp in her voice. "No. I know she was enjoying it. I know it," she said firmly as she closed her eyes tightly.

Riley held her breath, waiting for Kai to respond. *Please let her not think I'm a freak.*

In a very soft voice, Kai said, "That's just the way I feel whenever we...you know."

A wave of relief washed over Riley. "I know! Me, too."

"Have you read the whole book, is there more stuff...you know, like that?"

"No, I haven't read very much, but I think I better. Don't you?"

"Yeah, I think we should both read it, but I won't have time until Christmas break. My science final is gonna be a bitch."

Riley closed the book and put it down. She grabbed Mr. Rat and hugged him.

"Kai, I don't know about you, but I sure have a lot of strange stuff going on in my head—about you, and Mrs. Byrd. On top of that, the biggest event in my whole life coming up next week. If it wasn't for you..."

"I know. Me, too. I'm there for you Ri, just like you were for me today. She was right, you are my protector."

"And you're mine. I'm so lucky have you—"

"Lucky to have who?" said Rebekah, pushing open the door.

Riley sat up. "I gotta go, my jerky big sister just came in. See you tomorrow."

Rebekah threw her bag on the bed and tossed her coat on the desk chair. "Who were you talking to, your friend Kyle?"

Riley tossed a pillow at her and stuffed the book under her comforter. "You know you're a gigantic pain in the butt, don't you?"

Rebekah flopped on the bed and grinned at her. "I do what I can, baby sister."

"I don't know how Mr. Wonderful can stand you."

"Because he thinks I'm beautiful, brilliant, and extremely sexy." She flung the pillow back at Riley.

"Aaack, he must be stupid."

"Eat your heart out, sis. We may be moving in together next year." Rebekah got up and began to put her things away. "We can't staaand to be apart."

Riley watched with mixed feelings. She might miss her sister, but…if Bekah moved in with her boyfriend, she wouldn't have to share her room anymore. Maybe Kai could stay over sometimes.

❧❦❧❦

Kai crumpled up the scratch paper and launched it across the room to the wastebasket. She rolled over on her back, completely unable to focus on science. All she could focus on was the excerpt Riley had read to her. Just talking about a kissing scene from a book made her feel sort of loose and giddy at the same time.

Resting her hand on her chest, Kai smiled, wondering what it would be like if she could put her hand on Riley's chest. Her fingers tingled and felt hot.

When Riley kissed her on Sunday, it was the first kiss she'd ever had in her entire fifteen years, and it was perfect. Too perfect. It would be so great if they could be together without interruption.

The photograph on her dresser caught her attention. It was a picture of Tilley and her at the county fair, the souvenir photo taken when they rode the roller coaster two summers ago. They were both laughing and their hair was flying everywhere. She smiled at the memory because they had such a great time that day.

Kai closed her eyes and thought about the wonderful memories she had shared with her aunt. She was lucky; Tilley took such good care of her even though she had a hard job, and Kai could always count on her.

She looked at the picture again, then sat up. Thinking as far back as she could, there was never a memory of Tilley with anyone. She thought her aunt was beautiful and couldn't imagine why she had never married. She didn't even remember any dates. She was probably just too busy.

Kai closed the science book, vowing to get up early and study. She took a shower and pulled on her favorite tee and warm-up pants. She glanced at the photo one more time before turning out the light. *I think I'll put a picture of Riley on my dresser too.* She closed her eyes and thought about Riley's laughing face surrounded by soft auburn hair.

In her dream, she slipped the bonds of earth and soared on the west winds with white wings extended, the fading sunlight dazzling her.

# *Chapter Sixteen*

I am so furious I could spit!" Riley continued stomping through the crusted snow, evidently for the mere pleasure of hearing the icy surface crack.

Kai remained a few steps behind on the sidewalk. "I don't get it. Why do you think she has the wand?"

Riley stopped and whirled around. "Because. She was teasing me, she kept hinting about something she'd found. Then she never left our room so I couldn't look for it." She threw her arms in the air and yelled, "I hate her!"

Kai just kept walking. She knew better than to interrupt that tirade. Besides, there wasn't much she could do to help.

"What am I gonna I do?" Riley said, catching up to her.

"Ri, I don't even know your sister and even if I did, I don't think she'd listen to me. I think you need to tell Mrs. Byrd."

"Can't you tell her?" Riley said.

"No. I've got the game after school and then I have to go to the mall with Tilley, remember?"

Riley followed along in silence for a few moments. She finally caught up and said, "So, what are you going to buy?"

Kai cringed and shook her head. "I have no idea. What are you going to wear tomorrow?"

"We went shopping before school started and I

got a bunch of stuff. I had to have a black skirt for the chorus, but Mom found a really pretty green sweater that she thought would look good for Christmas." Riley reached for Kai's arm and turned her around. "Mom even let me get a pair of heels! They're only a couple of inches, but at least I'll be taller. How cool is that?"

Kai smiled and gave her a shove. "You're still gonna be Shorty," Kai said and took off running.

"Hey come back here!"

ೋೋೋೋ

Riley dropped her Mr. Rat backpack as she pulled open her locker door. The books spilled out, adding to her aggravation. "Damn it! I don't wanna miss the tip-off." As she bent down to grab them, a booted foot kicked her math book down the hall. She looked up and saw Dick Chiclet laughing at her.

"What's the matter Ri-ley, ain't your freaky friend around to help you?" Zach laughed.

Riley was on her feet. "You don't wanna go there, Coho, you pathetic dickhead."

He took a step toward her then stopped, looking over Riley's shoulder. Riley turned around to see Mrs. Byrd moving down the hall quickly and he turned the other way.

"Ms. James, I'm so glad I caught you."

*Oh shit. I'll be late for sure.* "Hello, Mrs. Byrd."

"Do you need some help, dear?"

"No, I'm good," Riley said, shoving the last book into her backpack.

"I saw you and it reminded me that you had inquired about a lost item that you thought belonged to me."

"Yes ma'am, I did. Well, we did. And I…you know, I just keep forgetting to bring it to school. I'm really sorry."

Mrs. Byrd tipped her head to one side with a curious expression on her face. "I understand. It is actually a rather significant piece and it was very careless of me to leave it behind." She stepped closer. "Would you mind calling me when you think of it." She handed Riley a business card that read "Mrs. Loliy Byrd, Consultant."

"I will. See you Monday," Riley said, closing her locker. She turned around and Mrs. Byrd was gone. *How does she do that?*

She turned and ran back down the hall toward the gymnasium, hoping Kai wouldn't notice her absence. *Kai.* Just thinking about her made Riley remember the silky shorts and tank top Kai wore for home games. It made her look lean, tan, and strong. Whenever they hugged, Kai had such a gentle touch almost like a large cat making her purr. *Then get moving!* She picked up the pace.

❧❧❧❧

"Tiva, get out there. Focus."

Kai had been nervously scanning the bleachers for any sign of Riley. She'd all but given up hope when she saw the rust-colored sweater Riley had worn that day. She felt her heart skip a beat. With a quick wave, she ran out to center court.

The girls from St. Luke's weren't much of a challenge, but three of Lindan's best players were home sick. Coach warned them to be extra careful.

Being the tallest player on the floor made winning

the tip-off easy for her, sending the team off to a good start. The Lindan Polecats took an early lead, with Kai scoring almost half of the points. Coach took her out to give her some rest.

Kai sat on the end of the bench where she could see the court and Riley sitting three rows up behind her. She lifted the ponytail from her neck to towel off the sweat, then wiped her face. As she glanced over her shoulder she saw Riley wave, and she blushed knowing that she always watched her very carefully.

St. Luke's scored twice and Coach put Kai back in. Each team pushed hard toward the final buzzer. Kai scored a rebound and the tallest girl on St. Luke's snatched the ball and raced down court for a quick bucket. A tie score with one minute to go.

Lindan surged ahead and on the final foul shot, Kai twisted her ankle and fell. She jumped back up but the coach was right there and helped her off the court. When she looked up in the stands, she saw Riley on her feet with her hands covering her mouth.

Kai gave her a wave and thumbs-up. The assistant coach checked her ankle, taped it, and told her it was a light sprain. She agreed to take it easy for week, but felt like a complete dork for falling on her ass in front of Riley.

As soon as the final whistle sounded, Riley was at her side. "Are you okay?"

"I'm fine, I just feel stupid. The guard was so short I didn't see her."

"Will you ever be able to play again?" Riley said with a panicked look on her face.

Kai laughed. "Of course I will, I just have to stay off of it for a while." As she said that, she looked up to see her aunt walking toward them. She looked so out of place in the school gym with her high heels and business suit. She had her coat over one arm and a briefcase in her other hand. Tilley usually wore her hair up at work and looked very professional.

"Nice game, Kai. Sorry I missed the first half. Is your ankle all right?" Tilley said.

"I'm okay, I just have to take it easy for couple of days." Kai was grinning. Aunt Tilley and her best friend were both at her game, and she fell on her ass. *Great.*

"I hope you didn't do that on purpose just to get out of going to the mall," Tilley said, tugging her ponytail. "It's good to see you, Riley."

Riley stood up. "It's nice to see you, too."

Tilley sat down on the end of the bench. She put her hand on Kai's ankle, then said, "I don't think a mall trip is in your future."

"I'm okay, really. I'm sure Coach will get me some crutches."

"No sweetie, it's slippery. I'll just drop you off at home and run over by myself. Riley, can I drop you off?"

"You could just drop me at your house. Maybe I could get Kai something to eat and then I can walk home," Riley offered.

Tilley stood up and looked at them both. After a minute she said, "All right. Kai, you wait here while I go get the car. Riley, if you could go and get Kai's belongings from the locker room, you girls can meet me in front."

Kai looked at Riley, who just nodded.

Tilley put on her coat and headed for the door.

"Ri, you don't have to do that," Kai said.

"It's okay, I don't mind. It's Friday night, my

folks won't care. I'll just call them."

❧❧❧❧

Riley took off for the locker room while Kai waited patiently on the bench. In ten minutes, they were waiting in front as Tilley drove up.

"I see the coach gave you some crutches," Tilley said.

Kai laughed. "After Riley left, Coach came out and found me sitting there all by myself. I guess she felt sorry for me so she went back to the office and got them. She said it might help for the next day or two."

"All right, let's get you in the backseat with your leg up. Riley, you can hop in front. Why don't you call your folks and tell them you'll be over at our house?"

"Okay." Riley called her mom while Tilley arranged Kai's leg.

Both Riley and Tilley fussed over Kai, getting her into the house and settled on the couch. "There's some leftover turkey and ham and the refrigerator, and some hard rolls on the counter—if you're hungry, and I know Kai is." Tilley winked. "I shouldn't be more than an hour or so. Call me if you need anything."

Riley hung up Kai's jacket and arranged a large cushion under her leg. She looked around, seemingly confused. "What should I do now?"

Kai laughed hard, covering her mouth with one hand. "Riley, I'm fine. I went along with all this so I didn't have to go shopping. You don't have to do anything."

Riley sat on the foot of the couch and lightly touched the bottom of Kai's bare foot. "I was sort of worried. I'm glad you're okay." She stroked the side of

Kai's foot with her thumb.

Kai could feel the heat through the elastic wrap on her foot. It tingled all the way up her leg. The tender expression in Riley's eyes melted her heart. Kai was supremely happy at that moment. Tilley had actually come to her game and her best friend came back to the house to take care of her. "I really am kinda hungry, but I might be able to settle for a kiss," she said with a grin.

Riley stood up, laughing. She bent down, kissed the top of Kai's head, and went out to the kitchen. "A turkey sandwich it is."

Kai folded her hands behind her head and smiled. *An hour. It won't take me that long to eat a sandwich.* The ankle was a little swollen, but it was no worse than other injuries she had in the past.

Riley returned with two sandwiches, then went back for two glasses of milk. She also brought an ice bag and draped it ceremoniously over Kai's ankle.

"With all that happened I forgot to tell you, I almost had a run-in with Dick Chiclet. I was in a hurry and dropped my books, and he kicked one of them down the hall. I was so pissed. He was all macho trying to get in my face, and I was just about to nail him when he backed off. Know why?"

Kai shook her head.

"The magical Mrs. Byrd showed up. Scared him half to death, and off he went."

Kai wiped her mouth with the back of her hand. "This is really good, thanks. So did you talk to her?"

Riley put her sandwich down and picked up the milk glass. "Yes. I apologized all over the place and told her I forgot. She seemed kind of, I don't know, weird. Just said to call her and let her know. She gave me a card with her number."

Kai finished her sandwich and burped. "'Scuse me. Well, at least she knows you've got it, I guess that's good. So you better get it."

"I will. With all the craziness at the house tomorrow getting ready for the party, I'll be able to do some snooping." She sat up straight and looked horrified. "You *will* be able to go to the party won't you?"

"Of course I will. You think Tilley would be out buying me clothes if she meant to keep me home? She's really looking forward to this, and so am I."

⁂

Tilley returned right on schedule with a large bag from The Gap. She dropped it on the coffee table and went to hang up her coat.

Kai sat up and opened it. She reached in and pulled out a package of underwear that she promptly stuffed back in the bag.

"What was that?"

Tilley laughed. "I got her a new bra and some underpants."

Kai felt the heat rise up her neck. "Tilley!"

"Tell me what you think of the slacks," Tilley said, unfolding the grey tweed, skinny boot-cut pants.

Riley reached over to touch the fabric. "These are really nice."

Tilley handed them to her as she pulled out a federal blue long-sleeved shirt tapered at the waist. "I think you can wear your loafers if your foot isn't too swollen.

Kai shrugged. "Those are really nice, thanks for

shopping." She replaced the ice bag on her foot.

"You wanna try them on?" Tilley asked.

"Not right now, I'm kinda tired."

"I should probably get going," Riley said. "It's late."

Tilley stood up. "I really appreciate you babysitting my little niece. Let me grab my coat and I'll run you home."

"Oh, you don't have to it's not that far—"

"It's no problem. Besides, it's gotten quite a bit colder." Tilley went to get her coat.

Riley gently squeezed Kai's foot and winked. "Guess I'll see you tomorrow, Stretch. I can't wait to see you in your new outfit."

Kai felt embarrassed and a little awkward. "Thanks for helping me tonight and coming to my game. It meant a lot."

Tilley's stuck her head around the door. "Kai, stay put and I'll be back in a few minutes."

Kai flopped back on the couch with one arm draped across her forehead. She liked the clothes Tilley bought except they were so fancy. But at least Riley wouldn't be freaked out when she saw her.

As her mind wandered, she tried to envision Riley in a long black skirt and a tight green sweater. Her eyes grew heavy.

In her distant memory, the score from *The Nutcracker* began to play. Tilley had taken her to the ballet in Minneapolis over Christmas when she was ten. Kai had been enchanted by the dancing and frightened by the rat soldiers. Of course.

Every year since, they listened to the music on Christmas.

❦❦❦❦

Riley waved good-bye as Tilley drove off. She really liked Kai's aunt. She was smart and pretty and really cool with kids.

"Riley, is that you?" her mom called from the kitchen.

"Yeah, Mom, it's me," Riley said as she tossed her jacket on the banister and headed into the kitchen.

Her mother had the kitchen counters covered with trays of appetizers and the whole house smelled great. "So tell me again what happened to your friend."

Riley grabbed a piece of cheese and started to eye the Christmas cookies. "The game was really good, right up until the end. Kai turned into her guard and fell, twisting her ankle. It was really gross and swollen, so the coach wrapped it up and put her on crutches."

"Did you get a ride home?"

"Her aunt was at the game, so we helped Kai to get home and I stayed with her while her aunt went to the store. Then she brought me home."

"Do you have homework? Because tomorrow will be too busy."

Riley deflated. "I should study my math. The exam is Monday."

Her mom covered one tray with Saran wrap. "Okay. I need one of you girls to go with me to pick up the turkey and the roast beef. Your father has to get chairs and go to the liquor store. Oh, I hung your skirt and sweater in the closet. Get some rest, sweetie."

Riley dragged her backpack. She always had fun at the Christmas party, but all the preparation was exhausting. Realizing she was alone, Riley took the opportunity to search through her sister's luggage.

Bekah didn't really unpack for her two-week visit home. Her suitcase was on the floor next to her backpack filled with schoolbooks. Riley laughed. *Like she's really gonna do any studying when her boyfriend's in town. She's probably making out with him right now.*

She went through each zippered section of the suitcase to no avail. Her backpack had nothing but a lot of junk, a bunch of books, and…birth control pills! She smiled. *I wonder if mom knows about this? Could be helpful.* She zipped the bag closed and looked around. *It's got to be somewhere.*

The dresser drawers revealed nothing but more clothes. She knelt down and looked under the bed, then under the mattress. "Damn."

She heard the front door shut and voices the kitchen. This was not a good thing to be caught doing, and Riley scrambled to get into her pajamas.

# *Chapter Seventeen*

I'm exhausted. We spent all day fixing this house up, and now I can hardly move." Riley switched her cell phone to the other ear.

"It probably looks great. I'm getting excited about coming over. What did your mom fix to eat?" Kai asked.

Riley sat up on her bed. "You won't believe how much food there is! I'm sure the whole town of Lindan could be fed with just the appetizers. Mom went nuts this year. I hope you haven't eaten all day because there's tons of food. I helped to make the little sandwiches, so try one of those, okay?"

"If you made them I'll eat them all. What time should we come?"

"I think Mom's expecting people around four. At least that's when we're supposed to be ready. I'm really glad you're gonna be there, at least I'll know somebody." She squeezed Mr. Rat.

"Did you have time to study for the math test?" Kai sounded serious.

"No, I was supposed to last night and I fell asleep. How's your ankle?"

"Oh, it's much better today. The swelling's gone down a lot and I can get a normal shoe on. Tilley had some weird cream that she rubbed on it last night. I think that's what helped. If you want, maybe we could study on Sunday."

"That's a great idea, unless I die from all this partying." She sighed.

Kai laughed. "Are you kidding? You'll be in your element. Everyone knows you're great at a party."

"Who told you that?"

"Brock Jones."

"You jerk!" Riley bolted upright.

"Tilley is calling, I gotta go. But I'll see you soon."

"Bye, Stretch." Riley hung up and stuck the phone in her pocket. She rolled over and hugged Mr. Rat. "Almost showtime, Mr. Rat."

"Take your shower, Riley. People will be arriving in less than an hour."

❧❧❧❧

"This won't take a minute," Tilley said, getting out of the car. "I just want to get a bottle of wine as a hostess gift. You can stay here or come with me."

Kai thought she might as well go on in and see what her aunt decided to get. The store was surprisingly busy. Kai thought maybe everybody bought liquor on Saturday afternoon. Tilley took off down the wine aisle and Kai limped slowly over to the chips and snacks. She picked up a package of corn nuts, put them back, and grabbed some pork rinds. Suddenly Riley's words of warning came back to her to save her appetite for the little sandwiches.

She sighed heavily. It had been hours since breakfast and she was starving. If Riley was teasing her about the amount of food, it could be serious. Tilley was gone from sight. Kai leaned against the beer cooler and was startled a tall man bumped into her. A prickling sensation alarmed her.

The man was clearly Native American and stood her height less than a foot away. A strong odor she couldn't identify assaulted her. She tried to step back but was blocked by the cooler.

The stranger's one eye was almost black, the other covered by a patch. His hair was pulled back and tied behind his neck. A raspy pinched voice squeaked out of a mouth curled in a sneer.

"You have something I want, and I'm growing impatient."

Unable to swallow, Kai weakly protested. "What are you talking about? I don't know you." A chill enveloped her entire body and her throat tightened. It was like a premonition—a dream or a nightmare she couldn't quite identify. Frighteningly familiar.

He leaned even closer. "You have been chosen. That should be me. Chay tried to take it from me—and now you. Give me what I want or you will meet the same fate," he growled.

Kai felt an uncomfortable vibration and then there was a bright flash. When she opened her eyes she only saw spots of light, yellow light. She shook her head and looked around, There was no one near her. Tilley was at the checkout counter and Kai moved quickly to her side, looking around at every face. There was no dark-haired, one-eyed man anywhere. *Shit.*

"We're all set," Tilley said, sticking her wallet back in her purse. "I found a rare eighty-seven Pinot Noir. It's a little pricey, but I think they'll like it. Kai? You want me to pay for that?"

Kai looked down and found a bottle of root beer in her hand.

Tilley pulled out a five-dollar bill and paid for the soda. "I never knew you liked root beer." She took the change and started for the door. "It's kind of odd, your dad loved root beer when he was younger. We'd better hurry."

On the front porch of Riley's house, Kai shifted nervously as Tilley straightened her collar. There was no point in being so nervous, but she couldn't help it. What she wanted was a chance to tell her aunt what had happened in the liquor store. Or did she? "Are you sure I look okay?"

Tilley smiled and smoothed the hair on the side of Kai's head. "You look really nice and I'm proud of you. A little makeup might have helped, but..."

Kai glowered at her just as the front door opened.

Mr. James looked very festive in a red and green plaid vest. "Merry Christmas. Please come in. It's good to see you, Kai. This must be your aunt?" He offered his hand. "I'm Richard James, Riley's dad."

"Thank you so much for inviting us. I'm Tilley Tiva, Kai's aunt." She shook his hand as they stepped into the brightly decorated hallway. "I brought a little holiday cheer." She handed him the wine in a festive bag.

"Thank you, that was thoughtful."

Christmas music was playing from several speakers, and the house smelled like cinnamon and pine. Kai quickly looked around, hoping to find Riley.

"Let me take your coats," Mr. James said. He took both their coats to a coatrack at the end of the hall. Kai and Tilley waited as he hung them up then returned. "The girls are in the kitchen helping their mother, but let me get you started with some punch."

They walked into the large dining room, which was decorated beautifully with evergreen boughs around the doorways and on the buffet. The wall sconces glowed with colored bulbs, and an elaborate centerpiece glittered with twinkly white lights.

The fairyland atmosphere and the music enchanted Kai. "Thank you," she said when handed the punch cup.

"Riley tells me you're a lawyer with Bartels and James. Excellent firm. I've played golf with Cedric James—no relation."

Kai was listening, but was much more interested in the mixed nuts and bacon-wrapped water chestnuts.

"I was fortunate to be offered an associate position shortly after I graduated. They've treated me very well, and I just made partner in June."

Her aunt looked beautiful. She'd worn a really simple purple dress with a short magenta jacket. She did something amazing with her hair. It was pulled up in big loose curls and just a few bangs. The turquoise necklace and long, dangling earrings accentuated her neck.

Kai cocked her head and smiled. Every once in a while, she remembered that her aunt was a darned attractive woman, not just her caregiver. Today was one of those days.

Mr. James excused himself to get the door just as Riley came in carrying a tray of hot appetizers. When she looked up and saw Kai, she broke into a grin. "Boy, you look terrific," Riley said. Kai couldn't breathe. Riley's eyes sparkled. She set the tray down and walked over.

"I'm glad you guys are here. Mom wanted to know when you arrived so she could meet you. Wait here a second." She hurried to the kitchen.

"Your description must've made quite an impression." Tilley nudged Kai with her elbow.

Kai could feel the heat wave burning across her neck as the fluttering started in her chest. *Oh my God, Riley looks incredible. That's sweater is absolutely gorgeous and I never realized that she was so, that they were so—*

Riley returned with her mother in tow. Elizabeth James was tall, almost as tall as her husband. She had on a long holiday skirt with a pretty blouse.

"Mom this is Tilley, Kai's aunt, and of course you know of Kai." She jerked her thumb toward Kai.

Tilley reached her hand out. "I'm Tilley Tiva. Happy to meet you, Mrs. James."

"Oh please, call me Elizabeth. I'm so glad you girls could make it. Kai, you look very nice."

Kai watched as the two women strolled into the living room as they talked.

"Riley you look totally awesome," Kai whispered. "That sweater is incredible."

"You look cool. Those pants fit you perfectly, and how'd your aunt fix your hair that way? I love the small braid in the back," Riley said.

The green sweater made Riley's eyes and even deeper shade of green. She had a little makeup that accentuated the beauty of her face. She even had lipstick on. Kai felt dizzy and put her hand on the table.

"Are you okay? You look a little pale, is it your ankle?"

"Ankle, yeah. I think a better sit down a minute."

Riley steered her to a dining room chair against the wall. "I'm going to go get you some water, so don't move."

Kai could feel little beads of perspiration on her forehead and the back of her neck. Maybe she should've had breakfast. *But damn, Riley looks so good. It's gonna be so hard not to touch her.*

Riley brought the water and sat down next to Kai. It seemed like just minutes and suddenly there were dozens of people milling around. The music had gotten a little louder and the punchbowl had become a very popular place.

Mr. James was also providing mixed drinks for many of the guests. The latest two arrivals were a priest and a nun. Kai elbowed Riley and pointed.

Riley whispered. "That's Father Portus and Sister Mary Agnes. She was the principal at Saint Mark's. Mom always wants to invite her over. She thinks it's good for me to remember the discipline. I had plenty of it. Bekah was the perfect child and I was the spawn of the Devil, according to her." Riley shuddered.

Kai tried to imagine her beautiful friend as the iconic troublemaker, then realized it wasn't that hard to do. An image appeared of Riley taking down Zach Coho in front of the whole school. Kai started to giggle and put her hand over her mouth.

"And what's so funny?"

Kai leaned over. "I just remembered you punching out Dick Chiclet."

Riley laughed. "That was fun. Hmm, maybe I am the spawn of the Devil."

Mrs. James walked through the dining room. "Riley, would you help me for a minute please?"

Riley sighed, got up, and headed for the kitchen. "I'll be back in a minute."

After several minutes, Kai could no longer resist the food calling her. She sampled everything with gusto. She bit into a bacon-wrapped scallop and hoped that no one had noticed she'd eaten six of them already. Mrs. James was an amazing cook, and these scallops were about the best thing she'd ever had. She quickly scanned the room looking for Riley, but didn't see her yet. Mr. James had begged his youngest daughter to help him get Great-Aunt Molly situated in the living room and as far away from the eggnog as possible. *Bet there's a story there.*

Wiping her fingers on a cocktail napkin, Kai saw Aunt Tilley involved in an animated conversation with a striking redhead in the living room. When she moved closer, she recognized her as Mrs. James's friend Sela. Kai grinned to herself as she watched her normally demure aunt throw her head back in laughter. *I'm glad Tilley is having little fun tonight. Boy, does she deserve to let loose a little.*

She looked up and saw Riley making her way through a gauntlet of white-haired old ladies who all wanted to pinch her cheek and touch her hair. She gave her friend a sympathetic smile. *Can't blame them. I totally want to touch her, too.*

With a burst of speed, Riley broke free of the gaggle of old ladies and rushed past Kai, grabbing her hand. "Follow me."

Even with her long legs, Kai had to hop-step after Riley, who pushed open the kitchen door at full speed. "Ri…"

"Where are you two going in such a rush?" Mrs. James glanced over her shoulder as she removed a tray of appetizers from the oven.

Riley stopped and looked at Kai, then back at her mom. "Uh, Kai spilled some punch on her blouse, so we're going to the laundry room to treat it before it stains."

Kai looked at Riley with a surprised expression on her face. "I did?"

Riley elbowed her hard in the ribs.

"I did." Kai got the message. "Yes. I did spill dip—"

"Punch," Riley corrected.

Kai winced in anticipation of another elbow that didn't come. "Punch. I spilled punch. On my shirt." She pointed vaguely to a place on her side that was partially hidden behind Riley. "Here."

Mrs. James looked at Kai and blinked three times in rapid succession. The oven timer buzzed, and she turned toward the stove to shut it off and started arranging the appetizers on a serving tray. "There's a stain stick next to the detergent, and a few Tide pens in the drawer with the fabric softener sheets."

Riley gave Kai's hand a tug as she sprinted for the back of the house. "Thanks, Mom!" she yelled over her shoulder.

Kai tried to focus on not taking a header into the doorjamb as Riley yanked her at full speed. "Hurry up, this way."

"Where are we going?" Kai murmured as Riley opened a door, shoved her in, and reached for the light switch.

"Close that behind you, will you?"

As soon as the door latched, Riley spun Kai around until her butt smacked against the washing machine. "What's going on, Ri?"

Riley's eyes had an almost feral look to them. She stepped toward Kai and slipped her hands over her shoulders and behind her neck. Kai raised an eyebrow. "Ri?"

"Will you just shut up and kiss me?" She pulled Kai's head down and kissed her with an unexpected passion. Kai melted into Riley's warm lips as some shadow of logic reminded her to raise her arms and wrap them gently around Riley's waist, pulling her closer. Kai felt the muscles in her belly tighten as Riley moaned into her mouth, and the last hints of conscious thought evaporated.

Before she was ready for it to stop, Riley's fevered kisses began to slow into a succession of soft pecks, gentle nibbles, and playful nips. Slowly, Riley pulled back, still breathing heavy. Kai leaned forward and placed a soft kiss on her forehead, and then pulled back to stare into the familiar green eyes. "Better?"

Riley shook her head.

Kai raised her eyebrow. "No?"

Riley shook her head again.

"Do you want to kiss some more?

Riley nodded in agreement as her tongue darted out to wet her swollen lips.

Kai felt a sudden jolt between her legs that threatened to make her knees buckle. *What is she doing to me?*

Breathing deeply, Kai looked into Riley's glassy eyes as heat blossomed across her chest. "Ri?" she whispered as she stroked her left thumb in a small arc across Riley's ribs. Riley blinked, clearly trying to control herself. Kai looked down at the firm, round breasts covered in soft green cashmere. "Can I..." She looked into Riley's eyes. "Touch them?"

Riley licked her lips again, and nodded her consent.

Kai slowly slid her left hand up and cupped a supple breast. *Oh, man, that feels good.* She released a soft groan as she squeezed lightly and felt a hard nipple press into her palm. Kai lowered her head to Riley's and met her lips with a searing kiss.

The pressure of Riley's lips against hers grew in intensity, and Kai felt herself becoming lightheaded. She tightened her grip, and heard herself moan as Riley deepened the kiss. Kai slipped her hand from Riley's breast to the bottom of her sweater. Her fingertips felt the warm, soft skin of Riley's belly, as she inched her fingers up to slowly trace the lace along the top of her bra. Her fingertips dipped inside the soft satin, and she stroked a firm nipple.

Riley broke the kiss and pulled back, causing Kai to lean back against the washer to keep herself upright. Riley was breathing heavily. "What are you doing?"

Kai blinked twice. "Huh?"

Riley looked from Kai's dazed eyes down to her chest and then back up. "Your hand."

Kai blinked again, and then looked down at her left hand.

"Kai."

"Yeah." Kai was mesmerized by the feel of Riley's nipple against her fingertips.

Riley tugged on a strand of Kai's dark hair. "Hey, look at me."

"I am." Kai's mouth began to water. *I wonder if it tastes as good as her lips.*

Rolling her eyes, Riley gently put her fingers beneath Kai's chin and lifted until their eyes met. "What are you doing with your hand?"

Kai looked down to Riley's chest, and then back up into Riley's soft green eyes. "You said I could touch you."

A smile tugged at the corner of Riley's lips. "I meant on the outside of my sweater."

"Oh." Kai blinked.

Riley moved her hand up to Kai's face and

brushed a strand of hair behind her ear. "Are you going to move it?"

Kai looked back to Riley's chest and brushed her fingertips against soft satin. "I'd rather keep it here." With her thumb and index finger, she gently rubbed the hard nipple, and looked back up into Riley's eyes.

With a growl, Riley surged into Kai, bringing their lips together in a deep and sensuous kiss.

Kai continued to roll the nipple between her fingers, and Riley gasped and parted her lips as she tugged Kai closer. The unexpected contact of Riley's tongue on hers made Kai moan again. Every nerve ending in her body lit up, and she felt the surge of something molten rising deep inside.

"Hey, are you in there, Riley?"

Kai pulled back as the pounding on the laundry room door registered like a klaxon her in her brain.

"Riley!" Bekah's voice rose above the pounding. "Are you in there?" More. Pounding.

Kai looked at Riley; her eyes were huge.

"Come on, open up." The door handle jiggled.

"Ow!" Kai grimaced as Riley slapped at her left hand.

"Behave!" Riley whispered as she pointed at Kai and stepped back to put some space between their bodies.

The door opened, and Bekah peered in. Kai whispered a silent prayer that she didn't look half as guilty as she felt. "Why didn't you answer me?" Bekah looked from Riley to Kai, and then back to Riley.

"I, uh." Riley looked up at Kai, and then back to Bekah. "I didn't hear you."

"The door was closed?" Kai tried to help. *Oh, God. When did my voice start sounding like Mickey*

*Mouse?*

Bekah gave her a funny look, but thankfully turned back to Riley. "Whatever. Anyway, Mom says Father Portus is about to leave, and she wants you to invite him to the concert to hear your solo."

Riley rolled her eyes. "Why can't she just do it?"

Bekah shrugged. "I don't know. Anyway, you'd better hurry up. She said if you weren't there in five minutes she'd send Sister Mary Agnes to find you."

"Oh, God." Riley whined as she looked up at Kai. "She'll make me pray the Rosary before I even get to the kitchen."

"Bet-ter hur-ry," Bekah singsonged as she stepped aside. "Dad said she was into the single malt again."

With a dramatic sigh, Riley brushed past her sister. "Okay, okay. I'm going."

Bekah watched Riley scurry around the corner into the kitchen, and then turned back to Kai. She smiled. "So you're the infamous Kyle."

*Kyle?*

"I'm Bekah." She thrust out her hand.

Kai looked down at the hand, and then back up into Bekah's blue eyes. She was several inches taller than Riley, and looked like a younger version of their mom. "It's Kai." She shook the offered hand. "My name is Kai, not Kyle."

Bekah folded her arms across her chest and leaned on the doorjamb. "Did you go to Saint Mark's with Riley?"

"No." Kai leaned back against the washer. "I went to Avoca Middle School."

"Oh, okay." Bekah nodded. "I didn't think I recognized you."

Kai shrugged. "We only met a little while ago."

Bekah raised an eyebrow. "Really?"

"Yeah." Kai shoved her hands in her pockets. "In the principal's office."

Bekah looked surprised. "Why was Riley in the principal's office?"

Kai shrugged again. "They made her meet with some guy from the newspaper. It was for the concert."

"Oh, yeah. Mom sent me that article." Bekah bit her bottom lip. "Why were you there? Are you in the concert too?"

"Uh…" Kai looked down at her shoes. "No. I kinda punched some kid in the nose for being a jerk." She looked back up and Bekah.

Bekah scrutinized her for what felt like an eternity. "You do know Riley is one of those people that everyone likes to be around?"

Kai nodded. *Heck, I sure know I do.*

"She's always been pretty popular."

Bekah's eyes were focused on her, and Kai nodded again, wondering where she was going with this.

"When you're popular, everyone wants a piece of you."

Kai bit her bottom lip and nodded a third time. *She thinks I'm using Ri.*

"But a lot of people don't really care about you, just what you can do for them." Bekah's eyes continued to bore into Kai. "You know what I mean."

Kai swallowed hard and considered her words carefully. "Riley's the first real friend I've ever had."

Bekah nodded and squared her shoulders. "If anybody hurts her, for any reason, they're going to have to answer to me."

Kai felt a lump rise into her throat, and she met

Bekah's eyes. "And they'll have to answer to me, too."

A moment passed as the two stared at each other.

"Mom says you've been tutoring Riley in math and science." Bekah seemed to relax a little.

Kai followed her lead, and leaned back against the washer again. "Yeah, but she's been helping me in English, as well."

Bekah smiled lightly. "Dad can't figure out how the daughter of a CPA can suck that bad at math."

"Yeah, but Ri is really smart." Kai smiled back. "Her brain's just wired differently from mine. Have you ever read any of her short stories or seen her sketches?"

"She's been doing that since she was little." Bekah's smile grew a little brighter. "I've always been a little jealous. She makes it seem so easy."

Kai reached up and brushed a strand of hair behind her ear. "Ri makes a lot of things seem easy."

Bekah cocked her head and considered Kai. "You call her Ri."

A blush crept up Kai's neck and her heart thudded against her chest.

"You, uh…" Bekah pointed up at Kai's lip and then back to her own. "Have something here."

Kai reached up and brushed her fingers over her lips. When she looked at her fingers she saw traces of Riley's lip gloss. There was no stopping the full-on blush that had to be making her ears red.

Bekah wiggled her eyebrows. "Looks like things got a little out of control." She paused for dramatic effect. "Maybe you should work on your technique."

Kai's eyes were huge as she stammered out. "H-h-huh?"

"Your technique." Bekah winked. "You know, for applying lip gloss." She pointed at her lips.

A thousand-pound weight slipped from Kai's shoulders. "Lip gloss. Yeah. I should practice." She was grinning like an idiot, but couldn't shut up. "Applying it. On my lips. Lip gloss. That is."

Bekah laughed out loud and she turned to leave the laundry room, motioning for Kai to follow. "Come on, Einstein. Let's go save Riley from the pious and diabolical Sister Mary Agnes."

Kai wiped her mouth again and straightened her shirt, hoping she didn't look as disheveled as she felt, then followed Rebekah back through the kitchen. As soon as they entered the dining room, Rebekah glommed on to her boyfriend. She looked over his shoulder at Kai and winked.

It was all she could do to muster a smile. It was mortifying, absolutely mortifying, to have been caught making out the laundry room. Kai wanted to die. She looked around and finally spotted Riley cornered on the couch by the schnockered sister. She wanted to help but she was too upset.

She spotted a half-empty wine bottle on the end of the bar and grabbed it. Pulling a plastic cup from the stack, she poured a healthy amount into the cup and drank it as quickly as possible.

Alcohol was not routinely available at her house. Tilley drank on occasion but not very often. The dry red wine probably would've tasted better with 7UP but, even as she thought about it, she could feel the effect warming her bloodstream. After a minute or two, she felt able to make a sandwich. The warm turkey smelled wonderful. She added servings from several of the salads including the creamy green Jell-O mold with pineapple.

❧❧❧❧

Father Portus was looking impatient and very uncomfortable as Riley tried to steer the giggling nun toward the door. "I know Sister, this really was the best party ever and I'm so glad I had a chance to talk to you."

"You know Riley, in spite of all of our difficulties, you are still one of my favorite students." She leaned forward, pinching Riley's cheek for the hundredth time.

"Thank you, Sister," Riley said, making a will-you-please-hurry look at her dad, who was trying to separate one black coat from a dozen others.

He finally arrived and helped their guest into her coat as Riley ducked into the dining room. She spotted Kai in the corner with a plateful of food, went over and sat down. "How can you eat a time like this?"

Kai looked up from the seven-layer salad and grinned.

"Are you drunk?" Riley said looking at Kai's bleary eyes. "Oh my God, you are."

"Not. Jus' had a little wine."

"Are you nuts? My mom would kill me." Riley looked around, and smiled.

Kai sat up a little straighter and looked serious. "Then I think…we better not tell her." She went right back to eating.

❧❧❧❧

It wasn't much longer before Tilley came to find them. "You two still awake? I thought you'd be bored by now." She sat down next to Kai. "I just talked to your mom, Riley, and asked her if she thought it would be a good idea for you to come back to our house tonight. This party is not winding down anytime soon and I think you two could use some sleep."

Riley could hardly believe her ears. *A sleepover, what a great idea!* They could talk as much as they wanted to without Rebekah. She looked at Kai who just nodded. "Okay, let me run upstairs and grab some stuff. I'll be right down."

"Don't forget your math book," Kai said, quite seriously.

# *Chapter Eighteen*

Tilley put clean towels on Kai's dresser. "Kai, remember to show Riley where things are and then I think you girls should get to sleep. Do you have everything?"

"Yes, I'm good," Riley said. She hung her backpack on the chair next Kai's desk.

"Okay. Good night." Tilley closed the door and they could hear the steps creak as she went back downstairs.

"Kai, what's that circle thing hanging over your bed?" It looked like a decorated spider web.

Kai pointed above her. "You mean this?" Riley nodded. "It's a dream catcher. Almost every child gets one over their bed. There's a rich legend that goes with it, but the basic story tells about a spider that created one for a wise Elder so the good dreams are captured in the web of life and carried with them, but the evil dreams escape through the center's hole and are no longer part of them. Or, depending on which version of the legend you believe, the center allows the good dreams through to the dreamer, and the bad dreams are caught in the web."

"Does it work?" Riley was intrigued.

Kai looked up. "I sure hope so. I've had some pretty strange dreams."

"Huh." Riley began unpacking clothes, books, iPod, pajamas, and a bathroom bag. "This is so fun. I don't remember the last time I got to have a sleepover." She paused and looked at Kai. "It might've been Tiffany's birthday last year. Her mom was really strict. Lights out at ten and she waited outside the door to make sure were asleep." Riley laughed suddenly. "I almost forgot." She giggled again. "We had a really gross pizza and after we played karaoke Amber hurled all over the kitchen floor."

Kai sat with a puzzled expression on her face.

Riley kneeled next to her on the bed. "Come on, haven't you been to some heinous sleepover?"

Kai shook her head. "No. I've never been to any sleepover. I went to Dorinda's house for lunch once in fifth grade. We just had peanut butter sandwiches and chicken noodle soup."

"I never thought about it, maybe you didn't want me to come over? Is this a bad idea? I mean maybe after—" She stood up.

Kai reached for her hand. "I do want you to be here. I was glad that Tilley thought of it."

Riley sat back down. Something felt off and maybe it was because of the whole incident in the laundry room. It had gotten a little out of control and Riley felt like it was all her fault. Maybe Kai was angry. *I never should have dragged her down there. I came on so strong and then made her stop.*

"Kai, I'm really sorry about the whole scene, you know, before Bekah barged in."

"It's really okay. I mean it was embarrassing, but then Bekah was really nice. I'm pretty sure she knows what's going on."

"Ya think? Five minutes later and she would've known for sure," Riley said.

Kai bit her lower lip and looked at Riley with a

curious expression. "I guess we better get ready for bed. Do you wanna use the bathroom first?"

"No, you go ahead. I still have to find my retainer."

Kai stood up and took her shoes to the closet where she grabbed her nightclothes off the hook. "Be back in a minute," she said and headed for the bathroom, closing the door behind her.

Riley groaned and shook her head. This was incredibly awkward. She looked at the door and tried to decide what to say. They needed to clear the air and talk about what happened. Riley felt so confused. Butterflies filled her chest and her skin felt all tingly just being in the same room with Kai—but there was a cold lump in her stomach. She didn't want Kai to be mad at her.

She stripped off her jeans and socks then pulled on some blue flannel pants. She tossed her sweatshirt on the desk and took off her bra, peeking over her shoulder, and quickly pulled on the flannel jersey. She had debated what to wear and vetoed her favorite tee because it was so old and grody.

Riley just stood there with the bathroom bag in her hand. Her feet were getting cold on the wood floor and she wished she hadn't taken her socks off. She put the bag down and decided to turn back the bed. *I wonder which side she sleeps on?*

The beautiful quilt looked homemade and barely covered the queen bed. Riley liked the navy blue sheets—they looked new. As she folded back the top sheet and fleece blanket, a warm wave washed over her as she pictured the two of them lying together. How many nights had she thought about this very thing, being able to talk and whisper, wrapped close together under a blanket…

The door opened.

"Your turn." Kai stood there in a tank top and baggy shorts, her shiny black hair down.

Riley stood staring, then swallowed hard. "Okay…" She grabbed her bag and hurried toward the bathroom, then ran back to grab the towels.

*How am I going to do this? God, I'm so nervous.* Riley dried her face and hands then dropped the toothpaste cap in the sink. "Crap."

She brushed her teeth way longer than necessary.

"Okay, I'm just going to do it," she announced to the mirror.

Riley closed the bedroom door behind her. Kai was lying on the far side of the bed, so Riley crawled in, pulled up the covers, and folded her hands across her chest. "I guess we're all set."

"Are you warm enough?" Kai asked.

"Yes, I'm fine." *But I think I'm going to have a heart attack I'm so nervous.*

Kai reached over and turned out the light. "Ri? I'm really glad you're here."

Riley's whole body relaxed. "Me, too. Do you think we could talk about what happened?"

A long pause.

"Yeah, it's probably a good idea."

Riley rolled over on her right side. "I'm really sorry. You must've been like, totally confused when I hauled you into the laundry room to make out with me and then pushed you away." It sounded stupid but it was all she could think of at the moment.

Kai folded one arm behind her head. "I have a lot of confusing feelings. Sometimes I don't even know what my own body is doing. I really wanted to kiss you and then…I wanted, well I wanted more. You know? Then when you said I could touch you…oh shit, it was amazing, and I—"

Riley reached over and touched her shoulder. "I know, right? That's exactly what happened. I was so into it and then I wasn't. I mean, when I realized you were touching me I really liked it, but I thought we shouldn't be doing it." Riley sat up as her throat tightened and tears began to run down her cheeks. She covered her face and began to cry.

Kai immediately sat up. "What's wrong?"

"Nu…nothing. Oh Kai, I was just so scared."

"Of what? Did I do something wrong? Did I hurt you?" Kai sounded panicked.

Riley took a breath. "No." She grabbed a tissue off the nightstand. "It was me—I don't know what happened, but I felt so out of control. It felt like my body was taking over and I couldn't think anymore, I just…I wanted. I'm not sure what I wanted, but I didn't want you to stop. Do you understand?"

Kai took her hand. "I think so. I sometimes feel that way too, and it is a little scary. But you know I wouldn't ever hurt you."

"Oh, Stretch, I know you wouldn't. It's just…" Riley sat cross-legged facing Kai. "Do you remember the book I was reading to you the other day?"

Kai nodded. "How could I forget?"

"At the end of that scene, after the kiss, she talks about how they touched each other and other stuff. But it was really good and they were both really happy." Riley paused. "In the morning, the other girl got up and went somewhere with her mom. She never said anything and they never spoke again. It was like they just had that one night." Riley began to cry. "I don't wanna lose you."

Kai squeezed Riley's hand then turned on her side and pulled Riley in front of her so they were spooning. "Ri, it was just a story in a book. We're real people, and I would never do that to you. We can always talk and we don't have to do anything if you don't want to." Kai leaned forward and kissed the back of Riley's neck, then moved her arm around her waist.

Riley put her hand on top of Kai's and scooted back to get closer. "I don't wanna stop kissing you but maybe we should just go slower, or have some rules."

This time Kai sighed. "I guess that means you won't let me touch them again, will you?"

Riley smiled. "Well, I wouldn't say never. Maybe we could say…nothing below the waist, how's that?"

"I guess I could live with that," Kai said, then yawned.

"I feel better we talked. I was really dreading it, but it's always better to discuss this kind of stuff, how about you?"

No answer but deep slow breathing.

Riley stroked Kai's hand and sighed. She felt safe in Kai's arms. Behind her, the warm strong body supported her. She liked the way that felt.

As tired as she was, she didn't want the moment to end. She looked around the semi-dark, unfamiliar room, and felt peaceful as though she had been there before, lying in Kai's arms.

The bedroom door opened partway and Tilley looked in on them. Riley saw her nod her head and smiled at her. The door closed.

"Good morning," Tilley cracked another egg. "Did you sleep all right?"

Riley sat down at the table. "Like a rock. Kai is much quieter than my noisy sister. I had no idea people could sleep that quietly. Twice I had to check to see if she was breathing."

Tilley laughed. "She's a quiet one all right. You know what they say, 'still waters run deep,' and she certainly does."

Riley cocked her head and picked up the glass of orange juice. "She really is kind of deep isn't she? I mean she's fun and everything, but it always seems like there's something on her mind."

Tilley wiped her hands on a towel and glanced at Riley. "You know her better than most people, Riley, do you think there's something bothering her lately?" She pulled out a chair and sat down at the table. "I've noticed a change, evidently you have as well."

Riley didn't know what to say because she didn't know how much Kai had shared with her aunt. "Well, there is a lot going on a school now, you know with finals and all."

"Yes, and, of course, her basketball—"

"Somebody say basketball?" Kai walked in and pulled out a chair.

Tilley looked from one girl to the other. "Good morning, honey. Riley and I were just wondering if you had something on your mind lately, since you seem to be a little distracted."

Kai immediately shot a glance at Riley, who just shrugged.

"What did you say to her?" she whispered

Tilley got up, turned off the stove, and poured a little more coffee. "Honey, we don't keep secrets and something has been bothering you for the past couple of weeks. Now I'm pretty sure Riley knows what's going on but I'm not going to put her on the spot, because I'd rather have you tell me."

Riley started to stand up. "Maybe you guys would like—"

Tilley put a hand on her arm. "I think Kai would be more comfortable if you stayed."

After a moment, Kai folded her arms on the table and took a deep breath. She glanced at Riley, then looked at her aunt. "It's no big deal, but there's just been some weird stuff going on. On top of that, I've been having more of those creepy dreams—like the ones I had this summer?"

"I've been expecting this. I didn't know it would be so soon." Tilley sighed. "How much have you told Riley?"

At this point Kai looked up at Riley and gave her a quick smile. "Pretty much everything."

"Riley, I won't expect you to stay and listen if you don't want to or if you're uncomfortable. We can do this later."

Riley leaned forward in her chair and put her hand on Kai's arm. "No, I really wanna know what's going on. I mean, this kind of involves me, too."

Tilley leaned back and pinched the bridge of her nose. "Okay. Kai, why don't you start at the beginning?"

"I told Riley about Dad and about last summer in the Badlands. And remember I told you we went to the magic shop?"

Tilley nodded. "Go on."

"Well…it was kind of weird. When we were upstairs, the old guy running the store got pissed off and tried to chase us. We were just looking around, we didn't do anything wrong. Anyway, we escaped to the alley and there was all this yelling, and this guy was beating up an old lady, and I jumped him but he banged me into the wall." She smiled at Riley. "That's when Riley came to my rescue and scared the guy off. But a gigantic one-eyed rat jumped on me and totally skeeved me out. I mean, I thought he was gonna kill me. But Riley just pulled him off and threw him into the Dumpster. Man, she was awesome."

Kai's face suddenly drained of color and she sat up. "Yesterday at the liquor store. I completely forgot." Her hands were trembling.

"What happened?" said Tilley.

Kai was hyperventilating.

Riley grabbed her hand. "Tell us what happened."

Kai shook her head and looked at her aunt. "I was waiting for you by the beer cooler. This tall dude, with a patch on his eye, cornered me. I think he was Sioux, and he was really angry. He told me I had something he wanted, and he mentioned somebody named Chay, and then he, like, vanished. I forgot about it till right now."

Riley and Kai both watched as Tilley's face became stonelike.

"Oh, Kai, I really don't want to go into all the details right now, but I will. Your father's death was not an accident. Everyone agreed that it was best to take you away, and I hoped this day would never come. Remember when Wakanda told you about your dreams—the dark and the light?"

Tilley stood up and started to pace. "Was there anything else that happened in the alley?"

"Tell her about the lady, and the…you know," Riley said.

Kai got up for a glass of water. She stood facing Tilley. "The lady that was being attacked—she was little and old and wearing a bright yellow coat and hat. Well, she disappeared. We looked for her, but she was gone. Instead, we found this fancy, heavy wand thingy." She went back to a chair, but squeezed Riley's shoulder.

"We were pretty freaked out." She looked up at Tilley. "Now, I don't want you to think I'm crazy, but on the way home, a really huge ugly vulture bird swooped down on us and I thought it was gonna kill Riley." She took a breath and scrubbed her face with both hands. "All I could do was throw that wand thing and when it hit the bird, everything kind of exploded and a little finch flew away instead."

Riley was nodding her head. "It's true, I swear, just the way Kai said it was. And then we saw a bird just like it, again on the way to school."

Tilley made no comment and just said, "Is there anything else?"

Kai actually laughed, hard. She shook her head and looked at Riley. "Okay, you are really not gonna believe this. I swear I am not doing drugs. That little lady in the yellow coat? She's the new chorus director for the school show."

Riley laughed. Then Kai laughed. Pretty soon all three of them were laughing.

Kai was the first to stop. "But that's not all. She remembered us from the alley and took us to tea. She told Riley and me that we had past lives together and that she was sent to be our teacher, and that what was happening was dangerous…"

Tilley sighed and began to massage her temples. "Okay. That's good to know." She looked up at Kai and then to Riley. "I was told someone would come.

Honey, I don't understand all this, but you were born with a gift, a very important gift. I don't have it. Your dad did, and it was passed on to you. My job was to keep you safe. But I was told others would come when you turned fifteen. At that age you would be ready."

Kai pushed her chair back. "Ready? Ready for what? Ready to freeze my ass off on a desolate plateau with some crazy woman? Did anybody think to ask me? What if I don't want to, what if I wanna have a life?" She stood up. "What if I wanna play basketball and go to college and have...have a relationship with someone and be normal? What about that?"

Riley had never heard Kai raise her voice.

Kai collapsed in the chair with her head on her arms.

It was all Riley could do to keep from moving closer and putting her arms around Kai. Instead, she reached for her arm and squeezed it. "It's okay, Stretch, you don't have to do anything. Your aunt won't make you do anything horrible, will you?"

Tilley shook her head. "I need to tell you something, sweetie. Chay was your dad's name."

"No! His name was Chet." Kai scowled and looked at her aunt with a confused expression.

"That was what they called him in Minnesota. His Lakota name was Hotah Chayton—it means White Falcon. There was a prophecy a long time ago that the White Falcon would save the Oglala." She leaned her elbow on the table and rested her head against her palm. "We—your dad and I—had a brother. He was insanely jealous of your father. They fought most of their lives. I was younger—and a girl—so nobody paid any attention to me."

She reached across the table and took both of

Kai's hands. "No one really knows what happened. Many believe your uncle was responsible for your father's death."

Kai screamed. She kicked out her chair and ran upstairs.

Riley started to get up and Tilley grabbed her arm. "Let her go."

She took Riley's hand and squeezed it. After a minute she said, "I always hoped someone would come as her protector. That's always the way." She smiled. "I never realized such a great gift would come in such a small package. Riley, the lady you rescued was right. You two have been together before, many times, but I think this will be your biggest challenge. We have to be careful for now, because it will take time for you two to amass enough strength to defeat him."

Riley felt tears burning her eyes. "Oh Tilley, I don't understand any of this but I don't want anything to happen to Kai—ever."

Tilley's soft brown eyes and her head tilt reminded Riley of her beloved Mr. Rat.

"See, you do understand. Don't worry, you won't be alone." She stroked the side of Riley face. "I'm very glad that Kai has you and that you have her."

Tilley stood up. "I'll have to go out in a little while, but you can stay. Kai mentioned studying for a math exam and maybe that would be a good thing to get her mind off all this. Let me run upstairs and make sure she's better and then we can eat. Okay?"

Riley nodded. The kitchen was quiet. The table had been set for three and it looked like Tilley had gone to some trouble to plan a nice meal. Oranges and the juicer sat on the counter next to a plate of freshly baked rolls. It looked so perfect.

Squishing her eyes together, she tried to loosen the tight muscles around her forehead. Her brain felt like a tossed salad. The growing urge to grab her things and bolt was overpowering, but at the same time she wanted to stay for her friend—Kai might need her. Besides, Aunt Tilley was incredibly supportive and it seemed like she totally understood what good friends she and Kai had become.

A small ember warmed Riley's heart as she thought about her Kai. She glanced at the ceiling, then closed her eyes remembering the comfort she felt snuggled close through the night. She was almost afraid to sleep out of fear she might move and disturb Kai.

Sleep had come, but the imprint of Kai's soft breathing and their warm bodies touching made her feel as though she had been floating but in a vast sea of warm pudding.

# *Chapter Nineteen*

K ai, Can I come in?"

"Sure." She didn't look up. She stayed on her stomach until she felt the mattress give. Tilley sat beside her, quiet for a moment.

"I wanted to make sure you were all right. You haven't been that upset in a very long time." Her voice held that I'm-going-to-be-patient-until-you're-ready-to-talk tone. "If I'm not mistaken, the last time was when I said you couldn't ride your Rollerblades to school."

Kai groaned. "That was ugly, and a long time ago."

"Exactly my point. All this new information has to be a little overwhelming, and I feel terrible I didn't prepare you better. There never seemed to be a right time. I'm sorry, Kai." She gently rubbed Kai's back with one hand. "I promise you, we will talk about it and I'll answer every question I possibly can. If we need to call somebody, we will."

"You know, everything was going along okay this semester and then bam! All this weird stuff." Kai rolled onto her side to face Tilley. "I don't blame you. It's just, well...I didn't know who to talk to about all this." Her throat tightened, threatening to betray her brave-little-soldier outside.

Kai swiped her Henley sleeve across her eyes. "You never talked about Dad, or anybody else. It's almost like I don't have any other family. Then all of a sudden, I find out I've got some uncle that's bat-shit crazy…how am I supposed to handle that?"

Tilley changed position, bringing Kai's head into her lap. She held her and stroked her forehead. "Oh honey, I'm so sorry. I know this is confusing." Her sigh was one of deep resignation. "I probably should have said something earlier, but there's no handbook for being a single mom. It was my decision to withhold information until I thought you could handle it. I underestimated you and how grown up you had become. I hope you'll forgive me."

The warmth of Tilley's arms comforted her. Their relationship had always been close, but in the last few years, Kai had pulled away a little thinking she no longer needed cuddling like a little girl. She forgot how good it felt.

"Your good friend Riley is sitting downstairs alone right now. If you're okay, I think we should go ahead and eat. I asked her to stay a little longer hoping you two might get some studying done. I'm going to have to go out for a little while, but I'll be back for supper."

Kai sat up, feeling puzzled. "You have an appointment on Sunday?"

Tilley stood up. "Not exactly an appointment. I promised a friend we'd meet for coffee."

She sounded mysterious but her eyes were twinkling.

"Come on down when you're ready." Tilley leaned down and kissed her cheek.

Kai stacked the dirty dishes next to the sink and turned on the hot water. Riley watched, unable to read this odd behavior. Breakfast had been fine right up until Tilley got ready to leave, and then Kai got very quiet.

"If you're washing, I'll dry," Riley said, offering a verbal olive branch.

Kai motioned with her head. "The towels are in that drawer."

"My mom called earlier, she sounded exhausted. Said the Flynns didn't leave until almost one a.m. Sounds like we missed all the fun. Not that I'm complaining. I'm glad we came over here, you know?" Riley grimaced as she pulled a dishtowel out of the drawer. *That sounded so totally lame.*

They continued washing and drying and stacking in virtual silence. Riley could only assume that Kai didn't want small talk. But after twenty-five minutes, she had to say something.

"Kai, I don't know what's going on, but if you want me to leave I will. I thought we could study, but maybe you'd rather be alone." It wasn't at all what she wanted, but it didn't seem like she had much say in the matter.

Kai folded the dishtowel and draped it across the front of the sink. She leaned heavily on both hands with her head down. In a very small voice she said, "I don't want you to leave. I don't know what I want to do."

Riley took her hand. "Maybe we could just go in the other room and sit down."

Kai nodded.

Riley did her best to distract Kai with stories her mom had told her about the party and eventually produced a math book. Once Kai was engaged in the subject of mathematics, her sullen, stubborn, pouty self disappeared, and she changed into a patient math tutor.

Riley had no patience for the beautiful logic of mathematics. Still, she had to pass the exam on Monday, and sitting next to Kai watching her explain it made it all worthwhile. It was amazing how easily Kai could break down some of the complex formulas into understandable examples.

Besides, her eyes were beautiful. "Can we take a break for a minute?"

Kai's gentle face took on a worried expression. "Is anything wrong?"

"No. You've done a wonderful job, I'm just kind of distracted…"

"By what?"

"Your lips."

Kai fell back on the couch, laughing hysterically. "You kill me. How can you be so serious one minute and so damn funny the next?"

Riley straightened up rather indignantly. "Funny? You thought I was being funny." She tossed the math book on the table and leaned over the partially reclining, giggling Kai.

Kai cocked her head. "You weren't joking?"

"Nuh-uh," Riley said and leaned close enough to hear Kai swallow.

A very tiny smile started around Kai's eyes and moved down to her lips. "Does that mean…you might wanna kiss?"

Riley nodded.

Kai pulled her forward into her arms. The expression in her eyes softened as she studied Riley's face. "I'm so glad you're here," she said and touched the side of Riley's face. "And we were awfully well behaved last night, don't you think?"

Riley could feel herself melting into Kai's arm and shoulder. She tucked her legs closer and felt the heat between them. "We were very good. It felt so good to have you cuddle me like that…please kiss me."

Kai leaned forward until her warm lips made contact, and Riley felt her eyes close and her head fall back. Their connection crackled like a summer storm and electricity flooded her body.

They pulled apart for the briefest of moments. Kai's expression became intense. When she pulled Riley's body even closer, Riley surrendered.

⁂

It was almost dark when Tilley opened the front door. "I am so sorry I'm so late," she said, closing the door and stamping her feet on the mat. "Riley?" she called from the front hall. "Would you like me to run you home, or do you want to stay for supper?"

"That's okay. I think I'd like to walk," Riley said, getting up from the couch and grimacing at Kai.

Kai wore a self-satisfied grin.

Tilley came into the living room looked at the two girls and slowly nodded her head. "I guess you finished studying?"

Riley nodded and looked at Kai as they both blushed furiously. It was obvious to her that Tilley totally knew what was going on and that they were finished, all right. A long walk in the cool night air was exactly what she needed.

"Yes, Kai did a terrific job of explaining those

complex formulas. And...uh, thank you so much for breakfast, and letting me stay over. It was fun." *Just shut up, James.*

"See you tomorrow, Ri," Kai said and stood up.

"You, too. Bye."

ༀ ༀ ༀ ༀ

Tilley closed the door and smiled at Kai. "I think I'll have a glass of wine," she said and started toward kitchen.

Kai watched her, curious about the odd expression on her aunt's face. Tilley looked kinda giddy. "M'kay."

Kai returned to the living room, and a short time later Tilley came and sat down in her leather chair, threw her legs on the ottoman, and sighed.

"How was your afternoon, honey, are you feeling better?" Tilley took a sip of the straw-colored wine in her glass.

Kai scooted back into the couch and crossed her legs. The question sounded a little more serious, but she couldn't be sure. Direct confrontation was not the way they communicated; it wasn't considered polite. She'd wait. "Yeah, I feel better. Riley tricked me into studying, but once we began, I felt better. How about you, how was your meeting?"

"It wasn't exactly a meeting. I had coffee with someone I met at the party." Tilley took another sip over wine and held the glass with both hands. "It was more like a date."

Something streaked across Kai's mind-screen. In all these years, she couldn't remember Tilley ever going out on a date. She saw the beautiful woman in the chair across from her in a whole new light. "A date..."

Tilley raised one eyebrow. "Is that a problem?"

"Of course not! I mean I'm thrilled. It just occurred to me that all these years together, you've never dated, and I'd never really thought about it. I feel so stupid."

Tilley laughed. "It's not a problem. It's a choice I made. I wasn't sure I could do both, and at the time… well, you were more important. But you're a little older now, and I thought it might be okay to give it a try."

"Sure, that's a good idea. Did you want to get married, I mean before you had to take care of me?"

"Not exactly." Tilley put her empty glass on the table and began to fidget the hem of her jacket. "Do you remember this morning when I told you that you could ask me anything and I would tell you the truth?"

"Yes." It sounded like two syllables when she said it. *What is Tilley going to tell me now?* A cold knot began to form.

"When I was in college I dated a little bit before I discovered…" She tipped her head back and squeezed her eyes closed, then opened them. "I found that I was more attracted to girls than boys."

A nanosecond became millennia. Kai felt her jaw drop open like a baby waiting for a spoon. "Attracted to…"

"Girls, women."

"Oh…"

"I'm gay."

"Oh."

Tilley got up, picked up her glass, walked out to the kitchen, and returned with two glasses of wine. She handed one to Kai and then sat down next to her.

"Turning fifteen did not qualify you to drink legally." Tilley chuckled. "But I did notice you had indulged a little at the party. This glass is more of a celebration—let's call it a little 'coming out' party. Okay?"

Kai felt herself blushing again. "Okay."

"Think we should talk about it?"

Kai took a sip of the semisweet wine and nodded her head. "I think so."

Tilley just smiled

"You know, huh?"

"I suspected, yes."

Kai took another sip and put the glass down. "Maybe you could tell me something. When did you know you were…" She gestured vaguely, not knowing how to ask.

Tilley put one arm across the back of the couch and bit her lower lip. "I think I always knew, but I wanted to be like the other girls, so I acted like they did and I had no trouble getting dates. When I went away to college, I met someone very special. She was a girl in my dorm and we became, well, very good friends."

"But how did you know that she felt the same way?"

"We talked about it. A lot. It took all year."

"What happened? Where is she?"

Tilley looked down at her lap and her voice softened. "We moved in together the whole second year. Everything kind of ended when she transferred to NYU to go to medical school. We made promises, but somehow it didn't work out. We still keep in touch a couple of times a year."

Kai felt a sharp pinch in the deepest part of her heart. "And that was it? You never met anyone else?"

"Your dad called me and needed my help."

# *Chapter Twenty*

Riley ran almost all the way to the park on snow-packed streets. The growing darkness was almost complete. She stopped at one of the benches as the streetlights began to come on. Tiny pieces of memory snapped through her brain like fresh popcorn. It seemed the more time she spent with Kai, the stronger their connection grew.

She pulled her hood up to deflect the wind and glanced at her booted feet. Her warm breath bloomed on the frigid December air and she deliberately blew out the clouds of steam. Whatever new circumstances had rearranged the wiring inside her body made her feel happy.

Her grades were good and she actually enjoyed going to school every day. The Christmas program was back on track. Rebekah was home—but thankfully gone most of the time. And the growing realization that her new best friend might actually be her girlfriend made her giggle. Kai Tiva was the coolest girl ever.

Riley smiled a half grin as the streetlights seemed to flicker in time with her heartbeat.

Then they went out, one by one. *That's weird.* As she sat there watching, the park got darker and darker. Even the ice rink in the center looked like a black mirror, just like the one in *Sleeping Beauty.*

Her senses sharpened as the hair on her neck prickled. She smelled it before she saw anything—the rancid odor of something dead. Her instinct was to run, but something told her to stay very still. Whooshing air currents brushed her face.

Then she heard it: a low growl. It got closer.

Riley looked around frantically for someone—anyone—but didn't dare make a sound.

Without warning, her body hurled forward to the ground. Something sharp grazed her forehead and she felt herself growing faint.

The growl turned into a shriek.

❧❧❧❧❧

"You're going to be fine," a soft voice whispered.

Her head hurt when she opened her eyes. She was in a warm car parked in front of her house. She pivoted quickly and was stunned to find Mrs. Byrd behind the wheel.

"What the…"

"You had a little accident, Riley. As luck would have it, I was in the neighborhood at the right time," she said, unbuckling her seat belt.

"Mrs. Byrd? What were you—?"

She smiled. "I think when we're outside of school you can call me Loliy. Meanwhile, let's get you inside and take care of that scratch on your head. I think it's best to just tell your folks that you tripped on your way home. I'll take care of everything else."

"Was it…Was it that bird again? I heard it, I even smelled it, it was gross!" Riley shivered at the memory.

Loliy put her hand on Riley's arm. "I'm not sure what's going on exactly. I think for a while you girls should try very hard not to be alone when you're out. All right? Excellent," she said in a voice that assumed the conversation was over.

"Mom, this is Mrs. Byrd. She's the new music director," Riley said when her mother opened the door.

Mrs. James looked from Riley to the little lady in the yellow coat and hat and back to Riley. "I'm pleased to meet you, but I'm not sure I understand why—"

In a very clipped brogue, Mrs. Byrd explained. "I was driving past the park and happened to see Riley had taken nasty spill near one of the benches. I'm sure she'll be fine but she did get a bit of a bump on the head. I feel lucky that I just happened to be in the neighborhood, but I really must run or I'll be late."

"I really appreciate you doing this. Are you sure you can't stay for some eggnog?"

"No, I must be off, but I'm sure I'll see you on Thursday."

Before Riley could speak, her rescuer was already halfway down the sidewalk. "Bye, thank you."

Loliy waved and kept moving.

Her mom closed the door and said, "Let's get that scrape taken care of. Are you sure you're all right?" She took Riley's coat and backpack, set them on the stairs, and guided her out to the kitchen.

Riley was almost too confused to speak but took the hug her mother offered. "I'm okay, just glad to be home."

After a brief Q and A, Neosporin, a bandage, two Tylenol, and a turkey sandwich, Riley was excused to go upstairs. She couldn't wait to tell Kai what had happened. Her line was busy. "Shit." She impatiently texted, "Call me," and waited.

Two minutes later Kai called.

"Hello?"

"Hey, guess what?" Kai asked.

"Why was your line busy?"

"I was calling you with news."

"And I've got news you won't believe."

"Go ahead," Kai said.

"No, you go ahead." Riley felt flushed and a little anxious, but took a breath.

"Mine can wait. You sound crazy."

"I'm not crazy! But you won't believe this—"

"Okay."

Riley started cursing. "Bekah's home. Crap." She lowered her voice. "I can't talk now. Listen, meet me early for school, okay? Promise."

"I'll be there, but are you okay?"

"Yes—hi Bekah—we can review that tomorrow. Gotta go."

❧❧❧❧

Kai hung up the phone and shook her head. "That girl is whacked," she said under her breath. She flopped back on the bed and sighed. The conversation with Tilley had really kicked her off kilter. She wasn't surprised so much that her aunt was gay, just that she had been so clueless for so long. She folded her arms over her forehead. To no one she said, "How could I have been so selfish for so long? Tilley should hate me."

Riley would be so freaked out when she got to tell her, but in a good way. After all, she liked Tilley a lot and Tilley had been so cool when she talked about Riley.

She glanced at the clock and realized she still had some time to study. Finals Monday. Math and science were solid and Riley promised to help with *To Kill a Mockingbird.*

Riley. Riley Beth James. A torch ignited in her chest, and Kai reached for the pillow Riley had slept on the night before and hugged it to her.

❧ ❧ ❧ ❧

Kai stamped her feet in the slushy snow. Overnight some of the snow had started to melt, leaving a mess on the streets and sidewalks. When a neighbor took the corner too fast, a wall of dirty slush sprayed up on the sidewalk, causing Kai to jump back, shouting, "Hey, you creep!"

"Stretch!" Riley called as she jogged closer.

Kai grinned. A hood surrounded Riley's pink-cheeked face and her backpack bounced as she ran.

After they slept together on Saturday night, Riley was all Kai could think about.

"Morning, Shorty. You're sure in a hurry."

Riley took hold of Kai's arm as she bent over and took some deep breaths. "Yeah, boy that was hard. I couldn't wait…" Another deep breath and she stood up. The pink cheeks made her look like a little angel, but her eyes were dark with what Kai imagined to be fear. "The bird, the scary bird tried to get me last night. It knocked me down and I must've fainted."

Kai grabbed her arms. "Oh my God, are you okay? Ri, no wonder you couldn't say anything. This is terrible…" Just then, she noticed the bandage on Riley's forehead. She touched it gently and felt her eyes tearing up. Without thinking, she wrapped her arms around Riley and hugged her close.

"I'm okay, Stretch, really," she muffled into Kai's coat.

Kai pulled back and looked at her. "Are you sure?

This totally sucks—"

"Wait, wait, that's not the weirdest part!"

Kai refocused. She felt like she was gonna jump out of her skin she was so freaked, but Riley was clutching the front of her jacket.

"Listen. When I came to, I was in a warm car, and guess who was driving?"

Kai slowly shook her head, unwilling to hear any more strangeness.

"Mrs. Byrd! And she told me to call her Loliy."

"What?"

"I know. She told me she was in the neighborhood and that I should just tell my parents that I fell down. Kai it was awful. All the streetlights went out. I felt like I knew it was there before I could even see it, and then I smelled it. Yuck, it was awful. I'm not sure what happened, it must've knocked me to the ground because I knew I hit my head on something. Mrs. Byrd said we should be very careful and not be alone. Then she took me home."

Kai hugged her again and felt something expanding inside her chest as if she had grown taller and stronger in just seconds. "We have to talk to somebody about this."

Riley hugged her back. "You know what was really weird this time? I wasn't as scared. When I smelled that rotten smell, I felt like a cat or dog sniffing something, and then I got real still. You know, like I knew not to move."

"We better get going or we're gonna be late."

They started walking quickly. Kai looked around and all of her senses tingled.

Riley looked up at her. "What was it you were gonna tell me last night?"

Kai chuckled and kept walking. "Oh, I was just gonna tell you that Tilley's gay and she knows about us."

Riley stopped in her tracks. "WHAT? Hey, wait up!"

❧❧❧❧

Heinous was the only word to describe the math exam. Riley hoisted her backpack and slapped the exam on Mr. Forkbinder's desk. It was a good thing she had study hall now. She'd need it to clear her head.

Tiffany caught up with her. "How do you think you did on the test?"

"I have no idea. I studied hard, but some of that stuff was not in the book, and I really need a good grade in this class."

"I so get that," Tiffany said, sweeping her blond hair out of her face. "My dad threatened to ground me over Christmas break if I didn't get at least a C. He's such a toad. Amber, wait up."

Riley hurried into the study hall, hoping to get a seat near the back window. She knew Kai had PE third hour, and sometimes she could see her class across the courtyard.

Kai was easily as good at volleyball as she was a basketball. Some kids were just natural athletes, and Kai was one of them. No matter what she did, she was graceful and still aggressive. More important, she loved playing.

Riley settled in and then checked the window. Nobody was in the gym yet.

She opened her history book and thought about Kai's news. She never would've guessed that Aunt

Tilley was an actual lesbian.

Even though she'd had a ton of studying to do the night before, Riley had read a little bit more from the book they got from the library. After thumbing through it, she thoroughly read a pretty amazing scene between the two girls. Even thinking about it now, she felt flushed with an ache between her legs.

She looked around nervously. After reading that section she had decided she better start at the beginning of the book to understand the story.

Now, thinking about Tilley, she realized there would actually be someone they could talk to about… stuff. She tried to remember who Tilley might have met from the party. Then it dawned on her. Aunt Sela! She had to be the one. She was perfect. She was really pretty and was even part Native American. She played softball with Mom and worked for the police department.

Tilley spent a lot of time talking to her during the party. *I wonder if they did any kissing on their date. Probably not, since they were in a coffee shop.*

❧ ❧ ❧ ❧

Kai stood waiting when Riley came bounding up the stairs to the auditorium. She laughed. "I was beginning to wonder where you were. I couldn't imagine you'd forget rehearsal."

"No, Ms. Schultz wanted to talk to me after PE. She thought I wouldn't stumble as much if I had a better pair of shoes. I didn't have the heart to tell her new shoes wouldn't make much difference. Have they started yet?" she asked, panting.

Kai bit her cheek to keep from laughing. "Uh, no, I just wanted to get here early. I was hoping to see Mrs.

Byrd. You better get in there. I'll be waiting here for you."

By the time Riley dumped her stuff and ran upon the stage, Mrs. Schumacher had started warming them up and Mrs. Byrd, brand-new yellow hat perched squarely on her white bouffant hairdo, marched in from stage left, baton in hand.

There were a few students and teachers in the audience, and Kai had to choose a row on the side to be unnoticed. It was an unobstructed view to where Riley would stand for her solo. A gleeful grin started deep in her chest and moved up to cover her face. Ever since she first heard Riley sing, she could hardly wait for the practices.

Kai didn't have much opportunity to hear choir singing. She and her aunt weren't churchgoers, but they followed some of their traditional spiritual practices as best they could, even though they were a long way from the reservation and their leaders. And not much music. But after she talked with Tilley about her heritage, Kai felt strongly that she needed to learn more, whatever it took. She hoped it wouldn't mean more sessions on the butte with Wakanda, but if that's what she had to do, she'd do it.

She pressed her thumbs into her temples as a sharp pain crossed her through head. She had no clue what the tribe expected of her, but if her father died because of it, she would do whatever she could to honor his memory.

Her throat tightened as she remembered a gentle man who raised her until she was six. His laugh was like rippling water and his eyes twinkled when the teased her. Mostly she remembered his hands because they were strong but soft. He would braid her hair before school and brush it at night, all the while singing in a lilting voice. He told her they were the hunting songs that the warriors would sing to bring luck.

A few hot tears rolled down her cheeks. She reached into her shirt, pulled out the medicine bag, and clutched it in her hand as she swiped at the tears. Riley's voice floated through the auditorium. The sound felt like a kiss, and her heart swelled like a helium balloon.

# *Chapter Twenty-one*

Hurry up," Riley said, looking nervously back at the school.

Kai fumbled with her backpack and tried to get her coat buttoned as she trotted behind her short friend, who was seriously trucking. "When did you get this note?"

"Right after seventh period. I told you, she said it was important." Riley lost her balance on the snowdrift and Kai grabbed the shoulder of her parka. "Thanks."

"Tell me again what she said, because I don't wanna go anywhere near that magic shop!"

They had reached Main Street, and Riley finally stopped and leaned against the window box in front of the sweet shop. She pulled a folded piece of paper out of her pocket and read aloud. "Riley—I would like you and Kai to meet me at Agrippa's Natural Magic on Mystic Lane at 4:00 P.M. punctually. It is necessary to discuss two items that will be very important. L.B."

Kai tipped her head to one side. "Two items, huh? Did you ever get a chance to talk to Bekah about the wand? God, I hope that's not what she wants to ask about."

Riley rolled her eyes. "I told you, I tried. Bekah just laughed and made faces at me. I was gonna ask her tonight, but Mom said she's gonna stay with Wesley at his grandparents' house. So no, I didn't. I wish I could ask Dad, but I don't want the 'rents to hear anything about a magic wand—they'd lock me up for sure. Besides, with her gone, I can go through her stuff tonight. Don't worry." She grabbed Kai's sleeve. "C'mon."

The creepy little magic store looked no better today than it had the first time. Fast-moving clouds in the winter sky made shadows that looked alive. The wooden sign dangled precariously in the wind. The grime that covered front windows looked dark and menacing.

Kai pulled her collar tighter and squared her shoulders. She glanced over and smiled at the determined look on Riley's face; it was the face of a baby pit bull. Riley charged forward like a linebacker. In spite of her small stature, she would fight when she was provoked, and she certainly had.

Just before they got to the door, Kai grabbed Riley's arm and pulled her next to the building. "Listen, stay close to the front door and if anything creepy starts to happen, run like hell, and if we get split up, meet me by the sweet shop. Deal?"

Riley nodded, but looked scared. "Deal."

"It's gonna be okay, I just don't wanna take any chances. After all, I don't think Loliy would've brought us here if there was any danger." Kai winked and squeezed Riley's arm.

The antique bell tinkled as they opened the front door. It didn't seem possible there could be more dust in the antique-cluttered store. "Hel-lo," Kai said. Her voiced trembled like a sapling in a storm.

Riley moved closer to her. "I forgot how nasty this place smells," she whispered.

It seemed like a long time before the curtain to the back room opened, revealing a short little ball of sunshine that could be no one but Loliy Byrd.

"Good afternoon, girls. And right on time. Excellent." She walked closer with her yellow pillbox hat bobbing. "I've just learned that you two had a rather unpleasant experience in here the same day that you came to my aid. Tsk, tsk. Most unfortunate. But we shall set that right. You have nothing to be uncomfortable about when you come here."

She took them both by the arm and marched them to the back of the shop. "This establishment has been in my family for…a very long time. My brother Fergus took over when my father died. Anyway, I think if we all work together, we can solve some of the mysteries the seemed to be dogging you two. But, first we'll have tea."

Kai looked over Riley, who stared back with a glowering O-M-G expression. Kai shrugged and forced a weak smile. This was so not what she expected. The back room of the old shop was almost as large as the front half. The difference was like night and day. Literally. The space was carpeted with a beautiful oriental rug, and two tall windows in the back wall allowed generous amounts of sunlight to fill the space.

The antique wooden furniture glistened as though newly oiled. An oak table sat in front of the windows surrounded by six tall, beautifully carved straight-backed chairs with upholstered seats. A large doily covered the center, and an ornate silver tea service occupied one side.

Riley nudged Kai, nodded toward the table, and whispered, "Pretty fancy." Kai stared at the elegant rolltop desk near the doorway.

"Riley, Kai, I'd like to introduce my brother, Fergus O'Dwyer. Fergus, please say hello to Riley

James and Kai Tiva."

Kai turned toward the doorway and saw the cranky old man who had been minding the shop the first time they visited. He took a step forward and offered his hand to each of them. "Pleased to meet you." His low voice sounded like grit in a rock tumbler, and his dry, scaly hand seemed lizard-like.

"Wonderful. Let's all have a seat. I've prepared a lovely Irish blend," Loliy said and began to pour.

Kai couldn't take her eyes off the odd little man who was not much taller than Loliy. From their brief first encounter, she remembered his longish oily hair and the stray hairs in his ears, but sitting this close, she noticed that his ears were pointed on top, and his hair clean and cut,

Kai was sitting rigid in her chair until she felt a nudge under the table. She glanced at Riley briefly and turned back to her teacup. Then she felt a hard kick. Kai jerked and whipped her head around to glare at Riley. Under her breath she muttered, "What'd you do that for?"

Both Loliy and Fergus looked up from their teacups.

"I'm sorry. This tea is really good," Riley said, flushing and trying to cover. She reached for the tongs and added two lumps of sugar.

Loliy dabbed at the corners of her mouth with a starched white napkin. "Let me start with a little backstory. Much like you two," she said, nodding at Riley and Kai, "Fergus and I have shared past lives. The only difference is that our traditions were mainly in the British Isles. What is infinitely more important is that Fergus was chosen long ago to be a teacher for a young man who would lead his people. That young man, Kai, was your father."

Spoon and teacup clattered together in front of Kai as she fumbled to right them. "Wha…what?" She felt light headed, and both her hands trembled visibly.

Riley reached over and grasped her wrist.

"'S true. Your Da was a very talented healer," Fergus said with a pronounced burr.

Kai put both hands in her lap, twisting her napkin. "You…you knew my father?" Her voice sounded tight and higher than normal.

"Aye, I did. He was very brave and loyal to his people."

Kai's mouth was moving but no words came out. She slowly shook her head in disbelief.

"Kai listen to me," Riley said in a voice stronger than she recognized. "This is what you wanted to know. Kai, this man can tell you about your dad. Can you hear me?"

Kai's breathing slowed and she nodded. She looked at Riley and made eye contact.

"She's okay. It's really important to tell her what happened to her dad."

Fergus looked at Loliy. She gave a quick nod. He cleared his throat and looked at Kai. His dark blue eyes took on an odd kind of light.

"Your Da moved here about fifteen years ago—he was sent because of the prophecy. I was to train him, teach him to use the power he had been given." A soft expression washed over Fergus's face, causing a tiny smile to crack his craggy face.

"He was a good lad. Smart, clever, and eager to learn. He knew we didn't have much time before they'd come. He wanted to learn as much as possible. It wasn't his own safety he was concerned about, it was yours."

Fergus leaned forward. "He left his people and moved as far away as possible to protect his baby girl, because her mother left, afraid of the prophecy."

All the sounds in the room disappeared. It was totally silent. Kai felt a shiver creep up her spine and moved closer to Riley, who sat transfixed.

"What happened?" Kai said in the voice of a six-year-old.

"Black Raven was insanely jealous. He believed that his brother—your Da—was the favored child, and he wanted to take his place. He searched for years for him when he heard about the birth of a child. If the prophecy was true, that child would be the heir."

He went to the desk and returned with a bundle wrapped in a piece of deerskin. Reaching across the table, he handed it to Kai. "He left this with me and made me promise to give it to you, because he knew you would come."

Kai took the small bundle and put it in front of her reverently. A small, spherical, black stone glistened in the hazy light. It felt warm. When she looked up there were tears in her eyes. "It wasn't a magic accident, was it?"

Fergus shook his head and lowered his eyes. "No. Black Raven followed the energy source to the shop. It was a day your Da and I were working together. I shoulda known with the sudden change in weather. Clouds foretold a disturbance." His voice broke. "Hotah Chayton, White Raven, was not ready. He never expected it, and Black Raven never gave him a chance."

Kai began to shake and tears streamed down her face, but no words came out. Loliy moved quickly and placed both hands on the sides of Kai's head, chanting some unknown words.

Riley's eyes fluttered. "This is confusing."

Kai trusted Loliy, but her chest felt tight and it was hard to breathe. Everything in the room seemed to be spinning.

There was a loud crack. The building shook and the dishes rattled.

Just as quickly, it stopped. Loliy returned to her seat and Kai leaned forward with her head on her folded arms.

⁂

"What just happened?" Riley asked, looking at their hosts.

Loliy just nodded. "She'll be fine. That was a lot of information to absorb. Riley, she's going to need you now. She won't remember this conversation and you'll need to explain it. It would be better if you did that with her aunt present. Do you understand?"

"Why won't she understand?" Riley was angry. "I don't understand. My best friend is half in a coma because you just dumped some horrible news on her. I'll take care of Kai. I'll never let anything happen to her, but I need some answers!"

Loliy smiled. "Of course, this is why you are her protector. It will all be explained, I promise you. I want you to take that bundle and put it in your pocket. Protect it. Her father left that and the prophecy for a time when Kai was old enough to understand it. Now is that time."

Loliy folded her napkin and laid it on the table. "My car is in back and I'm going to drive you girls home. Get your things."

Riley carefully put the bundle in the pocket of her hoodie then roused Kai. "C'mon, it's time to go. Loliy's going to give us a ride home."

"I'll start the car, and Riley? Don't forget the final rehearsal tomorrow afternoon."

*Oh lord, can this woman be for real?* Riley pushed back her chair, and took Kai's arm. Kai looked totally confused but obediently stuck her arms in her sleeves as Riley held it. Fergus cleared the table.

❧❧❧❧❧

"Hi, Mom. I'm over at Kai's and we're studying for the English test. Is it okay if I eat here and come home a little later? Okay, cool. You and Dad have fun. Bye." Riley stuck her phone back in her pocket and looked across the table at Kai. She'd been completely quiet on the ride home and still looked a little pale.

"Stretch, are you okay?" She sat in the chair next her, took her hand and carefully stroked it. "I'm sure you're pretty weirded out by that whole event at Agrippa's. At least Loliy said you would be. She said you wouldn't remember anything—is that true? Do you remember what happened?"

Kai stared as if she thought Riley was speaking Urdu or Swahili. Her eyes brimmed with confusion, her eyebrows knitted together, and her lips parted as if waiting for question to spill out. "Ri, don't leave okay?" Kai said with a soft, pleading tone.

Riley felt her heart squeeze, a wave of tenderness nearly capsizing her. "I'm not going anywhere," she said with uncharacteristic fierceness, and knew she meant it. She pulled Kai's hand over and squeezed it tightly. "Do you wanna talk about what happened?"

Kai shook her head. "Not now. I think I need to sit with it for a little while until I understand. Maybe we could just eat and study or something. I need to focus on something real, you know?"

"Yeah, I get it. Can I pillage your refrigerator?" Riley said, already on her feet.

Kai chuckled. "Please do. You're obviously a little hungry, and I'm starving."

Within ten minutes, Riley had pulled out every leftover she could find and had the kitchen table stacked. She poured them each a glass of milk and they verbally dissected Harper Lee's classic book as they picked through the various dishes with fingers and forks.

Tilley's arrival interrupted the leftover-orgy. Kai heard the door first. "Hi, Tilley."

"Hi, Tilley," came Riley's echo.

"Hi girls," Tilley said as her jaw dropped, staring at the table loaded with dishes.

Both girls saw the expression and looked at the table. Riley swallowed hard, realizing the awful mess they had created. "Oh, wow, I am so sorry. Kai needed something to eat…I wasn't sure what she wanted, so I kinda pulled out everything. I'll put it back." Riley jumped up.

"No need," said Tilley, washing her hands. "Let me grab a fork and a plate, and I'll join you." After scooping a few items onto her plate, she sat down. "How was school? Only one more day of tests, I'll bet you guys are excited."

Kai glanced at Riley. "Yeah, it was okay. I'll be glad when tomorrow's over, I need a break."

Riley picked up on the cue. "Some of the tests were a lot harder than I thought they'd be, and the

English test will be an essay—I hate those." She looked up at Kai and realized that she still had that deer-in-the-headlights look. Tilley must've seen it too because she put down her fork and was watching Kai.

*Crap.*

"Is everything all right, Kai?"

Riley looked quickly from one woman to the other. Kai was not responding. She just stared at the Jell-O mold. *Tap dance.* Riley stabbed her fork into the Jell-O and scooped some onto a plate. "Essay tests, you know, there's all that writing and it takes a long—"

Tilley reached over and put her hand on Kai's arm. "Honey, are you okay? You look a little pale."

Kai slowly turned her head toward her aunt's touch.

Riley tried to run a block. "She did say she was awfully—"

Kai looked at her and shook her head sharply. "We went to the magic store. The owner…he knew Dad." She stopped, then pointed at Riley.

"What's going on?" Tilley sounded tense.

Riley bit her lip and looked into Kai's pleading eyes. She couldn't decide what to say. She believed Kai wanted her to let Tilley know what happened. But earlier she said she didn't want to talk about it until she could think about it some more. Riley's heart pounded in her chest and her hands were cold. She closed her eyes momentarily and had a tiny unrecognizable vision that strengthened her.

"Mrs. Byrd has been a kind of…mentor, of sorts, and she wanted us to meet her at the magic shop." She looked at Kai, hoping for some direction. Kai nodded. Riley sat up a little straighter and took a breath. "We met there this afternoon. It turns out, the owner is her brother, Fergus. We thought he was kind of creepy, and he is, but not as bad as we first thought. He's kind of a wizard or something, I'm not sure what he is. Anyway, he told us the story of how he was supposed to train Kai's dad, and there is a bad guy who's like an uncle, and he wants the power he thought his brother had…I mean Kai's dad…I mean I guess it's your brother, too. Anyway her dad left this deerskin…" She suddenly remembered she still had it and removed the bundle from her sweatshirt. She looked left and right, then handed the bundle to Kai. "Loliy said it was time, and that Kai should hold onto this."

Riley slumped in the chair. "That's when there was this crack and the building shook and I thought were having an earthquake and Loliy said everything was gonna be okay, then she drove us home and told me to stay with Kai…" Riley gleaned from the look on Tilley's face that she should wrap it up. "Anyway, that's the gist of it."

Tilley sat with her mouth open, staring in what appeared to be utter disbelief. Then she turned to Kai, who simply nodded. There was a long pause. A really long pause.

"I see. Kai is there anything you want to ask me? It's really important you understand what's going on."

Kai scrubbed her face with both hands and shook her head. "Tons, but I wouldn't know where to begin. You know, right now I don't think I understand it enough to ask any questions. I just really need to sit with everything for a bit."

Tilley folded her arms tightly and leaned forward, shaking her head. "I'm so sorry. I probably should've talked to you long before this." She looked up. "I thought I was doing the right thing and that you were too young. I was wrong."

Kai's face relaxed a little and she shook her head once. "It's okay. I wouldn't have understood any better a year ago or two years ago. It's probably better you waited. When I get this sorted out, I know I'll have questions, but in the meantime, I really just want to focus on school and tomorrow's tests. Would you take the stone and hide it somewhere safe?"

Tilley chewed her lower lip then said, "Yes, I have the perfect place. It'll be safe."

# *Chapter Twenty-two*

Riley giggled as Kai shoved the mammoth floor polisher out of her way and closed the door. "Hush! You don't want anyone to hear us, do you?"

"I can't help it. The janitor's closet. Really?"

Kai moved a carton of paper towels so they could sit down. She whispered loudly, "The yearbook staff is having a meeting."

Riley sat down and her expression became serious. She bit her lower lip. "Crazy, I know, it's just that I haven't seen you all day and the exams were horrible."

"I know. Me, too." She put her arm around Riley's shoulder pulled her close. "Are you nervous about the concert tomorrow?"

"Not yet. We'll see how rehearsal goes today. It may be different with my folks and Bekah there."

"Tilley's coming, too," Kai said, stroking Riley's hair.

Riley felt the fluttering in her chest and the warmth in her belly. She leaned closer and slid her fingers behind Kai's neck. "I really need—"

Kai's mouth finished the sentence.

Riley groaned as she felt Kai's tongue touch hers. It was soft and warm and it made her feel tingly. She arched her back as Kai's hand slid down to her waist and she leaned even closer as her mouth opened wider.

Kai broke the kiss. She was breathing hard, and her eyes were wide. She clasped the side of Riley's head and crushed their mouths together hungrily. Riley could feel her head drop back as her muscles relaxed into the embrace. Prickles of light danced behind her eyes.

*This has to be the most wonderful feeling in the whole world.*

Kai slowed her attack to small soft kisses. She finally stopped and pressed her forehead against Riley's. "Oh, my God. You are the most wonderful kisser. I wish we could just stay here all night." She stroked Riley's damp face and let out a huge sigh. "I guess we better stop so you can get to rehearsal. But I sure like kissing you."

Riley took hold of Kai's shoulder and shook her head. "Wow. Have you been practicing? Day-m." She held Kai's face and kissed her one more time. "That's so I remember what you taste like." Then she giggled. "Let's go, and if rehearsal gets out early…"

❧❧❧❧

The auditorium hummed with about fifty people—teachers, office staff, and a few parents who couldn't make the performance the next night. Kai had to pick a seat closer to the front.

It was still early, and most of the chorus were mingling around onstage. She immediately spotted Riley in her red and white ski sweater. Riley looked around the auditorium, but Kai knew she couldn't see her with the house lights dimmed. She slumped down in her seat with her knees on the back of the chair in front of her, and smiled. She touched her delightfully tender lips. *I kissed Riley James in the broom closet. That will be a story for our grandchildren.* She laughed out loud and then looked around nervously.

Riley was standing off to one side, and Kai noticed immediately when Brock appeared and walked over to her. He leaned over the chair in front of her—much too close for Kai's comfort. Riley nodded her head, and then began to smile.

Kai sat up straight and leaned in. She wished she'd chosen a seat a little nearer; she wanted to know what they were talking about. Riley seemed to be just listening, and occasionally shook her head or nodded. Brock sat facing her and scooted the chair closer.

Kai's neck hairs bristled, her chest burned, and her hands shook. "Damn it!" she said through clenched teeth. For the first time in her life, she actually felt jealous. They were just kissing less than twenty minutes before. Why was she talking to him?

She struck the seat back with her hand and shifted her position so she was sideways in the chair. *How can Riley do this to me?* Her heart ached in her chest and her throat tightened. She would have run from the school except that she'd be embarrassed. *Shit.*

Mrs. Byrd was talking to the choir but Kai heard nothing except the sound of her heart breaking in two. Her best friend—her girlfriend—still liked Brock. Kai feared she might die from the pain. Her whole world was coming apart and now she couldn't even trust Riley. *What else could possibly go wrong?*

The rehearsal went straight through from beginning to end. Kai heard very little because of the voices screaming in her head. At least they screamed until Riley started to sing. Kai wiped her nose with the back of her hand and sat up straighter.

By some miracle, Riley spotted Kai and sang directly to her. The ice encasing her heart began to melt. Her beautiful voice filled the auditorium and there wasn't another sound.

*No wonder she's the most popular girl in school. She's beautiful and her voice is magic.* Kai broke her gaze long enough to look around the audience. Everyone was watching intently with smiles on their faces. She just nodded. She started to look back to the stage, but did a double take toward the rear of the auditorium. In the shadows, she could make out the silhouette of a man in a black coat standing near the door. She squinted her eyes but couldn't make out details. When he shifted under the exit sign, she could see the patch. Then he slipped out the door.

She felt the sensation of icy fingers grabbing the base of her skull like a vice. Kai couldn't move. She looked quickly to the stage and Mrs. Byrd. The song was finished and the people in the audience were applauding. Mrs. Byrd turned around, took a little bow, then looked directly at Kai.

*She knows.*

Kai peeked around, hoping the one-eyed man was gone for good. What the hell was he doing there? She pulled out her cell phone and was about to dial, then shook her head. "Who in the hell am I gonna call?"

"What did you think?" Riley said trotting up the aisle toward her.

"I really liked it, everybody's gonna love it, it's a great show." She stood up and tried to smile, but it felt forced. Between the creepy guy and creepy Brock, Kai was seriously confused.

"I really love the new finale, and that bell solo is terrific. I had no idea Kennedy could play bells. I know he's a music major, but who plays bells?" Riley zipped her coat. "We have to hurry because Mrs. Byrd is gonna give us a ride home. She doesn't want us walking home in the dark."

Kai sighed as her shoulders relaxed and a sense of relief flooded her. This night, she did not want to walk home anyway. "Great, I'm really glad."

Riley cocked her head. "Really? I thought we might…uh, you know…take the long way home?"

A flash of Brock sweet-talking Riley made Kai clench her teeth together. "Not tonight," she said and picked up her backpack.

"What's wrong? You're acting weird."

"Nothing, let's go." This was not the time for a discussion.

⁂

"We really appreciate the ride," Riley said, looking at Kai in the backseat. "I'm sure my mom would have picked us up if I just called her."

"Don't think a thing of it. I don't mind and besides, I wanted to talk to Kai." Loliy glanced in her rearview mirror. "Are you feeling all right, dear? You had quite an ordeal and I was a little worried."

"I'm okay. We explained it all to my aunt." She paused, wanting to ask about the stranger. She looked at Riley and realized there was no point in keeping it from her. "Mrs. Byrd—"

"Loliy."

"Loliy. This afternoon at the rehearsal I thought I saw—"

"Yes, dear, I know. He was there"

"Who was?" Riley said.

"The one-eyed man Kai has seen, the Black Raven," Mrs. Byrd said and stopped the car in front of Riley's house. She turned in the seat. "I don't know what this means, but I think you're both perfectly safe at home and at school. Tomorrow morning, after you're dismissed, I'd like you to come to Agrippa's. We're going to need some help from Fergus. These events are most unusual, and I think we need to take some preventative action. I don't want you to worry; if we need additional help we can get it. Are you all right with that?"

Riley just nodded and looked at Kai.

Kai said nothing.

"Kai, would you be comfortable staying at Riley's until your aunt is off work? Perhaps she could pick you up."

Kai had never asked her aunt to do that, but knew she wouldn't mind if she called. "It's okay with me if it's okay with Riley."

"That's cool. We're having spaghetti anyway. C'mon in."

"Wonderful. See you girls tomorrow after class. Good night."

Kai and Riley stood on the sidewalk and watched as the huge blue Buick Electra slid away from the curb. As the car turned the corner, the streetlights went on, and Kai shivered. "We better get inside."

"Hey, Mom, I'm home." Riley tossed a jacket on the banister.

"Okay. Dinner will be ready in about an hour," Mrs. James said.

Riley took Kai's jacket and hung it on top of hers, then pulled her by the arm. Once in the kitchen she giggled. "Mom, she followed me home. Can I keep her?"

"Rileee..." Kai said, pulling her arm free.

"I'm not sure her aunt would like that. Hi, Kai. Of course, you're always welcome to stay for dinner. How was rehearsal?" she asked and continued to stir the sweet, spicy spaghetti sauce.

Riley looked at Kai and grimaced. "I think it was good, but I'm probably not the best person to ask." She nodded at Kai.

"Actually, Riley's right. It was a good rehearsal. Mrs. Byrd has done an amazing job, and she's added a couple of numbers. They even had a little audience today and I think they liked Riley's solo best." She received an elbow in the ribs as a reward. "Hey! That hurt."

"Why don't you girls go upstairs and wash up. I'll call you when it's ready."

Riley was out the door instantly. "Okay."

When they got upstairs, Riley's mood changed. She closed the bedroom door and pointed at Rebekah's bed. "Would you please tell me what's wrong with you? You have been seriously weird since we left rehearsal. Are you mad at me or something?"

Kai sat down on the foot of the bed and looked up at the diminutive figure threatening her. "I don't know, this whole day has been, like...irritating."

Riley stretched out on her bed facing Kai. She cocked her head to one side and scrunched up her eyebrows. "Sometimes I seriously don't get you. One minute you're dragging me into the janitor's closet to make out, then I turn around and you're not talking me. What is with that?"

Kai flopped back on the bed, covered her face with their arm, and chewed on her lower lip. All she could see was Brock Jones's pimply face leering at Riley before the rehearsal. Her fingers clenched into a fist. *Damn it.*

She sat up suddenly. "Do you like him better than me?" she said louder than she intended. Her voice shook.

Riley's expression changed from perplexed to stunned.

"Like who?"

Her jaw tightened and her breathing sped up. "Brock Jones."

"What in the hell are you talking about?" Riley sat up.

Kai jumped up and began to pace. Riley's bedroom felt too small, too confined.

"Kai, talk to me."

She stood next to the bed shaking with a combination of fear and anger. If she said the wrong thing, she could ruin their relationship. But if she didn't tell her, Kai thought she might explode.

"I saw him talking to you, and it looked like you were…I don't know, it looked like you liked him, like you were flirting."

Without a word, Riley hurled Mr. Rat, catching Kai in the gut.

"You big dork! What is the matter with you?"

Kai jumped, pushing the stuffed animal to the floor. "Hey! You know I hate rats!"

Riley picked him up and held him in her lap. "Mr. Rat, I have seriously bad news. My very best friend in the whole world is CRAZY!" She leaned closer and whispered in his ear. "But you know what? She is the best kisser in the universe. Yeah, really. You think? You may be right. All right, if you insist."

She stood up, carefully placed Mr. Rat on her pillow, turned around, and jumped onto Rebekah's bed knocking Kai onto her back and pinning her by the shoulders.

Kai struggled. "What the hell are you doing, Ri?"

Riley leaned very close. "Mr. Rat thinks I need to beat some sense into you. I told him that you are much bigger than I am, but he thinks I can take you." She moved closer, threw one leg over, and straddled Kai.

Kai started to push her off, then stopped as her anger trickled away. Riley's green eyes were focused, intent, and beautiful. "Ri…Your mom, she could… Don't—"

Riley put her head on Kai's shoulder and slid down, holding her. "I don't want you to be mad at me. Brock Jones is a dorky goat-boy who has a huge crush on me." She looked up at Kai. "You are the only one I care about. And I do. A lot."

Kai hugged her back. Her heart pounded and her throat burned. Tears threatened and she whispered, "I'm sorry, I was just so afraid you didn't wanna be with me. I was stupid."

Riley lifted her chin and kissed Kai's cheek. "Don't ever be afraid."

❧ ❧ ❧ ❧

After dinner, Kai called Tilley, who agreed to pick her up on the way home. She hustled up the stairs and joined Riley in her bedroom.

"Since Bekah is hanging out with Wesley, you can help me go through her stuff," Riley said in her most conspiratorial tone.

"Are you sure? It seems a little creepy to be going

through your sister's stuff."

"Wimp. Maybe you could go through the top shelves of the closet. I can't reach those."

They each started the search for the missing wand. Riley crawled around between the beds as Kai easily searched through boxes stored at the top of the closet.

"Do you think it's weird that your parents are totally cool with Bekah staying with Wesley?" Kai said.

"Why? They let me stay at your house."

"I suppose." She stopped and turned around. "Do you think your sister has…you know, done it, with Wesley?"

Riley sat on the bed and looked at Kai with a very serious expression. "I don't know. She has told me about some pretty hot make out sessions." Her lips tightened into a small impish smile. "Do you ever think about it? You know, what it would be like."

Kai shoved her hands in the back pockets of her jeans and felt the heat rise up the sides of her neck. "I think about wanting to do more, but I'm not really exactly sure what that might actually be. You know?"

"I know what you mean about wanting to do more. I sometimes feel like I wanna touch, you know, places to see what it feels like. Do you know what I mean?"

Kai shifted from one foot to the other. She knew exactly what Riley meant. What she didn't know was how to talk about it. "Yeah, I think I do."

Riley sat on the foot of Bekah's bed with her legs crossed and her elbows on her knees. "Well, have you ever? On yourself, I mean. And what did you feel like?"

Suddenly Kai felt a great burden of being seven months older. She slid down the doorjamb to the floor and tucked her knees up. It felt better to keep some distance from Riley. She carefully formed her thoughts, then cleared her throat.

"Well, sometimes in the shower." She felt perspiration forming on her forehead and her back. "I've kind of explored, you know, what things feel like. Some places feel really good when you touch them. This is really embarrassing, Ri. Maybe we should just find a book or something."

"Don't be embarrassed, Stretch." Riley's cheeks were pink. "Remember when we were in the laundry room and you touched me...here?" She put her hand over her left breast.

Kai flushed and swooned a little at the memory of where Riley's hand lay at that moment. She couldn't take her eyes off Riley's hand. In a hoarse whisper she said, "Oh, yes..."

"Have you done that?"

Kai nodded.

"Did you like the way it felt?"

Kai nodded and swallowed. "Yes...but it felt better when it was you."

"I liked the way that felt, too." Her voice was softer and she wasn't smiling. "So, I think it would feel good to be touched...other places."

Kai felt bolted to the floor. Part of her wanted to leap over the bed, pull off Riley's clothes, and touch every inch of skin on her body for as long as she wanted. Her heart pounded in her chest and she suddenly felt her clothes were suffocating her.

"Kai? Tilley's here."

# *Chapter Twenty-three*

Riley, you're going to be late."
"It's okay, Mom. I bet a lot of kids will be missing today because they are already on vacation." She picked up a piece of toast and shoved half in her mouth, then mumbled, "Did you know, Tiffany's whole family is going to the Bahamas, how awesome is that? How come we never get to go any place cool?"

"You know the answer to that question: your father's job. Accountants are busy at the end of the year. Now hurry up."

Riley leaned over the breakfast table reading the cartoons in the paper as she finished her toast. "I just love Garfield, don't you?"

Her mother dropped the last Ziploc into the insulated lunch bag. "Riley... Riley, would you listen to me for a minute? They're predicting snow all day so I'm going to bring your outfit to school on my way to work. Now, I didn't ask, but I'm sure Rebekah will help you with a little makeup before your performance..."

"Mo-omm, please—"

"Honey, I'm just excited for you and I want you to do your very best. If the roads aren't too bad, Gram and Grandpa may drive down from Minneapolis."

Riley wheeled around, mortified. "Seriously? Will they stay through Christmas?" She loved her grandparents—in very small doses. Whenever they stayed over it was a gigantic ordeal with a lot of fussing and fretting over nothing. It was exhausting.

"I don't know. It all depends on the weather. You are not wearing those jeans to school, so run upstairs and change."

"There's nothing wrong with these jeans!"

Her mother dropped the lunch bag on the table. "We are not having this discussion. Now go and change."

Riley stomped out of the kitchen muttering, "We won't even be there that long, and these look better than half the other jeans in school."

❧❧❧❧

Kai checked her watch for the third time. It was after eleven and most of the kids were scrambling to get out the doors. The new snow made everything look white and fluffy. That morning, the school secretary had permission to play Christmas music over the PA system, and every twenty minutes she reminded the students about the annual Christmas concert at seven in the auditorium.

Riley dashed down the front steps, slipped, and almost fell on her ass. She recovered just in time. "Stretch, woo hoo! We're done!"

Kai laughed as Riley waved her arms and spun in a circle. *Damn she's cute.* "I know. I'm guessing you're a little excited?"

"A little? I'm ecstatic. No homework, no rehearsals, and I can sleep late!"

"I know. I'm pretty psyched, too. Don't forget, we're supposed to meet Loliy."

Riley made a ridiculous face. "Whoops, I did forget. Guess we better hurry." As they walked toward

Main Street, Riley turned on her cell phone. "Message from Mom." Riley read the text and stopped.

"What's wrong?"

Riley hit speed dial. "Dunno, Mom just said to call as soon as I got this. "Hey, Mom, what's up?…No, I haven't…Of course, but I would've told you…I have no idea…What? I'll be right home…But I…Okay."

"Ri? What's wrong?" Kai had never seen Riley look so shaky.

"Wesley called this morning and wanted to know where Bekah was." She looked up at Kai. "She never showed up at his grandparents' house on Wednesday. He thought she was sick or something. Mom says she's not answering her cell phone and she's called the police!" She started to cry. "Kai, nobody knows where Bekah is."

"Come on, Shorty, we'll find her." Kai started walking toward home with her arm around Riley's shoulders. She had no idea where Rebekah could be, but she had very bad feeling about it.

"Wait, she wants me to stay with you. She doesn't want me to come home. Wesley is driving around and the police are going to the house."

"Then I think we better talk to Loliy. I'm not sure if it's related, but…she was the last one with the wand."

"Oh shit, what if—"

Kai took her by the shoulders. "Don't start making up stuff. C'mon," she said, pulling Riley around the corner to Mystic Lane. "I'll bet between Loliy and Fergus, somebody will have an idea. Don't worry, we'll find her." Her voice sounded a lot more positive than she felt.

Kai shoved the front door open and stopped so suddenly Riley bumped into her.

"What'd you do that for? Move." Riley pushed her aside and stopped just as quickly.

Loliy was standing at the foot of the spiral staircase looking about as scared as anybody Kai had ever seen. Fergus was on the floor in front of them, clearly messed up. Blood trickled from his nose and forehead.

Behind him stood the one-eyed man—her uncle, Black Raven. Between him and Loliy stood the guy from the alley.

Kai tried to make out what was going on, but her heart was beating so loudly she could hardly think.

Riley gripped her arm and then screamed.

She looked in the direction Riley pointed and saw Rebekah tied up on the floor beside Loliy.

"Well little warrior. Exactly the person I wanted to talk to," her uncle said, stepping closer.

Kai squared her shoulders but said nothing. She focused on her breathing and tried to stay calm. That's when she saw it. A hologram-like image of her father superimposed on her uncle and with it, a sense of comfort that he was with her.

Black Raven held up the bejeweled magic wand, gloating. "All of this would've been so much simpler if you—" he stabbed the wand toward Riley—"had learned how to mind your own business and not take things that didn't belong to you," he said, sneering at her.

Riley started to lunge. "What have you done to my sister?" she yelled.

Kai grabbed her sleeve. "Ri, don't."

He stepped over to where Rebekah sat on the floor and nudged her with his foot. "She was worthless. She knows nothing about this wand or where it came from…Or anything else for that matter."

Riley flew at him, her fists flying as she screamed.

Kai watched in wonder until the guy from the alley grabbed Riley and yanked her back.

Riley spun on him so fast that her elbow caught him in the face, knocking him backward. He tripped when Fergus grabbed his ankle and Riley jumped squarely on his chest. When he lunged at her face, Riley reached up, grabbed a wooden bear statue, and cracked him on the side of the head.

Out of the corner of her eye, Kai saw her uncle turn around and she rushed to Riley, shielding her. "What is it you want?" she said, jabbing a finger at him.

"You know perfectly well. This wand has limited power, but combined with the Black Obsidian it will be limitless. I want that, I deserve it, and I will have it, regardless of what it costs."

Fergus stood up. "It's not here. I've told you that a dozen times, and these children know nothing about it."

"Somebody knows. Tell me and no one will have to die." Now he was shouting.

"I believe we have tried to tell you, none of us knows where it is," Loliy said, speaking for the first time.

Lightning-fast, he slapped her across to face, knocking her back.

Before his hand dropped, Kai was on him. She grabbed him around the waist and her momentum sent them flying into the tall glass bookcase. The glass door cracked, raining shards, slashing his face.

He snarled and shoved the wand into the base of Kai's throat. "Get. Off. Of. Me."

She knocked his hand away and reached to her

back pocket, producing the hand-carved elk bone knife from her father. The hilt was wrapped with beaded leather, the tapered balance was ground, and the blade was polished to a sharp point. She placed it just at the bottom of his sternum. In a barely contained low voice she said, "Your time is done. The darkness is over and it's time for the light."

He raised both hands over his head with the wand and screamed with a voice that sounded more like a screech. He lunged forward but Kai stood firm. As the tip punctured his skin, his form imploded into a black ball that catapulted backward, smashing out the front window.

Riley screamed.

As Kai turned, the unconscious man on the floor rose up in the form of a grey wolf. The animal bared its teeth, snarled, then jumped through the front window. Both forms disappeared in a flash of black and silver and a high-pitched squeal.

After what seemed like a silent eternity, Fergus walked to the front window and looked out. He turned around and shrugged his shoulders, then went out the door.

Kai slipped to her knees as her whole body began to shake. She looked down at her hands and the elk bone knife, stunned to see it was clean. She was overwhelmed with the terror that she had actually stabbed someone, and yet there was no blood. She looked up to see Loliy standing behind her.

Riley pulled off the blindfold and untied her sister's hands and feet. "Oh my God, Bekah, are you okay?"

Fergus returned, locked the front door, stuck up the closed sign, and pulled a heavy drape across the front window. "They're gone, as near as I can tell. Is everyone all right?" he said to Loliy.

"I think so. Kai, are you all right, dear?"

Kai could only nod numbly.

"I think we should all go in the back and have some tea. Riley, I think you might want to call your mother and let her know that your sister is safe. I'm sure they will want to pick you both up right away." She turned and marched through the curtains to the back.

Riley stood up, glanced at Kai, and then escorted her sister into the back room. "Just sit here with Loliy. Why don't you call Mom, I'll be right back."

Fergus had straightened up the shop a little. "I'll just get the dustbin for that glass," he said and disappeared into the back.

"Kai? Kai are you okay?" Riley said, kneeling down and putting her arms around Kai's shoulders.

"What the hell just happened?" Kai said, leaning into the warmth. "Riley, I thought I killed him. I was so scared." She choked back a sob.

"I don't know. Can you stand up? Let's go in the back with the others." She pulled Kai to her feet. "I think you better stick that back in your pocket," she said, pointing to the elk bone.

As she got to her feet, all Kai wanted to do was hold Riley. She pulled her into a hug. The warm, soft body and sweet smell helped.

For several minutes earlier, Kai had felt like she was actually outside of her body. Almost like watching herself as she wrestled with Black Raven.

"Stay close, please," she whispered.

"I will, Stretch. Let's get some of that great tea." Riley took her hand and led her back to the office.

Loliy was sitting at the table with Bekah, pouring her tea and patting her hand. "Yes, you've had quite a fright. It was all a dreadful misunderstanding, you see."

Fergus walked through with a broom and dustpan, shaking his head.

"Girls, join us. Rebekah has spoken to your mother and as soon as they finish up with the detective, they will come down here." She poured each a cup of tea and passed around a plate of biscuits.

Kai fumbled the spoon twice and Riley immediately stirred in the cream for her. They exchanged glances and Riley nodded her support.

"Riley, I think when you get home you may have a better chance to explain a few things to your sister. For now, I think it's best not to alarm your parents. In time, I will be happy to talk with them." She rearranged a biscuit on her plate into four pieces, wiped her fingers, and picked up a teacup. "I think the problem has been temporarily dealt with and there is, after all, a very special concert this evening. Everyone will have holiday plans, so I don't think we should worry."

Kai shook her head to clear the cobwebs. Loliy made this sound like it happened every day. "I don't understand. I just stabbed my uncle and he vanished. How is it you think I'm not gonna worry? My aunt is gonna be furious."

Riley giggled. Then Rebekah chuckled. Pretty soon they were both laughing hard.

"I don't get what's so funny," Kai said, feeling indignant and angry.

"Stretch, think about what you just said. Your aunt is gonna be furious? Well, duh!" Riley said and laughed again. "I think maybe we could find a better way to explain what happened, that's all."

"I'm sure that's how you remember it, but that's not actually what happened and I'm not going to go into that right now. Your uncle is not dead. But he is, in fact, not going to be around."

Fergus sat down. "I've been giving it some thought, and I believe it's best if we just agree that there was a break-in. Two men broke in to the store to rob me. There was a scuffle and they took off." He picked up a biscuit, broke it in two, and nodded at Loliy. "I'm not sure how to explain the kidnapping."

Loliy leaned back in her seat and tented her fingers together. "I think for the most part we tell the truth. You girls found the wand in the alley. You thought it belonged to me and you planned to return it. Rebekah unknowingly took it as a prank. The men were able to track it because of the GPS chip."

Three voices chimed in unison. "GPS chip?"

Loliy stood firm. "Yes, that is how they were able to track it. They knew there was another piece to the wand and hoped to extract that information from Rebekah. Of course she didn't know, so they returned to the scene of the crime"—she waved her arms expansively—"and discovered it was not here. They fought with Fergus and he chased them away." She folded her hands and smiled victoriously.

Kai looked at Riley and they shook their heads. The story was basically true, but it still sounded weird as hell.

The phone rang. Fergus groaned, went to the desk to answer it, muttered a few comments, and hung up. "The police are on the way over."

# *Chapter Twenty-four*

The backseat was crowded with all three girls. Riley's dad was driving. He came home from work as soon as he got the call. Riley couldn't remember the last time she saw her parents so upset. Kai was completely silent. Riley was pretty much dismissed. All they wanted to do was talk to Bekah—naturally.

"Richard, there's no point in talking about pressing charges, the men are obviously gone. Sela said until they have a good description they can't even begin to look for them." Her mom's voice sounded tight and kind of high-pitched. Riley didn't like it.

Her father struck the wheel. "Lizzie, a young woman was snatched in broad daylight in Lindan. That has never happened before. We have to see to it that it doesn't happen again. These men have to be apprehended and prosecuted."

Bekah squeezed Riley's knee. Riley looked at her and could see the question in her eyes. She didn't know what she was supposed to tell her parents.

Elizabeth James turned around in the front seat. "Kai, I hope you don't mind, but I thought it was best to let Tilley know what was going on. She's leaving work early and will meet us at our house. You girls understand that we just want you to be safe."

"Yes, ma'am," Kai said into her lap.

Riley bit her lip. The person she was most worried about was Kai. Bekah seemed okay and Loliy...who knew about Loliy? She and Fergus probably teleported back to Ireland by now.

Kai didn't look good. Her face looked pale and she seemed sort of weak or shaky.

Riley tipped her head back and closed her eyes. The whole day had gone so fast. The last thing she remembered was reading Garfield and eating toast before Mom made her change her jeans. Then seeing Bekah and those creepy evil dudes…she shivered involuntarily. And poor Fergus, he probably got the worst of it.

Her eyes snapped open. How did those guys vanish? More importantly, were they coming back? At least they didn't have to worry about the wand. That was gone for good. A wave of guilt sloshed up as Riley realized that if they had just returned it immediately, none of this would have happened. *Crap.*

Tilley's Beamer sat in front of the house when they turned down Riley's street. Kai sat up.

"You girls get out and I'll put the car away."

"I'm so glad you could come on short notice," Elizabeth said to Tilley, who was standing on the sidewalk. "I just thought you'd want to be here. It seems everyone is fine."

Tilley watched carefully as Kai got out of the car. "No problem. I'm glad you called." She walked over to Kai and put an arm around her shoulders. "Honey, are you okay? I'll take you home as soon as I talk to Mr. and Mrs. James."

"I'm okay, don't worry."

⁂

Once inside, everyone shed their coats and sat

down at the dining room table. Mrs. James defrosted some of the hors d' oeuvers from the party while Tilley asked about everyone's health.

Within a few minutes, the phone rang and Mr. James went into the kitchen to answer it. Both he and his wife returned with some plates and a pitcher of iced tea. "That was the Lindan Police. They finished questioning the owner and are coming back over here."

Mrs. James poured tea for everyone.

"I don't think I can drink another sip of tea," Kai said.

"Riley I think I better call the school and tell them you won't be able to perform tonight—"

"NO! I have to. I've waited all year for this. Pu-leaze Mom, I have to."

"Pumpkin, your mom is probably right. This has been quite an ordeal."

"Daddy please, the program is only an hour and I only have one song. It's so important to me and I promise I'll come right home and go to bed." She looked from one to the other.

Kai jumped in. "Mrs. James, Riley's worked really hard for this and she's really the best part of the show."

"We'll see. If this interview doesn't take too long you may have time to rest."

On cue, the doorbell rang.

"Tilley, you remember Sela Whitehorse from the party? She's also a detective on the case. Please come in." Mrs. James took her coat and pointed. "And of course you remember Riley's friend, Kai."

Detective Whitehorse sat down across from Tilley and they exchanged a look. Kai looked at her aunt and saw what looked like blushing.

"Thank you all for waiting to talk to me. I

promise it won't take long because we got most of the story from Mrs. Byrd and Mr. O'Dwyer. Let me start with Rebekah. Would you tell me what happened on Wednesday?" She opened a notebook and began to write.

Rebekah looked quickly at Riley. "Well, Wednesday afternoon I was going over to Wesley's grandparents' house over on Euclid. I took the bus most of the way and then it's only two blocks after that." She looked at her mother, who just nodded. "I started to walk and a car pulled up. The driver asked me about an address and I had no clue where it was. I never even noticed there was a man on the sidewalk. He grabbed me and pushed me into the backseat of the car."

Riley started to cry. Kai handed her napkin and moved her chair a little closer.

"Please continue."

"I was blindfolded and had something in my mouth, and then he tied up my hands. We drove for a long time. They took me inside of some house and took off the blindfold. It must've been vacant because there wasn't very much furniture, and when we drove back into town the next morning, it seemed like we were out by the old Newcomb farm."

The detective wrote everything down. Tilley watched her the whole time.

"Rebekah, tell us what happened at the abandoned house," Detective Whitehorse said.

"The shorter guy, the one with the eye patch, asked me if I knew about the wand. I said I didn't know anything about it, but the other guy was already going through my backpack and found it." She stopped and looked at her mother. "I was just goofing around when

I took the wand from Riley, I didn't know it was a big deal, I thought it was a prop for the school show. I was gonna give it back."

Riley gave her weak smile.

Kai had a chilling thought that if Bekah hadn't taken the wand, they would have taken Riley instead.

"So they had the wand, presumably the one they were looking for. What next? Why did they keep you so long?"

"I don't really know. They kept asking about something called the Black Obsidian. I had no clue what they were talking about."

Tilley dropped her napkin and bent over to pick it up. Kai thought she looked oddly nervous or something.

"What did the men do when they found out you didn't have the other object they wanted?"

Rebekah looked tearful and a little scared.

"The taller guy yelled at me over and over. He said it was really important and as soon as I told them where it was, they would let me go. Daddy, I told them the truth, I didn't know where that thing was."

"Did they ask you where you got the wand?" said the detective.

Tears fell, and Rebekah nodded. "I told them I took it from my sister. I'm sorry, Riley. The men went into another room and I could hear them talking about some alley and two girls. They tied me up and put me in one of the bedrooms, and then they left."

Detective Whitehorse turned her attention to Kai and Riley. "Which one of you would like to tell me what happened in the alley?"

Riley sat up and put her shoulders back. "I will. We went to Agrippa's Natural Magic a couple of weeks ago and heard somebody crying for help in back. Kai ran to help her—Mrs. Byrd—and fought with the man, the tall guy we saw today. When he ran off, we went to help the lady but she was gone, and all we found was the wand. I didn't mean to keep it, honest. I forgot about it and then when I wanted to find it to give it back to Mrs. Byrd, I couldn't find it. I asked Bekah and she told me she didn't have it."

Detective Whitehorse rubbed her forehead. "I think that's all I need for now. Mrs. Byrd told me what happened in the shop. Does anyone need medical attention? We probably should've done that first, but you girls were already home by the time I got there."

"Rebekah, you should see the doctor," Mrs. James said.

"I'm okay. I wasn't hurt, I was just scared," Bekah said. "Can I please call Wesley and ask him to come over? I'm sure he's worried sick."

"Go ahead." Mrs. James looked at her watch. "It's almost four thirty. Riley, we don't have much time, but I think you girls should go upstairs and rest for a while. We still have a few things to talk about."

⁂

When they reached the top of the stairs, Kai said, "I need to use your bathroom."

Riley turned on the light in her bedroom. It looked the same but it suddenly felt warmer and safer than it ever had before. She curled up at the head of her bed and tucked Mr. Rat under her arm. "Boy, am I glad to see you." She hugged him tightly.

Next door, she heard the toilet flush and the water run. Kai came into the bedroom and closed the door quietly. She kicked off her shoes and lay down on Rebekah's bed. She looked terrible.

"Are you okay? Were you sick?"

Kai just nodded.

Riley slipped off the bed and knelt on the floor. Kai's beautiful hair was damp and matted around her face. There were dark circles under her eyes and her lips were pale. Riley stroked her face. "I think I better get your aunt. Wait here."

"No, I'm okay."

"You're not okay and I'm going to get you something to drink." She hurried out.

"I just need to get some 7UP, Mom," Riley said. With glass in hand, she passed behind Tilley and whispered, "Could you come upstairs, please?"

They entered the bedroom at the same time.

"I think Kai is really sick. She threw up," Riley said, sticking a straw in the glass and kneeling beside the bed. "Here drink some of this. It'll make you feel better."

Tilley sat down beside Kai and put her hand on her forehead. "Sweetie, what's going on? Whatever it is, you can tell me."

Kai sat up and took a drink of the soda. She handed the glass back and began to shake. She fell sobbing into Tilley's arms.

Tilley held her, but looked at Riley, astonished. "It's all right, I've got you."

Riley got up and sat on her bed. She grabbed Mr. Rat with one arm and handed Tilley the tissue box with the other.

It was unsettling to see her best friend totally lose it. Kai was always the calm one. Riley felt tears burning her own eyes as she sat powerless to help.

Tilley pushed the hair back from Kai's face and handed her a tissue.

The sobs became less and less intense. Eventually, Kai gasped two short breaths and sighed. She put her head back on Tilley's shoulder and Tilley kissed her forehead.

"Why don't you tell me what happened? I've never seen you this upset."

"It was Black Raven. I thought I killed him. Oh God, I was so scared. Loliy thought we should keep the story simple. But it was awful. Bekah was tied up and Fergus was bleeding on the floor. Loliy looked like she'd seen a ghost." Kai reached for the soda and took a big swallow.

Kai's eyes met Riley's.

A weak smile appeared on Kai's face. "Riley was amazing. She totally tackled the other guy and knocked him in the head with a statue. She was really fierce." The smile disappeared and she looked at her aunt. "Black Raven scared me. He yelled because he couldn't find that obsidian thing, and threatened to kill people if he couldn't."

She got very still and said, "Something bizarre happened to me. First, there was a strange floating image of Dad right over his face. And then he went all kind of crazy and hit Loliy. When he did that, I was kind of out of my body, do you know what I mean?"

Tilley nodded and took her hand. "Yes."

"I grabbed him to keep him from hurting Loliy, and when he stuck the wand at my throat I thought he might really kill me. I grabbed Dad's elk bone knife—I don't remember putting it in my pocket—and I...and I stabbed him." Her hands trembled and her voice sounded strained. "And then he disappeared out the front window."

Tilley leaned her head against Kai's and whispered, "It's over now and you're all right." Then she suddenly hugged her very tight.

Riley felt the tears on her cheeks and the death grip she had on Mr. Rat. They both waited for Kai to respond.

After several minutes, Tilley asked, "Do you want to go home?"

Kai shook her head. "I'm okay. I really wanna see Riley sing."

They all laughed and Riley said, "Stretch, you're the best."

Tilley stood up. "I think Elizabeth was right, you two need to rest. I won't say anything about this. Kai, we can talk about it more tonight, if you want. I think you're both very brave. Remember, you are stronger together than separate." She closed the door behind her.

"Kai, do you think we could rest together?"

"Yeah, I think that's a good idea." She climbed onto Riley's bed and wrapped her arms around her protector.

# *Chapter Twenty-five*

Kai waved as Riley got in the car with her parents, then climbed into Tilley's car. "Could we make a quick stop on the way?"

"Sure thing. Did you get some rest? Because you look a little better."

"Surprisingly, I actually slept for a while. Til, I'm sorry about the meltdown."

Tilley squeezed her arm.

The auditorium bustled with noise and excitement. Kai and Tilley had arrived early to get good seats.

Bekah waved to them from the third row. "We saved two seats for you," she said. "You got some flowers?" She winked at Kai. "That was really nice. Mom, look what Kai got for Riley. Isn't that sweet?"

Kai hung back so Tilley would go first. Just as a precaution, Kai scanned the audience to make sure they were okay.

The house lights dimmed and Mrs. Byrd entered from stage left. In addition to her Mary Sunshine yellow suit, she had a stunning red velvet Santa hat complete with jingle bells. Kai groaned. She had never ever met anyone like Loliy Byrd. As she watched her, she wondered if Loliy was one of the Irish magical little people. There was kind of an elfin quality about her, not to mention the fact that her brother Fergus looked like a gnome. Still, they were allies, and Kai felt a little better knowing they were on her side.

The students paraded on to the stage from the wings and made their way to their assigned places on the small risers. Kai quickly scanned the faces until she found Riley on the side near the piano, front row.

Her jaw dropped. Riley looked beautiful. Her auburn hair was pulled back and pinned up. Her eyes were made up and her lips looked luscious. The long-sleeved blouse tapered the waist, and the floor-length black skirt made her look much taller.

They were halfway through the concert before Kai stopped staring at her. Tilley glanced at her two or three times, but said nothing. What could she say? Riley James was the most beautiful girl on that stage.

Her solo was coming up, and the audience hushed. Riley walked closer to the piano, scanning the first few rows. Kai hoped she could see her grinning face and not her sweaty hands.

"O, holy night, the stars are brightly shining…"

All Kai could see was the beautiful green eyes looking directly at her. Tingling started in the back of her neck and went straight down her spine. She must've been grinning because her cheeks hurt.

The sound of Riley's voice was crystal clear and filled the auditorium. By the final verse, the choir was humming behind her. It sounded perfect, just like a real angel would sing it. Kai thought her heart might melt into a puddle and she didn't care. She didn't want this moment to end.

Mrs. Byrd moved them seamlessly into *Silent Night* and invited the audience to sing along at the end. Everyone sang. Kai's heart beat in her throat along with the music. When she glanced at Tilley, she saw tears in her eyes. *Yeah, she knows how this feels.*

The noise of the applause shook the floor. Kai was immediately out of her seat and through the side exit. On Wednesday she had looked for the route that would take her backstage as quickly as possible. She'd planned it all out.

As the chorus filed offstage chattering, Kai scanned the tops of their heads looking for those beautiful auburn curls. She waited until Riley almost passed her, then quickly pulled her behind a curtain. "You were fantastic! Here, these are for you." She handed Riley two long-stemmed roses—one red and one white, nested in baby's breath, and tied with a red ribbon.

"Flowers? For me?" Riley looked at the flowers, then up at Kai, then back to the flowers. Tears flowed softly down her cheeks. "They're beautiful. No one has ever given me flowers. Thank you so much. You're the best friend anyone could ever ask for."

Kai felt her cheeks burn and shifted from one foot to the other. "I just wanted you to know how special you are. And not just tonight, although you were amazing! It's the best you've ever sounded. But I think you're special every day."

Loliy appeared out of nowhere, as usual. "Riley, I am very proud of you. Everything went perfectly. Wasn't that concert fun? Must run. Merry Christmas."

"We better go, your folks will be waiting. I'll text you before I go to bed." Kai looked around, wishing they had some privacy because she really wanted to kiss Riley. But there were tons of people everywhere. *Damn it.*

❧❧❧❧

Riley cracked open one eye and listened. A

strange noise had wakened her. The alarm clock read 11:33 a.m. *I must've been tired.* She rolled onto her back, stretched, and closed her eyes as she clutched Mr. Rat with one arm. It felt good to be snuggled a warm bed instead of getting ready for school.

*But what is that noise?* The process of deduction led her to only one conclusion: the vacuum cleaner.

After several moments, she managed to put the facts together. It was Friday, school was out, the concert was over, and her sister was still home for the holidays and…must be vacuuming the downstairs.

Connecting thoughts was a challenge. And her hands were stiff, and the right one badly bruised. *Oh yeah, punching out creepy guy.* She flexed her fingers and winced.

As the events of the past twenty-four hours flooded back in with all of the Technicolor wonder of a B-grade teen thriller movie, Riley sat up quickly. Yep, it was her room and it was safe. The new furniture arrangement and the peach colored walls with white accents looked perfect. Her clothing strewn artistically around the room and schoolbooks dumped beside her desk left her feeling secure and grateful. She had grown up and shared this room with her sister for many years. Smart, beautiful Rebekah. Her best friend…until now.

They needed to talk. Bekah must have a thousand questions by now and Riley was thankful she hadn't said any more to the police or to their folks. She dressed quickly, then trotted downstairs to scrounge up something to eat.

Bekah was dancing around the living room with her iPod in one hand and the vacuum cleaner in the other. Whatever ordeal she suffered must have been resolved because she sure looked better. Riley waited to get her attention and finally gave up, opting for the kitchen.

*When was the last time I had anything to eat?* She leaned heavily on the open refrigerator door, surveying shelves of Tupperware. The assortment of foods reminded her that Christmas was only two days away and her parents would once again be entertaining. *That's why she's vacuuming.*

"Hey, whatcha doin'?"

Rebekah was standing in the kitchen door wrapping the ear buds around her iPod.

"Trying to find something to eat. I'm famished."

"There's some ham in the middle drawer. Would you make me a sandwich?" Rebekah brought over two plates, an open bag of potato chips, and two sodas.

"Do you want mustard?"

"Dijon, if we have any."

Riley put the plates down and grabbed a handful of potato chips. "Did we actually eat last night?"

"Yes, don't you remember? Dad stopped for hamburgers."

She groaned. "Just barely. I can't remember the last time I was so tired." She stopped eating long enough to look at Bekah. "How are you?"

"I'm pretty tired, too. I didn't sleep all that well last night."

Riley laughed. "You sure were busting some moves a few minutes ago. Just sayin'."

Rebekah snorted, choking on a mouthful of soda. "Brat. Why do you always wait until I have a mouthful? So rude."

"Sorry." Riley handed her a napkin. "I really feel bad about, you know, all the scary shit you went through. I probably should've told you about the wand, but I really was gonna return it."

"I know. It was my fault for taking it and not telling you." She sat back in her chair and pulled one leg up to wrap her arms around. "Riley, what the heck is going on? I wasn't gonna say anything and I really like Kai, but those were some really creepy dudes, you know? Are you sure you should be hanging around with her? I mean, I know you really like her. *Really* like her. I just don't want you to get hurt."

The ham sandwich was sitting like a lump in her stomach. She wasn't sure how much to say, because she didn't understand it all herself. Still, she needed Bekah's help, and she wanted her to like Kai. "It's complicated."

"Well, d'oh! Magic wands, disappearing people, kidnapping, death threats...am I missing anything else?"

"You didn't mention Loliy and Fergus. They're kind of odd."

Riley looked up when she heard Rebekah laughing and realized how absurd the whole thing was. "I know, right? I guess complicated is an understatement, huh?"

"Ya think? Geez, Ri, what have you gotten involved in? Are you bewitched or something?"

"No, it's nothing like that. In fact, up until a few weeks ago I didn't know about any of this stuff. I suppose if we'd never gone to the magic shop in the first place, we wouldn't have met Fergus or Loliy, we wouldn't have found the Dreand, and we wouldn't have been in a fight with those guys. But we did and there's nothing we can do about it now."

"Ooo-kay. What can you tell me?"

Riley chewed on her lip, wishing Kai were there. "I'm not really sure. But I promise you that I'll talk to

Kai and Tilley."

"When?"

"I don't know. Soon. I haven't even talked to Kai. I'm sure she's pretty upset, too."

A quirky smile grew on Bekah's face. "Soooo, how long have you and Kyle been together?"

Riley startled then glared at her sister. "Her name is Kai, and you know I just met her this semester."

"Right, and the laundry room? Are you two, you know, serious?"

"I don't know what you're talking about, serious about what?"

Rebekah just smirked. "Dude." She pronounced it so it somehow sounded like two syllables. "Serious about each other?"

She hesitated. "We're really close friends and we've shared an awful lot."

"I guessed that much. Hey Riley, it's totally cool. You know, if you're gay, that's cool." Rebekah's smile wasn't snarky; it was warm and accepting as she nodded. "Do you remember Jason Brightman, captain of the swim team? As soon as we got to the university, he came out to everybody. Now he's so much happier. I'm glad for him. I mean, we all suspected that he was gay in high school. But he was so uptight about it, man. Now he's just totally relaxed and cool."

Riley remembered him from the few times he'd hung out with Bekah and her friends. At the time, she thought he was the most handsome man she'd ever seen. *He's gay, huh? Go figure.* She continued to rearrange the bread crust on her plate. "The thing is, I don't really know. I mean, we don't. We just, we just really like each other a lot. Like more than anybody. And I can tell her anything, you know?"

"I know. It's how I feel about Wesley. We like each other, but we like each other physically, too."

Riley could feel herself beginning to blush. Just the word "physically" made her feel a little fluttery.

Rebekah waited then finally asked, "So, you've kissed, right? Anything else like—"

"Bekah!"

"Just asking. I mean you're not a little kid anymore. You told me about kissing Brock, and I have a pretty good idea what happened in the laundry room."

Just the mention of his name made her shudder. "The thing is, it's just really hard to figure out and we haven't really talked about it much. We will, it's just… well things have been kinda crazy. I'd really appreciate it if you didn't say anything to Mom. I don't want to get her upset, especially with everything else going on."

"No problem, kid. If you guys are happy, I'm happy. I just wanna know little bit more about her and this weird shit going on. Okay?"

"Did you tell Wesley?"

"Are you kidding?" She laughed. "Wesley asked me if you guys were together."

"Why would he even ask that?"

"Ri, haven't you ever noticed the way Kai looks at you? She just beams. It's pretty obvious."

Riley groaned. "Oh, God, my life is over. Does everyone know?"

"No. I'm not sure I would've noticed if Wesley hadn't mentioned it. I'm pretty sure nobody else would get that. But who cares? You need to think about this a little." Bekah stood up and picked up the dishes. "I promised Mom we'd have the downstairs cleaned up before she got home. Emphasis on the word 'we.' So shake your tail feathers and let's get to work."

# *Chapter Twenty-six*

Kai kicked her feet against the top step, shaking loose most of the snow on her boots. Once inside, she peeled off her jacket, knit cap, boots, and wet jeans. Fortunately, she'd remembered to wear long underwear, but she was still freezing.

Tilley had woken her up before she left and asked that she shovel the walk and driveway. "Please don't forget, Kai." Through the pillow she'd groaned something unintelligible and gone back to sleep.

It was after ten when she started the driveway, which took hours. The snow from yesterday had added another eight inches of snow to the base already on the ground. She only stopped once to come in and warm up, and then finished the front walk. According to the kitchen clock, the whole project had taken way longer than it should have. It was almost two thirty.

She stretched her arms above her head and twisted from side to side. The muscles in her back and shoulders burned from the exertion. It was like giant, overwhelming fatigue, both physical and emotional. Without any warning, her thoughts migrated to Riley standing on stage the night before. Kai couldn't believe how beautiful she looked. The little glow started again, the one that ignited whenever she thought about Riley.

On autopilot, Kai went through the steps of making hot chocolate. The steam from the heating milk warmed her hands as she rubbed them together.

As soon as she had feeling in her fingers she texted Riley, who responded immediately. The back and forth continued as Kai sipped her cocoa with one hand and the phone in the other. They agreed to meet the following morning at the Avoca Coffee Shop.

Her smile only grew wider as she thought about getting together the next day. They had both agreed that it might be hard to see each other over the winter break. It made them even more determined to come up with some plan, whether it was going to the mall, meeting for breakfast, or trying to arrange sleepovers.

With the second cup of hot chocolate in her hand, Kai curled up in the recliner with a heavy knit throw. Tilley had left a copy of one of her books, *The Lakota Way*, by Joseph Marshall. Kai smiled at the sticky note on its cover. *I know this won't answer all your questions, but it may help. :) T.*

Her feet began to thaw out as she tucked them underneath her. The warm blanket, the sun beaming through the window, and the hot liquid wrapped her in a comfortable envelope. *I sure like school breaks,* she mused as she read over the back cover of the book. Within a half hour, she parked the empty cup on the table and closed her eyes. The living room fell away.

*The wind howled. Hot sun warmed her face and the wool blanket was tucked around her shoulders. Far off in the distance she could hear nickering and whinnying from a herd of horses.*

*The air smelled of spring grasses and the familiar scent from the smudge stick burning nearby. She inhaled deeply the mixed scents of tanned buffalo hide, strong coffee, and warm skin.*

*Now there were sounds of children and laughter.*

*It was a good sound; the people were happy.*

*She went deeper and felt herself pivoting around clockwise. She faced west and saw the history. She grew colder facing the north and the source of her power. Soon she was moving fast to the dawn and the hope, and as she rotated to the south she felt the darkness descend. She was riding hard and being pursued by three horses. Her hands clutched the mane of the horse beneath her as the wind whipped strands of horsehair across her eyes. Over her shoulder there were even more coming and they were coming faster. She tightened her legs around the galloping stallion and reached both hands to the sky.*

*A thunderbolt struck, plunging the pursued and the pursuers into the depths of the earth.*

Kai jerked. Her eyes flew open and her body vibrated with electrical energy. The visions had become more frequent and more frightening.

ঝঝঝঝ

Tilley had changed her clothes four times. Kai looked at the kitchen clock and sighed. "We're gonna be late."

"I'm coming. What do you think, should I wear my hair up or down?"

"Down. What difference does it make? You look beautiful, and I really like those new jeans, they fit you perfectly. Geez, Tilley, you act like you've never been on a date in your life. Sela seems cool, I bet she won't be dressed up," she added with a smirk.

Tilley took one more look in the mirror then slipped on her jacket. "I guess this will have to do. Will someone pick you girls up after breakfast, or do you want to call me?"

Kai laughed out loud. "Are you serious? You really think I'd call you when you're out on a date? No way, we'll be fine."

"It's not like a date, we're getting together to go look at the new art project at the library."

Kai raised one eyebrow. "Really. You know, I'm not ten years old. I saw the way you guys were looking at each other."

Tilley smiled with one of those 'oh really' smiles. "Well, thank you, my wise little I've-had-my-first-kiss-ever niece. Suddenly you're an expert?"

Kai felt the heat in her cheeks. "Now I wish I'd never told you."

Tilley pinched her leg.

"Heeeyy, that hurt."

Tilley pulled over in front of the Avoca Coffee Shop. After fishing through her purse, she handed Kai thirty dollars. "I'd like you to pay for breakfast. The James's were kind enough to have us over to their holiday party and tomorrow's Christmas dinner. I'm going to pick up some champagne and a card."

"Okay, thanks." Kai unbuckled her seat belt and started to get out.

Tilley put her hand on her arm. "I love you and I'm very proud of you."

"I know. Me, too." Kai stood at the curb and waved as Tilley drove away.

A rap on the window caught her attention. Riley was waving at her from a table inside.

"Hi, Stretch. Have you ever eaten here? The menu's amazing. They have ten different kinds of pancakes. And look at these omelets!"

Kai hung up her coat and sat down. She didn't even pick up the menu. All she wanted to do was look at Riley. Her sweater was red and green with little brown reindeer across the top. Thump, thump. She was sure everyone could hear that sound coming out of her chest.

Once again, she regretted not choosing a more private meeting place. *Damn. I should've had her come over to my house and then we could've—stop it. You sound like one of those horny jocks. Riley looks so good. After all that shit Thursday and she can still be excited about pancakes? I am seriously hooked on this girl.*

"...so that's what I'm going to have, how about you?"

Kai fumbled with the menu then noticed a hulking presence beside their table. The gigantic waitress had to be at least six feet tall. Her bright red hair made her look like Lucille Ball, and she was cracking her chewing gum.

"What'll it be, kids? Wanna hear the specials?"

She pulled an index card out of her order pad, cleared her throat, and stuck her pencil behind her ear. "We got venison hash with mushrooms, eggs, and Wisconsin cheddar. We've got a nice mushroom quiche, and real blueberry pancakes."

Kai just stared with her mouth open. The woman's voice was so high-pitched that it sounded fake.

Riley pointed. "I'll have the combo plate, with eggs over easy and two buckwheat pancakes. And sausage. Oh, can I have orange juice, too?"

Betty—that's what her nametag read—scribbled something and turned to Kai, smacking her gum. "How 'bout you kid?"

"Umm, I guess I'll go with venison hash." She closed the menu.

"To drink?"

"I'll have a glass of… I'll have coffee." Kai leaned back and smiled.

"I didn't know you drank coffee." Riley handed the waitress her menu.

"I didn't."

Riley turned sideways in the booth and rested her chin on her hand. "So how did it go when you guys got home on Thursday?"

"Tilley made me more tea and asked me more questions about what happened. I think she was pissed, but not at me. She didn't say why. We've never really had a big talk or anything about my family or what happened before they all left Pine Ridge. Whenever I'd ask questions, she just reassured me that someday she'd explain it all to me. Kinda looks like that someday just showed up."

The waitress returned with the orange juice, coffee, and two glasses of water. "Your food shouldn't be too long. Anything else?"

"Do you have any cream?"

"Ya, you betcha."

Kai added a packet of sugar and a generous pour of cream to the steaming cup of coffee, then tasted it. It was strong and kind of bitter so she added several more packets of sugar.

Riley just giggled. "So, Ms. Tiva, how's your coffee?"

"Better now. I'm guessing this must be an acquired taste. Last summer when I was with Wakanda, she made some really strong stuff, and even with sugar it was hard to drink."

"I'm guessing Tilley might've been mad because she didn't know what was going on."

"That's what's really weird. Wouldn't you think

that at some time or another she would've mentioned they had another brother?" Kai hadn't thought much about it, but now wondered if there were other things she hadn't been told. Did she have a brother or sister?

"Good point." Riley sat up straight and picked up her orange juice.

Betty The Amazon appeared with two heaping plates. Kai almost drooled at the sight of the food. "Thanks, I'm starving."

"I know. You know what's weird? When I got up yesterday morning, I couldn't even remember that we'd gone out to eat after the concert. I must've crashed hard."

Kai stopped chewing and tried to remember what they'd eaten. She couldn't. "What'd your folks have to say? Were they mad?"

Riley tapped her lip with her fork. "I don't think mad as much as worried. It was good that we went to the concert so that they could see I was all right. Know what? Bekah really thought I nailed it. She couldn't stop talking about how much she liked my solo. I was pretty stoked."

Kai watched as Riley's face lit up and got bright pink. "She's right, you were awesome."

Her expression changed dramatically. "Oh my God, you know what else? Wesley told her that he thought we were together, like together-together, and she asked me."

Kai choked. "What did you say?"

"I didn't know what to say. I told her I was confused, we both were."

This wasn't the time or the place. Kai finished the last piece of toast as the waitress appeared with the coffee pot.

"Warm that up for you, honey?"

"Just half, thanks."

"Will there be anything else?" she asked, fishing for her order pad.

Kai looked at Riley, who shook her head. "I think we're good."

"You kids have a Merry Christmas," Betty said, laying the check on the table.

Kai scooped it up and reached in her pocket for the cash Tilley had given her.

"I've got some money here—"

"That's okay. Tilley wanted me to get this for you."

"How nice, but you don't have to."

"I want to. Listen, can you come back to my house for a while? Tilley won't be back till later."

"That's cool. My mom's freaking out about cooking and has Dad running errands. I'll text her, but I don't think they'll care."

❧ ❧ ❧ ❧

Riley waited outside while Kai paid the check. The village was crowded with last-minute shoppers. Two days before Christmas until the day after the bandstand speakers played nonstop carols twelve hours a day. Tons of lights and garland filled every store. She looked around as though she had never seen this before and wondered why it made a difference this year.

"All set. Are you ready to go?" Kai asked as she joined her outside.

"It looks kind of pretty with all the decorations and the music and stuff, don't you think?"

Kai finished buttoning her coat then glanced up

and down the street. "You know, it does. Wonder why I never noticed that?"

"I totally thought the same thing. It looks like a little Christmas wonderland, like the kind you see in it snow globe."

"Hey, great idea. Maybe we should get one of the store owners to market the idea." She held her hands up framing an imaginary sign. "Get 'em while they last. All new. Lindan Snow Globes!"

Riley pulled her arm. "Too bad Loliy lost her wand, she could probably zap one, or even a hundred of them. We could all be rich."

"Ri, what do you suppose Loliy and Fergus'll be doing for Christmas?"

"Well I suppose it would depend on where they teleported to. Ireland, Germany, could be anywhere."

"I didn't think about that. I just feel kinda sad. I mean they really tried to help us. They might not have known that my uncle would turn out to be creepy bad guy, with an even worse attitude, who'd wreck their store."

"Hey, Stretch, don't be bummed. I was just messing with you, Mom invited them both for dinner tomorrow and I'm pretty sure they'll be there."

"Really? That's great." She flung her arm around Riley's shoulders. "I feel much better now."

"Are you finished shopping?"

Kai groaned. "No, I still have to find something for Tilley. She's just kinda hard to buy for because she has such good taste and I don't. Besides, she has everything she needs."

They had turned a corner and were approaching Walgreens. "I've got an idea, let's go in there." Riley pointed to the entrance.

"The drugstore?"

Riley turned to face Kai. "You are like totally clueless. They have all kinds of fun gift stuff. You know—perfume, makeup, bubble bath, scarves, jewelry. Haven't you ever been in there?"

It took forty minutes to interest Kai in a few items. She finally agreed to perfume.

"Kai, I've already put on four of them. If you can't pick from there, then you'll have to try some on yourself. And that might be better. You have closer chemistry to your aunt."

"What in the world does chemistry have to do with it?"

"Haven't you ever heard of pheromones?"

Kai just shook her head and started turning in circles. "Can't we just pick one? She can bring it back if she doesn't like it."

Riley punched her in the arm. "I like these two." She pointed to her left wrist and the left side of her neck.

Kai leaned over and held her wrist, taking a long whiff. "This is just too flowery." She continued to hold the wrist but moved up to Riley's neck. She gently pushed the hair out of the way and leaned in.

"Well?"

"I'm deciding," Kai said. "Okay, I like this one. At least I really like it on you."

"That's a start. Does she like the spray or the kind you dab on?"

Kai scrunched up her face.

"What's the matter now?"

"I'm trying to remember what's on her dresser."

Riley banged her head on Kai's shoulder. "Aaaaaahhh."

# *Chapter Twenty-seven*

"That was really a good idea to have her gift wrap it," Kai said.

"You really don't get out much do you? I'm surprised you've made it fifteen years. How do you normally buy gifts?"

"We don't really exchange gifts that much. If I need stuff I just tell Tilley and she gets it. We've never made much of a deal out of Christmas, except for her Christmas party. And we don't have a lot of friends."

"That's kind of sad." They turned down Kai's street and watched some neighbor kids make a snowman.

"Why? I don't feel like I've missed anything."

"I guess. We've just always made a big deal out of Christmas. My folks love to decorate and entertain. You've probably figured that out by now."

Once inside, Kai said, "Let me take your jacket, and I'll start the fireplace."

Riley noticed a fresh garland draped across the built-in bookcases. It had dozens of small handmade ornaments hanging from it.

A few of the shelves were backlit and held some lovely artifacts. Most of the pieces were natural stone or wood. Some were sculpted, some more plain. "Is this a geode?"

Kai glanced over her shoulder. "Uh-huh."

One shelf held what looked to be geological

samples: a large piece of turquoise, some lovely green stones that were probably malachite, polished pieces of onyx, and a round pink stone the size of a baseball. Riley picked it up from the carved metal stand. "What's this?"

Kai walked over. "I'm not sure, Tilley's had it forever."

Colored lights framed each window in the living room. "Can I plug in the lights?" Riley asked.

"Sure, go ahead." Kai turned on the fireplace insert and lit the gas flame. Satisfied it was working, she flopped down to the couch. Riley joined her. "Ri, were you upset by what your sister said about us?"

"Not really. Mostly I was surprised, then a little embarrassed that her boyfriend had to point it out, but I guess I was worried because I don't really understand the labels."

"Me neither but, after you said that, I started thinking and maybe…well maybe we should talk about what we're doing. And what we want."

Riley tucked her knees up and watched the fire for a few minutes. She sighed heavily. "This is hard. Maybe you could start, okay?"

Kai really wanted Riley to start because she wasn't sure what she wanted to say. "I'm really nervous but I'm just gonna say it. Please don't laugh at me, promise?"

"I promise."

"Riley, I really like you a lot. I mean you're my best friend, which is totally cool. But, you know, I think about you all the time and I think I'd like us to be more than best friends, more like girlfriends. I'm not sure if that's what you want, and I'll be really disappointed if you don't, but I'd still want you to be my friend." Her heart was jackhammering in her chest and she felt sick to her stomach. *Please let her like me the same way.* She wiped her sweaty hands on her jeans and avoided Riley's shimmering green eyes.

"That's pretty much the same way I feel, but I don't know what that really means. Does that mean we're dating or like going steady or something?"

Kai wished she had talked a little more about this with Tilley or maybe gotten a library book. There must be some kind of book about this. "I think we both have to be pretty clear about the fact we like girls—not boys."

Riley nodded. "I don't know any girls I've ever liked as much as I like you. And I like you way better than any of the boys."

"Me, too. Then I think we should probably agree not to go out with other people—boys or girls."

"I agree. So does that mean we're dating?"

Kai had to laugh. *How can we date if neither one of us can drive and there is nowhere to go? I really needed talk to Tilley.* "Well, kind of, since we can't really go anywhere without somebody driving us. But like, breakfast was kind of a date. It's more like a chance to get to know each other better, in private. I think."

"So, if we were officially dating, would that include more, you know, kissing and touching and stuff?"

Kai felt the fluttering and then the room felt really, really warm. She turned sideways and tucked one leg under her. She put her arm on the back of the couch and looked Riley in the eye. "I really hope that's what it means because it's getting much harder for me not to touch you."

Riley's face flushed immediately and her lips

parted. "I know. Me, too. Kai, I'm a little scared."

"I would never hurt you, honest."

Riley put her head down and started to fidget with the hem of her sweater. She always fidgeted when she got nervous.

"Do you remember at the party when we were in the laundry room?"

Kai nodded.

"Do you remember when I told you that I was scared because I wasn't sure I could stop?"

"I remember."

Riley looked up and a tear rolled down her cheek. "Do you think that you could be the one to say stop, even if I wanna do more?"

Kai's chest ached, and she knew at that moment she would never do anything to take advantage of this wonderful girl. "I promise you, Riley."

Riley reached out her hand and Kai took it.

Kai pulled Riley closer and kissed the back of her hand, smelling hints of the perfume she had tested. A need began to grow inside of her like an impending thunderstorm. She took Riley's face with both hands, took a breath, and pressed their lips together, at first very lightly and then a little harder.

Riley responded immediately, wrapping her arms around Kai's neck and pulling them tightly together. "Please kiss me harder," she said.

Kai was breathing fast as she pressed into Riley, pushing her backward on the couch. The soft noises Riley made only increased her desire until she felt Riley's tongue touch hers.

Their bodies shifted as Riley stretched out on the couch. Kai sat up and yanked her crewneck sweater over her head.

Riley reached for Kai's hand and pulled it to her breast.

"Are you sure?"

"Yes."

Kai gently caressed the soft tissue and watched as Riley closed her eyes. The muscles in her belly tightened as she leaned forward, capturing Riley's lips with a groan.

She felt Riley's hand on her back moving down below her waist and pulling her. At the same time, she carefully moved under Riley's sweater to feel the soft skin on her side.

Riley gasped and then raised her arm to Kai's shoulder, giving her unspoken permission.

"Damn, Ri, you feel so good," she moaned, and moved her mouth to the soft skin below Riley's ear. Her fingers slipped under the side of the bra.

Riley shifted onto her side. "Unhook it."

Kai jerked her head up. "Seriously?" Her excitement was just barely contained.

Riley smiled and nodded.

Kai reached behind her with one hand and fumbled miserably.

Giggling, Riley sat up. "Try using both hands."

Kai kissed her and reached around under the sweater to unhook the bra.

"Whatever you do, don't ever stop kissing me." Riley reached behind Kai's neck and pulled her down into a searing kiss.

Gradually Kai felt more comfortable and was able to do more than one thing at a time. They took turns kissing, exploring, and experimenting. Kai rolled up on one elbow to brush a lock of hair behind Riley's ear. Her face was flushed and her lips swollen. Her beautiful green eyes were glassy and half-lidded. Kai stroked her face with the back of her fingers. "You are so incredibly hot. And I really like touching you. Would you let me kiss 'em?"

Riley reached up and put her hand on Kai's chest. Both of them were breathing hard. "I don't know, I mean I'm a little shy and we are in the living room. Sometime, I just don't think we should right now. Could you just hold me for a while?"

Kai snuggled down next to her, kissed the side of her face, and held her tight. "Okay. I love the way you feel in my arms, kind of like you fit perfectly."

"I know I love the way your body feels on me." Riley ran the tips of her fingers along Kai's face, touching each feature gently. "And what you can do with your mouth is amazing."

Riley ran her hands under Kai's shirt, causing her to shudder with pleasure. Her fingers were delicate and warm and curious. She whispered in Kai's ear, "I never imagined this could be so wonderful. I wish I didn't have to leave."

Kai deflated.

❧ ❧ ❧ ❧

Riley glanced over her shoulder and waved. Kai was still standing on the front step. She touched her lips again, surprised at how tender they were. Yes, dating was definitely fun. She wished she could have stayed longer, but had promised her mom she'd be home early to help with Christmas wrapping.

In addition to all the entertaining and decorating, her mother always shopped for small new or gently used toys for the children's hospital. Then Christmas Eve the whole family would wrap them and deliver them so the kids would have something to open Christmas morning. As a little kid, Riley never understood why they had to give away all these presents. When she was old enough to go with her parents and see how sad it was for the families who had to spend Christmas at the hospital, she began to take more pride in their tradition.

Besides, she had something special to wrap for Kai.

※ ※ ※ ※

Kai hurried back to the couch because she was cold. She curled up in one corner and pulled a heavy blanket over her. She couldn't remember the last time she felt this good, really good. This was the best day of her life. Her skin still tingled with the memories. The whole nasty magic store episode felt like a dream. Totally unreal.

A loud bang startled her and she jumped up.

"I'm home. Where are you?"

"In here," Kai panted.

Tilley joined her on the couch, tucking her stockinged feet under her. "Boy, am glad you've got the fire going. It's getting really cold out there. The wind almost blew the door off."

Kai shared half the blanket. "Here, take this. How was your date?"

Tilley raised one eyebrow and pursed her lips. "It was just fine. We both enjoyed the exhibit and had a wonderful lunch at Dunwoody's on Main." She reached over, picked up Kai's sweater from the floor, and began to fold it. "And how was your date?"

Kai felt heat rising up her neck. She never left clothing lying around the house, ever. It was surely clear to Tilley that it had been carelessly flung on the floor, so the way she folded the sweater spoke volumes. Kai grimaced. "Fine."

Tilley started laughing and soon Kai joined her.

"This is a little awkward isn't it?" Tilley laid the sweater on her lap and smoothed it with her fingers. "You know Kai, we're in a different spot than we used to be. You've grown up differently than other children and turned into a pretty amazing young woman. You're a lot smarter and I think a lot more mature than I was at your age." She folded her hands in her lap. "I guess what I'm trying to say is, since we both have…well, started dating, at the same time, it would be foolish to act as if you didn't understand what was going on, right?"

Kai looked up and swallowed hard. "I guess I agree, but there's a lot I don't know. I've been thinking today that there might be some questions I want to ask you. I mean, if it's okay."

Tilley nodded. "You can always ask me anything you want, you know that. As long as you understand that I may not have the answer immediately."

"I understand."

After a little pause, Tilley asked, "Is everything okay with Riley?"

The blushing started again. "Oh yeah, it's good. We had a long talk today."

"I can tell." Tilley nodded to the sweater.

Kai blushed. "Well, first we talked. I've never dated anybody, nobody's even asked me. Riley is a little more experienced, but not that much. The deal is, neither one of us knows anything about how dating is supposed to happen, and we don't know…well, you know…Crap! How are girls supposed to do it?"

Tilley nodded as she bit her lower lip. "I see. It is an awkward thing whether you're a boy or girl. I'm not going to insult you by reciting facts about how your body changes when you become a teenager and all that. Suffice it to say, many of the decisions you have to make will be affected by hormones." She looked around and crossed her legs. "I suspect you figured that out already."

Kai nodded. "Yeah."

"What you need to remember is that you have plenty of time. You both have the rest of your lives to meet people, date people, and fall in and out of love. It will happen many times."

"I think Riley will be the only one."

"I'm sure you do. She very well may be, but remember you're only fifteen, and there's a good chance you'll fall in love with several people before you settle down."

That was not what Kai wanted to hear and not what she wanted to ask. She really wanted to know why her body reacted the way it did and why she felt so crazy sometimes, especially when Riley touched her.

"What's wrong? You look worried."

Kai refused to look her in the eye. "It's just, I sometimes feel so out of control. I mean my heart pounds and I sweat and I can't get my breath and there's this terrible ache…"

"I know, honey, that's normal. Those feelings you get are because right now your body wants to reproduce. That's why human beings have sex. Well, there are a couple of other reasons." She winked. "It's certainly pleasurable and intimate."

*I can't believe we're talking about sex.* Kai blinked a few times because of the dizziness. She looked at her sweater lying on Tilley's lap and groaned. "So, you're not mad that we were…" She gestured at the couch. "You know we were just kissing, we didn't do anything. I don't want to do anything that would upset her."

Tilley shook her head. "No, I'm not. I just want you to be careful—both of you. This is a very emotional time and it's easy to miscommunicate and for someone to get hurt feelings. Honestly, it would be a little hypocritical of me to lecture you in dating behavior."

Kai grinned. "'Zacly."

"Do you think you can stop thinking about Riley long enough to help me with dinner?"

Kai stood up. "Can I do both? 'Cause I'm really hungry, but I'm still pretty happy."

"You really are going to be insufferable aren't you?" Tilley said and started for the kitchen, tossing Kai her sweater.

# *Chapter Twenty-eight*

The kitchen table was covered with Christmas wrap, ribbons, and boxes. Kai rubbed her eyes and yawned. "Hmm, I guess I caught Santa in the act."

Tilley looked up, her eyes wide. "Merry Christmas, honey. Just wrapping a few odds and ends. I do think Santa might have left something for you in the living room. Would you like something to eat first?"

"I am kinda hungry." Kai pulled out a stool at the kitchen counter.

"I made the casserole you like. It's in the oven," Tilley said, trying to tie a bow with one hand as she held the ribbon together with the other.

Kai leaned over. "Here let me help you."

"Thanks."

"Is it the one with eggs and potatoes and green chile?" Kai rolled off the stool toward the oven.

"Yeah, I hope it's not too spicy." Tilley took the gift to a large bag by the back door. "Most of these things are little thank-you gifts for Riley and her family. They've been awfully nice to us."

Kai tore a tortilla in half and scooped up some of the eggs. "This is really good." She watched as Tilley wrapped up a can of mixed nuts and remembered the present she bought was upstairs.

"Did you get something for Riley?"

"I made her something along with a card I designed."

Tilley looked up and smiled at her. "I bet she'll like that."

"Til, do you like Sela?"

"I guess so." She put down the tape. "We don't know each other too well, yet. But we seem to have things in common. You know, interests."

"Are you going to invite her over here?"

"Would you like me to?"

Kai suddenly felt a little protective. "I guess. I mean if you're gonna see her a lot and you like her, I'd like to know her better."

Tilley folded her arms remove and tipped her head to one side. "I believe you're right. And I think you'll get the chance a little later today. Sela told me that Elizabeth invited her for dinner as well." She continued wrapping. "It seems that they've been friends for quite some time. They both work for the Department of Public Safety and play on the same softball team."

"Seriously? Mrs. James plays softball?"

"Hard to believe, I know. Someone that *old…*" Tilley laughed and shook her head. "Having children doesn't mean the end of all fun."

"I didn't mean that, it just surprised me." Kai took a dish to the sink, rinsed it, and put it in the dishwasher. She glanced over her shoulder at Tilley. *So I'll get to see them together, which should be cool.* She realized she had no idea how many people would be at this dinner.

"Do I have to dress up again?"

A genuine belly laugh bubbled up from Tilley. "I don't think you need to do too much, but just be aware that other people will be a little dressed up. Your nice jeans and a sweater would be fine." She put the wrapping supplies away and took Kai's arm. "Let's go see what Santa brought us."

"Okay, I just have to run upstairs quick."

"Meet me in the basement, will you?"

When Kai returned, she found her aunt piling a few packages on the ping-pong table. "Are we having Christmas in the basement?"

"Why not? We went to a lot of trouble to decorate this place two years ago, and we never come down here."

"I suppose." Kai had really enjoyed the space when it was first decorated. They moved the TV down, there was a good sound system, and it was all wired for video games. Tilley had partitioned off part of it for an eventual workshop. Neither of them had done anything about that.

Tilley handed her an oblong box. "Start with this one while I get some coffee."

"Would you get me some, please?"

Tilley stopped on the stairs. "When did you start drinking coffee?"

"Yesterday." Kai grinned. "But I still need a lot a cream and sugar."

Kai ripped into the box and found two new pairs of jeans and Superman lounge pants. She held them up. They seemed long enough. That was always the biggest problem with getting pants: girls pants were all too short.

"Here you go," Tilley said, handing her the cup. "Merry Christmas."

It tasted perfect. "This tastes really good, what did you put in it?"

"Eggnog. Do the pants fit all right?"

Kai put her cup down and held up the black jeans. "I didn't try them on, but they look okay."

"Let's be sure, because those would be nice to

wear this afternoon. Why don't you go in the shop and try them on?" Tilley sat down on the recliner and didn't have to wait long.

"Oh. My. God!" Kai shrieked. "I can't believe this. When did you…How come I didn't…Wicked!"

Tilley followed the sound of ripping paper, giggling, interspersed with hoots. The jeans lay on the floor and Kai was seated on the bench of the Nautilus home gym.

Kai looked up with tears in her eyes and shook her head. "Wow. You are so awesome!" She jumped up, threw her arms around Tilley, and spun her around. "How did you know? I really wanted to work on my strength training and Coach won't let us use the free weights because the upperclassmen always get 'em." She stopped jumping. "This must've cost a fortune. I know, I'll get a job and I can help pay for it. You shouldn't have done all this, it's too much."

"Honey you've grown so much taller in the last year, and I know you're going to need to work out a lot harder to stay in shape. You're a gifted athlete, but it's gonna take a lot of work to be competitive." Tilley put her arm around Kai's waist as Kai leafed through the brochure. "You showed me how responsible you can be this year with your studies and your practices. This is as much of a reward as it is an incentive to keep going."

Kai hugged her. "I love you, Tilley."

"I love you, too. There are a few more packages if you wanna open them, or they can wait. We'll need to leave by one thirty."

❧ ❧ ❧ ❧

Christmas music echoed throughout the house

and Riley barely heard the doorbell. "I'll get it." She'd been looking out the window, looking for Tilley's car.

"Come in you guys, and put your coats right there. Hi, Kai."

"Hi, Riley," Kai said and gave her a quick hug.

Riley felt herself blushing, but damn, Kai looked really hot. The sharp crease in her jeans indicated that they were new. The black V-neck sweater fit perfectly, and Riley was at the right height and close enough to notice Kai's boobs. *Whoa.* She felt her throat dry up. Suddenly she looked up into Kai's twinkling brown eyes. She smiled lamely. "Nice sweater."

"You look nice, too."

"I think I'll just go find Elizabeth," Tilley said.

"What's in the bag?" Riley asked.

"Oh, Tilley got some stuff for people."

Riley giggled. "I guess we could put it under the tree, huh?"

They moved into the living room and sat down. One by one they read the tags and placed the small packages under the tree.

After reading the last two gift tags, Riley pointed to the dining room. "Did I tell you that my mom invited Loliy and Fergus? Wasn't that sweet?"

"Yeah, you did. I was really worried about them. They haven't had the best holiday season either. I mean, the shop's kind of wrecked and they're not young."

Riley leaned back on her outstretched arms and nodded. "I know what you mean. I wish there was something we could do."

Kai looked around. "Ri, I have something for you." She reached into the bag and pulled out a small box and a large envelope. "It's nothing fancy, I just wanted to make something for you."

Heat crept up Riley's neck to her cheeks. It wasn't the package she had in front of her, it was the way Kai said it that made her heart skip in her chest. "Thank you." She laid the card in her lap and carefully opened the small package. Even the paper looked homemade. Wrapped in tissue sat a braided leather bracelet with a series of red, black, yellow, and white seed beads woven through the middle. She blinked back a tear. "Kai, it's beautiful. Wherever did you find this?" she said as she draped it over her left wrist.

"I made it for you. Here let me get that." Kai reached over to tie the bracelet.

Kai had her back to the door and blocked them. Riley leaned forward and kissed her cheek. "I love it and I'll never take it off."

Kai bent over, took Riley's hand, and kissed it. "The card is part of the present."

The card was an ornately decorated winter scene and said "For Someone Very Special." Riley read the verse and touched the inscription Kai had written. Her handwriting was neat and legible.

Dear Riley,
You are the best thing that has ever happened to me in my life. I hope we will always be friends for the rest of our lives (this one, and all the others).
Love, Kai

She wiped a tear from her cheek and sniffed. Setting the card down, she put her arms around Kai's neck. "Me, too, Stretch. Me, too."

Kai hugged her back.

"Wait a second." Riley crawled around the other side of the tree and then came back with a candy-cane-striped package. "This is for you."

"You didn't have to—"

Riley punched her in the arm. "Of course I did. I wanted to."

Kai opened the box and took out a small scrapbook. As she turned each page, her eyes grew wider. They were all sketches that Riley had worked on for weeks.

"Did you really do all of these? They're beautiful. Look at this, it's my house." She turned the page. "And this is me playing ball, and the park, what's this...? Riley, is this a broom closet?"

Riley could no longer contain herself and burst out laughing. "I couldn't wait until you got to that one."

Kai looked around and giggled. "You are so bad." She continued through the sketches, smiling and nodding. "I think this is my favorite present ever." She carefully put it back in the box. "Oh my God I forgot to tell you! Tilley got me a Nautilus home gym! It is un-friggin-believable. I can do a whole workout downstairs so I won't need to fight with the upperclassmen for the weights at school. You won't believe how good I'm going to look by summer."

Riley just watched as excitement radiated off of Kai. She'd never seen her so energized except during a game. She glanced again at the sweater and licked her lips. *I think you look pretty good right now.* She imagined Kai's body even more buff, in the summer, tan, in a bathing suit...

"Are you okay?" Kai asked.

"Of course. Why?"

"Your face got all red, I was worried."

"I was just thinking about summer. And heat."

She looked suggestively at Kai.

Kai cleared her throat nervously and stood up. "Maybe we can get something to drink?"

❧❧❧❧

The kitchen was crowded with both Elizabeth and Rebekah cooking. Sela and Tilley were working on a salad. Richard was in the dining room opening wine bottles and Wesley was bringing in firewood.

"Is there anything we can do?" Riley asked.

"Yes, would you girls get the new napkins out of the dryer and fold them, please?"

Kai didn't need to be directed to the laundry room. She knew where it was, and she winked at Riley.

"Okay, Mom, then should we put them on the table?" Riley said as Bekah turned around and smirked. Riley stuck her tongue out and Kai shoved her toward the door.

"Come on, Shorty, we have work to do."

Once in the laundry room, Riley opened the dryer. "Still a little damp," she said, resetting the dryer.

Kai hoisted herself up on the washer.

"Your new clothes are very flattering, especially that great sweater," Riley said walking closer and slowly latching the door.

Kai looked down and nodded. "Tilley has pretty good taste. I wasn't sure this would be comfortable," she said, smoothing her hands over the front of the sweater. "But it really is. It's so soft."

"Really?" Riley placed both hands on the front of Kai's sweater.

An electric jolt shot through Kai's body.

Riley wedged between her knees and slid her

hands up to just below Kai's breasts.

"What are you doing?" Kai rasped.

"Don't you want me to?"

Kai felt like she was sitting on an electric stove and she was burning up. Riley's hands were hot and she was leaning hard enough to push Kai's legs apart. All she could do was nod.

Riley's fingertips brushed softly across her breasts, causing an instant reaction through her body. She reached for Riley's face.

"Not yet."

The ache grew as Kai groaned. "Ri, please…"

She continued stroking, squeezing, and pinching. "You have really nice boobs, and I think they like me."

Kai squirmed in discomfort. "You're killing me."

The timer went off and Kai jumped off the washer, pushing Riley back against the shelving unit. She grabbed Riley's head and pulled it to her, crushing her lips with a savage kiss.

Riley responded in kind, her open mouth begging.

Kai felt crazy. She kissed and grabbed and pulled, trying to eliminate any space between them. Something clicked. Kai pulled back, panting hard. "Stop," she said and grabbed hold of the wire rack. "I have to stop or I won't be able to."

Riley leaned her head back and let out a huge breath. "I know. I know…I didn't know, my God, you feel so good. I just didn't wanna stop touching you."

"We have to be careful. I know what you mean, but we can't. Not now."

"You're right."

Kai stroked her hair, the side of her face, and kissed her forehead. "Let's fold the napkins."

# *Chapter Twenty-nine*

While they were messing around in the laundry room, Loliy and Fergus had arrived, the music had been cranked up, and everyone was enjoying a glass of wine. Kai and Riley looked at each other, shrugging. Evidently, no one noticed they were gone.

Riley handed half the napkins to Kai and nodded with her head toward the table. Mrs. James whispered, "Just prop them like this." She circled one napkin, tucking the ends together. "And put one on each plate."

Kai struggled to duplicate the action, and finally got it. She looked around and thought the table looked beautiful. Pine boughs ran down the center of the long table, there were red candles placed at intervals, and the napkins matched the runner. She looked across the table, watching Riley as she placed each napkin carefully and cocked her head to be sure it was perfect. Kai's heart swelled in her chest.

When Riley looked up they both smiled.

Mr. James's voice rose above the noise. "Elizabeth and I are delighted you could all join our family for Christmas dinner. When you get to the table, there will be a small card in front of each plate with your name on it. And unless someone objects, we've selected a nice champagne to have with dinner."

"Did you see the cards? Mom put us next to each other, isn't that cool?"

"I saw that and I'm really glad. That way I won't be so nervous." Kai pointed to the glassware on the table. "They gave us wine glasses. Do you think we'll get wine?"

"I doubt it. They usually have kids' wine, you know, nonalcoholic stuff. It's pretty good."

"Kai." She turned when Tilley put a hand on her back, and smiled. "You remember Sela?"

"Nice to see you again, Detective." Kai stuck her hand out.

"Please call me Sela, I'm only called that at work. Besides, we already know each other a little." She took Kai's hand and smiled. "But, your aunt's told me a lot about you, Kai. You're quite the basketball legend around here."

Her hand was strong but warm. Her blue eyes stood out against her dark skin and hair. Kai thought she was attractive. She wore her hair short and had on a pressed pair of navy Dockers, a white shirt, and a blazer. She stood a few inches shorter than Kai, but was about the same height as Tilley. Kai thought they made a nice couple.

"I enjoy it, but I wouldn't go so far as to say I was a legend." She felt Riley move closer.

Tilley said, "And of course you know Riley."

"This woman I've known since she was maybe seven? Not the chubby little girl I remember," she said, reaching over to pat her cheek, then winked. "You're all grown up aren't you?"

"I'm working on it," Riley said. "And I was not chubby."

"Let's all sit down," Mr. James said.

Kai and Riley found themselves sitting across from Loliy and Fergus. Kai was next to Tilley, Riley on the other side, and Mrs. James at the head of the table. Sela, Rebekah, Wesley, and Mr. James rounded out the other end.

Loliy smiled like a Cheshire cat. "Merry Christmas, girls. Isn't this a delightful surprise? Riley, your parents were so kind to include my brother and me at your family gathering."

"We're glad you could come," Riley said.

"I'm really glad you're here because I feel like we didn't really get to talk after, you know, stuff happened, and the concert and all," Kai said as softly as possible.

Loliy nodded. "I think we'll have a chance to talk. I've spoken to your aunt and your parents, Riley." She unfurled her napkin and guided it to her lap with a dramatic flair. "Fergus and I are going to need a little help with the shop. We thought perhaps over your break you might like a little part-time work—in case you need money for something."

Kai looked at Tilley sitting next to her, but she was busy talking to Sela. Riley's parents were up again, shuttling dishes to the table.

"That could be kinda fun," Riley said, poking Kai.

"Sure. It's okay with me." Kai pulled her napkin into her lap.

"Excellent. Perhaps we could have a little meeting sometime tomorrow, would that work for you girls?"

Kai looked at Riley and nodded. "Okay. Riley?"

"Works for me."

Dishes passed, plates filled, and everyone tucked into a plateful of food. Kai thought the number of dishes offered was astounding. She'd seen paintings of gigantic feasts, and this sure ranked right up there with the best of them. Along with turkey and ham, there were different kinds of potatoes, yams, two vegetable dishes, and a green Jell-O salad. A cut glass dish with a bunch of different olives, celery, and carrots made its way around the table and landed in front of her. *Wow.*

She helped herself to a little bit of everything as her stomach growled in anticipation. Tilley looked at her and winked.

"It's our tradition to say grace. I hope everyone is comfortable with that," Mr. James said.

Kai watched as everyone put down their silverware and bowed their heads. He recited a grace she had once heard in a movie. It sounded vaguely similar to the prayers she remembered her father offering.

She closed her eyes and for a moment could see the lean handsome face of her father. Her throat tightened and she swallowed. Sometimes she missed her dad. When she opened her eyes, Tilley was looking at her.

"Mom," Rebekah said. "If it's okay, Wesley would like to offer a toast."

"Of course, that would be nice."

Wesley stood up holding his half-full glass. "I would like to offer a toast to Mr. and Mrs. James for their wonderful hospitality and for having such wonderful daughters, especially Rebekah." He leaned down and quickly kissed her.

Everyone raised a glass and drank. Kai looked at Riley and they picked up their water glasses.

Riley turned to her mother. "Since this is such a special occasion, don't you think we could have just a little champagne?"

"Richard? Riley would like to know if they could have a little bit of champagne."

"I don't see why not, if that's all right with you,

Tilley?"

She nodded.

He stood up and brought the bottle down to the other end of the table, then poured half a glass of champagne each for Kai and Riley. "Riley, you've worked hard this semester and made us very proud of you. And Kai, you have proved to be a good influence and we're happy to welcome you and your aunt into our little family. Cheers."

Once again, everyone raised their glasses, and Kai could feel herself blushing. "Thanks," she said and picked up the champagne flute. She smiled at Riley and they each took a drink.

The bubbles tickled her nose and then felt like they expanded in her mouth. It was different from the red wine she had tasted which had been kind of sour. This was sparkly and fruity.

So much commotion during a meal was unusual and a little unsettling for Kai. Instead, she focused on the tastes of all the new and different foods while everyone around her was busy talking. Richard was talking to Wesley, Sela to Rebekah, Tilley to Fergus, and Loliy to Elizabeth. In her head, it sounded like the drone of bees.

Riley leaned over. "Are you okay?"

"Sure, why?"

"You're just being so quiet. Do you like the food?"

Kai lowered her voice. "I've never seen so much food my life, and it's all good."

Riley giggled. "What do you guys usually do for Christmas?"

"We fix a nice dinner and sometimes rent a movie or go out. A few times we've gone up to Minneapolis for a couple of days, mostly to look around. Sometimes we shop, once we went to the ballet. Tilley's firm has an office in the cities. They even have a hotel suite that we've used."

"That would be fun. I wish we could go somewhere," Riley said as she put her hand on Kai's knee.

The gentle touch shot right up her leg and into her belly. Kai wished Riley would leave her hand there, but she pulled away.

Kai watched for a minute as Riley continued to eat. The colored beads on the bracelet caught the candlelight. It looked nice on her.

"So Kai," Richard said. "I understand from Coach Logan that you've been asked to try out for the girls' varsity team."

In unison, Riley and Rebekah both said, "Awesome."

"You didn't mention that," Tilley said.

Sela grinned and gave her a thumbs-up.

The table conversation stopped.

The muscles in Kai's chest began to tighten and the turkey she was chewing became too dry to swallow. She grabbed her water glass, bumped against a plate, and splashed water on her sweater. She took a swallow and then pulled her napkin up to wipe it off.

She looked at Tilley. "I am not sure I should do it. I don't think I'm that good."

Richard continued. "It's your choice of course, but I don't think the coach would've suggested it if she didn't think you're up to it."

Riley chimed in. "Remember how much stronger you're gonna be because of your workouts."

Sela leaned forward with her left arm on the back of Tilley's chair and her right hand leaning very close to Tilley's on the table, fingers almost touching. "I say go for it. Heck, if you don't make it you can still play for JV. Don't you agree, Tilley?" Their eyes met for a brief moment, but Kai noticed immediately.

Richard nodded. "Sela knows what she's talking about. I think she has a trophy for just about every sport she played at Lindan High. Let's see…" He held up his hand and ticked off each finger. "Basketball, softball, track and field, and what was the other one?"

Elizabeth spoke up. "Swimming."

Sela laughed. "Oh, let's not forget debate club. That was a groaner. Really Kai, Coach Logan thinks you have natural athletic ability and she thinks you could take them all the way to State."

Her face stung with embarrassment. "Yeah, well, we'll see." Kai stuck her fork in the Jell-O mold.

"We can talk about this later," Tilley said and rubbed her back reassuringly.

Kai looked at her, nodded, and saw Sela's hand on Tilley's leg. *Hmm.*

As dinner wound down, Rebekah and Wesley left in order to meet his grandparents for dessert. Tilley volunteered to help clear the table. Sela joined her.

Kai was on her third helping and feeling more relaxed since almost everyone had left the table. Fergus joined Richard in the living room for brandy, leaving Loliy and the girls alone.

"Did you girls have a nice Christmas?" Loliy asked.

"Yes," Riley said. "Mom decided to let me do my own shopping and just got me a gift certificate. Dad said if I wanted I could have some voice lessons. He was really proud of me after the concert."

"I can't say that I blame him, even I was impressed.

Your voice is lovely and you did a remarkable job." Loliy was beaming with pride.

Kai's mouth was finally empty. "I agree, you sounded awesome."

"And how was your Christmas, Kai?"

"Really nice. I got some new clothes and stuff but my aunt went all out and got me a home gym. It's incredible."

Loliy just smiled and nodded. "No more, shall we say…troubles?"

Kai thought about the dream she'd had, but decided to talk to Tilley about it first. "No, not really. How about you guys?"

"Fergus had the window replaced and oddly, the commotion must've attracted a few people because the store has been a little busier."

Riley leaned forward. "So will you be teaching next semester?"

"No, I'm afraid not. I certainly enjoyed myself, but Mr. Winkler will be back and I'm sure he's terribly disappointed to have missed the performance."

"Oh, that's too bad because you did a really good job and the kids liked you." Riley smiled.

"Thank you, dear. I really enjoyed myself. But since the shop has gotten busier I think it's best that I help Fergus."

Tilley appeared at the kitchen door. "Would you girls bring the rest of the dishes in so we can get them cleaned up?"

Loliy excused herself to go to the living room while Kai and Riley cleaned the rest of the table.

"The table is clear, Mom. Is there anything else you need?" Riley said.

"Are the candles blown out? We don't want a

fire."

"I'll do it," said Kai. She watched as Tilley picked up all of the napkins and took them to the laundry room. Right after that, Sela slipped into the laundry room and closed the door. Her curiosity and her thoughts created a vision of Tilley and Sela together… in the laundry room. *I can't wait to tell Riley.*

"All set, no fire danger Mrs. James," Kai said. She nudged Riley.

Riley looked at her for a minute, shrugged, and then said, "Mom, can we go upstairs?"

"Sure, I'll call you when we decide to have dessert."

❧ ❧ ❧ ❧

"What's so important?" Riley said, closing the door.

Kai flopped onto Rebekah's bed. "You'll never guess who I saw sneaking into the laundry room."

Riley jumped onto her own bed. "Who?"

"Sela."

Riley grabbed Mr. Rat and shook her head. "And that's a big deal because?"

Kai snickered. "Because a few minutes earlier I saw Tilley go in with an armful of dirty napkins. Just sayin'."

"Shut. Up! Are you kidding me? Your aunt and Mom's oldest friend. Say it isn't so."

"I would never have said anything, but they've gone out for coffee a couple of times, and…" Kai held up her hands in testimony. "If they're sneaking around at the party, hiding in the laundry room…well, we know what goes on in laundry rooms." Kai started to giggle and Riley joined in until they were both laughing hysterically.

"What is it with you slinky Tiva women seducing innocent girls everywhere?"

"Hey, I had no clue what was going on with her, honest. I mean if it hadn't been for me gorking out hopelessly about you she might never have said anything to me. But since she and Sela went out a couple of times, I finally asked her."

Riley sat up with Mr. Rat in her lap. Her head was spinning and she had trouble focusing. She rubbed her head with the heel of her hand. "This is too weird you know. What are the odds that both you and your aunt are gay, a trillion to one?"

"It is kinda weird. I wonder if there's a genetic thing, although my dad didn't seem to have that problem, I don't think." She rolled over onto her back. "Nope, I don't care if it is a genetic problem. Riley James is too damn hot to give up."

"Be careful what you're saying there, my tall sexy basketball player, because we are alone in my bedroom. My rules."

Kai laughed. "All except for the part where you made me promise to stop you if you got out of control." She looked at Riley and wiggled her eyebrows.

Riley narrowed her eyes and tried to make herself look mean. "Don't mess with feisty girls liquored up with champagne."

Kai giggled and closed her eyes. "Okay, okay, I won't." She sighed heavily. "Listen, I'm just going to rest a minute."

Riley watched as Kai's breathing slowed. The muscles of her face relaxed and if possible, she became even more attractive. She lay flat on her back with her legs crossed at the ankle and one arm folded behind her head. Her belly, the same flat abdomen Riley had groped earlier, rose and fell rhythmically.

She continued to watch until she was sure Kai was asleep. She tiptoed over and lay down beside her with one arm across her waist. She gently rested her head on Kai's shoulder. A comforting warmth enveloped her as the fluttering in her chest slowed. At that moment, Riley felt safe and cared for in a very special way. She looked at the bracelet on her wrist and felt more than ever that the two of them were connected. "I love you, Kai," she whispered softly and closed her eyes.

# *Chapter Thirty*

Tilley stepped carefully along the salted sidewalk. "I'm sorry I didn't wake you girls for dessert, but you both looked so peaceful, I didn't have the heart. Elizabeth sent us home with tons of leftovers including dessert."

"No problem. I didn't realize I was so tired and God knows I had more than enough to eat," Kai said as Tilley unlocked the car doors. "Have you ever seen so much food in your whole life?"

Tilley got in and buckled up. "Actually I have, but it's usually a catered event. The Jameses certainly know how to throw a party, don't they?"

"I like them. They're really nice people."

"They are nice people, but I'm guessing you would like Riley's parents even if they were trolls."

Kai laughed at the lame joke but knew she agreed. Her heart belonged to Riley James and with the girl came the parents. "You're probably right. Riley is a special person and I really do like her."

"I think Loliy and Fergus had a good time, but I'm glad they chose to take a cab. I offered them a ride home but they declined. You know, it's too bad she's not going to be at the school next semester." Tilley backed up and started toward home.

"I know. They kinda grew on me. At first we thought they were totally whacked. But, I guess with all that's happened, it's a good thing they showed up."

Kai glanced out at the dark sky and shivered. "Tilley, is it really okay with you that I work for them?"

Tilley turned in the driveway and looked at Kai. "It is as long as you keep your grades up and try to limit it to holidays and weekends."

"No problem. I think it's mostly just help with things they can't do, like heavy lifting and stuff like that."

"And in return they might have some good insight about the other thing. They seem to have some experience with that…world, for lack of a better word."

"Frankly, at this point I'm so confused, I'll take whatever help I can get."

"You and me both." Tilley unbuckled her seat belt and opened her door. "Okay. Why don't you go on up and get ready for bed. I'll be up and a little while to say good night."

Tilley took the bag of leftovers to the kitchen and Kai headed off to her room. She really wanted to run down to the basement one more time is to be sure her Nautilus was still there. First thing in the morning, that was what she would tackle, if for no other reason than to burn off the million calories she ate. Her stomach still hurt.

Once she snuggled comfortably in bed, Kai texted Riley to say good night. The instant response was a photo of Riley making a scary face and a message to call in the morning. Kai smiled and tucked her cell phone under her pillow.

She carefully opened the box containing the scrapbook. One by one, she studied each sketch, amazed at the detail. In the sketch of Riley's house, there was a tiny little face in Riley's bedroom window. On closer inspection, she saw it was Mr. Rat. She had to laugh.

One of the last sketches was of Agrippa's. It must've been done a couple of weeks earlier. Again, Kai was amazed at the details Riley remembered. They had only been there once before but the details of each shelf and display cabinets were almost perfect. It was uncanny.

"Knock, knock," Tilley said. "Can I come in?"

Kai motioned her over. "Yeah."

Tilley stretched out on the bed next to Kai. "I'm exhausted. Good thing I only have half a day tomorrow. Will you be okay?"

"I have a new gym and a serious workout to do. And if Riley's mom lets her, she may come over. Is that okay?"

Tilley took out her silver hoop earrings and gave her an are-you-serious look. "Of course. Just remember not to overdo the first time you work out. You'll be using some different muscles, I suspect."

"I'll be okay. So did you have a good time tonight?" Kai turned on her side to watch Tilley. If possible, she thought Tilley looked even prettier. Regardless of the sad circumstances, Kai was grateful that Tilley had taken such good care of her all these years.

"You know, I really did. I wasn't sure if they were just being nice because of you. But Elizabeth and I really hit it off. She's a very interesting woman. Did you know she graduated magna cum laude from Vanderbilt University? She had a double major in psychology and political science. She met Richard in Minneapolis at a community planning seminar. I think it's fascinating." She looked over at Kai. "I'm guessing you don't find that as interesting as I do, right?"

Kai nodded. "Anything else you've found

interesting?" Kai was blatantly fishing and she knew it, but Tilley didn't seem to be catching on.

Tilley pinched the bridge her nose and closed her eyes. "You know I have to admit, and I don't want you to repeat this, but I think Loliy and her brother Fergus are two of the strangest people I've ever met, and yet there's something comfortably familiar."

"Yeah, I know what you mean. Maybe it's because they've known me and Riley from past lives. So they say."

It was Tilley's turn to look confused. "What?"

"Another story for another day. On another note, I guess I'll just ask you. Sela and the laundry room?"

Tilley snapped her head up. "Pardon me?"

"Nothing, I just saw Sela follow you in there and shut the door. You guys were in there for a while."

"Kai, I'm not sure—"

Kai held up her hands. "I have been in that laundry room a couple of times..."

Tilley's poke in the ribs came as a surprise.

"Ow!"

"So Rebekah wasn't kidding."

"About what?" Kai was horrified that Bekah would've told her aunt about the laundry room incident. *Crap. What else had she said?*

Tilley was on her side now, facing Kai.

It was impossible for her to lie to somebody two feet from her face. Kai remembered the incident like it was yesterday. Wait a minute, it was today. A scorching smile covered her face. Riley's hands, her lips... "Okay. Yes. Riley and I have spent some time getting to know each other a little better, on one or two occasions, in the laundry room."

Tilley burst out laughing then grabbed Kai's

hand. "You are so damn cute. No wonder Riley has fallen for you."

"Tilley, isn't this embarrassing enough?"

"Honey, remember this moment, remember these days and the blush of first love. It's so important." Tilley rolled on her back and folded her hands over her stomach.

*First love? Is that really what was happening?* Kai sat up against the headboard. A warm tingling moved around her chest. She swallowed hard and cleared her throat.

"So I noticed that Sela was getting kind of friendly with your thigh at the dinner table. What's up with that?"

Tilley gave her another look. "As a matter of fact, she claimed she couldn't get enough of the wonderful perfume you gave me. Evidently, it's very alluring."

"Truthfully, Riley was the first one to pick it out but I made the final approval. It does smell nice." Kai thought about how Sela seemed sort of chivalrous, holding Tilley's chair and helping her with her coat. "Do you like the way Sela treats you, you know, kind of protectively?"

"I do. It seems like I've spent my whole life being the strong one and taken care of myself and everyone else. It's really is nice to have someone be attentive to my needs. She's very good about that. Always senses when I'm getting tired, remembers how I like my coffee, sends me little notes, laughs at my jokes." She smiled. "Sometimes it's just the little things in life that make the difference."

Kai watched. "Have you been in love before?"
Tilley nodded.
"Was it the girl from college, was she your first?"

Tilley sighed. "No, it was much earlier. Her name was Silent Springs. We called her Odessa, I don't remember why. She was my first friend. I loved her so much. I think I'll always remember how we cared for one another. She was tiny, not even five feet tall, but so strong her personality made her seem so much taller. Even the boys were afraid of her, not because she was mean, because she was powerful." Tilley closed her eyes. "I don't remember when we became friends. Must've been when we were very young.

"Every major event in my life I remember because of her; she was always there. From the very beginning, she was there for me. She was my shield, no matter what. Every day I woke up excited to meet her because we laughed so much in spite of the constant pain of our lives. It wasn't an easy time.

"Odessa came from a large family—seven brothers and two sisters. So many days there was no food for them. I would take her what I could, but it didn't really make a dent. And you know what, it didn't matter because she was always happy and full of joy. The most unbearable days we all managed because of Odessa. It was a very hard life for all of our people."

Tilley's voice became thick with emotion and she reached for Kai's hand.

"We didn't have a lot of money. Daddy worked the oil fields when we were little. I was the youngest, the baby, but even though both of my brothers were older, they got more attention because they fought a lot. Our mother raised the three of us without any help. Daddy sent checks that were barely enough. When I turned fifteen, it was an especially bad time on our reservation. Girls weren't safe and I had no father to protect me, and my brothers...weren't around. Mother sent me to a boarding school in Minnesota."

Kai watched helplessly as her aunt began to cry. Tilley had never shared her past, never cried, and Kai had no words to help. She reached for tissues and stuffed them into Tilley's hand. "It's okay…"

"On my last day off before school, Odessa and I walked to the river to say good-bye. She would stay and I had to leave." Tilley's voice caught in a gasp. "I cared for my family, but I think Odessa was the only person I ever truly loved. I had to leave her, and to this day I miss her."

Instinctively, Kai hugged Tilley into her arms. She had no words of comfort. She ached for her aunt, but hearing the story also made her worry about her own situation. The terrifying thought of losing Riley crushed her chest to the point of pain. How could someone survive that kind of loss? How had Tilley gone on to raise her brother's child, all alone, without support, without her first love? Especially now knowing the hardships she had faced, Kai had a deeper respect for her aunt.

"I had no idea. I'm so sorry."

"Of course you didn't. It's not the worry for a child. Now you're more grown up. It was a long time ago." Tilley patted Kai's hand, blew her nose, and sat up. "What were you looking at?"

"Riley's present. She made a sketchbook for me. I'm kinda surprised because I had no idea she drew, but she's really good."

"Can you show me?"

Kai thought about it and decided the only questionable picture was the janitor's closet. She handed it over. "Look at the one of her house. Isn't that amazing?"

Tilley sat up. She flipped a couple of pages. "These are extraordinary." She turned a few more pages and saw the one of Agrippa's. "Is this…?"

Kai sat up too. "Yes. That's where it happened."

"Do you wanna tell me about it…the magic shop?"

Kai could feel her heart accelerate thinking about the confrontation with her uncle. "I guess. It was pretty awful. The same guy I saw in the liquor store—Black Raven—I can't believe he's my uncle, and that he'd wanna kill me. Tilley, honest to God I don't know what he wants from me!"

"Tell me what he said," she said calmly.

"He was totally demented. He screamed and carried on. He told me the wand was useless without the Black Obsidian. I told him we didn't know what he was talking about. It didn't matter. He was out of his mind and having some kind of delusions of grandeur. He scared me, Tilley, but I don't know how to give him what he wants."

"You're okay. I think I'd better call Wakanda. Kai, I'm so sorry this legacy has really come to fruition. I hoped it was just an old story people told about the old battles between the dark and the light. After your dad died, I thought that the story would end. No one heard from your uncle for years, so we all thought he was dead, too. I'd just hoped you would have many years to enjoy your youth." And more softly. "Just when you found someone to love…"

"Why does he want this so badly? Enough to kill people…I don't get it. What the heck happened?"

Tilley rubbed her shoulder. "I don't know, honey. This was never explained, they never told me. The school was so strict about visitors and letters, I rarely got news from home. When your dad moved here with you he was very angry, absolutely furious, but he wouldn't talk about it. Whenever I asked, he simply told me it was safer for both me and you to just let the stories die."

"What stories?"

Tilley took a breath. "Wakanda said the heir would follow the line from her grandmother Wind Horse to a girl bred from the loins of your father, Hotah Chayton. You are his only offspring, but I guess I felt like it would be years in the future, when you were an adult, before we would ever have to think about it. If it's even true at all."

"Wow. But even if it's true, I still don't know what the hell I'm supposed to do!" Kai felt red hot anger rising from her toes. "And what about Riley? She's supposed to be some 'past lives partner.' How come I can't remember any of them? And neither does Riley."

Tilley shrugged. "I don't know. There's so much unknown, and it's so much sooner than I anticipated. It hurts my heart that this has fallen to you, especially now. However, I believe with all my heart: if you are the one, you'll have all the guidance and wisdom you will need. If Loliy and Fergus are correct, Riley will be here to help you, as will I. Please know, I'm already so very proud of you."

Kai pulled back, nodded, and looked her in the eye. "It isn't over. I had a dream night before last. He's coming back someday, and he's not coming alone. Tilley, I'm scared."

# Chapter Thirty-one

The snowplow sprayed slush across the sidewalk in front of them. "I was going to say I enjoyed the warmer weather." Riley jumped toward the bushes.

Kai snickered. "Careful. The next wave might wash you away."

"Shut up, Stretch!"

"I can't believe Tilley was okay with you working on the magic shop cleanup."

Kai looked around as they turned down Mystic Lane. It was empty. She shuddered, remembering their last visit.

"You okay?" Riley stopped and put a hand on her arm.

Kai pulled her collar tighter. "I will be. I didn't realize how creeped out I'd be." She stopped. "I had another dream about my uncle and he's gonna be back. I just don't know when."

Riley moved closer. "We need to get some answers from Loliy and Fergus. You're not alone. Remember that."

Kai let out a big breath. "Thanks, but that's the thing. If we shared past lives or whatever...how come neither one of us has a clue? Tilley didn't have any answers when I asked her, but she admitted she'd all but dismissed the old stories when my dad told her to forget about it. It wasn't until after he died that she gave them a second thought, and then…well, it was simply too late to get any answers from him."

"That's so weird your dad never said anything to her. I mean, if he knew their brother was whacko, wouldn't he want to warn his sister?"

"Right? We better hurry."

They hurried to the door and saw that the raggedy sign was hanging menacingly on one hook. The window was covered and the bell above the door was gone. Kai shivered.

"Hello?" Riley said.

"We're back here." Loliy's lilting voice. "Tea is ready."

The back room looked untouched. Sunlight shone through the dust motes and the tea set shined as steam rose from the pot. Fergus and Loliy were seated with a large sheet of paper between them.

"Come sit. We've been expecting you." Loliy smiled. "We were just working on some remodeling ideas."

Kai looked at Riley and shrugged.

They each shrugged off their jackets and took a seat.

Riley smiled. "Smells good."

Loliy handed them each a cup and saucer while Fergus passed the cream and sugar. "I want to thank you and your family for including us in your holiday. It felt so warm and welcoming."

"I sure enjoyed chatting with your Da. Fine man, aye." Fergus lifted his cup with both hands to sip.

Riley gave Kai the sugar. "Everyone enjoyed meeting you. Considering the weird circumstances, it was probably good for us all to be together."

Kai focused on her tea as the silence grew. After

an interminable wait, Loliy looked at her. "Kai, I'm a little concerned about you. Perhaps we should address the proverbial elephant in the room."

Kai choked a little, grabbed her napkin, and glanced at Riley, who nodded. "I really need to know what's happening. My aunt told me about her life growing up and what it was like for her and my dad and why they left and what happened to his wife and what a freaky jerk my uncle is." She paused, winded, and took another breath. "But he keeps showing up and demanding I give him something." She wiped away a tear. "Can you please tell us what the heck this has to do with me and Riley? Please?" She took a tissue from Riley, blew her nose, and wiped her eyes.

Riley moved her chair closer.

Loliy looked at Fergus and folded her napkin. "Yes, girls. I think I must."

The room stilled and Kai watched a small rainbow in the steam from the teapot as the sun danced through the window.

"As I told you, you and Riley have shared several past lives, and always to help right some egregious wrong. We can discuss those sometime, because Fergus and I were usually around in some form. But right now we need to develop a plan."

Fergus stood up and carried the teapot to the hot plate to refill.

"Your uncle was badly hurt by your attack and it will take time for his power to return...if it does. Clearly he is still determined to intimidate you. I have asked for some powerful help. Your great-aunt Wakanda has agreed to come and help."

"Really? I knew she had powerful medicine, but can she really help us?" Kai sat up and grabbed the edge of the table.

Loliy chuckled and nodded. "Yes, dear. She might be the most helpful of all."

"I don't get why I'm involved. I don't know any of these people," Riley said.

"I'm afraid it might take a very long time to describe every incident the two of you have shared. Suffice it to say, the two of you have touched many lives with your good work. Riley, this time seems to focus on Kai, but trust me, there will be a pivotal role for you to play. Kai cannot do this without your strength."

Kai fidgeted. "Were we always, um, friends?"

Loliy smiled. "Well, let's say there was always a connection. A very strong one. You are a powerful force together."

Riley poked Kai in the shoulder. "See, you need me."

Kai smiled. "Oh, I knew that a long time ago."

Fergus brought a large trash barrel in from the alley. "How 'bout using some a' that power to shovel up some broken glass and junk? We got a business to run."

"And much work to do," Loliy added.

Riley tugged Kai through the heavy, dusty, velvet drapes and into the shop. She spun around and took hold of Kai's shirtfront. "Listen," she whispered. "If we're on some weird fated journey with this crazy crew, I'm okay as long as I'm with you."

Kai leaned in and kissed her forehead. "Me, too. Loliy's right. When we're together I feel pretty invincible. You're the most amazing person I've ever met."

Riley hugged her, and Loliy popped her head through the drape and smiled. Kai smiled back. As anxious and uneasy as she felt surrounded by all this unsettling confusion, she knew that this family, both the one she was born into and the one she had chosen—*her family*—would be at her side through whatever lay ahead. Armed with that sense of comfort, she closed her eyes and squeezed Riley tighter.

# *About the Author*

After sixty years in the Midwest, Barrett packed up her life and her chocolate lab Murphy and moved to the high desert of New Mexico. With a long nursing career behind her, she began making up stories and writing them down.

Today, there are eight novels, two novellas, and a new one on the way. Retirement has been a good thing.

http://www.facebook.com/Barrett-Writes

http://barrett-writes.com/

https://twitter.com/BarrettWrites

http://www.sapphirebooks.com/barrett

***Books by K.M. Scott and Anina Collins***
In The Darkness (Project Artemis #1)
After The Storm (Project Artemis #2)
Behind The Scenes (Project Artemis #3)

***Books by K.M. Scott***

Hard Work (Standalone)

If I Dream (Corrupted Love #1)
If You Fight (Corrupted Love #2)
If We Fall (Corrupted Love #3)

Crash Into Me (Heart of Stone #1)
Fall Into Me (Heart of Stone #2)
Give In To Me (Heart of Stone #3)
Heart of Stone Volume One Box Set
Ever After (Heart of Stone #4)
A Heart of Stone Christmas (Heart of Stone #5)
Return To Me (Heart of Stone #6)
Forever With Me (Heart of Stone #7)
Heart of Stone Volume Two Box Set

Temptation (Club X #1)
Surrender (Club X #2)
Possession (Club X #3)
Satisfaction (Club X #4)
Acceptance (Club X #5)

Crave (Addicted To You #1)
Adore (Addicted To You #2)

Shatter (Addicted To You #3)
Claim (Addicted To You #4)

**_Books by K.M. Scott writing as Gabrielle Bisset_**

Blood Avenged (Sons of Navarus #1)
Blood Betrayed (Sons of Navarus #2)
Longing (A Sons of Navarus Short Story)
Blood Spirit (Sons of Navarus #3)
The Deepest Cut (A Sons of Navarus Short Story)
Blood Prophecy (Sons of Navarus #4)
Blood Craving (Sons of Navarus #5)
Blood Eclipse (Sons of Navarus #6)

Stolen Destiny (Destined Ones Duology #1)
Destiny Redeemed (Destined Ones Duology #2)

Love's Master
Masquerade
The Victorian Erotic Romance Trilogy

**_Books by Anina Collins_**

The Eleventh Hour (Poppy McGuire Mysteries #1)
After Hours (Poppy McGuire Mysteries #2)
Top of the Hour (Poppy McGuire Mysteries #3)
The Darkest Hour (Poppy McGuire Mysteries #4)
Happy Hour (Poppy McGuire Mysteries #5)
The Witching Hour (Poppy McGuire Mysteries #6)
The Finest Hour (Poppy McGuire Mysteries #7)